Orders made to be broken ...

He didn't know what the whole story was. Maybe the SEALs were being deliberately sacrificed in the service of some grand, global vision. More likely, the *Nimitz* had been ordered to deliver that alpha strike and pick up the SEALs, but someone higher up had countermanded the order and the SEALs had fallen through the cracks.

Either way, the bastards were throwing away good men like carelessly moved game pieces.

Slowly, he crumpled the orders in his fist.

Not on my watch! ...

FIRST TO FIGHT

Edited by
MARTIN H. GREENBERG

JOVE BOOKS, NEW YORK

FIRST TO FIGHT

A Jove Book / published by arrangement with
Martin H. Greenberg/Tekno-Books

PRINTING HISTORY
Jove edition / July 1999

The Penguin Putnam Inc. World Wide Web site address is
http://www.penguinputnam.com

ISBN: 0-515-12528-8

A JOVE BOOK®
Jove Books are published by The Berkley Publishing Group,
a division of Penguin Putnam Inc.,
375 Hudson Street, New York, New York 10014.
JOVE and the "J" design
are trademarks belonging to Penguin Putnam Inc.

PRINTED IN THE UNITED STATES OF AMERICA

10 9 8 7 6 5 4 3 2 1

CONTENTS

FIRST TO
FIGHT

The 17th Day

STEPHEN COONTS

Stephen Coonts is the author of six New York Times *bestselling novels, the first of which was the classic flying tale* Flight of the Intruder. *It spent over six months on the* New York Times *bestseller list. He graduated from West Virginia University with a degree in political science, and immediately was commissioned an ensign in the Navy, where he began flight training in Pensacola, Florida, training on the A-6 Intruder aircraft. After two combat cruises in Vietnam aboard the aircraft carrier U.S.S.* Enterprise *and one tour as assistant catapult and arresting gear officer aboard the U.S.S.* Nimitz, *he left active duty in 1977 to pursue a law degree, which he received from the University of Colorado. His novels have been published around the world and have been translated into more than a dozen different languages. He was honored by the U.S. Navy Institute with its Author of the Year award in 1986. His latest novel is* Cuba. *He lives with his wife, Deborah, in Highland, Maryland.*

"WHAT'S A YANK doing in the bleedin' RFC anyway, I'd like to know," Nigel Cook asked between slurps of tea. "As if the bleedin' RFC didn't have troubles enough, eh, with the Diggers and Canucks and provincials from all over. Wouldn't the Frogs take you for that Lafayette outfit?"

Paul Hyde had had more than enough of Nigel Cook the last two weeks. Two weeks and two days. Sixteen days of fun and games since he'd reported to the squadron in France. "I don't speak Frog," he muttered at Cook, because he had to say something. After all, Cook was the squadron pilot with the most service-time at the front.

Cook thought Hyde's retort screamingly funny. He elbowed the pilot next to him at the breakfast table and giggled soundlessly. Finally he regained control of himself and managed, "Doesn't speak Frog." Then he succumbed to another silent giggling fit.

"Looks like ol' Cook's nerves are about shot," Robert MacDonald murmured to Hyde.

"Has he really been in the squadron a whole year?"

"A week short. He should go home any day now."

Hyde chewed his toast mechanically, sipped at strong, black tea. Down the table, Cook was pouring brandy into his tea and still giggling. He wiped tears from his eyes, managed to get a cigarette going.

"They ought to have sent him home months ago," Hyde whispered to MacDonald.

"No doubt, Tex, old man. No doubt." The Brits all called Hyde "Tex," although he was from Boston and had never been west of the Hudson. Mac motored on: "Cook isn't much good to us now, I'm afraid. Has the wind up rather badly."

Having the wind up was an occupational hazard, Hyde had learned. He grunted in reply.

"But we've got you and those two virgins who arrived yesterday, so we'll give the ol' Hun a bloody good go today, eh?"

"Yeah."

"Today you go over the hump, I believe."

"Today is my seventeenth day," Hyde acknowledged, and finished up the last of his toast. Seventeen days was the average life expectancy of a British aviator at the front, according to army statistics compiled during the grim days of 1915 and 1916.

"We've got better machines now, thank God," Mac said cheerfully. He had two months at the front under his belt and liked to play the role of veteran warrior. "If a chap learns the trade, stays fit and reasonably sober, snipes his Huns only after a careful look all about, why, I think he could grow old and gray in this business. It's the new men getting potted who ruin the averages."

"Quite so," said Paul Hyde. He had fallen in love with these meaningless little phrases of conversational British and salted them around at every opportunity.

"After all, the average was made up of a few old birds who'd grown positively senile and a lot of young ducks who couldn't see a Hun until he opened fire."

"So they say."

"Why, some of the new fools they send us these days get potted on their very first snipe."

"Not very cricket, that," Hyde said, as British as he could.

"Enough philosophy." Robert MacDonald slapped the table. "They tell me you're going up with me this morning. Keep your eyes peeled, don't go swanning off on your own. We've got a push on and the Huns will be quite curious. The old man will be most unhappy if I come back without you."

"I should hope."

"Let's not be overly keen, Tex. Not good form. Watch for Huns, obey my signals, don't get the wind up."

"Righto," said Paul Hyde. As he left the table he saw Nigel Cook nipping brandy straight from the flask.

Rain had fallen the previous night. In the hour before dawn the cool, invigorating June air had a tangible substance and a pungent, earthy scent. Dew covered everything. Wisps of fog drifted through the circles of light.

"Bugger fog," Mac said.

"Getting down through this stuff will be a little chancy, don't you think, Mac?"

"The general staff isn't going to call off the war. Might as well do our bit for the king, hadn't we? Maybe this lot will burn off by the time we come back to land."

"I was wondering about the getting off. Perhaps we should get off separately, then get together on top. What do you think, Mac?"

"Quite sound, that. I'll go first, of course."

They walked to the planes, which were already parked in the takeoff position.

The sky in the east was turning pink when Paul Hyde completed his preflight inspection. The mechanics seemed quite proud of the bullet-hole patches they had completed overnight. Hyde mouthed a compliment, fastened the collar of his leather flying coat tightly, and automatically held his hand a few inches from the exhaust pipe, which ran along each side of the cockpit and ended just behind it. The pipe was cool this morning, of course, but Hyde always checked. He put his left foot in the stirrup on the fuselage and swung his right leg into the cockpit, as if he were mounting a horse. When that exhaust pipe was hot, getting in or out of an S.E.5 was a task for a careful man. Hyde's first burn, on the inside of his left thigh, was still tender.

Seated, strapped in, Hyde looked around carefully in the predawn gloom. The glow of a nearby light mounted on a pole behind him helped.

The S.E.5A had two guns, an air-cooled Lewis on a Foster mount on the top wing, which fired over the propeller arc, and a synchronized water-cooled Vickers mounted in front of the pilot, slightly to the left of the aircraft's centerline. The Lewis used a 97-round drum that mounted on top of the weapon, the Vickers was belt-fed. Both guns were .303 caliber.

The Lewis was an anachronism, mounted above the top wing in the S.E.5A because it rode there in the Nieuport-17, a rotary-engined scout now obsolete. At the full forward position on the Foster mount, the gun fired above the prop arc along the axis of the aircraft. To clear a jam or change the drum, the pilot pulled the gun backwards and down on the mount. Flying the plane with his knees and fighting the 100-MPH slipstream, he cleared the jam or wrested the empty drum off and replaced it with a full one. While still in the retracted position, the weapon could be swiveled through a limited arc and fired upward into the unprotected belly of another aircraft.

Sitting in the pilot's seat, Hyde checked the circular drum magazine of the Lewis, made sure the cocking mechanism was lubricated and moved easily, made sure the trigger cable was properly rigged, and pushed the gun forward on the circular mount until it latched. An extra drum was carried in a case above the instrument panel.

Then he turned his attention to the fixed Vickers, which was much easier to reach. The Vickers was dependent upon the proper functioning of the Constantinesco synchronization gear. If the hydraulic gear developed a leak that hand pumping couldn't overcome, the weapon was useless.

The cockpit in which he sat had been modified by the squadron. The armored seat had been removed and a wooden bench installed that allowed the pilot to sit much lower in the cockpit. The original huge windscreen was gone; in its place on this particular machine was a small, flat piece of glass that deflected the slipstream over the pilot's head.

One of the mechanics leaned in and shone an electric torch on the instrument panel. Hyde studied the levers, dials, and switches in front of him. On the seventeenth day, they seemed like old friends. Mounted on the panel were an airspeed indicator, altimeter, compass, tachometer, switch and booster mag, and petrol shutoff. Gauges informed him of oil and air pressure and the temperature of the radiator coolant.

The mixture and throttle controls were on the right side of the panel. For reasons no one could explain, they worked exactly opposite of each other. The throttle lever was full forward for full throttle, but full rich required that the mixture control be all the way aft.

A fuel pump was on the left of the panel, and a hand pump for the synchronization gear was between his knees.

The control stick had a ring mounted vertically on the top of it, hence its nickname of "spade handle." In the center on the ring were two toggle switches, one for each machine gun.

Hyde thanked the mech, who moved away. Hyde didn't need the light; he knew where everything was.

He turned on the petrol, made sure the switch and booster mag were off.

"Gas on, mag off," he called.

The linesmen took the prop and moved it back and forth several times. Finally fuel began running out of the carburetor.

"Contact," the linesman called.

"Contact," Hyde echoed and turned on the mag switch.

The linesman seized the prop and gave it a mighty heave. As he did, Hyde rotated the booster mag handle and the engine started with a gentle rumble. It ticked over nicely at 500 RPM, the tach needle barely twitching at the bottom of its range.

The 200-HP liquid-cooled Hispano-Suiza engine took a while to warm up. On Hyde's right the linesmen were trying to get Mac's engine started. They pulled it through repeatedly.

Hyde settled himself into his seat, stirred the controls around, and visually checked the ailerons, elevator, and rudder. All okay.

The Hisso rumbling sweetly in the false dawn. The fog stirred by the spinning propeller, the smell of the earth, the waiting sky, life pungent and rich and mysterious—Paul Hyde had dropped out of college for this. Took a train to Montreal and joined the Canadian armed forces. In England he had wrangled a transfer to the Royal Flying Corps, which was looking for volunteers for pilot training. The whole thing was a grand adventure, or so he had assured himself at least a thousand times. Friends had died in accidents, some before his eyes, and the Germans had killed both the young pilots who'd accompanied him to France just weeks ago.

An adventure . . . the word stuck in his throat now. If by some miracle he lived through this . . .

The truth was, he probably wouldn't. Hyde knew that, and yet . . .

The best way was to take it a day at a time. Live through Day One, Day Two, etc. He was up to Day Seventeen now. If he made it through today, he had beaten the odds. If he made it through today—who knows?—he just might pull it off, live through the whole obscene bloody mess. Well, there was a chance, anyway. But first, make it through today.

The radiator thermometer indicated that the engine was warming nicely. In the cool, saturated morning air a thin ribbon of cloud developed at the tips of the slowly swinging prop and swirled back around the fuselage of the plane. The windsock hung limp.

To Hyde's dismay, as the dawn progressed, the fog seemed to be thickening.

Mac's engine was not going to start anytime soon. The sweating mechanics pulled it through a dozen times while Nigel Cook and one of the new puppies charged into the fog and got airborne. Finally Mac climbed from the cockpit in disgust and threw his leather flying helmet on the ground. He stomped over to Hyde's plane, leaned in to make himself heard.

"Bloody Frog motor won't start. Take a few minutes to set right, the fitters say. You go on and I'll meet you in our sector."

Hyde nodded.

"Wish we still had our Nieuports," Mac added savagely.

Hyde didn't share that opinion. The squadron had re-equipped with the new S.E.5A's only two weeks before Hyde arrived, and in truth, the S.E. was a better plane in every way—faster, easier to fly, more maneuverable, with two guns. . . . The only weak point was the S.E.'s geared French engine. The Hissos were temperamental. Worse, the metallurgy was substandard and quality control poor.

Now the linesmen waved Hyde off, so with his right hand he fed in throttle as he enriched the mixture and with his left he shoved the spade handle stick forward. The S.E. began to roll. Almost immediately the tail came up. Flames twinkled from the exhaust pipes on both sides of the plane and illuminated the underside of the top wings with a ghostly yellow glare.

There, tail up, accelerating, bumping along over the uneven grass as the engine's song rose to a promising growl, not too loud. The prop turned so slowly on take-off—only 1,500 RPM—that almost no right rudder was required.

After a bit over three hundred feet of run, Paul Hyde gave a gentle tug on the stick and the nose came off the ground.

He concentrated fiercely on flying the plane. If he lost contact with the earth or the dawn in this poor visibility, he was a dead man. And if the engine stopped for any

reason—he had mentally prepared himself—he was landing straight ahead regardless. Just last week an old dog
died trying to turn back to the field with the motor popping, barely turning over.

When he was safely above the fog layer, Paul Hyde
looked back into the gloom. And saw nothing: the field
had disappeared.

The dawn's glow would be his reference this morning,
for the compass was impossible to read in the dark cockpit. Hyde flew north, parallel to the trenches, with the
dawn off his right wing as he climbed.

Mainly he looked for other aircraft, but he also
scanned the gauzy sea below for landmarks. Here and
there were towering pillars of cumulus cloud, monsters
half hidden amid the patchy stratus. Hyde steered around
these. In the east the sky was yellow and gold—in just
moments the sun would appear.

German observation planes would be along when the
light improved. Hyde's mission was to prevent German
crews from photographing the front, and, if possible, to
shoot them down. The job sounded straightforward
enough, but it wasn't. When they weren't taking pictures,
German observers could give a good account of themselves with machine guns. And there were often enemy
scouts perched above the two-seaters, ready to pounce on
any British mice attracted to the cheese.

This morning the air was dead calm, without a bounce
or burble of any kind. The engine ran sweetly and the
ship obeyed Hyde's every whim. The slightest twitch of
the stick or rudders brought forth a gentle response.

Hyde charged each gun and fired a short burst. Everything was ready.

The plane swam upward past various layers of pink

and gold patchy cloud, turning gently from time to time to avoid the cumulus buildups. Swatches of open sky were visible to the north and east.

The eastern sky drew Hyde's attention. It was quite bright now as the rising sun chased away the night.

Hyde was searching for specks, little black specks in the bright sky that moved slowly this way and that. Those specks would be airplanes.

Finally he remembered to search the gloom in all the other directions. The Huns could be anywhere.

The altimeter recorded his upward progress. After about sixteen minutes of flight he passed fourteen thousand feet. Further progress upward would be much slower. Hyde wanted to be as high as possible, so he kept climbing.

Below he could occasionally catch a glimpse of the ground. Once he saw the ugly brown smear of trenches.

He was near Grommecourt, he thought, but nothing was certain. He couldn't see enough of the earth to be sure. He must be careful this morning not to let the wind that must be at altitude push him too deep behind enemy lines.

He swung west, let the ship climb into the prevailing westerlies. There was enough light to easily see the altimeter now, which was moving very slowly upward. The temperature in the radiator was rising, so Hyde opened the radiator shutters to let more air through. Up, up, up as the minutes ticked past and the engine hummed sweetly. He leaned the fuel/air mixture, tightened his collar against the cold.

He was breathing shallowly now, and rapidly. The air here was thin. He must make no sudden movements, make no serious demands upon his body or his body would rebel from the lack of oxygen.

At seventeen thousand feet he let the nose come down a degree or two. The plane was slow, sluggish on the controls, and he was a touch light-headed.

He let the left wing drop a few degrees, let the nose track slowly around the horizon until he was again flying east. The sun was up now, filling the eastern sky. All the clouds were below him.

God, it was cold up here! He checked his watch. He had been airborne for forty minutes.

He put his hand over the sun, looked left and right, above and below. Out to the left, the right, behind, below, even above. His eyes never stopped moving.

Another quarter hour passed. The day was fully here, the sun a brilliant orb climbing the sky.

There, a speck against a cloud. No, two. Two specks. To his left and down a thousand feet or so.

He turned in that direction.

Definitely two planes. Flying south. Hyde was approaching them from their right front quarter, so he turned almost north, let them go past at about a mile, hoping they didn't see him. As the specks passed behind his right wing, he turned toward them and lowered the nose a tad.

Two. One alone would have been more than enough, but Hyde wasn't going to let the Hun strut about unmolested just because he had brought a friend.

At least there were no enemy scouts above. He looked carefully and saw only empty sky.

He was going fast now, the wires keening, the motor thundering again at full cry, coming down in the right

rear quarter of those two planes. The distance closed
nicely.

He fingered the trigger levers inside the round stick
handle.

The victims flew on straight, seemingly oblivious to
his ambush.

At three hundred yards he realized what they were:
S.E.5's.

He turned to cross behind them. If the pilots had seen
him, they gave no indication.

Perhaps he should have flown alongside, waved. But
they would rag him in the mess, say that he thought they
were Germans and had come to pot them. All of which
would be true and hard to laugh off, so he turned behind
them to sneak away.

He kept the turn in.

There! Just off the nose! A plane coming in almost
head on.

He was so surprised he forgot to do anything.

The enemy pilot shot across almost in front of him, a
Fokker D-VII, with a yellow nose and a black Maltese
cross on the fuselage behind the pilot.

Hyde slammed the right wing down, pulled the nose
around, used the speed that he still had to come hard
around in the high thin air. Unfortunately the S.E. turned
slowest to the right—maybe he should have turned left.

When he got straightened out he was too far behind
the Fokker to shoot.

The enemy pilot roared in after the pair of S.E.'s.

If only he had been more alert! He could have taken
a shot as the enemy scout crossed his nose. Damnation!

Now the Hun swooped in on the left-most S.E. A slender feather of white smoke poured aft from the German's nose—he was shooting.

The S.E.5 seemed to stagger, the wings waggled, then the left wing dropped in a hard turn.

The Fokker closed relentlessly, its gun going.

The S.E. went over on its back and the Fokker swerved just enough to miss it, then lowered its nose even more and dove away.

Paul Hyde kept his nose down, the engine full on.

Out of the corner of his eye he saw the S.E.'s nose drop until it was going almost straight down. It couldn't do that long, he knew, or the wings would come off when the speed got too great.

He checked the Hun, going for a cloud.

Brass. The enemy pilot had brass.

But Hyde was overtaking.

He looked again for the stricken S.E., and couldn't find it.

Only now did the possibility of another Hun following the first occur to him. Guiltily he looked aft, cleared his tail. Nothing. The sky seemed empty.

He was two hundred yards behind the Fokker now, closing slowly, but closing.

The Fokker was going for a cloud.

Suddenly Paul Hyde knew how it was going to be. He was going to get a shot before the enemy pilot reached the safety of the cloud. He moved his thumb over the firing levers, looked through the post and ring sight mounted on the cowling in front of him. The enemy plane was getting larger and larger.

Without warning the nose of the enemy plane rose sharply, up, up, up.

Hyde automatically pulled hard on the stick. He was

going too fast, knew he couldn't follow the Fokker into the loop, so he pulled the nose up hard and jabbed the triggers. Both guns hammered out a burst and the Fokker climbed straight up through it.

Then Hyde was flashing past, going for the cloud. He jammed the nose down just as the cloud swallowed him.

He throttled back, raised the nose until the altimeter stopped unwinding.

The S.E.5A had no attitude instruments whatsoever. All Hyde could do was hold the stick and rudder frozen, wait until his plane flew through the cloud to the other side.

His airspeed was dropping. He could feel the controls growing sloppy. He eased the nose forward a tad. The altimeter began unwinding.

God, he was high, still above thirteen thousand feet. The altimeter was going down too fast, his speed building relentlessly.

He pulled back on the stick. To no avail. The altimeter continued to fall. He was in a graveyard spiral, but whether to the right or left he could not tell.

Panic seized Paul Hyde. He tightened the pressure on the stick, pulled it back further and further.

No. No! Too much of this and he would tear the wings off.

He had no way of knowing if he was turning left or right. He could guess, of course, and try to right the plane with the stick. If he guessed wrong he would put the S.E. over on its back, the nose would come down, and the plane would accelerate until it shed its wings. If he guessed right, he could indeed bring the plane upright, or nearly so, but it would do him no good unless he could keep it upright in balanced flight—and he had no means to accomplish that feat. All this Hyde knew, so he fought the temptation to move the stick sideways. What he did do was pull back even harder, tighten the turn, increase the G-load.

Oh, God! Help me! Help me, please!

Something gave. He felt it break with a jolt that reached him through the seat, heard a sharp sound audible even above the engine noise.

Eleven thousand feet.

He kept back pressure on the stick. Instinct required that he do *something,* and he sensed that if he relaxed back pressure, the plane would accelerate out of control.

Ten thousand.

Fabric flapping caught his eye. A strip of fabric was peeling from the underside of the left wing. He looked, and watched the wind peel the strip the width of the wing.

Nine thousand.

Before his eyes one of the wing bracing wires failed, broke cleanly in two.

Eight.

Another jolt through the seat. Wooden wing compression ribs or longerons or something was breaking under the stress. If a wing spar went, he was a dead man.

Seven.

Hyde was having trouble seeing. The G was graying him out. He shook his head, fought against the G-forces, screamed at the top of his lungs, although he wasn't aware he was screaming.

Six . . .

Five . . .

Four . . .

And then in an eye-blink he was out of the cloud, spiraling tightly to the left. The ground was several thou-

sand feet below. He raised the left wing, gently lifted the
nose. He was so frightened he couldn't think.

Below he saw farmland. Squares of green, trees, roads,
carts, horses. . . .

Was he east or west of the trenches? *Think, man, think.*
He was so cold, so scared he wanted to vomit.

A sunbeam caught his eye. He turned to place the sun
on his tail, checked the compass. It was swimming round
and round, useless.

At least two lift wires were broken, a wide strip of
fabric flapped behind the upper wing, one of the struts
was splintered, and the damn plane flew sideways. Not a
lot, but noticeably so. Hyde used right rudder and left
stick to keep it level and going west.

Up ahead, the trenches. Clouds of mud and smoke . . .
artillery!

The artillery emplacements were impossible to avoid.
The guns roared almost in his ear. If a shell hit him, he
would never know it; he would be instantly launched into
eternity.

He hunched his shoulders as if he were caught in a
cloudburst, waited with nerves taut as steel for the inevitable.

Then, miraculously, he was past the artillery and out
over the trenches, jagged tears in a muddy brown landscape. He saw infantrymen swing their rifles up, saw the
flash of the muzzle blasts, felt the tiny jolts of bullets
striking the plane. No-man's-land lay beyond, torn by artillery shells which seemed to be landing randomly. The
land was covered with men, British soldiers. Hyde
weaved his way through the erupting fistulas of smoke
and earth while he waited for a chance shell to smash
him from the sky. After a lifetime he flew clear.

He recognized where he was. The airfield was just ten miles southwest.

He sweated every mile. Once he thought he felt another jolt of something breaking.

At least the fog had burned off a bit. Visibility was up to perhaps three miles.

When he saw the hangars and tents of the aerodrome, a wave of relief swept over him. With the sun shining over his shoulder onto the instrument panel, Paul Hyde eased the throttle and let the S.E. settle onto the ground. It bounced once. When it touched the second time he pulled the tailskid down into the dirt. When the plane slowed to taxi speed he used the rudder to turn the steerable tail skid, and taxied over in front of the maintenance hangar.

He was unstrapping, getting ready to climb from the cockpit, when three more bracing wires on the left side snapped and both the left wings sagged toward the ground.

A maintenance wallah came trotting up as Hyde pulled off his leather helmet and wiped the sweat from his face and hair.

From twenty feet away the damage was obvious: a strip of fabric was peeled from the lower right wing too, one of the bracing wires for the tail was broken, at least one of the fuselage stringers behind the cockpit had snapped, the tip of the lower left wing hung only inches above the grass, the plane was peppered with several dozen bullet holes that he had picked up flying over the trenches.

The horrified M.O. didn't say anything, merely stood and looked with a forlorn expression on his face.

Hyde didn't care. He was still alive! That was something grand and exciting in a subtly glorious way.

He turned and walked across the field toward the mess. He desperately needed a drink of water.

"Rough go, old chap," the major said, eyeing the broken S.E. out the window as the mechanics towed it off the field with a lorry. "What happened?"

Hyde explained. "Went out of control in the cloud," he finished lamely.

"Albert Ball died like that, or so I've heard," the major said. He ran his fingers through his hair and looked at Hyde carefully. "Are you fit?"

"I suppose," Hyde said, taking a deep breath and setting his jaw just so. He didn't want the major to think he had the wind up.

"There's a push on, I needn't tell you. Going to have to send you up again. We've got to do our bit."

"Where's Mac?"

"He got off just a few minutes ago. If you hurry you can catch him in this sector here." The major showed him on the wall chart.

"I got a short burst into a D-VII just west of the Hun trenches."

"Plucky lad you are, Tex. If someone reports one going down, I'll let you know. Now off with you."

The next machine was older and had seen more rough service than the one he had just bent. The engine didn't seem to have the vigor it should have.

Paul Hyde coaxed it into the air and turned south. He was passing through five thousand when the engine popped a few times, then windmilled for a second or so before it resumed firing. He pulled the mixture lever full out and frantically worked the fuel pump handle.

Perhaps he should go back.

But no. The major would think . . .

The engine ran steadily enough now. Perhaps there was just a bit of dirt in the carb, maybe a slug of water in the petrol.

On he climbed, up into the morning.

He saw the German two-seater when he was still several thousand feet below it. He had been airborne about an hour and had seen a handful of British machines and several German kites, but they were too far away to stalk. This LVG was weaving around cloud towers at about twelve thousand feet. Hyde let it go over him, then turned to stalk it as he climbed.

Idly he wondered if that burst he had fired at the German scout earlier this morning had done any damage. Or if it had even struck the Fokker.

No way of knowing, of course.

In the past sixteen days he had destroyed two German machines. The first, a two-seater, he'd riddled before the observer finally slumped over.

Not willing to break off to change the Lewis drum, he'd closed to point-blank range and shot the pilot with the Vickers. The machine went out of control and eventually shed its wings. Before he died the observer put forty-two holes in Hyde's S.E.

"As a general rule," Mac had commented as he looked over the plane when Hyde returned, "it's not conducive to longevity to let the Huns shoot you about. Sooner or later the blokes are bound to hit something vital. Perhaps you should get under them and shoot upward into their belly. S.E.'s are very good in that regard."

"I was trying to do that."

Mac pretended that he hadn't heard. "Shoot the other

fellow, Tex," he advised, "while avoiding getting shot oneself. That's my motto."

Hyde's second kill was a Fokker scout. Hyde didn't even realize he had fired a killing shot. He got in a burst as the Fokker dove away after riddling Hyde's leader, who fell in flames. Apparently Hyde's burst hit the German pilot, who crashed amid the British artillery behind the trenches. By the time the Tommies got to him he had bled to death.

It was all very strange, this game of kill or be killed played among the clouds. And here he was playing it again.

The two-seater this morning was looking for him. The pilot was dropping one wing, then the other, as the two men scanned the sky below. Hyde turned away, put a towering buildup between the two planes as he continued to work his way higher into the atmosphere. The air was bumpy now as the sun heated the earth and it in turn heated the atmosphere. At least the fog was gone. Visibility was six or eight miles here.

He got a glimpse of the LVG through a gap in the cloud. It was still going in the right direction, about five hundred feet above him.

When next he saw it, he was at an equal altitude but the Hun was turning. Hyde banked sharply and kept climbing. If possible he would get well above it, then dive and overtake it, settling in beneath to spray it with the Lewis. The Brits assured him this was the best and safest way to kill two-seaters.

The Hun had turned again when next it loomed into view amid the cloud towers. It was close, within a quarter mile, and slightly below his altitude. He could see the heads of the crew. Fortunately they were looking in the opposite direction.

Hyde scanned the sky to see what had attracted the Germans' attention.

Ah-ha. An S.E. swanning closer. That might be Mac. Good old Mac!

Paul Hyde turned toward the LVG, pushed the nose forward into a gentle dive. His thumb was poised over the trigger levers.

He came in from the left stern quarter, closing rapidly. With the Hun filling the sight ring, he opened fire with both guns.

The Vickers spit five or six bullets out before it stopped abruptly. In less than a second the Lewis also ceased firing.

Holy damn! He backed off the throttle to stop his relative motion toward the enemy.

He tugged at the bolt of the Vickers. The damn thing was jammed solid. He hammered at it with his hand.

Now the observer began shooting at him. Streaks of tracer went just over the cockpit.

Cursing aloud, Hyde turned away.

He tried to get the Lewis gun to come backwards on the Foster mount. No. The damn thing was stuck!

Cursing, Hyde unfastened his seat belt, grasped the stick between his knees, and eyed the German, who was a quarter mile away now. The pilot stood up in the cockpit and used both hands to tug at the charging lever. The windblast was terrific, but he was a strong young man.

The Lewis was also jammed good. Old, inferior, shoddy ammo! What a way to fight a war!

Perhaps he could get at the bolt better if he took off the magazine drum. He pulled at the spring-loaded catch, tugged fiercely at the drum. It was jammed too.

He was working frantically to free the drum when he realized the plane was going over on its back. The right wing was pointing at the earth.

His lower body fell from the cockpit. He latched onto the ammo drum with a death grip. His back was to the prop, his feet pointed toward the earth.

If the damned drum comes loose now . . .

The rat-tat-tat of a machine gun cut into his consciousness. Hyde heard it, but he had more pressing problems. If he fell forward into the prop, the damn thing would cut him in half.

He tried to curl his lower body back toward the cockpit. The windblast helped. He had his left foot in and his right almost there when the nose of the plane dipped toward the earth. The S.E. was going into an inverted dive.

He was screaming again, a scream of pure terror. He was still screaming when the plane passed the vertical and he got both feet inside the cockpit combing. Still screaming when the force of gravity took over and threw him back into the cockpit like a sack of potatoes thrown into a barrel. Still screaming as he pulled the plane out of its dive and looked about wildly for the Hun two-seater, which was far above and flying away.

He lowered the nose, let the plane dive as he struggled to get his seat belt refastened.

Praise God, he was still alive.

Still alive!

Just then the engine cut out.

"It's these bloody cartridges, sir. All swelled up from moisture." The mechanic, Thatcher, displayed three of the offending brass cylinders in the palm of his hand. "They jammed the gun and the drum."

"Uh-huh."

"Bad cartridges."

"And a dud engine. The damned thing cut in and out on me all the way home. It's junk. I'm up there risking my neck in a plane with a junk motor that runs only when it wants to. The bloody RFC has to do better, Thatcher."

"We're working on it, sir," the mech said contritely. He was used to carrying the ills of the world on his thin shoulders. "But what I don't understand, Mr. Hyde," he continued, "is how you acquired two bullet holes through the pilot's seat. Came right through the bottom of the plane and up through the seat. Or vice versa. Don't see how those two bullets missed you."

"It's quite simple, Thatcher," Paul Hyde said softly. "Perfectly logical. Obviously I wasn't sitting in the seat when the bullets went sailing through."

Without further explanation he walked toward the mess tent for lunch.

Mac was already there. "I heard you've had an exciting morning, Tex."

"Much more excitement and my heart is going to stop dead."

"Oh, I doubt it. Heart attacks are rather rare in this part of France." Mac sipped a glass of red wine. "Lead poisoning and immolation seem much more prevalent."

Hyde grunted. The wine looked tempting. One glass wouldn't hurt, would it?

"You remember the new man, Cotswold-Smith? Reported last night and sat in that chair right there for breakfast? Hun shot him off Nigel's wing this morning."

Hyde helped himself to the pudding as the dish came

by. "Too bad," he said politely. He didn't have any juice left to squander on Cotswold-Smith.

"Nigel says you came galloping to the rescue, chased the bleedin' Hun off."

"Little late," Hyde remarked, and tasted the pudding.

"Not your fault, of course. Did the best you could. Can't blame yourself, old man."

"Oh, shut up, Mac."

"It's these new lads that ruin the average," Mac mused. "Don't know how to take care of themselves in the air. Disheartening, that."

The major wanted him to fly after lunch, but the plane was dud. Paul Hyde went to the little farmhouse room he shared with Mac and collapsed into his bed fully dressed. He was so tired. . . .

He couldn't sleep. The adventures of the morning were too fresh. To get so close to death and somehow survive seared each subsequent moment on the brain. The way people moved, every word they said, the way something looked, all of it took on enormous significance.

His hands still trembled from this morning.

The worst moment was when the plane rolled over with him hanging onto the Lewis drum. If that thing had come off . . .

Well, he would have had a long fall.

He lay in bed listening to the hum of engines and the noises of the enlisted men banging on machinery and wondered how it would have felt, falling, falling, falling, down toward the waiting earth and certain death.

He was dangling from the ammo drum, nothing but clouds and haze below his shoetops and his fingers slipping, when someone shook him.

"Mr. Hyde, sir! Mr. Hyde! They want you in Ops." The batman didn't leave until Hyde had his feet on the floor.

Four-thirty in the afternoon. He had been asleep almost three hours. He splashed some water on his face, then left the room and closed the door behind him.

Three pilots stood in front of the major's desk: MacDonald, Cook, and one of the new men, Fitzgerald or Fitzhugh or something like that. Hyde joined them.

"HQ wants us to attack the enemy troops advancing to reinforce their line," the major explained. "Nigel, you'll lead." He stepped over to the wall chart and pointed out the roads he wanted the planes to hit.

MacDonald's face was white when he stepped from the room into the daylight. "There must be two divisions on those roads marching for the front," he whispered to Paul Hyde. "I saw them earlier this afternoon. The roads are black with them. This is murder."

"I wouldn't quite call it that," Hyde replied. "The damned Huns will be shooting back with a great deal of vigor."

"The bloody Huns are going to murder *us*. We don't stand a chance." Sweat ran down Mac's face. "God, I'm sick of this," he muttered.

"Maybe we'll get lucky," Fitzgerald said. He was right behind the two.

"I've used up all my luck," Nigel Cook said dryly. He had followed Fitzgerald through the door. "Come on, lads. Nobody lives forever. Let's go kill some bloody Huns."

Hyde snorted. Cook could act a good show on occasion. "This morning, Nigel, did you see that Fokker before he gunned Cotswold-Smith?"

Nigel Cook's face froze. His eyes flicked in Hyde's direction, then he looked forward. He walked stiffly toward the planes, which the mechanics had already started.

"Why did you ask him that?" Mac demanded.

"Everybody's a damned hero."

"You bloody fool," Mac thundered. "Nothing is going to bring that puppy back. You hear? Nothing! Cook has to live with it. Don't you understand anything?"

Mac stalked away, the new man trailing along uncertainly in his wake.

Hyde glanced at his watch. He had a few minutes. He sat down on the bench by the door of the Ops hut and lit a cigarette. The smoke tasted delicious.

One more hop today. If he lived through that, the seventeenth day was history. He had beaten the odds. Tomorrow he could worry about tomorrow.

Filthy Huns. This next little go was going to be bad. The S.E.'s were going to be ducks in the shooting gallery.

He would live or he wouldn't. That was the truth of it.

He remembered his family, his parents and his sister. As he puffed on the cigarette he recalled how they looked, what they said the last time he saw them.

His hands were still trembling.

Nigel Cook led them across the lines at fifty feet. Hyde was on Cook's wing, the new man on Mac's. The plan was for Cook and Hyde to shoot up everything on the left side of the road, Mac and Fitz to shoot up the right. When the Lewis drum was empty, they would climb and change ammo drums, then select another road.

Each plane had four bombs under the wings that the pilot could release by pulling on a wire. With a lot of practice, a man might get so he could drop the things accurately, but to do it at two hundred feet with a hundred bullets a second coming your way was more than most men had in them. Hyde hated the things. If a bullet hit one as it hung on your wing, it would blow the wing in half. He planned to drop his at the very first opportunity, and whispered to the new man to do likewise.

Fitzwater his name was, or something like that. He looked pasty when Hyde shook his hand and wished him luck.

Hyde's plane this evening was running well. Motor seemed tight, the controls well-rigged, the guns properly cleaned and lubricated.

What else is there?

"The M.O. asked that you try to bring this bus back more or less intact, Mr. Hyde," the linesman said saucily. "He said you've been using them up rather freely of late."

Hyde didn't even bother to answer that blather.

Flashes from the German trenches—the scummy people were already popping away. . . .

The clouds were lower and darker than they had been this morning. Perhaps it would rain tonight.

The four S.E.'s crossed above the trenches and headed for a supply depot that the major had marked on the map.

A bullet shattered the altimeter on the panel. Slivers from the glass face stuck in the glove of Hyde's left hand. He used his right to brush and pull the slivers out. Specks of blood appeared on the glove.

Several lorries ahead, some tents and boxes piled about. That must be the dump. Hyde gripped the bomb release wire. Cook and the others were shooting at the lorries, but Hyde didn't bother. He flew directly toward

the dump and toggled the bombs off. He checked to ensure they had fallen off the racks, but he didn't look back
to see where they hit. He didn't care.

Tiny jolts came to him through the seat and stick.
Those were bullets striking the aircraft, bullets fired by
the men he saw just a few feet below the plane blazing
away with rifles.

Fortunately most of the airplane was fabric and offered
little resistance to steel projectiles. The frame was wood,
however, and bullets would smash and break it. Then
there was the motor and fuel lines and the fuel tank, a
steel container mounted on the center of gravity in front
of the pilot, under the Vickers gun. Bullets could do horrible damage to fuel tanks and engines.

And there was the petrol in the fuel tank.

Of course the whole airplane was covered with dope,
a highly flammable chemical that pulled the fabric drum-
head tight. The smallest fire would ignite the whole plane,
make it blaze like a torch.

A truck loomed on the road ahead, amid the running
men. Dipping the nose a trifle, Hyde lined the thing up
with the bead and ring sight and let fly with the machine
guns. He put in a long burst, saw the flashes as the bullets
struck the metal. He ceased fire and pulled up just enough
to let his wheels miss the top of the truck.

Gray-clad figures were everywhere, lying on the
ground and running and kneeling and shooting. He
pushed the triggers and kicked the rudder back and forth
to spray his bullets around.

He heard the Lewis stop and knew it must be out of
shells. He waited until Cook raised his nose and followed
him up in a loose formation. Only when well away from
the ground did he pull the gun back on the Foster mount

so that he could get at the drum. It came off easily enough. He put it in the storage bin and lifted another drum into place with both hands while he flew the plane with his knees.

Fumbling, straining to hold the heavy drum against the wind blast, he got the thing seated, worked the bolt to chamber a round, then pushed the gun back up the rail until it locked. All this while he maneuvered the stick with his knees to stay in Cook's vicinity. Cook was similarly engaged changing his Lewis drum, so his plane was also flying erratically.

After the gun was reloaded Hyde looked around for Mac and Fitz-something. They were a mile or so to the left, under a gloomy cloud, descending onto another road.

He would stay with Nigel, who was going to fly back over the supply dump again! The blithering fool.

More fire from the ground, machine guns this time—the muzzle flashes were unmistakable. If Cook wasn't careful the Germans were going to be shooting Big Bertha at him.

A hatful of bullets stitched Hyde's right wing, broke one of the bracing wires. Hyde wiggled the plane instinctively, then settled down to slaughter troops on the road ahead.

He opened fire. Walked the bullets into a mass of men and saw them fall, shot down a solitary grey figure in a coal-scuttle helmet who was shooting at him, toppled a team of horses pulling a wagon, gunned men lying in a ditch. . . .

A bullet burned the back of his hand, furrowed a gouge through the glove and flesh and blood welled up.

Cook flew lower and lower, his guns going steadily. Hyde saw him out of the corner of his eye as he picked

his own targets from the mass of men and horses and
lorries on the road ahead.

His face felt hot. He ignored it for a few seconds, then
paid attention. Hot. Droplets of a hot liquid.

The radiator was holed. He was losing water from the
radiator.

And he was again out of ammo for the Lewis. He had
another drum, so without waiting for Cook, he pulled up
and soared away from the fray.

The Germans opened up with a flak gun. The bursts
were so close the plane shook. He got the empty ammo
drum off the gun, tossed it over the side. Got a fresh drum
up and the gun ready.

As he turned to descend, he saw Cook's plane go into
the ground. One second it was skimming the earth, the
gun going nicely, then it was trailing a streak of flame.
An eye-blink later the plane touched the earth and came
apart in a welling smear of fire and smoke.

There were enemy troops everywhere he looked. Paul
Hyde picked a concentration ahead and opened fire.

The hot water from the radiator was soaking him.
There wasn't enough of it to scald him, just enough to
get him wet.

Wiggling the rudder, holding the trigger down, Hyde
shot at everything he saw. The Vickers ceased firing. Out
of ammo, probably.

When the Lewis jammed he instinctively turned for
the trenches. The water was hotter now, so it was coming
out of the radiator in more volume. The needle on the
water temp gauge on the panel was pegged right. The
engine was going to seize in a moment.

And his feet were wet. Hyde looked down. Liquid running along the floorboards, toward the rear of the plane.

A lot of liquid. His shoes and socks were soaked.

Water?

Sweet Jesus, it must be petrol. There must be bullet holes in the tank! He flew with his right hand while he worked the fuel pump with his left.

When he crossed the German trenches the motor started knocking. A cylinder wasn't firing—he could hear and feel the knocking. Backfires from the exhaust pipe. And some Hun was blasting away at him with a machine gun.

A violent vibration swept through the plane, then another.

The last enemy trench was behind. Ahead he could see the British trenches. At least this time he wasn't going to cross in the middle of an artillery barrage.

He crossed the trenches twenty feet in the air, the engine knocking loudly and vibrating as if it were going to jump off the mount.

He didn't have much speed left. He tried to hold the nose up and couldn't.

The wheels hit something and he bounced. Pulled the stick back into his lap and cut the switch. The noise stopped as the ship slowed and settled.

It bounced once more, then the landing gear assembly tore off and the fuselage slid along the mud and smacked over a shell hole and came, finally, to rest.

Paul Hyde was out and running before the plane stopped moving.

He was gone about seventy feet when fuel vapor found the hot metal parts of the engine and burst into flame. The *whuff* of the whole ship lighting off pushed Hyde forward on his face.

He lay there in the cold mud gripping the earth with both hands.

Finally he turned over in the slime and looked up at the evening sky.

Two Tommies found him there.

"Are you injured, sir?" they demanded, running their hands over him, feeling his body for wounds or broken bones.

He tried to answer and couldn't.

One of them held Hyde's head in his hands and looked straight into his eyes.

"It's all right, laddie," he said. "You're safe. You can stop screaming now."

UNODIR

H. Jay Riker

Bill Keith is the author of over sixty novels, nearly all of them dealing with the theme of men at war. Writing under the pseudonym H. Jay Riker, he's responsible for the extremely popular SEALS: The Warrior Breed series, a family saga spanning the history of the Navy UDT and SEALs from World War II to the present day. As Ian Douglas, he writes a well-received military–science fiction series following the exploits of the U.S. Marines in the future, in combat on the Moon and Mars. A former hospital corpsman in the Navy during the late Vietnam era, he draws on his personal experience for many of his characters, his medical knowledge, his feel for life in the military, and his profound respect for the men and women who put their lives on the line for their country.

THEY CAME FROM the sea, six black shapes clad in shadow, all but invisible against the night. Four rode ashore on their CRRC, engine muffled as they guided the craft through the low, booming surf. As the bottom scraped hard-packed sand, they rolled out, grabbed the carry lines to either side, and dragged the rubber boat farther up the beach.

They were met by two more, who'd swum in ahead of the CRRC to reconnoiter, then signal the come-ahead with a carefully hooded flash. Each man in the squad wore a black combat vest and harness over his wet suit. Their masks, like much of their other gear, were commercial, privately purchased, with the bright colors and chrome strips carefully covered over by black or dark olive tape; and their faces were coated with green and black paint.

U.S. Navy SEALs, the best of the best.

And it was time to go to work.

The sky was completely overcast, but a soft glow against the cloud ceiling toward the southeast faintly illuminated the crashing rollers and wet sand. Stowing the rubber boat well above the surf line, the SEALs gathered several large, waterproof cases and began hauling them toward the crest of the island.

Island? The thing was barely worthy of the name, a fifty-yard-long fishhook of sand and coral rock and stinking black seaweed that just edged above the foam-swirl and crashing surf at low tide; four hours from now, as the tide came in, this island would literally disappear.

By then, the SEALs' job would be done, and they would be long gone.

Chief Gunner's Mate Hugh Warren pulled the sea-proofing plugs from his SEAL-modified H&K SD5, then crawled the last few feet flat on his belly, reaching the weed-draped spine of the island and slowly edging his head high enough to see what lay beyond, to the southeast.

A dazzling glare greeted him, work lights brilliant against the night casting flickering reflections in the water beneath. They appeared to be clustered near the horizon, perhaps four miles away. *Right on the money,* he thought. *Now we find out what the hell they're hiding.*

Lieutenant Carter McCullough crawled up on Warren's right, cradling a PAS-7 IR viewer in his arms. Peering into the thermal imager's eyepiece, he slowly and carefully scanned the bright-lit patch of ocean.

A few moments later, without comment, he passed the viewer to Warren. Bringing it to his eye, the chief zoomed in on the scene, eerily silent across four miles but magnified enough that he could see individual people moving among the lights.

AMPET-89S was an oil platform, originally the joint property of American Petroleum and a Filipino energy consortium. It had been taken over five weeks earlier by a naval task force of the People's Republic of China, one of the events leading to the current crisis.

The Chinese, Warren noted, had been busy since then.
A kind of awning had been erected from the derrick
tower, beneath which was moored a Dajiang-class submarine support vessel. *J302* was painted on her bow.

And tied up alongside, a black and menacing stream-
lined shape, was a Kilo hunter-killer submarine.

Jackpot. . . .

In the darkness a few yards down the shelf, RN/2 Gionetti and TM/1 Knox were setting up the team's LST-
5C, while the other SEALs, BM/1 Sheehy and GM/2
Dustevich, mounted guard. The ten-pound SATCOM
transceiver would give them a solid, data-encrypted communications link with Special Operations Command, Pacific. In another few moments, they could deliver their
report, then wait for pickup. An easy mission, slick in,
slick out.

Piece of cake, Warren thought as he continued to study
the Chinese submarine base . . . and then he frowned. He
didn't usually allow himself to think that any part of a
mission was simple or routine until he was safely back
at base delivering his after-mission report. In his experience, doing so was a great way to end up dead. He wondered if the gods of war had heard his uncharacteristic
mental gaffe. A nasty lot, that bunch.

Especially the all-powerful King of the War gods,
Murphy.

2

COMMANDER Gene Dahlgren stared unbelievingly at the
VLF message printout that the U.S.S. *San Antonio*'s communications watch had just handed him.

YOU ARE HEREBY ORDERED TO ABORT MISSION RE-
PEAT ABORT MISSION IMMEDIATELY AND DEPART
CURRENT STATION. PROCEED YOKOSUKA AT ONCE
FOR PROVISIONING. DO NOT REPEAT DO NOT RISK
ENGAGEMENT WITH POSSIBLE PRC NAVAL ASSETS
KNOWN TO BE IN YOUR AO.

It was signed by Admiral Charles Cuttler, SOCOM-
PAC.

Dahlgren didn't like this . . . not one bit.

Without comment, he handed the printout to Lieutenant Commander Brad Vincent. "PRC naval assets?" The
San Antonio's exec scowled as he read the message. "We
knew Beijing had ships in the area. What the hell's
changed to make SOCOM throw a conniption like this?"

"Whatever it is, it can't be good." The captain
glanced at his watch, then, as if for confirmation, at the
big clock on the comm shack bulkhead set to local time.
"Three more hours until we're supposed to recover the
SEALs."

"Maybe SOCOM has another boat in the area we
don't know about," Vincent suggested.

"We would know," Dahlgren replied. "Unless . . . I
guess they *could* be sending in the *Nimitz* battle group."

"That's gotta be it, Captain. They could send in helos
to pick our SEALs up. Maybe they just want us out of
the way." Vincent's eyes widened. "They might even be
planning an alpha strike on the AMPET platform. They'd
want us well clear if they were sending in the Hornets."

"Maybe." Slowly, Dahlgren crumpled the message
printout. "Maybe."

But he wasn't convinced. Alpha strikes were not the
current administration's style.

Followed by his exec, Dahlgren stepped out of the *San Antonio*'s communications shack and walked aft along the portside passageway into the attack sub's control center. The *San Antonio*—the *Big Tony* to her crew—was a 688I Los Angeles–class attack sub, a vessel Dahlgren liked to think of as the very tip of the U.S. Navy's spear . . . and the meanest wet son of a bitch in the ocean. Three hundred sixty-two feet long, displacing 6,900 tons submerged, she was capable of nearly thirty knots underwater while carrying an arsenal of Harpoon and Tomahawk missiles and Mark 48 ADCAP torpedoes that made her the terror of any foreign power during wartime.

Of course, this was not wartime . . . not the real thing, anyway. CNN and the other news networks were calling the situation simply the Spratly Island Crisis.

Most of the Navy personnel of Dahlgren's acquaintance had other, somewhat saltier terms for it.

"Mr. Yates," Dahlgren said, addressing the Officer of the Deck. "Take us up to periscope depth. Do it nice and easy."

"Take us up to periscope depth, make it nice and easy, aye, Captain," Lieutenant Yates replied in the precise read-back of commands employed by Navy submarine crews. The OOD began giving the commands to the boat's diving officer, who repeated them back again. The officers and men in *San Antonio*'s control room worked with a smooth and polished perfection that made Dahlgren proud.

Damn, he was going to miss them.

Gene Dahlgren had been wrestling with his decision to leave the Navy for a long time now. It had been his whole life . . . well, his life for the past eighteen years, not counting the four years at Annapolis. It was going to be hard to leave.

But the Navy had been on a downhill slope for a long time, now. Downhill? More like a crash dive! Tailhook, contractor scandals, slashed budgets, an administration that seemed hell-bent on destroying the service. . . .

In the mid-eighties, the United States had deployed a navy numbering six hundred ships. Now here it was, the dawn of the new millennium, and America could barely float half that number—with fewer and fewer each year as old vessels were scrapped with no budget for procuring new ones. And as for the *real* heart and soul of the Navy, more and more trained and experienced men and women were leaving each year. That meant longer deployments and greater hardships for the personnel who stayed behind.

Dahlgren had hung on as long as he could . . . but if the longer deployments were hard on him, they were hell on Meredith, Kenny, and Melissa. Damn it, he owed it to his family to let them *see* him once in a while. . . .

He looked at Vincent, who was watching him with a shuttered expression, then gave a sketch of a grin. After five months he could damned near read the man's mind. SSNs didn't approach the surface unless they had a hell of a good reason. He didn't have to justify his command decisions to anyone, but Gene Dahlgren believed in keeping his people informed. ''This isn't one I'm going to take without confirmation, Brad.''

''Did I say anything, Captain?'' He shook his head. ''Damn it all, though. I smell something rotten on the Potomac.''

''That's a roger.''

U.S. naval personnel weren't supposed to express political opinions, but that didn't mean they didn't have them. Brad Vincent was a Democrat and a liberal in a traditionally conservative branch of the service, something Dahlgren lightly ribbed him about from time to time. Even he didn't like what had been happening lately.

What the hell are they thinking back in Washington?

Everyone had known that the Spratlys were going to cause trouble sooner or later. There were perhaps a hundred of them scattered across the southeastern corner of the South China Sea: total land area, less than five square kilometers; total population, zero, except for the military garrisons. Some of the reefs and smaller cays were still uncharted, and many existed at all only during low tide. The surrounding waters were shallow and poorly mapped, making the region one of the deadliest navigational areas in the world.

But that deadliness had taken on new proportions when oil and natural gas had been discovered here. The Spratly Islands, long ignored by everyone, were claimed by Vietnam, the Philippines, Taiwan, Malaysia, and by the newly expansionist and aggressively assertive People's Republic of China. Even little Brunei had had a claim to one of the islands since 1984. Within the last few years, China had begun garrisoning several of the islands, ignoring a 1992 treaty that theoretically had resolved the dispute. In one instance, the move had led to air strikes by the Philippine Air Force.

But Beijing had announced that the NanSha Islands, as they called them, were Chinese territory, and it appeared that they were more than willing to go to war to enforce that claim. They'd beefed up their army garrisons in the region, deployed a task force from Zhanjiang, the headquarters of their South Sea Fleet, and seized several foreign assets in the region—which was to say AMPET-89S and a number of other major oil drilling and pumping facilities.

U.S. spy satellites had spotted unusual activity in the vicinity of several of the oil platforms in recent weeks, but a long stretch of bad weather had precluded their learning much beyond that. The *San Antonio* had been dispatched from Pearl Harbor two weeks before, with six men from SEAL Team One embarked on board. The *Tony*'s orders were precise and direct. Avoid all contact with Chinese naval elements, and take no action that might betray the presence of U.S. forces in the region. At a spot on the map designated Point Nevada, the SEAL squad had locked out of the submarine, swum to the surface, inflated their CRRC, and departed for their planned OP some ten nautical miles to the southeast.

Dahlgren's orders had been most specific; he was to come no closer to AMPET-89S than Point Nevada. Washington feared that the People's Republic of China was attempting to draw the United States into a shooting war in the NanSha Islands—or at least an international incident. Such an incident might give Beijing an excuse to claim American imperialist warmongering . . . and move into the Spratlys in even greater force.

It was frustrating, though. The *San Antonio* could easily have carried out a point-blank recon of the objective through the Type 18 periscope, complete with 70mm photos, low-light video, and EMS data, without involving the SEALs, an operation which, to Dahlgren's mind, was a lot riskier and more likely to be discovered. *San Antonio*'s skipper had nothing but admiration for the Navy's premier commandos—even if they had to be a little crazy to do what they did—but there were some situations where the Silent Service could get the necessary intelligence with much less chance of being heard.

Ah, but SEALs were sexy, despite their preference for staying low-profile. Likely, someone in the Special Operations Command had seen an opportunity to boost SOCOM's budget and had drawn up the op to include the SEALs.

"Captain?" the OOD said, stepping back from the Type 18 periscope. "We're at sixty feet. Periscope and EMS mast up. Surface is clear."

"Very well." He picked up a microphone. "Sonar, conn. What do you hear?"

"Conn, sonar," came the reply. "Background traffic only." The South China Sea played host to one of the busiest shipping lanes in the world, one reason for Washington's interest in the area. There was a brief pause, and then the sonar supervisor added, "We're still tracking Sierra Five-niner. Bearing two-zero-five, range . . . Busy One makes it forty-nine thousand yards, on a heading of one-nine-five, at ten knots."

Which placed her twenty-four miles away and headed in the opposite direction. "Very well. Keep your ears on." Sierra 59 was a Vietnamese warship, identified by *Tony*'s HULTEC data base as the *Nguyen Khahn*, a Petya III frigate purchased a few years ago from the perennially cash-strapped Russians. The *San Antonio* had been picking her up—"Sierra" was the designation for a sonar contact—off and on all day.

Hanoi wasn't about to let China's claim to the Spratlys pass unchallenged. No wonder Washington wanted to stay clear of this damned powder keg.

With *Tony*'s EMS mast now above water, Dahlgren could communicate directly via satellite with headquarters—SOCOMPAC at the H. M. Smith Naval Reservation, just outside of Pearl Harbor. Dahlgren hated doing it; every submariner detested the very idea of giving away his position with even a burst-encoded transmission, and even more Dahlgren hated opening himself to micromanagement by Washington.

But, damn it, they were telling him to abandon the SEALs he'd put ashore from his boat just two hours ago. An order like that *demanded* confirmation.

Fifteen minutes later, he had it. The message, transmitted via VLF and picked up over the *Tony*'s floating wire astern, was cold, concise, and clear.

ORDERS CONFIRMED. URGENT YOU ABORT MISSION, EXECUTE IMMEDIATE. MAINTAIN RADIO SILENCE REPEAT MAINTAIN RADIO SILENCE. INTELLIGENCE REPORTS PRC SSK YOUR AO. SPECIAL PACKAGE NOW RESPONSIBILITY CBG-7. AVOID BLUE-ON-BLUE INCIDENT.

Dahlgren gave a low, thoughtful whistle. "Blue-on-blue incident" referred to friendly fire in a naval engagement. It supported the exec's guess that the *Nimitz* was about to launch an alpha strike—a carrier air attack against Chinese naval or ground forces. "SSK" was a conventional hunter-killer submarine, probably a Chinese Kilo . . . quiet and deadly when running submerged on batteries. HQ evidently had decided that it was too risky to have the *Tony* pick up the SEALs as planned; if the American sub was spotted by a Kilo and possibly even attacked, it could tip off the Chinese that an American attack was on the way.

"Looks like we have our marching orders," Dahlgren

told Vincent. "Mr. Yates? Come to heading zero-three-zero, make for twelve knots. Set depth to one hundred feet."

"Come to heading zero-three-zero, make for twelve knots," Lieutenant Yates replied smartly. "Set depth one-zero-zero feet, aye, sir!"

"Twelve knots and a hundred feet. Skipper?" the exec said, eyebrows rising in the general direction of his receding hairline. "Doesn't sound like we're in much of a hurry."

"Let's just say I'd like to keep streaming the wire a bit," Dahlgren replied, referring to the VLF antennae trailing behind the attack sub from the port side of her fairwater as she cruised slowly toward the northeast. "Let's see what other radio traffic we can pick up before we leave the area. This *is* an intelligence op, after all."

The exec rolled his eyes toward the overhead. "That, Skipper, is a matter of opinion."

3

CHIEF Warren peeled back the cover of his diving watch and scowled at the luminous face: 0040 hours, three and a half hours after they'd locked out of the *San Antonio* at Point Nevada, and ten minutes past the time when they should have heard from the sub. Silently, he caught Gionetti's attention and made a questioning gesture. The radioman touched his earphones and shook his head. *No contact.*

The *San Antonio* was late.

This was not good. The SEALs had already moved both the CRRC and the radio further up the beach as the tide continued to roll in, each wash of the surf surging a bit further up the flat beach shelf. By 0130 hours, the island would be gone.

If that happened, there were not a hell of a lot of choices open to the SEALs. They could try a three-hundred-mile open-ocean paddle in their rubber duck to Palawan, the nearest uncontested Philippine territory. They could bob around at Point Nevada and hope to hell the *San Antonio* was simply running late. Or they could motor across to the ex-AMPET rig and turn themselves in. *Hi, there. We're Navy SEALs on a secret recon of your base, but we seem to have lost our submarine. Could we use your phone to call our embassy, please?*

Nope. No decent choices at all.

Quietly, Warren crawled back to the OP, where Lieutenant McCullough was peering through the eyepiece of the IR scope. There'd been quite a bit of activity at the oil platform in the past half hour; a Chinese Hainan-class patrol boat had motored up to the sheltered moorings with what looked like a Filipino fishing boat in tow.

McCullough handed him the PAS-7 and he took a look. It was hard to tell, but it looked as if there was an argument of some sort going down on the fishing boat's forward deck. Warren could see five terrified Filipino fishermen, a Chinese naval officer, and a number of PRC troops with assault rifles. He couldn't hear the shouting at this range, of course, but the officer was pointing and . . .

My God! Muzzle flashes flickered against the night; bodies toppled, three pitching into the sea with eerily silent splashes. Those splashes were followed by two more, as the remaining bodies were tossed over the side. Wordlessly, he handed the nightscope back, making a small slashing gesture across his throat. The Chinese meant *business*.

Surrender, if it had even been an option before, was out of the question.

4

"SKIPPER?" Vincent handed him a message sheet. "Sparks just picked this up on the VLF."

"Let's see." Dahlgren took the message and read it. It was an order to the *Olympia* and the *Bremerton*, the two 688s attached to the *Nimitz* battle group, directing them to go to periscope depth to receive incoming CBG orders.

"I think I'd like to hear those orders," Dahlgren said. "Mr. Yates! Bring us to periscope depth, if you please!"

With *San Antonio*'s EMS mast again above the surface, they could listen in on the encrypted satellite transmissions from Pearl. Fifteen minutes later, Vincent handed him a second message. The exec's face was unreadable, but Dahlgren could hear the tension in his voice. The *anger*.

CBG-7, the *Nimitz* carrier battle group, then on station north of Palawan some four hundred miles from the *San Antonio*'s current position, was ordered to withdraw from the Philippines area and proceed north to Japan.

"No alpha strike," Vincent said. "And no pickup."

"Jesus Christ!" Dahlgren said, crumpling the flimsy. Washington *was* abandoning the SEAL team the *Tony* had put ashore that evening.

"Skipper . . . we can't just leave them!"

"I don't intend to, Brad. OOD!"

"Yes, sir!"

"I've got the watch." As Yates acknowledged the order, Dahlgren snapped, "Conn!"

"Conn, aye!"

"Put us about! Take us back to Point Nevada! Set depth to two hundred feet!"

Orders and echoed orders sounded back and forth among the men manning the stations in the attack sub's control room. The deck tilted beneath their feet as the dive officer ordered ten degrees down planes.

Dahlgren met Vincent's eyes.

"What about our orders, skipper? Not that I'm complaining, mind you, but . . . well, technically this is mutiny."

Dahlgren smiled. "There's a word that covers situations like this, Brad."

"Yeah," Vincent replied. " 'Clusterfuck.' "

"Actually, the word I had in mind was 'UNODIR.' "

5

CHIEF Warren watched through the PAS-7 viewer. Under top magnification, he could see Chinese soldiers aboard the oil platform casting off lines as the sleek, black Kilo eased away from the dock.

"Looks like they're getting under way," McCullough said quietly, almost the first words he'd spoken aloud since they'd locked out of the sub, three and a half hours before. "Better report it."

"We're still not getting a thing on the LST-5C, Lieutenant," Warren pointed out. "I'm wondering if the damned thing's working."

"You check it?"

"Yessir. Seems to be fine."

"Well, uplink it anyway. SOCOMPAC's going to want to know about this."

"Those REMFs don't care! Another hour and we're gonna have to swim for it!"

Warren thought McCullough was going to give a sharp reply, but he seemed to reconsider, then shrugged. "Just send the report, Chief. It's our job. . . ."

"Aye, aye, sir." He backed away from the lookout spot and crawled back down the beach to where the other SEALs crouched at the edge of the advancing surf.

Yeah, they were professionals, and they would do their jobs.

Even if that meant *dying* because some pencil-necked bastard back in Foggy Bottom decided that a SEAL squad was expendable.

6

DAHLGREN stood in the communications shack, scribbling with a pencil on a blank message pad. Tearing off the sheet, he handed it to RM/2 Tom Weinman, the radioman of the watch. "Send it by SLOT. Make it a thirty-minute delay."

"By SLOT, Captain?" The sailor looked puzzled. "Sir, I could give you a secure SSIXS link, no prob!" SSIXS—the Submarine Satellite Information Exchange System—was the usual means by which submarines communicated with headquarters and other U.S. subs. SLOT—a Submarine-Launched One-way Transmitter— was essentially a buoy fired from a three-inch launch tube and floated to the surface. After a preset interval, in this case, thirty minutes, the buoy would broadcast Dahlgren's message . . . long after the *San Antonio* was out of the area.

He scowled at the RM. Dahlgren did *not* expect to discuss his orders with his crew. "We've been having some trouble with the sat feeds, Weinman."

"Huh? I just went over the gear top to bottom yesterday, Captain! There's no—"

He lowered the temperature of his voice by ten degrees. "We've been having some trouble with the sat feeds, Weinman."

The radioman gave Dahlgren a blank look. Then, "Ah." Weinman laid the message on his console. "Understood, Captain. Right away!"

As Weinman began taping the message for delayed transmission, Vincent joined them. "Skipper? We've picked up a new Sierra. Sonar says it might be another sub."

"You're just full of good news today." He thought for a moment. "I'd like Allen on sonar. Pass the word for me, will you?" ST/1 Allen was the best sonar technician in *San Antonio*'s company, a fine distinction indeed in a crew as good as this one.

"Aye, sir."

A few minutes later, Vincent returned, just as Weinman handed the message back to Dahlgren. "SLOT released, Captain."

"Very well."

"What did we just tell them, Skipper?" Vincent asked.

He handed the message to his exec, who read it.

To: COMSUBPAC
From: U.S.S. San Antonio, SSN 725
Re: UNODIR Operation

INTERCEPTED FLEET ORDERS DIRECTING ALL USN
ASSETS OUT OF SPRATLY AO. COMPLIANCE WILL
COMPROMISE USN PERSONNEL NOW ASHORE. UN-
LESS OTHERWISE DIRECTED, SAN ANTONIO WILL
REPEAT WILL COMPLETE RECOVERY OF USN PER-
SONNEL AS ORIGINALLY PLANNED.

CO USS SAN ANTONIO,
GENE R. DAHLGREN, CAPT, USN

Vincent looked puzzled. " 'UNODIR'?"

Dahlgren glanced at Vincent. Despite thinning hair,
the boat's exec looked terribly young. He still needed
seasoning before he accepted a command of his own.

Assuming he was ever offered one after this cruise.

"Unless otherwise directed." Dahlgren snorted.
"Sometimes, the trick to command is to decide what
you're going to do, tell your superiors what you're going
to do . . . and then do it, before they can go into micro-
manage mode."

UNODIR had originally been a SEAL idea, in fact.
They didn't talk much—they were about as closemouthed
as submariners, in fact, which was saying something—
but during the two weeks that the SEAL squad had been
aboard since departing Pearl, Dahlgren had exchanged
sea stories with some of them, especially Chief Warren.

"According to Chief Warren," Dahlgren went on,
"when SEALs in 'Nam wanted to pull an op that
would've made the brass go into collective meltdown,
some of them would log it as an UNODIR report, send
it off, and then head out on their mission. By the time
the brass got around to saying, 'Hell, no' and ordering

them to stay put, the SEALs were already back at their
base, mission accomplished.''

"And you figure to make our pickup before Washington can say no?'' He grinned. "You're playing it damned
close to the line, Skipper. If something goes down sour,
they'll hang your ass out to dry.''

"They'll only hang it out there if we don't pull this
off, Brad. And if we don't pull it off, we're going to have
a hell of a lot worse to worry about than dry asses.''

Despite the lightness of his exchange with Vincent,
Dahlgren was angry, with a cold, determined, and cal-
culating fury that he'd known few times before in his life.
Washington could cancel projects, strangle the Navy's
budget, and run good people back to the comfort, security, and *sanity* of civilian life . . . but this was different.

He didn't know what the whole story was. Maybe the
SEALs were being deliberately sacrificed in the service
of some sort of grand, global vision. More likely, the
Nimitz had been ordered to deliver that alpha strike and
pick up the SEALs, but someone higher up had countermanded the order and the SEALs had fallen through the
cracks.

Either way, the bastards were throwing good men
away like carelessly moved game pieces.

Slowly, he crumpled the message sheet.

Not on my fucking watch! . . .

7

ST/1 Randolph Allen was in his rack, a narrow, coffin-
sized space two feet high that, when he pulled the curtain
closed, was the one place in this submersible sewer pipe
packed with twelve officers and 118 men where he could

enjoy some privacy. The rap on the outside of his bunk stack brought him up out of a comfortable submersion in Bach's Toccata and Fugue in D Minor.

Like many sonar operators, Allen was a devotee of classical music—in his case, especially Bach, which he claimed helped sharpen his awareness of the relationships and harmonies of the sounds he was eavesdropping on. He yanked off the headphones of his portable CD player and jerked the curtain back. "What the—" He bit off an expletive. "COB! What do *you* want?"

Master Chief Pete Marcetti was the *San Antonio*'s Chief of the Boat, the senior enlisted man aboard. "The captain wants you on the watch, Allen. Drop your cock, grab your socks, and move it!"

He rolled out of the bunk, flipped up the mattress, and grabbed his dungarees and *San Antonio* ball cap. "What's the word, COB? I just got off watch an hour ago!"

"Hey, you want to be the best, you take the heartache that goes with it."

"Yeah, but they've had me pullin' one-in-three since Pearl, man!"

"The Navy. It's not a career, it's an *adventure!*" Marcetti shrugged. "Hey, *you're* the one with the four-oh quals! Don't gripe about it to me!"

Allen finished dressing, secured his CD player, then started for the control room. He was a tall, gangly man, taller than most submariners, and he had to watch both his head and his step. This early in the cruise, the head-room in *San Antonio*'s passageways was still sharply reduced by the boxes of canned food covering all of the available deck space, especially in and around the enlisted quarters, crew's spaces, and mess.

Up the forward ladder one deck, he swung off into the

passageway leading to the sonar room, blue-lit to increase the contrast on the CRTs. Taking a seat at the Number One BSY-1 sonar console, he glanced at Chief Kirby, the sonar supervisor.

"Didn't I just see you in here?" Kirby said, grinning.

"Gee, I don't know." He used a middle finger to shove his glasses further up his nose. "How's your vision? What's the skinny?"

"Skipper's taking us back to Point Nevada. Seems someone back home decided to leave the SEALs high and dry, and the Old Man is class-A pissed."

"All *right*!"

"We're tracking several Sierras . . . but the one that has Conn worried is Sierra Six-six."

He checked the target history, then his two BSY-1 monitors—"the waterfall"—which showed a sea of green static punctuated by intermittent white, vertical lines.

"We're not sure," Kirby continued, "but we think Six-six might be a Kilo."

"Shit," Allen replied. "It's gonna be a long night." Placing the headphones over his ears, he leaned back, closed his eyes, and tried to hear a hole in the water.

8

THE problem with Kilos was that they were *quiet*.

"Kilo" was the NATO code designation for the vessel, which was known to its Russian builders as *Varshavyanka*. A principal export item for the cash-hungry Russians, Kilos had been sold all over the world, to India and Iran, to Algeria and Libya . . . and to China. Just over 243 feet in length, with a submerged displacement of only

3,076 tons, Kilo was conventionally powered; like the infamous U-boats of WWII, she was propelled by a diesel engine on the surface, and she switched to batteries when she submerged.

And, running on batteries, a well-run and maintained Kilo—with no coolant pumps for a reactor—was quieter than a 688 boat, almost as quiet as a 688I.

The single advantage Dahlgren possessed as he ordered the *San Antonio* back into harm's way was sonar. Chinese sonar operators didn't have the training and experience of American crews; even if they had, or if Russian "advisors" were on board, Kilos lacked the towed arrays of 688s and were, by comparison, downright hard of hearing.

Dahlgren was going to have to squeeze the most out of that advantage if there was a Kilo out there, between the *San Antonio* and Point Nevada.

At the moment, the *San Antonio* was moving ahead at dead slow, barely making seven knots as the men in her sonar room strained against the hiss and rumble of background noises, trying to pick out a nearer but much quieter target. He'd taken the boat down to three hundred feet to take advantage of a convergence zone that might let them hear an enemy farther off. By running slow, he increased the sensitivity of the *Tony*'s ears and reduced the chance that they would be heard first.

Still, they couldn't continue at a crawl indefinitely. It was now 0100 hours, and, according to the tide tables, the nameless cay where they'd put the SEALs ashore four hours earlier was nearly under water.

The big worry on Dahlgren's mind was what he would do if he found the Kilo. Taking swimmers on board took time, and it was *noisy*; if the Kilo was in the area and listening, they would have no trouble at all picking up the *San Antonio* . . . and that would give the Chinese just the provocation they were looking for. Worse, the *Tony* would be a sitting duck for a Chinese 533mm torpedo.

The only thing he could do was find and sink the Kilo first . . . which would be an act of war, and the very sort of incident Washington wanted him to avoid.

It seemed like an impossible dilemma.

"Conn, sonar." They were using sound-powered phones now instead of the 1-MC. They were quieter. "Come to one-eight-five, please."

The sonar operators had full authority to have the sub maneuver in order to best position the various hydrophones of the boat's BSY-1 sonar suite to best effect.

Dahlgren passed the word quietly. "Helm, come to one-eight-five."

"Helm, coming to course one-eight-five, aye, sir."

An agony of minutes dragged past, before the sonar watch brought the *Tony* back to its original heading. "Conn, sonar."

"Go ahead, sonar."

"Sir, we've IDed Sierra Six-six. Definitely a Kilo at two-five-four, range estimated at ten thousand yards."

"Very well," Dahlgren said. "Designate contact Sierra Six-six as Master-one." Giving the contact a Master Number upgraded it to target status, a target that posed a potential threat to the SSN.

"Captain . . . sir, I think you should come to the sonar room, if you can. There's something you should see."

"On my way."

Seconds later, he stepped into the blue-lit sonar room, where ST/1 Allen and three other ratings sat at their glowing screens.

"Thought you should see this, Captain." Allen pointed at one of his CRTs, indicating a faint white line against the green static, a line almost lost in a much bolder, brighter contact.

"What am I looking at, Allen?"

"The bright contact is our old friend, Sierra Five-niner."

"The Vietnamese frigate."

"The *Khahn*, yes, sir. She's passing our line of approach, south to north, making turns for fifteen knots. Range twenty-two thousand yards."

"Okay. . . ."

"This faint line on almost the same bearing is Master-one. He just started up his screws a few minutes ago. Sir . . . I think he's maneuvering to intercept the *Khahn*."

"An ambush. . . ." The *San Antonio* had played that game plenty of times, though never in earnest. "Do you think the *Khahn* knows he's there?"

"Very unlikely, sir. The *Khahn* has not changed speed or bearing for some time. At fifteen knots . . . I doubt that she can hear much of anything at all."

"Do you think Master-one has heard *us?*"

"Hard to tell, but I don't think so. My guess is that the Kilo is lined up on Sierra Five-niner, and we're coming in on his baffles."

"Okay. Keep listening, and let me know the moment you hear any change at all."

"Aye, sir."

Dahlgren returned to the control room. "Maneuvering, conn! Make revolutions for twelve knots. Fire control officer!"

"Yes, sir!"

"Order tubes one and two ready in all respects and open outer doors."

"Make tubes one and two ready in all respects and open outer doors, aye, sir!"

He joined Vincent at one of the plotting tables. Though the tables were automatic, Dahlgren, like most SSN drivers, preferred to use tracing paper stretched across the light table, marking it with grease pencil to indicate targets and bearings.

Together, they reviewed the tactical situation, looking for the right move to make. The depth here was about six hundred feet—less than twice as deep as the *San Antonio* was long—but rugged and irregular, with deep canyons and suddenly looming seamounts, a chancy place for a submarine dogfight. As long as the Kilo kept stalking the *Khahn*, the *Tony* could barrel in right up his baffles.

Point Nevada was five miles from the *Tony*'s position and perhaps three miles south of the Kilo. There was no way they could proceed to the SEAL retrieval point and not be heard by the Chinese sub.

"What I want to know," Dahlgren said, "is what the Chinese skipper's orders are. Washington seems to think Beijing *wants* an incident."

"Well, if they could torpedo a foreign warship," Vincent said, "and *especially* if they could sink a U.S. sub in what they claim as their territorial waters, they'd score a hell of a propaganda victory and maybe scare off others who want the NanSha Islands."

"Which is why Washington wanted us out of the area," Dahlgren said, nodding. "Trouble is, we get the blame no matter what happens. If we sink the Kilo, we get the blame for starting a war. If they sink us . . ."

"Hell, the way things have been going lately," Vincent said with a sour grin, "if we get sunk out here, the White House'll apologize to Beijing for our submarine breaking their torpedo."

Dahlgren laughed. "Brad, we may make a liberal-baiter out of you yet!"

"What, and be forced to join the NRA?" A pained expression twisted his face. "Never *that,* Skipper. Please!"

"Conn, sonar. Sir, Master-one is flooding his tubes, sir. And . . . now he's opening his outer doors. Master-one's range to Sierra Five-niner is twelve thousand yards."

"How close are we to Master-one?"

"Estimate two thousand yards, sir."

If the Kilo was opening his outer torpedo doors, he was almost ready to shoot. Certainly, he could get off his shot long before the *San Antonio*'s warshots reached him.

Dahlgren had considered letting the Kilo fire, then launching his own fish while the Chinese sonar operators were concentrating on their outbound torpedoes. But . . . there might be another way.

He needed to enlist an unlikely ally.

9

"WHAT the hell's going on over there?" Warren ducked as cold water broke over him in an explosion of foam, then peered again into the nightscope's eyepiece. "Looks like they're readying helos on the rig's helipad!"

"Super-Frélons," McCullough replied. "French-made helicopters, rigged for ASW. Dajiangs carry a pair of them in a double hangar aft. Looks like they flew them both off and landed them on the oil platform.''

Another cold wave broke over them in a swirl of sea-weed and white foam. The island was almost gone now. ''We've gotta go, Skipper.''

''Yeah. . . .''

''Orders? Where are we gonna go?''

McCullough stared out toward the northwest, toward Point Nevada, for a long moment, as though trying to glimpse an answer. ''We'll never make Palawan,'' he said. ''The outboard has juice for maybe fifty miles. After that, we paddle, but the current's against us and the Chinese will spot us from the air as soon as the sun's up. I think all we can do is head for Point Nevada and wait for pickup.''

Warren nodded. ''Roger that. Besides, if our ride don't show, we can *still* paddle if we have to. I'm not so sure we couldn't make it.''

''We can sure try. Okay. Let's saddle up and get wet.''

A big wave broke across the crest of the island, and Warren had to grab hard and hang on to avoid being swept over the top. ''Don't know about you, Skipper, but I'm *already* wet.''

They started packing their gear into the CRRC, now bobbing in the water with each passing swell.

''What do you think's happened?'' Knox asked as they worked. ''The bubbleheads get lost?'' The word was surface-Navy slang for all submariners.

''Nah.'' He'd been thinking about that. Warren had nothing but admiration for the men of the Navy's submarine service—though anyone who allowed himself to be locked up for months on end inside a sealed sewer pipe had to be a little crazy. ''I smell a whiff of the White House in this one.'' He grinned in the darkness, teeth white against his face paint. "Whaddaya wanna bet Washington decided to leave us here as another cost-cutting measure?"

"Right now, Chief, I wouldn't be a bit surprised."

10

CROSSING to the forward end of the control room, Dahlgren stepped into the passage opening into the sonar room. "Chief Kirby," he said, addressing the sonar supervisor. "If we go active right now, do you think Sierra Five-niner will hear us?"

Kirby looked startled. Submarines only rarely switched from passive to active sonar, since the emission of a pulse of sound not only "illuminated" the sub's surroundings but also pinpointed the sub's precise position for everyone who might be listening.

"They'll hear us, Captain," he replied, "unless they have their whole sonar suite switched off! Uh, Master-one will hear us too. . . ."

"Obviously. Go active, please."

There was a pause of one cold heartbeat. "Going to active sonar, aye, aye, sir."

The sharp chirp sounded through the hull. *San Antonio*'s BSY-1 primary sonar, mounted forward in her rounded prow, mustered over 75,000 watts, one of the most powerful transmitters in the world—so powerful, in fact, that steam bubbles formed on the outer coating of the SSN's sonar dome with each pulse.

"Well," ST/1 Allen said, grinning, "the whole world knows we're here now!"

"Any response?"

"Sierra Five-niner is slowing," Allen announced.

"Range, thirteen thousand four hundred yards. Coming now to zero-eight-five. Master-one . . . maintaining bearing on Sierra Five-niner. No . . . correction. Master-one is speeding up . . . and he's coming to port. I think he's turning to meet us, Captain."

Dahlgren was counting under his breath. The days when a submarine had to line up on a target with periscope–cross-hair precision before firing were long gone. With wire-guided torpedoes, a sub skipper could fire on any target in any direction.

Still, the closer to bow-on a sub could come to bear on the target, the better, since a bow shot meant that the torps didn't have to swing around in a one-eighty . . . and perhaps risk acquiring the firing vessel and scoring an own-goal.

He would give the Kilo skipper twenty seconds into his turn. . . .

"Torpedoes in the water!" Allen called. "Two splashes! Sir, I've got two 406mm torps from the *Khahn*! They're searching . . ."

"Secure active sonar!"

"Secure active sonar, aye, sir!" Kirby said.

"Master-one is going deep," Allen added. "Looks like he's trying to hide on the bottom."

Dahlgren turned in the sonar doorway. "Helm! Come left to two-zero-zero!"

"Helm left, two-zero-zero, aye!"

"Down planes, ten degrees. Put us near the bottom!"

"Down planes, ten degrees, aye. Put us near the bottom, aye."

Unlike her WWII predecessors, the *San Antonio* could not rest *on* the bottom—not without fouling her coolant intakes—but she could get close enough to take advantage of the ridges and valleys, making her a more difficult target.

"Captain!" Allen called. "Torpedoes have acquired Master-one. They've gone active."

"Fire control! Firing point procedures, Master-one, tubes one and two!" One of the BSY-1 operators snapped off a string of targeting data. The Kilo was still making his turn, at a range of eleven hundred yards . . . point-blank for a Mark 48 ADCAP torpedo.

"Match sonar bearings and shoot, tubes one and two!" Dahlgren said, his voice tight.

"Match sonar bearings and shoot, tubes one and two, aye" was the echoed reply from the fire control coordinator.

"Tubes one and two fired electrically," Lieutenant Larabee, the combat systems officer, announced.

"Units one and two running hot, straight, and normal," Kirby added.

"Master-one is releasing countermeasures," Allen said. "He's still in descent. Leveling off now, close to the bottom. Sir! He's just fired one . . . no! Two torpedoes! Two 533mm torpedoes, in the water! I think we're the target!"

"One of the *Khahn*'s torpedoes has just gone dead in the water, Captain," Kirby reported. "Damned Soviet junk. . . ."

The Petya-class light frigate would be armed with lightweight 406mm ASW torpedoes from the old Soviet inventory. Never that reliable in the first place, they'd probably deteriorated in Vietnamese service.

"Our torpedoes have acquired Master-one."

"Cut the wires!" Dahlgren ordered. "Close outer

doors. Maneuvering! Ahead full! I want to close with Master-one!''

"Maneuvering, ahead full. Coming to new heading, two-two-three.''

"The second Vietnamese torpedo has gone for the decoy, Captain," Allen reported.

"It's up to us, then," Dahlgren replied. "So much for the wrath of *Khahn*.''

It was a feeble joke, but several of the men chuckled, the sound strained against the rising tension.

"Master-one's first torpedo has gone active. It's acquired us, sir!''

"Release countermeasures!''

"Release countermeasures, aye!''

"First Mark 48 is closing on target," Allen said. Removing his headphones, he added, "Watch your ears, boys. . . .''

Somewhere in the dark waters ahead, 650 pounds of PBXN-103 high explosive detonated with a deep-throated thump.

"Maneuvering!" Dahlgren called. "All stop! Let her drift, silent routine!''

"All stop, aye, sir. Silent routine.''

The second Mark 48 exploded, a hard thump, and a shudder in the water.

Allen had his earphones on again. "Master-one's first torpedo is still homing. Second torpedo . . . Captain, it's gone wild. Sounds like we killed Master-one before it acquired us and they cut the wire." Tense seconds passed. The Kilo's desperate snapshot could still reach out and sink her killer.

They all heard the high-pitched whine as the Kilo's first torpedo passed down the length of the *San Antonio*'s hull, bow to stern. Seconds after the sound faded out, an explosion shuddered through the SSN's hull, muffled by distance.

"Master-one's first torpedo has struck the bottom astern, sir. It was trying to nail our decoy. Second torpedo has gone inactive."

The release of tension in the sonar suite and the control room was palpable. There were no cheers—the *San Antonio*'s crew was far too well trained, too disciplined to break silent routine like that—but the grins and quiet high-fives and clenched fists said it all.

"I'm getting breakup noises from Master-one, Captain." Allen was still listening to the waters beyond the *San Antonio*'s hull, eyes closed, as though he were listening to his CD player. Dahlgren could hear the death-cry of the Kilo even without headphones, a kind of popcorn crackle as compartments flooded, and the low-voiced groan of rupturing metal. "And . . . I'm picking up something else, sir."

"What?"

"I think . . . sir, it's hard to make out, but I think it's cheering. From the *Khahn*."

The crewmen of the Vietnamese ship were celebrating their kill. . . .

11

THE SSN's sail rose from the black water less than fifty yards from the CRRC's position, and the SEALs began motoring for the spot. Normally, after acquiring the contact signal, the SEALs would have approached the sub's position while the sub remained submerged; they would don their rebreathers and follow a buoyed line to the for-

ward escape trunk, where they would lock in and be
greeted by towels, dry clothing, and hot coffee.

That evolution took time, however, and the *San Antonio*'s skipper was obviously in a hurry. As the SSN
surfaced, figures were already visible moving out along
her deck. Someone tossed a line that splashed into the
sea a few feet away; Knox grabbed it and the SEALs
began hauling themselves in.

They didn't bother trying to recover their equipment
or the rubber duck, not with every second the SSN was
surfaced a small and deadly eternity. As Warren slashed
the CRRC with his diving knife, he grinned at Mc-
Cullough. "They want to cut costs? I'll show them cutting costs!"

Eager hands reached down to haul the SEALs out of
the water. Within minutes, they were aboard and on the
mess deck, blankets draped over their shoulders and mugs
of coffee in their hands, as the deck tilted beneath their
feet and the *San Antonio* returned to her natural hunter's
habitat.

"Sorry we were late, fellows," the sub's skipper said,
entering the mess room.

"We heard some explosions to the north," Mc-
Cullough said. "A few minutes later, we heard the Chinese helos off the oil platform taking off like bats out of
hell. Was that you?"

"Call it a decoy," Dahlgren said with a boyish grin.
"While those helos were tangling with the Vietnamese
frigate, we could slip down here, surface, and pick you
guys up."

"Vietnamese frigate?"

"It's a long story."

"We'll want to hear it," McCullough said, "soon as

we get squared away. In the meantime''—he stuck out his hand—''thanks for not leaving us out there, Captain.''

"We do *not* leave our own," Dahlgren replied, grasping the SEAL lieutenant's hand and shaking it.

"That's the philosophy in the Teams, sir. It's not always followed by others."

"It is on my boat, Lieutenant. And now, if you'll excuse me, I've got to get back to the control room. Talk to you later."

"You think he's in trouble?" Warren asked McCullough after the SSN's skipper had left.

"I'd say that was a definite affirmative," McCullough replied. "Sometimes, the real enemy's not out front. He's at your back with a knife and a very bad attitude."

12

"WELL, Skipper," Brad Vincent said as they stood together in *San Antonio*'s control room, "maybe the bastards won't throw the book at you after all."

They'd just crossed the hundred-fathom line and were entering deep water, north of the Spratly Islands, their baffles cleared, the boat on course for Pearl Harbor. Sonar reported no signs of detection or pursuit.

"You know, Brad, I don't really care whether they throw the book at me or not."

Well . . . that wasn't true. As he thought about it, Dahlgren decided that he really *did* care. A lot.

Because he wanted to stay in. Long hours, scant thanks for hard work in frustrating circumstances, long absences from home . . . but he didn't want to give it up.

"Shoot, Skipper, they wouldn't dare keelhaul you now! That UNODIR ploy of yours was sheer brilliance.

If they decide to court-martial you, their orders to abandon the SEALs would come out. They're not going to want that to happen. And as far as the crisis is concerned, you *know* the Vietnamese are going to claim credit for sinking the Kilo. And even if they guess the truth, the Chinese aren't about to admit that an American sub sank their boat, when everyone knows the Vietnamese Navy did it. They'd look foolish. Hell, your peculiar brand of diplomacy might even be what defuses the Spratly Crisis. Make the different parties sit down and talk, instead of shooting at each other.''

''Maybe. More likely, we've just touched off a war out here, Brad.''

''Ah, but we're not involved. 'Plausible deniability,' as Washington likes to say. Either way, we come out smelling like roses. If the bureaucrats try to scuttle you, the whole story comes out . . . including their screwup with the alpha strike orders, and the fact that someone back there was doing so much micromanaging of the situation they lost track of the SEALs! No, I think they're more likely to give you a medal!''

''*That* I very much doubt!''

Dahlgren didn't care about medals. Chances were, Brad was right and he wouldn't face charges for his small act of mutiny in the South China Sea. Even so, his insubordination would be remembered. Chances *also* were, the *San Antonio* would be his last command, and he'd never make it to the captain's list.

He found he didn't care about that, either. What mattered was that one man *could* make a difference . . . maybe even call attention to what was wrong with the government's mismanagement and neglect of the Navy and the military in general right now. He already knew that he was going to demand a court of inquiry, no matter what the official reaction back home.

He owed it to men like Chief Warren and Lieutenant McCullough, to men like Brad Vincent and ST/1 Allen.

He owed it to himself, and his own peace of mind.

When the dust settled, it might well be that Meredith was going to be seeing a *lot* more of him than she'd been seeing lately.

And that, he thought, wouldn't be bad at all.

The Man Who Got
Khrushchev

JIM DEFELICE

Jim DeFelice is the author of several techno-thrillers, including Coyote Bird, War Breaker, *and* Havana Strike, *all of which are available in paperback. He has also written true crime books and a trilogy of historical novels, as well as more than a dozen books for children. He lives in upstate New York with his wife and their young son. You can send him e-mail at* Jdchester@aol.com.

THE PAIN HAD hacksaw teeth, ripping the soft inside of his head like diseased wood. It slammed him so hard his legs began to wobble. A white light seared his eyes as his brain began to pound; nausea pricked at the corners of his stomach, sending caustic plumes up his throat.

Fortunately, there was a bench directly in front of him. Jonathan Keller managed to pitch toward it, pirouetting as he plopped butt-first onto the graffiti-encrusted wood.

The attacks had been increasing in frequency over the past two weeks. Each one felt worse than the one before; there seemed to be no way to prepare for them.

A student—not one of his, fortunately—was sitting at the other end of the bench. Startled, she leapt up, spilling her books in the process. The young woman grabbed them and ran up the hill, toward one of the dormitories.

Keller didn't notice her. He had gripped his head with both hands and pulled it down between his legs, every muscle shaking with pain. The small part of his consciousness that wasn't completely overrun with the horrible pounding prayed that it would stop.

It did not. Instead, his skull seemed to split in half. He took two shallow breaths, then found himself sitting in a park in a foreign city, pulling a thin coat closed against the cold. Keller knew he wasn't really there, but the sensation was so visceral it seemed more than mere hallucination. Groaning, he saw, or thought he saw, an older man with a beard approaching him from across the way, a deep frown on his face. He pretended not to look at him. The man carried a briefcase identical to the one Keller had placed near his feet.

Keller saw and felt all this as if it were real, yet he knew it couldn't be. He knew it had never happened.

Something, someone, was doing this to him. But who and why was a mystery. Keller had been to several doctors over the last few months. They had run tests and given him pills, but the migraines had only gotten worse. He was a rational man—a college professor, after all— but he knew and felt these were attacks being made by some outside source.

It was the motive he couldn't understand. His life had been blameless. He'd never married; outside of a brief affair or two during his early days at the college—never with a student, even though that was all the rage for a while—he had lived his entire adult life alone, rarely even insulting anyone, and then nearly always apologizing. His parents had died so long ago he couldn't remember their faces. He'd been in advertising before coming to teach, working for one of the big multinationals in the sixties before this job fell out of the sky on a silver platter. Keller had grabbed it, even though the pay was nowhere near as good.

There was a heavy spook connection to advertising back in those days. Maybe he'd crossed the wrong man in some obscure way and now they were out to get belated revenge.

"Professor Keller?"

He drew a breath. The pain had subsided enough so that he was able to open his eyes. He looked up into the face of Jack Fitzgerald, one of the adjuncts in the Communications Department.

"Jack. Sneaking up on me when I'm vulnerable?"

"Professor?"

Keller waved his hand. "I'm joking, son." He smiled weakly. The last pangs of the headache rolled back, like the final wave at high tide. "What are you doing on campus in the middle of the day?"

"Have to turn in my grades," said the younger man.

Keller felt a little sorry for him. Fitzgerald was being paid about three thousand dollars to teach two freshman communications classes. It wasn't clear how he made ends meet, though apparently he did some freelance work for two local radio stations. The college ripped these young people off, stringing them along with hopes of finding a full-time position, though few if any ever materialized. It was a scandal, really—some of the best years of their lives stolen from them, with nothing in return. He'd suggested two or three times that Fitzgerald find another line of work; the young man agreed and hinted that he might try at the end of the semester.

"What are you up to?" Fitzgerald asked.

Keller could tell he was still concerned. "I'm on my way to the dungeon," he told him, trying to sound jaunty. The department offices were in the basement of the Watson Building, and Keller was hardly the only one who called them the dungeon. He rose from the bench.

"Want to grab a cup of coffee?" Fitzgerald asked.

"I'd love to, but I'm afraid I have to meet Dean Lanning." He glanced at Fitzgerald, who seemed genuinely disappointed. "Perhaps later. Will you be around?"

"I have a few things to run down at the library," said

the adjunct. "Maybe I'll stop by your office and see if you're there."

"I'd like that," said Keller.

Dean Lanning's secretary, Chris, looked up as he walked in. Her desk was so close to the doorway that Keller had to practically walk sideways to get in. A middle-aged woman related to one of the college trustees, she'd always been pleasant to him. Today, though, Keller thought he caught something sinister in her eyes, as if she were plotting against him. She must have sensed his apprehension; she tried to cover her face with a phony smile.

"You're looking cheery this morning," she told him.

"I'm not feeling cheery," he snapped. "Is Dean Lanning in?"

She kept the smile pasted to her lips as she picked up the phone to tell her boss Keller had arrived. The dean's bald, oblong head popped through the doorway as she hung up. He, too, wore a phony smile.

"Come in, John. Come in," said Lanning. "Christine, some coffee for Professor Keller. Black, no sugar."

Since the notice that Lanning wanted to see him had come in the form of a memo, Keller had concluded that the dean wanted to talk about a specific student's grades. Every so often a parent or someone in the college would apply subtle pressure to keep a grade point average pegged at a certain level. It had to be done with a certain amount of subtlety, but Keller had long ago realized it was best to bend to the collective will. The topic itself would be approached only indirectly, after some preliminaries about course offerings or something equally innocuous.

But now Keller wasn't so sure why he'd been called

in. The smile threw him off; it seemed too fake for the occasion.

"What is it?" he demanded, suddenly in no mood to play bureaucratic games.

"Have a seat," said Lanning, closing the door. "Please, John."

"I think I'll stand."

Lanning went around to his desk. Bare except for a large, multifeature phone in its upper right-hand corner, the surface gleamed with gnarled walnut patterns.

"You've been at this college a long time," said Lanning. "This must be, what, your twenty-fifth graduation coming up."

"Twenty-ninth. I never attend the convocation, Jep. You can't make me. It's a contract item."

"This isn't about the convocation," said Lanning. His smile was gone. The hollow of his cheeks seemed to narrow and redden slightly as he continued. No longer sugar-coating his words, the dean told Keller it was time for him to retire.

"Why? You can't make me."

"There have been complaints," said Lanning. "You've spent whole classes gazing at the walls. Several students say you have shouted at them, as if they were attacking you."

"They were."

Lanning said nothing for a moment. "We can have three years added to your time-in-service. It will take you to a seventy-five percent pension. It's quite generous."

Calmly considered, the offer was more than generous, but Keller was hardly in a calm mood. He left the office shouting and shaking, his head once more pounding. Everyone had turned against him.

His eyes were bleary with pain and rage, and his hands trembled as he took out the key for his office lock. He rammed the key into the hole, practically snapping the metal in two as he pushed inside. The pain came in waves; Keller collapsed his face against the surface of his metal desk, hands clasped as if bombs were raining all around. Foreign voices loomed at the edge of his consciousness. They were speaking a language he couldn't identify, let alone understand.

No, he could. It was Russian. He understood it perfectly. He was at a train station, being asked for papers.

He had the papers. Left breast pocket, inside his jacket. He had to be careful when he reached for them because there was a danger he would expose the bulge where his gun was.

Gun?

He'd never fired a gun in his life. He hated weapons, abhorred all violence.

It was a tiny Deer gun, a very-close-range single-shot pistol that fit easily in the palm of his hand. Three nine-millimeter Parabellum rounds were stored in the pistol grip.

Who would have such a weapon? Why would he even know about it?

Yet this seemed to be a real memory, not something made up. Keller's astonishment cut through the pain; he raised his head and with his hand felt to make sure he did not have such a gun. As he did so, he saw Fitzgerald standing in the doorway, a concerned look on his face.

"Your keys were in the lock," said the adjunct, holding them up.

"I've just had the most remarkable dream," said Keller. "Very remarkable—I dreamed I could understand Russian."

"Can you?"

Keller laughed. Once again the pain in his head was subsiding. "No. It must have come from an old movie. Very remarkable. Stress. I've been having migraines." He held out his hands apologetically. "An unfortunate sign of aging, according to one doctor. Another says it's not. They've given me medicine. I take it, but it does no good."

Fitzgerald nodded. Silently, he placed the keys on Keller's desk. Keller decided he felt a great affinity for the young man. Fitzgerald, too, was being screwed by the college, though Keller sensed that the young man might greatly prefer the terms he had just been offered to his present state.

"Want to have that coffee?" Keller asked.

"Sure."

As Keller started to rise, he realized that his legs were still unsteady. He sat back quickly.

"Are you O.K.?" Fitzgerald asked.

"I've just had some bad news. I'll recover."

"Why don't I go get something from the coffee shop and bring it back?"

Keller nodded.

"You take it black, no sugar, right?"

"With sugar. No, wait, you're right. No sugar. Funny thing to forget," he added. "Bring me a donut or one of those sticky things, will you? Maybe my unconscious is trying to tell me my blood sugar's low."

"Be right back."

Fitzgerald was right; he never had sugar in his coffee.

But suddenly he remembered pouring two spoonfuls in, every morning.

Every morning where? He'd grown up in Queens, but now he was seeing rural Virginia in his mind. A friend, Tommy Lang, pitched a baseball across the open field.

Tommy Lang. Yes, he had a firm memory of that. But had it happened in New York City or Virginia? The closest he'd ever been to Virginia was Washington, D.C., and that was as a tourist.

No, he had a firm memory of walking in the city. He was on J Street, not far from the executive office building. He was headed for the intelligence office building. The D.O. had told him to meet him there, and he was shaking with nervousness.

What did "D.O." mean? Outside of a two-year stint in the army as a private—barely remembered, but that was probably for the best—Jonathan Keller had never worked for the government. He'd certainly not done anything that would take him to the intelligence building. Was there even an intelligence building in Washington?

"I'm back," announced Fitzgerald, entering the office. "Is this roll sticky enough for you?"

Keller took the pineapple Danish. With the first bite he felt refreshed. The coffee helped, too.

"So what did the dean want?" Fitzgerald asked.

It occurred to Keller that the young man was interested in his job. Perhaps he had engineered some sort of putsch to get rid of him.

But no. Fitzgerald wasn't like that. He was completely without guile, naive to a fault. They'd had several long conversations over the course of the last semester and a half. He was intelligent and thoughtful—and certainly generous, for he listened to Keller's ramblings without complaint, even seeming to enjoy them. Fitzgerald was anything but a plotter.

Besides, he wasn't the type Lanning would hire full-time, not even to fill a temporary vacancy.

"They're asking me to retire," said Keller, deciding to put a positive spin on the situation. "I guess they think I'm over the hill."

"Are you ready to retire?"

"I suppose if the offer is attractive enough it will be hard to turn down. The main problem is that I don't know what I'd do with myself. I'm a bachelor, you know. No family. Oh, a few friends, but I've always found it best to keep to myself. Just the way I am. Never really could put down roots. To be honest, I've been dreading the summer. My main project will be to repaint my apartment—if I can get my landlord to spring for the paint."

Fitzgerald smiled.

"Do you have big plans?" Keller asked.

"Just to look for a real job."

"You should apply for mine." Keller decided he liked the young man very much. Why shouldn't he get his job? Assuming, of course, that he went ahead and retired.

There probably wasn't a choice, just a question of going quietly or not.

"I don't know if I'm cut out to be a professor," said Fitzgerald. "Besides, I don't have a Ph.D."

"I don't have a Ph.D. either. At least, not in advertising or communications." Keller let his voice trail off.

"Professor?"

Keller laughed. "You know, I almost said I had a degree in international studies. And Russian. I don't know what's come over me in the last few months. These migraines. Things fly through my head, as if they're memories. You probably think I'm nuts.''

Fitzgerald took a long sip from his coffee. ''What kind of memories?''

''Do you ever think you've been another person?''

''Like reincarnation?''

''No, more like—'' Keller stumbled, trying to find the words to describe what he felt. ''More like you're simultaneously someone else. A clone, maybe. You think I'm crazy, don't you?''

''Who do you think you are?''

Keller shrugged. The pineapple filling in the Danish filled his mouth and nose with a pungent, sweet odor, something like decay. ''A character in a movie.'' He laughed. ''I'm getting paranoid. I even feel persecuted.''

''Maybe you are.''

''I'm definitely eccentric. I've always been eccentric. But not paranoid.'' Keller's mouth felt very dry. He took a gulp of the coffee, then another. He looked over in surprise. ''You put sugar in it.''

Fitzgerald nodded.

Keller took another sip. He did like it that way, though he knew for a fact that he hadn't ever drunk coffee with sugar. Never.

''Do you remember who you were in 1964?''

Taken by surprise, Keller looked into the young man's face. There was a hardness there he hadn't noticed before, rather than the confusion or pity he expected. He'd thought Fitzgerald was in his late twenties; he realized now he was ten years beyond that.

''Why 1964?''

''That was the year Nikita Khrushchev fell from power.''

"He was supposed to be shot."

The words sprang from Keller's brain to his mouth unbidden. He stared into the room in front of him, as if he might see them, as if they were a strange animal that had leaped from a hiding place deep inside his soul.

"The plan was changed at the last minute," said Fitzgerald. "A deal was struck, though you weren't given the details. But then, it wasn't like you had a choice."

"Me?" Keller's hand trembled as he reached for the coffee cup. The younger man leaned across the desk and helped him bring it to his mouth, his fingers gently wrapping themselves around Keller's wrist. They were warm, slightly moist.

"You remember?" Fitzgerald asked.

"I—" As the word slipped from his mouth, Keller felt a stab of pain sharper than the one that had hobbled him outside. It pushed him back in the chair. But even as his body reverberated with the shock, his mind began to clear. He felt calmer. It was as if the trauma in his brain had been caused by a seedling struggling to break the surface of the earth; something inside had passed through a difficult barrier and was now free.

"I was given microfilm," he told Fitzgerald. "I had to deliver it to a man in a park outside Moscow. It was in the handle of a briefcase. I wasn't told all this exactly, but I knew what was going on. It went very smoothly, though I was panicked the whole time."

"Because you weren't a real operative. You were an analyst."

"They needed someone with a fresh face. Who could speak Russian."

"You volunteered."

The weight of the returning memories pushed against

Keller's shoulders and spine. He could feel his lungs laboring. Keller reached again for the coffee cup. This time Fitzgerald didn't help him. He pulled it up to his mouth quickly, drained the rest of the sweet liquid.

"I did volunteer. It was a difficult decision."

"Because you had a wife and a baby."

Keller nodded. "I was told they would be taken care of. You're from the Company, aren't you?"

Fitzgerald nodded.

"It wasn't just patriotism," said Keller. "You have to remember the times. Khrushchev had gotten Kennedy, and I was getting him. We would have assassinated him. I could have. I had a clear shot."

And now, suddenly, Keller remembered everything: the plane to England, the ferry across the Channel, Germany, Berlin, his two-week stay in Czechoslovakia. The car ride to Moscow had been the most exciting few hours of his life.

In the original plan, Keller—his real name was Kellog—had been assigned to help a sniper. It was truly a revenge killing, with the Soviet leader to be taken out the same way Kennedy had been: high-powered rifle in an open area. Soviet security was considerably more formidable than the Dallas police force, but the CIA had a collaborator, a very high-ranking Soviet official who wanted Khrushchev out of the way. Kellog never knew who it was. It wasn't his job to know, and besides, knowing would put him in even graver danger than he was in.

The plan had moved along perfectly. And then the morning of the assassination, a deep-cover contact approached him on the street and uttered the code word— "Rommel"—calling off the attack. Kellog started to protest, but the man slipped back into the crowd. He went and found the sniper several hours ahead of schedule. According to the plan they were to await further instructions. The sniper was an old CIA hand; he went to see if he could verify the command. Kellog waited in the apartment chosen for the killing.

The rifle was a specially constructed Barrett sniper weapon, semiautomatic, a very heavy piece with a precisely calibrated scope. The sniper had explained the logistics of aiming the day before, how the drop and wind had to be properly compensated for. At 119.02 meters from their target, and with eleven bullets in his magazine, the expert did not consider the shot particularly difficult. The trick was in their escape; he expected a double-cross from the Russians helping them. They had chosen the time and building themselves, but the general area would be obvious as soon as the shot was fired. Still, with an elaborate series of backup plans and precautions—to say nothing of youthful naiveté—Kellog believed they would get away.

Now he sat in the room, waiting. They had tied up the apartment's occupant yesterday; he was in a closet nearby as Kellog waited for the sniper to return. The man was so scared he shit himself, and the odor permeated the air. Kellog felt it sting his nostrils as the car carrying Khrushchev arrived in the square. He gripped the rifle on its mount, sighting through the scope. The sniper had carefully checked and rechecked the adjustments this morning. All Kellog had to do was pull the trigger. He even knew where Khrushchev would probably fall and where the error in aiming would likely be; he was prepared to swing the rifle in that direction. It took years of training and a certain natural skill to be a sniper, but the thin steel of the trigger against Kellog's finger told him he would catch the brown suit full in the chest. His shoulder and legs tensed against the expected recoil.

Khrushchev got out, he was in the clear, it was an easy shot.

But Kellog had been ordered not to fire. Khrushchev was in the open for a good five seconds, maybe as many as ten, an eternity. Kellog's heart did not beat the entire time.

When night fell, he realized the sniper was not returning. Finally panicking, he forgot even to wipe down the apartment before leaving. By the time he regained his composure, it was almost midnight, and he was on a train heading toward Leningrad—a freelanced variation of one of their escape plans.

He hid near the platform all night, clutching his small Deer pistol in his hand in case a guard found him. The specially made CIA weapon was designed to be used to incapacitate someone so you could grab their gun; it had to be used at handshake range and he didn't particularly trust it. But it was all he had. Finally morning came. Kellog got on the train to Moscow, making his way back to a small cafe at a time assigned for contact should Rommel be put into effect.

The waitress pointed at a briefcase on the floor. "Is that yours?" she asked.

Later that day he was told to drive to a park in a suburb, where a Russian agent exchanged the briefcases.

"And then you took the Medusa pill," said Fitzgerald as Keller's voice trailed off.

"No. I took it on the plane. I almost took it in Moscow. The police stopped me for my papers. But I kept my head."

"You knew what would happen."

"They told me."

"And still you took it."

"It was a direct order. I was to take it on the plane."

He could tell Fitzgerald didn't believe him.

"It was an order," said Keller desperately. "Whether I was captured or not. I always intended to take it."

The adjunct nodded, though he still seemed unconvinced. "Your wife and child?"

"I know." Keller felt tears coming to his eyes. He rubbed his hand over his face. "But they were supposed to be taken care of."

"They were."

"You know that for a fact?"

Fitzgerald nodded. Keller believed him. "Why have you come?" he asked.

"It's my job."

They were both silent for a moment.

"To have someone like me, a nobody, with nothing at stake but who knew everything; that would have been too dangerous," blurted Keller. "The choice was to forget everything, or to be killed."

"I understand."

"No, you don't. You can't. You must remember, the original mission was to kill him. For that I was prepared to give up everything."

"You were cheated." Fitzgerald's voice was flat and hollow, but if he harbored some other belief—that perhaps Kellog should have gone ahead and killed Khrushchev, or should have killed himself, or should have refused the mission—it was undetectable. "You were cheated, but your bosses didn't see it that way. In their eyes, you accomplished your mission beautifully. It worked very, very well. They had managed to strike the

deal at the very last moment. The microfilm you handed
off was used to discredit Khrushchev within the Kremlin.
He was ruined. Brezhnev came to power, and carried
through with a remarkably large part of his promise. To
your superiors, it was a fair trade—a President for a Premier, and détente. A very fair trade, since most of them
didn't like Kennedy to begin with. One for one.''

"And me?"

"You didn't enter into their equation."

Keller nodded. He knew that was so, had known it
then. "The sniper?" he asked.

"Mark McCalugh's body was found in a stream outside of Moscow a few days after you left the country."

"My wife—is she still alive?"

"She died a year ago."

"How?"

"Cancer."

"Did she remarry?"

Fitzgerald shook his head. He reached into his pocket
and pulled out three photos, pushed them across the desk.
The top was of a gravestone, an entire lifetime reduced
to a few disjointed words:

MARY KELLOG
"I'M COMING FOR YOU, DEAR"
1943–98

The next photo was of a girl, three or four years old.
The next was of a boy, a babe in arms.

"Your grandchildren."

"My grandchildren?"

Now it was emotion, not physical pain, that made his
body shake. Sadness mixed with a joy Keller had never

felt, at least not for the past thirty-five years. He held the two photos in front of him as his eyes grew blurry with tears.

"Grandchildren," he repeated. "Grandchildren." Finally, he looked up at Fitzgerald. "What about my son?"

"The Company took care of him. As promised."

"Can I go to see him?"

Fitzgerald said nothing. Keller knew for sure now why he had come, why he was being told all this.

It was a gift, really. They could have taken him out, or worse, let him go on.

"The drug was very good," he said.

"For its time."

"How long have they known it was failing?"

Fitzgerald shrugged.

"The gravesite? Can I go there?" he asked.

"It's in New Jersey. Your wife went back to her family. You'll be buried there, if you want." The young man paused, studying his face carefully. Fitzgerald's eyes seemed to bore into his skull, searching past decades of purposely cobwebbed memories. "Was it worth it?"

The question came as Keller felt himself being pushed down a long hallway. His mind was retreating, running away. The walls of his small office went from pale green to deep black. His throat was dry again, and tasted like roasted almonds. His eyes flicked down to the photos in his hands.

His wife dead, after grieving all these years.

Grandchildren.

"Was it worth giving up your family?" Fitzgerald asked. "Your identity? All your memories?"

Keller struggled to answer. He wanted to say it was. It was the answer the twenty-five-year-old who had volunteered for the mission would certainly have given. But his tongue was glued in his mouth, as if the weight of all that might have been pressed against it. He felt his chest quiver and start to shake, his heart growing large. His eyes were losing focus, a dark shadow was enveloping the room.

"Would you do it again?" Fitzgerald asked.

Would he? Would he give up a life to assassinate a foreign leader, to kill the man who had ordered his commander-in-chief's death? Give up not only his happiness but his wife's, his son's?

Had Brezhnev made that much difference to the world? Would real revenge have made that much difference to him?

He was back in the office of the Director of Operations, back in the room where he had accepted the mission to kill Khrushchev. Yes, he would do it, Yes, yes, yes.

And then the faces of his two grandchildren swam before his eyes, and the hollow emptiness of his last thirty years consumed him.

An hour later, Jack Fitzgerald pulled the car into the Burger King parking lot. He quickly reviewed his mental checklist. Everything had been taken care of; grades filed, lease canceled. His car had already been wiped clean twice. It was an unnecessary precaution, perhaps, but he always paid attention to detail. He took a handkerchief from his pocket and wiped the steering wheel, then used the cloth to pull open the door handle. He left the keys in the ignition; the four-year-old brown Honda Accord would sit here for only a few minutes before being driven away to its own special oblivion.

There was one more piece of business he had to accomplish. The agent walked inside the fast-food restaurant and ordered himself a cup of coffee. As he headed toward a table around the side, he stopped at the trash can and shoved in the Styrofoam cup Keller had drunk from. Unless a trained expert who knew precisely what he was looking for performed the autopsy within six hours of the body's discovery, the death would be diagnosed as a simple and very expected heart attack.

Keller would undoubtedly get a good funeral, at college expense. The wake would be packed.

Everyone in the department would blame the dean for suggesting that he retire. True, Keller had become increasingly eccentric, crazy even, over the past two years; still, the situation could have been handled more delicately.

But by the end of the service, they would all conclude that it was probably for the best that Professor Keller had gone out like that: quick, quiet, conveniently after he had turned in his grades. And he'd gotten out of another of those endless graduation ceremonies, which he deeply detested.

Undoubtedly a large number of students would attend the funeral. Professor Keller had always had a reputation for being very friendly; he treated most like the family he never had. It was what had made his most recent behavior so shocking.

Keller had told him he would do it again. Had he truly meant that? Or did he not want to believe he'd given up so much in vain?

The man had lost so much, yet a certain amount remained, certain shadows of personality that could never be erased. Watching Jonathan Keller for nearly a year now, Jack Fitzgerald had concluded that James Kellog had not been an overly heroic man, just one who felt compelled to do his duty as he saw it. He was intelligent, kind, not particularly outgoing and yet friendly. The old professor had treated Jack well, much better than any of the other full-time members of the staff had.

The agent took a sip of coffee. It had been a long, absorbing assignment. Not particularly dangerous, but difficult. One he'd volunteered for.

Would he do it again?

Yes, he thought he would.

He reached into his pocket and took out the pill. Science had come a long way since his father's day. Memory erasing was much more selective.

At least, he'd been told that was the case. There was always the chance the people who told him were wrong, or were simply lying. But you had to factor that in when you made your decision.

John Fitzgerald Kellog slipped the pill into his mouth, then took a big slurp of coffee, and another, waiting.

Drang von Osten

HARRY TURTLEDOVE

Harry Turtledove is best known for his meticulously detailed novels of alternate history and time travel, which include The Guns of the South, A Different Flesh, *and* World War: In the Balance. *Recent books include* Fox and Empire, The Two Georges *(coauthored with Richard Dreyfus), and* Colonization: Book One: Second Contact. *A scholar of Byzantine history, he originally published studies of historians of the Eastern Empire. He lives in California.*

BUCKETS OF RAIN poured down from the autumn sky. They turned the endless Russian plain into an endless swamp. The thick, gluey mud tried to suck the boots off *Gefreiter* Jürgen Sack's feet at every weary westward step he took.

The clouds and the deluge shut down visibility, too. The lance-corporal never knew the ground-attack plane was near until it screamed past just over his head, almost close enough for him to reach out and touch the big red star painted on the side of the fuselage. He threw himself facedown into the muck. A few of his comrades had the presence of mind to fire at the aircraft, but to no effect.

Half a kilometer west of Sack, the plane vomited cannon fire and rockets into the Germans retreating across the Trubezh. He swiped a filthy sleeve across his equally filthy face. "God help us," he groaned. "We'll never make it back to Kiev alive."

Beside him in the mud lay a staff sergeant who'd been at the front since the push east began in '41. *Wachtmeister* Gustav Pfeil said, "If you think the Reds are going to get you, they probably will. Me, I figure I'm still alive and they haven't got me yet." He pushed himself to his feet. "Come on. The sooner we cross the Trubezh, the safer we're liable to be."

Sack stumbled after him. You had to stay with your comrades, no matter what. Get cut off and dreadful things

were likely to happen. Like too many other German soldiers, he'd seen what the Reds sometimes did to men they
caught. Some of the roadside corpses had their noses cut
off, others their ears. Others had their pants pulled down
and were missing other things.

The lance-corporal lifted his face against the rain, letting it wash some of the dirt away from his eyes. Here
and there, through the downpour, he saw other hunched
figures tramping west.

A squeal in the sky, different from any aircraft noise.
''Rockets!'' he screamed, his voice going high and shrill
as a girl's. He dove for the mud again, in an instant re-
destroying a couple of minutes' approach to cleanliness.

He was near the rear edge of the salvo of forty truck-
mounted artillery rockets; no doubt they were all intended
to slam down on the Germans struggling to cross the rain-
swollen Trubezh. The noise and the blast were quite
dreadful enough where he lay. He felt as if he'd been
lifted and then slammed back to earth by a giant's hand.
Fragments of rocket casing screeched past his head. They
could have gutted him like a carp.

More rockets rained down on the crumbling German
position east of the river. The enemy must have lined up
a whole battery of launcher trucks axle to axle, Sack
thought with the small part of his mind not terrified altogether out of rationality. To either side of him,
wounded men's screams sounded tiny and lost amidst the
shrieks and explosions of the incoming rockets.

Just when he was certain his company's hellish fix
could not grow worse, shells began landing along with
the rockets. Mud and dying grass fountained up into the
weeping sky, then splashed down on men and on pieces
of what had been men.

Then German artillery west of the Trubezh—the last defensive positions in front of the Dnieper and Kiev—opened up in counterbattery fire. The eastbound shells sounded different from incoming ordnance; instead of growing louder and shriller, their track across the sky deepened and got fainter as they dopplered away. But any response to the barrage under which he suffered was lovely music to Jürgen Sack.

The enemy fire slackened: maybe the counterbattery work had smashed the rocket launcher trucks. Sack didn't care about wherefores; the only thing that mattered to him was that, for the moment, the heavens were raining only water, not steel and brass and high explosive.

"Up!" he yelled, scrambling to his feet. "Up and get moving!"

At the same time, *Wachtmeister* Pfeil was shouting, "Come on, you lice! Head for the river! We have a chance to hold them there."

Between them, the two noncoms bullied almost all the huddled, terrified Germans into motion. A few did not move because they'd never move again. One or two more, still alive and unhurt, refused to get up even when Sack kicked them with his muddy boots. They'd taken all they could; even capture by the enemy, with its prospects of Siberia at the best, horrid death at the worst, could not stir them from their fatal apathy. Sack hurried on. Delaying to force the laggards up would only mean dying with them.

A ragged German rearguard—men in flooded foxholes, three or four mechanized infantry combat vehicles, a couple of panzers—held a line on a low rise a couple of hundred meters this side of the Trubezh. A grimy lieutenant, his helmet knocked askew on his head, squelched

toward Sack. The lance-corporal gulped, fearing he was
about to be ordered to help hold that unholdable line. But
the lieutenant just waved him toward the river. "Go on,
go on. Get as many across as you can, while we keep the
verdammte Asiatics off your backs."

Sack nodded and stumbled on. But when he started to
come down from the rise toward the Trubezh, his feet for
a moment refused to carry him forward. The ground-
attack plane had caught German rafts in the water.
Wreckage drifted downstream. So did dead men, and
their fragments. Sack had read of battles where streams
flowed red with blood. Till that moment, he'd thought it
a novelist's conceit. No more.

Living soldiers still struggled in the Trubezh, too; a
couple of rafts and barges that hadn't been hit wallowed
up onto the western bank. Men in camouflage cloth and
field-gray mottled and filthy enough to serve as camouflage cloth scrambled off, glad to put any water barrier,
however small and flimsy, between themselves and the
uncountable Asiatic horde swarming out of the east.

The boats started back toward the eastern bank of the
Trubezh. Sack dispassionately admired their crews, just
as he admired the worn lieutenant in charge of that
doomed rearguard line. He admitted to himself that he
lacked the courage required to stick his head deliberately
into the tiger's mouth and leave it there while the fanged
jaws closed.

Boots splashing at the marge of the river, *Wachtmeister* Pfeil positioned himself where one of the barges
looked likeliest to ground. Sack stood at his left shoulder,
as if he were a feudal retainer. But chivalry in Russia was
dead, dead. This war had room only for ugliness.

An old soldier, Pfeil knew all the tricks. As soon as

the barge got close, he splashed out into the Trubezh and helped drag it to shore. As if by magic, that entitled him to a place on board. His big, rough hands pulled Sack in after him.

Germans swarmed on until the rough water of the Trubezh was bare centimeters from the gunwale. Even as the sergeant at the engine threw it into reverse and backed the clumsy vessel away from the riverbank, more men reached out beseechingly, though they had to know they'd swamp it if they managed to get aboard.

The cannon of one of the panzers posted on the eastern rise roared. A moment later, a couple of MG-3 machine guns opened up. With their rapid cyclic rate, they sounded like giants ripping enormous sheets of canvas. However many bullets they spat, though, there always seemed to be more short, stocky men who wore the red star on their fur caps.

Some of the Germans by the riverside turned and ran back toward the rearguard line to help buy their comrades time. Others threw down weapons, stripped off clothes and boots, and plunged naked into the chilly Trubezh: drowning looked to them a better risk than waiting for another boat where they were. They swam almost as fast as Sack's overloaded barge made headway across the river.

The lance-corporal became aware of an unfamiliar feeling. "Great God, I'm almost warm!" he bawled into Pfeil's ear.

"I shouldn't wonder," the senior noncom answered. "We're packed together tight as steers in a cattle car." Pfeil managed a worn grin. "I just hope we're headed away from the slaughterhouse."

Sack tried to laugh, but after what he'd been through

the past few months—and especially the past few days—
he couldn't force himself to find it funny. Hardly more
than a year before, German motorized patrols were operating east of the Volga and pushing toward Astrakhan
over a steppe that seemed empty of foes. Now the Volga
line was long forgotten. If the army couldn't hold the
Reds along the Dnieper . . . if they couldn't do that, where
would they stop them?

Deciding such questions was not a lance-corporal's
concern. Sack watched the western bank of the Trubezh
ever so slowly draw nearer. How long could crossing a
couple of hundred meters of water take?

Too long—the barge was still wallowing toward the
far shore when he heard another fighter-bomber screaming in on an attack run. Cannon shells whipped the river
to creamy foam; underwing rockets lanced down on
tongues of flame. Sack's scream was lost in those of his
comrades.

One instant he was huddled in the barge, the next flying through the air, and the one after that floundering in
the cold, muddy Trubezh. He must has swallowed a liter
of it before he clawed his way to the surface and sucked
in a lungful of desperately needed air. Then his boots
touched bottom. He realized he was just a few meters
from shore.

He splashed up onto the western bank and threw himself down at full length, more dead than alive. Or so he
thought, till a roar in the sky warned that the enemy plane
was coming back for another pass. He scrambled on
hands and knees toward a shell hole that might offer some
small protection.

He rolled in on top of another man who'd beaten him

to it. "I might have known it would be you, *Wachtmeister*."

Pfeil grunted. "You can get hurt around here if you're not careful."

Both men buried their heads in the wet dirt, waiting for another dose of guns and rockets. But it didn't come. The Red fighter-bomber sheered off and streaked away eastward, two *Luftwaffe* fighters hot on its trail. Moments later, a blast louder than shellfire said one enemy aircraft, at any rate, would never harass German ground troops again.

Sack and Pfeil both shouted like men possessed. They pounded each other on the shoulders, clasped hands. "The air force *is* good for something!" the lance-corporal yelled, in the tone of an atheist suddenly coming to Jesus.

"Every once in a while," Pfeil allowed. "Haven't seen much of those bastards the past few weeks, though." Sack nodded. Too many hundreds of kilometers of front, too few planes spread too thin.

The two battered soldiers used the momentary respite to get away from the riverbank. Sack spotted an abandoned farmhouse, half its roof caved in, that looked like an ideal spot to curl up and rest for a while before getting back to the war. When he pointed it out to Pfeil, the staff sergeant grinned. He hurried past his junior to take the lead in exploring the retreat.

He and Sack both entered with rifles at the ready, in case partisans were lurking inside. And indeed, the farmhouse was occupied—but by German soldiers in too-clean uniforms with the metal gorgets of the military police round their necks. "What unit, gentlemen?" One of them asked with a nasty smile.

"First platoon, third company, second regiment, Forty-first *Panzergrenadiers*," Sack and Pfeil answered in the same breath.

"Where's the rest of it?" the military policeman demanded.

"Back in the hospital, dead on the field, drowned in the f— in the Trubezh," Pfeil said, "Oh, I expect some of our comrades are still alive, but we got separated. It happens in battle." His tone implied, as strongly as he dared, that his questioner had never seen real combat.

If the military policeman noticed the sarcasm, he didn't show it. One of his companions might have, for he said, "At least they have all their gear, Horst. Some of those fellows have been coming back without a stitch on them."

"As if the quartermasters didn't have enough problems," Horst snorted. Sack wanted to pump him full of bullets—here he was in his dog collar, with a safe post back of the line, making the lives of fighting men miserable. But Horst went on, "You're right, Willi, we have worse things to worry about. You two—there's a road, of sorts, about a hundred meters west of here. A kilometer and a half, maybe two, down that road are more *panzergrenadiers*. Attach yourself to their *kampf gruppe* for the time being."

"Yes sir," Sack and Pfeil said, again together. They got out of the farmhouse in a hurry; the military police had almost certainly taken possession of it knowing it would attract tired soldiers.

The road, like too many Russian roads, was nothing more than a muddy track. Pfeil swore at the military police as he tramped along. Sack echoed him for a while— like any real soldier, he had only scorn for the dog-collar boys—but then fell silent. He didn't like what he'd heard back at the farmhouse. A *kampf gruppe* was like papier-mâché: bits and pieces of defunct units squashed together in the hope they'd hold. Also like papier-mâché, battle groups fell apart when handled roughly.

Somebody in a foxhole shouted, "Halt!"

Sack and Pfeil obediently halted. "We're friends," Sack called. He stood still to let the sentry see his uniform.

"Stay," the sentry said. They stayed—he had the drop on them.

He didn't get out of the hole to check them himself, but called to someone else. The other soldier approached from the side, careful not to get between the foxhole and the two Germans. He too kept his assault rifle at the ready as he carefully examined Sack and Pfeil. But when he spoke to them, what came out of his mouth was gibberish, not German.

Now the two noncoms exchanged glances. "Should he worry about us being the enemy, or should we worry about him?" Pfeil muttered.

Then Sack saw the rampant lion on the fellow's collar patch. "Norway?" he asked, pointing to it.

"*Ja!*" the other soldier exclaimed, and then more in his own language. Sack eyed him with increasing respect. Several western European nations had sent contingents to hold back the Red Asiatic flood, and those outfits had solid fighting reputations. Sack just wished their soldiers had picked up more German.

The Norwegian was a big blond fellow who might have posed for a recruiting poster if he'd been cleaner. He and Sack soon discovered they'd both studied English in school. Neither of them was fluent, but they managed to understand each other. The Norwegian said, "There is a—how do you say it?—a canteen? a kitchen?—down the road not far." He pointed to show the direction.

That cut conversation off at the knees, or rather at the belly. The German supply system had worked well for a while, with everyone having plenty of food and field kitchens keeping pace with the advancing armies. The armies were no longer advancing. Enemy aircraft had taken their toll on truck columns and supply trains. The long and short of it was that Sack hadn't eaten for more than a day.

The big bubbling pot smelled wonderful. Most of the soldiers gathered around it were Scandinavians of one sort or another: Norwegians, Danes who wore a white cross on a red shield, or Swedes with blue and gold emblems that were almost the same shades as those of the Ukraine's national colors. Some spoke German; more knew English. They all had the worn look of men who'd been through a good deal.

But the stew in the pot was thick and rich, full of cabbage, potatoes, and meat. Sack wolfed down a big bowl. "It's horsemeat," a Dane said apologetically in English. The corporal didn't quite take that in, so someone else translated: *"Pferdfleisch."* In civilian life, the idea would have revolted him. Now he just held out his bowl for more. The Scandinavians laughed and fed him.

He'd hardly begun his second helping when firing to the east picked up. Gustav Pfeil looked grim. "Eat while you can. I think the Reds are trying to force the river."

As if on cue, a German artillery battery not far away fired a salvo. Then Sack heard the heavy diesels of the self-propelled guns roar into life to move them into a new position before Red artillery could reply.

The Norwegian who'd led him to the field kitchen handed him a mug full of hot instant coffee. He gratefully held it under his nose. Even the rich aroma was invigorating. And the aroma was all he got, too, for a whistling in the air said the Germans hadn't knocked out all the enemy guns. Soldiers shrieked "Incoming!" in a medley of languages. Some, who'd been around here for a little while, knew where the slit trenches were and dove for them. Sack threw his coffee away and flattened out on the ground. The burst were thunderous, and less than a hundred meters from where he lay. Splinters flew by with deadly hisses; mud splattered down on top of his helmet.

Still on his belly, he pulled out his entrenching tool, unfolded it, and started digging himself in. The Red shells kept falling; it might as well have been a World War I bombardment. If it was going to be like that, Sack wanted himself a nice World War I trench in which to endure it.

Then Gustav Pfeil screamed.

Sack rolled out of his half-dug hole, crawled snakelike over to where the *Wachtmeister* lay writhing on the ground. Pfeil had both hands clenched to his thigh. His trouser leg was already reddish-black, his face gray.

"Medical officer!" Sack shouted. Then, more softly, he said to Pfeil. "Here, let me see it." His hands shook as he moved the staff sergeant's away from the injury. Pfeil had never been scratched, not in more than two years of hard fighting. How could he be wounded now? And if he was, how could anyone hope to come through this war intact?

The wound sliced cleanly into the meat of the thigh. Pfeil's flesh looked like something that ought to be hanging in a butcher's shop, not like part of a man at all. "I don't think the femoral artery's cut," Sack said inanely.

"Of course not," Pfeil replied with the eerie calm of a man in shock. "If it were, I'd already have bled out."

Sack dusted the wound with sulfa and antibiotics from his aid kit, wrapped a pressure bandage around it. One of the Danes came up to help a moment later. Along with his white cross on red, he wore a red cross on a white armband. He looked under the pressure bandage to see what Sack had done, nodded, and then rolled up Pfeil's left sleeve. He gave the *Wachtmeister* a painkiller shot, then said in good German, "Make a fist." When Pfeil obeyed, the Dane stuck the needle from a plasma unit into the bend of his elbow.

The medical officer turned to Sack. "I wish we could airlift him out, but—" A fresh barrage of incoming artillery punctuated the *but*. The Dane stood up anyhow, shouted, "Stretcher party!" first in German, then in English.

"I'm one," Sack said.

The Norwegian who'd guided the two Germans back to the kitchen came out of his hole. "I'm the other," he said in English. "I know the way back to the field hospital."

The medical officer pulled telescoping aluminum stretcher poles from his pack, extended them, and strung them with mesh. He fixed an upright metal arm to one of them to hold the plasma bag. Together, he and Sack got Pfeil onto the stretcher. "He should do well enough," the medical officer said, "unless, of course, we're all overrun."

Sack, for one, could have done without the parenthetical comment. He and the Norwegian stooped, lifted the stretcher, and started for the field hospital. Though they headed away from the fighting, no one could question their courage, not with artillery shells still falling all around. They would have been safer staying in their foxholes than walking about in the open.

Wachtmeister Pfeil was not a big man; he weighed perhaps seventy-five kilos. By the time Sack had hauled him through mud for more than a kilometer, it might as well have been seventy-five tonnes. He marveled that his arms didn't drag the ground like an orangutan's by the time he reached the aid station.

All the tents there were clean and white, with red crosses prominently displayed on the cloth. That wouldn't necessarily keep away artillery fire, but Sack did notice no bigger bombs had hit in the immediate vicinity of the tents. That raised some small measure of relief in him; too often, the godless Reds respected nothing.

An orderly took charge of Pfeil. Sack stood near the hospital tents for a couple of minutes. He windmilled his arms, trying to work the soreness out of them. The Norwegian did the same; they traded weary grins. The lance-corporal wondered what the devil to do next. He supposed he ought to go back to the *panzergrenadiers;* if any officer asked what he was doing there, he could say the military police had sent him.

The Norwegian rolled himself a smoke with old newspaper and coarse Russian *makhorka*. He offered Sack the tobacco pouch. Sack shook his head. "I never got the habit."

"Better for you," the Norwegian answered. He lit his own cigarette—no easy feat in the rain—and took a deep drag. "I like it, though."

"However you wish." Reluctantly, Sack started back toward the Trubezh River. Still puffing happily, the Norwegian followed. They hit the dirt whenever an incoming round sounded as if it might be close, but otherwise gave the bombardment only small heed.

Then a shell landed almost right on top of them, so suddenly they had no time to duck. The blast left Sack half deafened, and also with the feeling someone about the size of God had tried to pull his lungs out through his nose. Otherwise, though, he wasn't hurt. He looked around to make sure his new friend had also come through all right.

His stomach lurched. Only a burial party needed to worry about the Norwegian now, and they'd have to spoon him into a jar if they intended to send his remains home. It was worse than butchery; it was annihilation. The only good thing about it was that the Norwegian couldn't have known what hit him.

Dazed and sickened, Sack staggered on. This wasn't how he'd pictured war when he first donned the German uniform. It wasn't so much that he hadn't imagined the death and injury that went with combat. He had, as well as one can without the actual experience. What he hadn't imagined was the horror and terror and dread they left in their wake, nor the filth and exhaustion of long combat, nor, most of all, that Germany, having pushed her frontier east almost two thousand kilometers, would ever see the line begin to shift west once more.

Trucks rumbled past him, heading away from the Trubezh. One of them stopped. Its driver was one of the Scandinavians with whom Sack had eaten. He poked his head out the window and said in English, "How goes your friend? And where is Olaf?"

"My friend will make it, I think," Sack answered, also in English. "Olaf—" He grimaced, turned. "Back there, a shell—" Speaking of death in a foreign language helped distance him from it, make it feel unreal, as if it could not possibly touch him.

"Shit," the driver said, and then, as if English did not satisfy him, he spoke several sharp sentences in Swedish or whatever his native tongue was. After he spat into the mud, he said, "You'd better climb inside. We're pulling back toward the Dnieper."

"Already?" Sack said, dismayed.

The driver only answered, "*Ja.* That is how my orders are."

The men in the back of the truck helped pull the lance-corporal aboard. He sat on somebody's lap the whole way. He was not the only one packed in like that, either, and the truck grew more crowded the further west it went. The compartment stank of unwashed men, mud, and damp.

The Scandinavians told different stories. Some thought the Reds had forced the line of the Trubezh in large numbers, while others claimed the enemy was sweeping down from the north and threatening to cut off all the German forces still on this side of the Dnieper. Whichever was true—if either was—it meant another retreat.

"When will it end?" asked the medical officer who had worked on Gustav Pfeil. No one answered him. The silence was in itself an answer of sorts, but not one to ease Sack's foreboding.

It was indeed another retreat. Over the rear gate of the truck, Sack saw panzers, mechanized infantry fighting vehicles, and self-propelled guns rumbling westward cross-country, heading no doubt for the still intact bridges (he hoped they were still intact, at any rate) and the ferry links between the eastern bank of the Dnieper and Kiev on the far shore.

He'd passed through Kiev in the summer of '42, on his way to the front. German arms had still been winning victories then. He remembered the blue-and-gold Ukrainian flags everywhere in the city. He remembered the smiling girls who'd greeted and fed him at the soldiers' canteen across from the old Intourist Hotel on Vladimirskaya Street, some of them in the elaborately embroidered blouses, skirts, and headdresses of native Ukrainian fashion, others wearing dresses that had been the very latest styles in Berlin in the early thirties.

He wondered how many flags would be flying now, how many girls would want to have anything to do with soldiers who might have to pull out of their city at any minute. Not many, he suspected. Victory had a thousand fathers; defeat was always an orphan.

Just getting to Kiev looked like more of an adventure than he'd ever wanted. A shell hit the truck right behind his in the convoy, turned it into a fireball in an instant. He looked down at the tattered knees of his trousers, not wanting to watch his comrades burn. It could have been he as easily as they, and he knew it. Had the trucks not kept the ordained fifty meters' separation even in adversity and retreat, it could easily have been he *and* they.

One of the Scandinavians, a big burly Dane, pulled out a mouth organ and started playing American country songs. Sack was not the only one to smile when he heard them. Their incongruity here on a plain vaster than any in the United States somehow brought home the absurdity of war.

After jounces and jolts and halts where everyone scrambled out to put a shoulder to a wheel to get the truck out of the mud, it pulled to a stop not far from the

Dnieper. "All out," the driver called over the intercom. "I'm going back for another load."

"Good luck to you," Sack called as the driver put the truck back into gear. The Scandinavian waved to him and drove off. He never saw the fellow again.

If the bank of the Trubezh had been crowded, that of the Dnieper fairly swarmed with men. Panzers and other fighting vehicles still crossed over into Kiev by way of the motor bridges still standing, but that way was closed to mere infantry, who might clog traffic and impede the flow of the precious armor. Military police directed foot soldiers toward the boats boarding by the river.

The two biggest, the *Yevgeny Vuchetich* and the *Sovietskaya Rossiya*, were four-deck Dnieper excursion boats, seized when the Germans first took Kiev more than two years before. Along with a host of smaller craft, now they ferried German soldiers back to guard the city against recapture by the Reds.

The big boats each took aboard hundreds, maybe a thousand or more at a time. The smaller vessels added dozens, more likely hundreds, to that total. But the riverbank remained packed as men from the crumbling German positions east of the Dnieper streamed back to try to hold the line west of the river.

Such a concentration of men, unfortunately, also offered a delicious target for planes painted with the red star. Antiaircraft batteries fired furiously at the raiders, but bold pilots bored through to strike even so. The casualties were horrendous, but Germans still kept pressing down toward the bank. As at the Trubezh, the only alternative was to stand and fight, and that seemed a worse bet than trying to escape.

A ground-attack plane roared low overhead, firing can-

non and rockets into the crowd of men. Just above Sack,
it also let go with its chaff cartridges. But instead of strips
of aluminized foil to baffle radar, the cartridges were
filled with leaflets. They fluttered down on the Germans
like warnings of doom from the heavens themselves.

Sack snatched one out of the air almost in front of his
own nose. He read it quickly, before the cheap paper it
was printed on turned soggy in the rain. *THERE'S
MONEY IN WAR . . . FOR SOME,* the headline read.
Sack snorted. "Not for me," he said aloud. He collected
108 *Deutschmark*s a month, including his combat pay
bonus.

He read on: *For others, this war can only mean death
and mutilation. Maybe you think Berlin is fighting for the
European values your propaganda so loudly proclaims.
The hard fact is that you are carrying out Berlin's vicious
orders, and those of Mercedes. Siemens, I. G. Farben,
and other capitalists who drink your blood to fatten their
dividend checks. Where will that get you? Your armies
are marked down for defeat; all your sufferings are futile.
Your blood is worth marks on the stock exchange—but
what cost to your folks at home?*

Sack's folks had been bombed out of their homes a
few weeks before. With rising anger, he finished the leaflet: *We have common enemies. Every member of the People's Liberation Army hereby guarantees: if you lay down
your arms, you will not be harmed or humiliated. Your
personal belongings will not be touched. You will receive
any medical treatment you need. You will surely get
home. Come on over, soldier. Just put down your weapon
and say—*

Growling, Sack crumpled the paper and stuffed it into
his pocket. He didn't care how the Reds said "surren-

der.'' But one of the other *panzergrenadiers* gave him a half-curious, half-suspicious look. ''Why are you keeping *scheiss*?'' the fellow asked.

''*Scheiss* is right,'' Sack answered. ''How many better arsewipes have you seen lately?''

''None around here,'' the other fellow admitted. ''Last time I dumped, I scraped my backside raw with dry grass.''

The attack run of another Red fighter-bomber ended abruptly when a *Gepard* self-propelled antiaircraft cannon shot off its left wing. The plane slammed into the Dnieper with a tremendous splash. The Germans on the bank and on the boats cheered like wild men.

Little by little, Sack drew nearer the concrete stairway that led down to the embarkation point. As he filed down to the river, he fearfully watched the heavens—hemmed in as he was, he couldn't hope even to duck if shells or rockets started coming in or if another plane strafed the landing. He saw other faces also turned up to the rain. Knowing that comrades shared his fright made it easier to bear.

Down by the river, military police with submachine guns kept the troopers boarding the boats in order. When a man in camouflage gear tried to shove his way onto an already crowded boat, they did not argue with him. One of them fired a short burst from point-blank range, then rolled the corpse into the Dnieper with the toe of his boot. After that, the line stayed orderly.

''This way! This way! This way!'' a big fellow with a metal gorget shouted. Sack was among those whom he directed ''this way'': aboard the *Yevgeny Vuchetich*. The men packed the boat's four decks so tight no one had room to sit down. Combat engineers had mounted a 20-

millimeter antiaircraft gun at the bow and another on the
third deck at the stern, but the lance-corporal doubted
their crews had room to serve them.

The old boat's overloaded diesel roared flatulently to
life. Slowly, so slowly, it pulled away from the riverbank.
The *Sovietskaya Rossiya* was a couple of hundred meters
ahead. It had drawn close to the colonnaded mass of the
river station when a bomb or a big rocket struck it amid-
ships.

The excursion vessel seemed to bulge outward, then
broke apart and sank like a stone. Hundreds of soldiers
must have gone down with it. More hundreds thrashed in
the chilly water. Many of them quickly sank, weighted
down by their gear.

The *Yevgeny Vuchetich* slowed to throw lines to survivors and pull aboard those they could. Sack stared in
horror as men drowned within easy reach of a line because they were too stunned to reach out and grab it. The
boat did not save as many as it might have under other,
more peaceful, circumstances, both because it was already overloaded itself and because stopping would have
left it even more vulnerable to an attack like the one that
had sunk its sister.

At the Pochtovaya Ploshchad river station, more military police lined the docks. Like their fellows on the east
bank, they screamed, "This way! This way! This way!"
As he followed their pointing arms into the station, Sack
wondered if they knew how to say anything else.

Milling men in gimy uniforms filled the main hall.
Still more men in dog collars profanely urged them on
their way. One of the herd, Sack shambled sheeplike past
wall panels depicting big blond men in chain mail (Var-
angians, he supposed), men with guns under red and gold

hammer-and-sickle banners entering Kiev in triumph, and factories pouring smoke into the sky under the same Soviet emblem. The lance-corporal deliberately looked away from those. He had seen all the red flags he ever cared to look at.

The German military police *did* know how to say more than "This way!"—the ones at the rear of the station were shouting, "To the subway station! To the subway station!" That was an order Sack obeyed gladly; the further underground he went, the safer he felt from Red air attack.

More crowds of wet, stinking, dazed soldiers jammed the platform. When he'd been here last, the station had been immaculate now. It was a long way from immaculate now. The trains did not run on time, either. Advancing as much from the pressure of the men behind him as by his own will, Sack moved toward the track.

After a longish while, he boarded a train. It rumbled through the darkness of the tunnel, then came to a jerky stop at Kreshchatik Station, only two stops south of Pochtovaya Ploshchad. The few Ukrainian flags that draped the inside of the station were faded and stained; he'd have guessed they were the identical banners he'd seen when he came through Kiev heading east to the front. Now he was back, and the front with him.

When he walked outside into the rain, he met only silence. He looked around in confusion, then turned to the soldier nearest him and said, "Where the devil are the boys in the dog collars? I figured they'd be screaming at us here, same as everywhere else."

"Do you miss them so badly, then?" the other fellow asked, tugging at the straps of his pack. He and Sack laughed. They both knew the answer to that.

The lance-corporal started to say something more, but a public-address system beat him to the punch and out-shouted him to boot: "German soldiers detraining at Kreshchatik Station, report to Dynamo Stadium in Central Recreation Park. The stadium is north of the station. Signboards will direct you. German soldiers detraining at Kreshchatik Station . . ."

The recorded announcement ran through again, then shut off. Sack turned to the other soldier. "There, you see what they've done? They've gone and automated the bastards."

Sure enough, signs with arrows pointed the way up Zankovetskaya Street. Sack and his new companion, whose name, he leaned, was Bruno Scheurl, ambled toward the park with other weary men coming up out of the subway.

He glanced over at the Moskva Hotel, which had taken shell damage when the Germans forced their way into Kiev. It looked as good as new now, all the rubble cleared away, all the glass in place. He wondered how long that would last. If Germany held the line of the Dnieper, it might survive intact a while longer. If not—if not, the hotel would be the least of his worries.

The Palace of Culture was similarly pristine; the Museum of Ukrainian Fine Arts on Kirov Street had not been damaged when Kiev fell. Across Kirov Street from the museum lay Central Recreation Park. The trees, green and leafy when Sack last saw them, now were skeletons reaching bony branches up to the dripping sky. The grass in the park lay in dead, yellowish-white clumps.

"Ugly place," Scheurl remarked.

"It's nice in summer," Sack said. "But I'm damned if I know how even Russians—excuse me, Ukrainians—

live through winter hereabouts, especially when winter seems to run about eight months out of the year.''

Near the entrance to Dynamo Stadium stood a granite monument more than twice the height of a man. In low relief, it showed four stalwart-looking men in the short pants and kneesocks of footballers. A nearby plaque told who they were, but its Cyrillic letters meant nothing to Sack. He jerked a thumb at it, asked, ''Can you read what it says?''

''Maybe. I did some Russian in school.'' Scheurl studied the plaque, then complained, ''Ukrainians spell funny. I think it says these fellows were part of a team of Russian prisoners who beat a crack *Luftwaffe* team in an exhibition match during the last war—and got executed for it. The death match, they call it.''

''Ha!'' Sack said. ''I wonder what really happened.''

Shrugging, Scheurl headed into the stadium. Sack followed. Signs of all sorts in the stands and on the football field directed soldiers to their units. The rows of colorful seats were rapidly filling with field-gray. Military policemen served as ushers and guides. ''What unit?'' one of them asked Sack.

''Forty-first *Panzergrenadiers*, second regiment,'' the lance-corporal answered.

The fellow with the gorget glanced down at a hastily printed chart. ''Section twenty-nine, about halfway up. Haven't seen many from your division yet.''

Sack believed him. Too many comrades hadn't made it back over the Trubezh, let alone the Dnieper. He and Scheurl parted company, one of a thousand partings with brief-met friends he'd made since he came east.

The people who made the signs hadn't left a division's worth of room for the Forty-first *Panzergrenadiers*.

Maybe they knew what they were doing; only a company's worth of men rattled around in the area, so many dirty peas in a pod too big for them. Sack found a couple of real friends here, though, men he'd fought beside for more than a year. They all looked as worn and battered as he felt. He asked after others he did not see. Most of the time, only shrugs answered him; once or twice, he got a grim look and a thumbs-down.

Somebody asked him in turn about Gustav Pfeil. "He took a leg wound, not too bad," he said. "I got him to a doctor. He should be all right, unless"—he found himself echoing the Danish medical officer—"the field hospital gets overrun."

"He may be luckier than all of us," somebody else said. "If he does make it, they'll fly him all the way back to Germany." Everyone in earshot sighed. Germany seemed more a beautiful memory than a real place that still existed. Reality—mud and blood and rain and fear—left scant room for beautiful memories.

Sack nervously looked around at the ever-growing crowd. "If they land a salvo of rockets in this place, they'll kill thousands," he said.

"We've got our own rocket batteries in the trees east of here, on the far side of the square," one of the other *panzergrenadiers* assured him. "They've knocked down everything the Reds have thrown so far."

Sack nodded and tried not to think about the potentially ominous ring of those last two words. "I notice there aren't a whole lot of vehicle crews here," he said. "Did the damned Asiatics take out that many panzers and combat vehicles?"

"No, that's not as bad as it seems," the other *panzergrenadier* said. He was a little skinny fellow named

Lothar Zimmer, and seemed to have been born without
nerves. "There's a big vehicle park north of here, and
most of the crews are trying to get their machines ser-
viced. The fellows you see here are just the orphans, the
ones who had theirs blown out from under them."

"That's a relief, anyhow. I was beginning to wonder
if we had any armor left at all."

One thing the Germans knew almost instinctively was
how to organize. Without that skill, the campaigns across
the vast distances of European Russia would have been
impossible to imagine, the more so as the Reds had more
machines and far more men than did Germany or even
Europe as a whole. Even with it, the tide was flowing
west now, not east.

Still, as he watched Dynamo Stadium fill, Sack had to
believe Germany would hold the onrushing Communist
hordes out of Europe. Each of the men here was worth
two, three, four of his foes, thanks to the combination of
discipline and initiative the German army had mastered
better than any other. Given a spell to regroup and breathe
a little behind the barrier of the Dnieper, they'd surely
halt the Reds and keep most of what they'd won in these
past bloody two and a half years.

Yet no sooner had the sight of so many Germans sorting themselves out by unit boosted the lance-corporal's
confidence than whispers began running through that
crowd of soldiers. Sack could almost watch them spread
by the way the men turned toward each other like so
many stalks of wheat bending in the breeze. Where the
whispers had passed, silence lay heavy.

They came piecemeal to the forty-first *Panzergrenadiers*, a word here, a word there: *balka*s (the gullies that
crisscrossed the country on both sides of the Dnieper),

helicopters, Reds. By now, Sack had had a lot of practice at joining a word here with a word there and making a whole rumor of it. "They've crossed the river," he said. He sounded almost as stunned as *Wachtmeister* Pfeil had after the shell fragment laid open his leg.

Another word came: *bridgehead*. Then another: *breakthrough*. Lothar Zimmer could paste them together, too. "If they break through here, where do we stop them next?" he said. No one answered him.

The stadium loudspeakers began to bellow, ordering units to report to concentration points scattered all through Kiev. Chatter stopped as men listened for their own assignments. Eventually, Sack's came: "Forty-first *Panzergrenadiers* to vehicle park seventeen! Forty-first *Panzergrenadiers* to vehicle park seventeen!"

"Is that the one you were talking about?" the lance-corporal asked Lothar Zimmer. The little swarthy fellow nodded. He got to his feet and trudged off. Sack followed, glad to be with someone who knew where he was going.

What he found when he got to the vehicle park dismayed him. Only a fraction of the division's panzers, self-propelled guns, and mechanized infantry combat vehicles stood there. To eke them out and give the Forty-first *Panzergrenadiers* a fraction of the mobility they'd once enjoyed, a motley assortment of captured Red equipment and impressed civilian cars and trucks sprawled across the asphalt. Maintenance personnel were still slapping hasty tape crosses onto their doors and sides to identify them as German.

"Look at all this soft-skinned junk," Sack blurted. "The Reds won't need missiles to take it out. They won't even need machine guns. An officer's pistol ought to do the job nicely."

"They'll get some of us there, wherever 'there' is," Zimmer said, shrugging. "Once that happens, we're on our own, but that's the way it always works."

To Sack's relief, a lieutenant waved him into a mechanized infantry combat vehicle. He peered out through the *Marder*'s firing ports as it began to roll. At least he had a modicum of armor between himself and the unfriendly intentions of people in the wrong uniforms.

Somebody inside the *Marder* came up with a name for where it was heading: Perayaslav, about eighty kilometers south and east along the Dnieper. *An hour's drive on the Autobahn*, Sack thought. It took the rest of the day and all night. Not only did the alleged highway stop being paved not far out of Kiev—which slowed the impressed vehicles to a crawl—the enemy had it under heavy bombardment from artillery and rockets both.

An antitank missile fired at extreme range from across the Dnieper took out the lead panzer and forced everyone else to detour around its blazing hulk. That made delays even worse. Jets blazoned with red stars arrogantly screamed past overhead. They raked the column with cannon fire and more missiles. The *Luftwaffe* was nowhere to be found. The Germans expended their whole stock of surface-to-air missiles before they got halfway to Perayaslav. As far as Sack could tell, they hit nothing.

He must have dozed in spite of the racket and the rough ride, for he woke with a jerk when the *Marder* stopped. He had to piss so bad, it was a miracle he hadn't wet himself while he slept. Artillery boomed ahead. He licked his lips. The firing sounded heavy. It was almost all incoming.

Somebody banged on the combat vehicle's entry doors with a rifle butt. Lothar Zimmer was sitting closest to them. When he opened the metal clamshell, whoever was outside handed him a bucket full of stew. He took it with a word of thanks and set it down between the two facing rows of seats. Everyone dug in with his own spoon. It was vile stuff, mostly potatoes and grease by the taste, but it filled the belly.

Sack took advantage of the lull to leap out and empty his bladder. Another *Marder* had stopped in the mud a few meters away. One of its crewmen—likely the driver, judging by his fancy helmet packed full of electronics— stood by his machine doing exactly the same thing as Sack. The little the lance-corporal could see of his face looked gloomy. "We're for it now," the fellow said.

"What do you know?" Sack asked eagerly. Nobody bothered telling infantrymen anything, but a driver couldn't help but get the word over the radio net.

The man answered, "The Reds are pushing hard. You can hear the guns, can't you?" He didn't give Sack a chance to answer. "Their field engineers have done something sneaky, too. They've built their pontoon bridges half a meter *under* the surface of the fucking Dnieper. Makes 'em harder to spot, a lot harder to knock out, but men and panzers just keep on coming across."

"Bad," Sack said. The driver grudged him a nod, then climbed back into his fighting vehicle through the front hatch. He slammed the hatch down after him. The *Marder*'s diesel roared. Its tracks spat mud as it headed toward the fighting.

When Sack returned to his own *Marder*, he passed on the news the driver had given him. His comrades' faces said they were as delighted as he had been. The combat vehicle got moving again.

A roar from the turret announced the launch of an

antitank missile. Sack clutched his assault rifle and hoped it hit. If it didn't, the Red panzer would return fire, and the *Marder* wasn't armored against the big, fast, hard-hitting shells a 150-millimeter panzer cannon threw.

The *Marder* didn't blow up in the next few seconds, so the missile must have done its job. The combat vehicle stopped about a minute later. "This is where you get out, lads," the driver announced over the intercom. "Good luck. *Gott mit uns.*"

"*Gott mit uns,*" Sack echoed as he reluctantly left the relative safety of the *Marder*. He and his mates formed a skirmish line, each man six or eight meters from his comrades. The driver let them get a couple of hundred meters ahead, then followed, his cannon ready to deal with any threats their personal weapons could not handle.

Glancing left and right, Sack saw more men heading up into the front lines with his squad, more combat vehicles moving with them to provide covering fire. He and his comrades were pushing through the battered German trench lines when the real Red artillery bombardment began. He leaped into a hole (he had endless variety from which to choose), held his helmet on his head with one hand, and waited for the nightmare to end.

It lasted two solid hours that seemed two years long. The ground shook and jerked, as if in unending earthquake. The Reds were giving it everything they had, rockets, shells, all different calibers, every weapon firing fast as it could. They wouldn't have much ammunition left when the barrage was over, Sack thought dazedly somewhere in the middle of it, but that might not matter, either.

The pounding let up at last. When Sack raised his head, he saw the German lines, already cratered, now resembled nothing so much as a freshly plowed field. Through the rain, through the mud, through the rubble, seemingly straight for him, came the Red ground attack.

It was, in its way, a magnificent sight. The green-clad troops stormed forward almost shoulder to shoulder, assault rifles blazing, a wave of men to swamp the Germans who still survived. Panzers and armored fighting vehicles rumbled forward in their wake; jets and assault helicopters roared overhead with missiles and cannon to engage German armor.

Sack wanted to empty his magazine into the onrushing horde. But if he and his comrades opened up too soon, the Asiatics would just dive for cover before enough of them could be slaughtered. "Fire discipline," he said out loud, reminding himself.

He and his comrades showed their training. Almost everyone started shooting at the same instant. The pieces of German artillery that hadn't been knocked out added their voices to the firefight. The infantry in green went down like wheat cut too soon. But as the first wave fell, another took its place.

A brilliant white flash marked an enemy panzer brewing up; some infantryman's wire-guided missile had struck home. But it was like fighting the hydra; for every head cut off, two more took its place. Sack scrambled backwards to keep from being outflanked and cut off.

He looked back toward the *Marder* that had brought him into action. It was burning. How many divisions had the Reds managed to crowd into their fucking bridgehead, anyhow, and how much heavy equipment? *Too many and too much* was all he could think as he retreated past the combat vehicle's corpse.

Something moved behind the *Marder*. As if it had a

life of its own, his assault rifle swung toward the motion. But before he squeezed off a burst, he saw it was Lothar Zimmer. He pointed the muzzle of his weapon at the ground. "You still alive, Zimmer?" he croaked.

"I think so," the other German said. He looked as battered, as overwhelmed, as Sack felt. Staring at the lance-corporal as if Sack had all the answers, he asked, "What do we do now?"

"Try as best we can to get out, I guess," Sack answered. It wasn't going to be easy; firing came not only from in front of them and from both flanks, but from the rear as well. While their little piece of the battle hadn't gone too badly, overall the Reds were forcing the breakthrough they'd sought.

The two Germans started north, back toward Kiev. Sack hoped the enemy would take no special notice of them in the rain and the confusion. For a couple of kilometers, those hopes were realized. But just when he began to think he and Zimmer really might get away free, a burst of machine-gun fire sent them diving into a ditch.

The fire let up for a moment. "Surrender or die!" a Red yelled in mangled German.

"What do we do?" Zimmer hissed.

"What *can* we do?" Sack said hopelessly. But if he stood up, even with his hands in the air, he was afraid the machine gunner would cut him in half. Then he remembered the propaganda leaflet he'd stuffed in his pocket, intending to use it for toilet paper. He dug it out, scanned it quickly. *"Tow shong!"* he shouted, as loud as he could. *"Tow shong, tow shong!"*

"Tow shong?" The Red pronounced it differently; Sack hoped he'd been understood. Then the enemy switched to German: "Surrender?"

"*Ja*, surrender. *Tow shong!*" Now Sack did stand. After a moment, Zimmer followed his lead. Their assault rifles lay in the mud at their feet, along with their dreams.

Several green-clad soldiers ran up to them. Grins on their flat, high-cheekboned faces, their almond eyes glittering with excitement, they searched the Germans, stripped off their watches, their aid kits, and everything else small and movable they had on their persons.

One of the Reds gestured with his weapon. Hands high, Sack and Zimmer stumbled toward captivity. A soldier of the Chinese People's Liberation Army followed to make sure they did not try to escape.

Flyboy

S. M. STIRLING

Stephen Michael Stirling has been writing science fiction and fantasy for the past decade, collaborating with such authors as Jerry Pournelle, Judith Tarr, David Drake, and Harry Turtledove, as well as producing excellent novels by himself, such as Marching Through Georgia, Snowbrother, *and, most recently,* Against the Tide of Years. *Born in Metz, Alsace, France, and educated at the Carleton University in Canada, he currently lives in New Mexico, with his wife, Janet.*

"As you know, ladies and gentlemen," Craven began.

The scientist stopped, looking around the table at the collection of military bureaucrats. *They probably don't know any such thing.* He had a depressingly long list of meetings like this stocked in his memories, and they'd all started to blur together. Even the paneled, windowless rooms and the smell of aftershave and bad coffee were always the same; the only real difference from his first was that nobody was smoking.

"As you know, the working life of a fighter jock is as limited as that of a fine athlete. That's a lot of talent and training going to waste."

Well, *that* they knew. He could see Brigadier General Ohlsen's eyes begin to glaze.

But hell, they never read the science briefings; figuring they might as well leave it to the experts to explain rather than struggling through some mass of technical jargon. Still, maybe his opening statement was too obvious. After all, everyone at the table *but* Craven had experienced the ordeal of being forced out of the air. He had to find the balance point between seeming to condescend and talking way over their heads. They might be idiots, but they were idiots with the power to say no.

Grapefruit and peas, he reminded himself.

"It's a fact that hand-eye coordination deteriorates with age. But the mental acuity remains sharp, enhanced

by experience—the 'aces' are invariably experienced pilots, and most of the casualties are just out of flight
school. We retire fighter pilots when the physical effects
of aging begin to outweigh the benefits of experience. I
believe that I have found a way to take advantage of that
acuity and experience, while bypassing the physical.''

Colonel Nagakura's jaw dropped. His head came forward as he asked in disbelief, ''Are you talking about
E.S.P.?''

There was a flurry of smiles around the table, but he
felt a slight chill at the base of his stomach as the officers
began to look at watches.

Craven laughed and shook his head. Time to hook
them, obviously.

''I'm talking about a brain/machine interface,'' he
said. Ohlsen was back from whatever report he'd been
composing. ''We're ready to move up to human tests and
naturally it makes sense to seek out a subject that has the
attributes that we want to test.''

Lieutenant General Ignazio looked directly at Craven
for the first time, pinning him like a bug against his chair.

''A human being for use in your experiment,'' Ignazio
rumbled, his heavy-featured face daring the scientist to
disagree with that assessment.

Craven swallowed visibly, but spread his hands like a
reasonable man.

''At some point, sir, every experiment comes down to
that. Yes,'' he continued carefully, ''we need a human
subject to complete our experiment. But''—Craven
leaned forward and folded his hands before him—''it
must be the *right* subject, or it's wasted effort. Which is
why we've come to you.''

''Dr. Craven,'' Ignazio said quietly, ''it's our job to

send men, and women, into dangerous, even deadly situations. But before I put one of our people on your butcher's block you're going to have to give us a *lot* more information than you put in your report."

The doctor's brows went up in surprise at that, and the general grinned lopsidedly.

"We do read, Doctor," he said dryly.

"Our work is very sensitive, General. We felt it would be inadvisable to release information outside of controlled conditions."

There was a long pause as the military contingent exchanged glances. Brigadier General Ohlsen said, "Then you'd better proceed, Doctor. This is about as controlled an environment as you can get."

Craven pushed up his glasses and leaned forward, resting his elbows on the table, hands clasped before him.

"For a long time now scientists have been working on biochips and the idea of a molecular computer. But up to now even the molecular studies have been based on silicon. And yet, part of the problem with implanting anything in the human body is the rejection factor. There's always the risk that whatever you've placed there will suddenly be attacked, even after a period of years, by the body's defenses. And we want whatever we put in place to remain unmolested for years on end." The doctor paused, looking at the faces around him. Well, at least they seemed to be awake. "So, in this case, we naturally turned to constructing a biological counterpart to ordinary silicon-based computer chips. We succeeded in creating extremely efficient biological facsimiles. However, as you might expect, these components had a very short life span. Now, thanks to the telemarase experiments, we've created what is, to the best of our knowledge, an immortal biochip, built on cellular material extracted from the subject himself.'' The doctor sat back, smiling, his dark eyes alight with excitement.

If he was expecting the outburst of questions, disbelief, and delight that any gathering of scientists would have made, the military men around the table sorely disappointed him. They gazed back at him with blank expressions and guarded eyes.

"Go on, Doctor," Ohlsen said.

"Uh." He leaned forward for another try, holding his hands palms out as he addressed them. "Okay. We implant an interconnected series of these chips into the pilot's eyes and brain. The network is powered by a new type of miniature fuel cell that taps the blood for oxygen and hydrogen, returning distilled water to the bloodstream."

He was losing them again; they just didn't see the potential.

"The vehicle itself," he went on doggedly, "has a complex of sensors that transmit information to the implanted chips, which interact directly with the brain and nervous system. This allows the pilot to respond to stimulus, literally, with the speed of thought." Craven spread his hands and shook them once as if to say *ta-da!*

"Just how many chips are we talking about?" Nagakura wanted to know.

"We've estimated that for a human subject four hundred and eighty should do the trick. Only an actual working experiment will tell us more."

"It seems very invasive, Doctor," Major Klien said dubiously. "I mean, the eyes I can see"—he gave a quick grin in answer to the pained smiles his remark brought—"but the brain? How many in the eyes, how many in the brain, and how big are these things, any-way?''

"We've achieved a high level of miniaturization," Craven reassured him. "We're talking no more than six or seven neurons. . . . Two hundred would be implanted in the eyes, the others throughout the brain."

Ignazio raised a brow. "*Throughout* the brain?"

Craven licked his lips.

"We've learned a lot about the brain in the last ten years, gentlemen. But there's an awful lot that we don't yet know. This experiment will provide us with invaluable information for general brain research as well as telling us specifically which areas of the brain will be most useful to us in this specific case." He tapped the table. "We're talking about a pilot firing his weapons with a thought. We're talking about, when a pilot straps on a fighter, *becoming* the fighter."

"Come again?" Klien said.

"That's the reason for the extended neural net," the doctor said. "There will be sensors throughout the vehicle, exterior and interior, which will be relaying information directly to the pilot's brain. In effect the fighter will become a physical extension of the pilot. He will *feel* the motion of the vehicle as though it's a part of his own body."

"Nice," Nagakura said. "But what's the point?"

Craven seemed nonplussed by the question. "Well, information," he said rather sharply. He blinked at his own temerity and went on more calmly. "It's based on work that NASA was doing for the Mars project. They know they're unlikely to get approval for using human subjects for this, or for sending humans to Mars for that matter; and our work was actually quite similar, so to save time and funds we combined what we'd been working on. My team felt that this plane-body interface would increase situational awareness,'' he added.

"The clue bird,'' Klien murmured, speculation in his eyes.

The military men glanced at each other and Craven leaned back, knowing instinctively when to stop talking.

"You've gotten your research to this point without air force help, Doctor,'' Ohlsen said quietly. "So what is it, exactly, that you want from us?''

"Your approval for performing the experiment under the air force's purview. We already have a short list of possible subjects from the active and recently retired lists. There's one in particular''—the doctor shuffled through his papers—"a Captain Lamy,'' he said. Extracting a dossier, he handed it to the brigadier general. "He was in an auto accident. Not his fault, he wasn't driving. But it left his legs paralyzed. He was actually extremely lucky; such injuries are usually much more devastating. He's continent, for example, and sexually functional.''

At a sound Craven looked up from tidying his papers, licked his lips again, and fell silent under the brigadier general's cold stare.

"Uh . . .'' The doctor folded his hands before him, visibly rallying, and continued, "He's well recovered and the most recently active flyer on our list. We think, because of this and his age, that Captain Lamy would make an ideal candidate.''

"His age?'' Kline asked. "I thought the whole idea was to extend the flying life of older pilots.''

"It is,'' Craven said. "Eventually. But we're still in the experimental phase. It's advisable to reduce risks wherever we can.''

"And just what are the risks?" Ignazio demanded.

"Stroke, leading to paralysis, blindness. Possibly some sort of emotional disturbance." Craven spread his hands. "We honestly don't know for sure. In our animal experiments we've gotten the gross physical risks down to below a four percent possibility. The truth is, when you're dealing with the brain, to a large extent you're flying on instruments and instinct. I have no guarantees for you. And yes, I will make that clear to Captain Lamy, or any volunteers we may have."

"Oh, you'll have volunteers," Klien said. "I'm tempted to be one myself."

The military men shifted in their seats at that and suddenly Craven realized that all of them were tempted. He felt something loosen inside himself and his usual serene confidence in his superiority returned.

These flyboys would do anything to get back into the sky.

Elwood Lamy took another sip of his lemonade and leaned his head back against the padded seat of the motorized wheelchair. He was looking forward to getting back into his own chair. It was smaller and more maneuverable and he worked it with his arms. But he'd been weak after the operation, and leaning his aching head against the backrest had felt good. It also felt good to be back in his own home after five weeks in the hospital, even if he was blindfolded and under twenty-four-hour nursing supervision.

It was even better that those bandages around his eyes would be coming off tomorrow. He was certain that his sight would be just fine. He could tell dark from light, even through the thick dressing, and according to Dr.

Craven all of the implanted biochips were still active and perfectly functional.

When the doctor fired them up El was sure that he could feel something. Even in the legs the accident had left useless.

"You're a perfect candidate," Craven had assured him. "You're young, you're healthy, except for your spinal cord injury, which doesn't matter in this case. There's not much worse that we could do to you, so you can be at ease on that point."

No, sensitivity and bedside manner were not Craven's long suit. But that was refreshing in a way. El had become so damn sick of sympathy. The too quiet voices and the uneasy smiles were like salt in the wound after a while.

"I don't see how you can stand to drink that stuff," his nurse, Selena, said. "You don't let me put hardly any sugar in it. It's too tart for me."

"More for me then," he said with a grin and saluted in the direction of her voice with his glass.

"Yo!" Mark, his night nurse, said from the doorway as the screen door clapped shut behind him.

"Oh, you're early," Selena said in pleased surprise.

"Whatcha bring me for dinner?" El asked.

"Chicken, mashed potato, and green beans," Mark answered, bringing it over to him.

For the third time this week.

"Again?" Selena protested, beating him to it.

"I think I'll order a pizza instead," El muttered.

"I dunno," Mark muttered. "The doctor—"

"He's twenty-seven!" Selena exclaimed in disgust. "He can eat a pizza. If I was twenty-seven again I'd be eating pizza with both hands, believe me."

"Nobody'll deliver a pizza way out here," Mark protested.

"Yeah, they will. Tony's will anyway," Selena assured him.

Lamy grinned. "Thank you for your support," he said.

"See you tomorrow," Selena answered on her way out.

"For real," El answered her.

"That's right," she said after a moment, her voice, faintly surprised, came to him from the porch. "I'll look forward to it." He could sense the smile in the words.

"So will I," he assured her. "G'night."

"Night." And she was gone.

"Whaddaya want on your pizza?"

"Who're you?" Mark asked.

Lamy heard the screen door crash and a woman's voice answered.

"I'm Petra Connoly."

El sensed from her voice that she was looking at him, though she was answering Mark.

"Where's Selena?" Mark asked, sounding suspicious.

"I'm afraid there's been an accident," the woman murmured, obviously trying not to be overheard.

"Please speak up, Ms. Connoly," El said. "What's happened to Selena?"

"She was in an accident last night," Connoly said more loudly.

Lamy turned his chair in the direction of her voice.

"Is she all right?"

"I honestly don't know," she answered. "All the agency told me was that your regular nurse had been in an accident and that I was to fill in for her.''

"The agency?" he asked.

"Professional Home Nursing," she said.

"Yeah," Mark said. "That's who we work for."

"You're rentals?" Lamy asked in disbelief. *Ultimate suicide-before-reading secret and they* contracted out *the nursing care?* If he hadn't spent most of his adult life in government service, he wouldn't have believed it.

"So?" Mark asked sullenly. "What were you expecting? Florence Nightingale and her sisters?"

"I just thought . . . that you were with the hospital," El finished lamely.

"Nah," Mark said.

"Hospital nurses," Connoly said dryly, "by definition, work only in hospitals."

Maybe it's some kind of cost-cutting measure, he thought. *Craven must know what he's doing, and if he thought this wasn't a security risk then, who the hell am I to doubt him.* Still . . .

"But why weren't we informed about Selena?" El asked uneasily.

"If they hadn't been able to find someone to cover for Mr. Tubbs here," Connoly said, "they would have called."

Lamy thought for a moment. "I'd like you to call and find out what's going on," he said to Mark.

"Sure," Mark agreed. "I wanna know too."

"I assure you I'm well qualified to take care of you," Connoly said over the murmur of Mark's voice on the phone. "I've a master's in nursing, and I've specialized in intensive care. If anything"—her voice smiled— "judging from your condition, I'm overqualified for this assignment. But"—cloth rustled as she apparently shrugged—"it was short notice and I was free."

"Thanks," Mark said and the phone clattered into its cradle. He walked over to join them. "Selena's okay," he said. "She was hit by a car and she's badly banged up, a twisted knee and a sprained wrist, but no broken bones or anythin'. She won't be back for a while though."

"Is she in the hospital?" El asked.

"Nah, she's home. I guess her husband's takin' care of her. I'll give her a call and let ya know tonight how she's doin'."

"Thanks," El said.

"No problem. Well. I gotta go," the man said nervously. "See ya tonight."

"See ya," Lamy agreed. He sat frowning, listening to Connoly walking around. There was the rustle of paper and then silence for a moment.

"Hm," his new nurse said, neutrally, "I see you have the doctor coming at ten o'clock."

"He's taking the dressing off my eyes," Lamy explained. "You sound almost disappointed."

"Oh, no," she said with a little laugh. "I just hope the agency informs him about the change. From your reaction and Mr. Tubbs's I'm not looking forward to the doctor's if they haven't cleared this with him."

Sounds reasonable, El thought.

"Well," Nurse Connoly said cheerfully, "have you had breakfast?"

"I don't eat breakfast," he informed her, liking her voice, but disliking the false chirp in it.

"I'm surprised the doctor lets you get away with that," she said disapprovingly.

"It must have something to do with my being old

enough to make my own decisions about when I'm hungry," El said tartly.

There was silence for a moment, then she gave a little *hmph*.

"What about coffee, then?" she asked, the more genuine smile back in her voice. "I'd kill for a cup about now."

"You're on," El said and settled back in his chair. Craven would be here in two hours; maybe Connoly could keep his mind off the possibilities. Such as, maybe all he'd ever be able to do from now on was distinguish light from dark.

"So, why are you a rental nurse?" he asked.

The phone rang and Petra answered. "Hello," she said with professional pleasantness, then more coldly: "Ah. One moment, please."

"It's for me," she said to Lamy.

Well, what does she expect me to do about it? he wondered. *Am I supposed to leave the room or turn my chair around and pretend that I can't hear her?*

"Go on," Petra said.

For a moment Lamy wondered if he'd spoken aloud, then realized she was again speaking into the phone. He could hear the caller from where he sat, though he couldn't make out the words. Whoever it was sounded royally pissed off.

"The doctor will be coming by at ten to remove the bandages from my patient's eyes," she interrupted. "There's nothing else on the schedule until Mr. Tubbs returns at six this evening." There was a gabble of response and she interrupted again. "Perhaps you could find someone else," she suggested. "Someone better qualified for this position?'' Silence, or perhaps they were speaking in a more normal tone of voice. ''That's what I thought,'' Connoly purred. ''It's only temporary, you do understand that, don't you?'' There was a pause, then, ''I always do, don't I? I certainly won't let you down. Yes. Yes. I have to go. Certainly. Good-bye.'' She hung up the phone and blew out an impatient breath.

''Who the hell was that?'' El asked.

''That little martinet down at the office,'' Petra growled. ''Seems I was supposed to call in as soon as I arrived here. But nobody told me that I was supposed to do that. Apparently, by not doing so I've upset the whole agency. I'm really not happy with these people.''

He believed her, the annoyance rang clear in her voice.

''Amateurs,'' she muttered.

El raised his brows and said, ''You take nursing pretty seriously, don't you?''

''It's a serious profession,'' she answered coldly, then walked away. ''I'm going to make your bed,'' she told him.

I'll just sit here quietly and try not to irritate you, he thought sarcastically.

Petra was back almost instantly.

''I'm very sorry,'' she said. ''I had no right to speak to you that way. He was just so . . . awful.'' He heard her hand slap against, he supposed, her thigh. ''That doesn't mean I had any right to take it out on you.''

''Apology accepted. Especially if I can get another cup of coffee.'' He held out his cup and felt her lift it away.

''Thanks,'' she said and went into the kitchen.

''Who the hell are you?'' Craven asked, staring in disbelief at the beautiful dark-haired woman sitting with Lamy.

She rose and walked towards him.

"I'm Petra Connoly," she said. "Selena's been in an accident and the agency sent me as a last-minute replacement."

"Well, nobody told me!" Craven snapped.

"I was afraid of that," Connoly said. "They didn't inform Mr. Tubbs either. I apologize, Doctor. Professional Home Nursing doesn't seem to be living up to its name today."

"No. They don't." The doctor hesitated. "I'll have to call them," he said after a moment.

"Look, I don't see what the big deal is," Lamy put in. "I was a little surprised that you were using a nursing agency in the first place, but since you are, why are you so surprised that they're acting like one?"

"I've still got to check in," Craven insisted.

"Okay, sure, whatever. But could you take these bandages off first?" El asked.

"Patience is a virtue," Craven replied, putting down his bag and picking up the phone.

El could hear the smug little smirk the doctor must be wearing. *Prick,* he thought. Five weeks without seeing, five weeks without knowing if he ever would see again, and the little bastard was going to drag it out five minutes more.

"What's this?" Craven asked.

"The agency's card," Petra replied. "Mr. Tubbs must have used it this morning when he called PHN."

There was a "Hm" and the sound of numbers being punched.

"This won't take but a minute," Connoly said to El. "I wish they'd taken care of it before, though. I'm looking forward to seeing your whole face."

"I'm looking forward to seeing yours too," he said. "What do you look like anyway?"

"Me," she said with an audible grin.

"Mrs. Webber isn't in," Craven snarled. "No one is. They're supposed to be at some seminar."

There was silence for a moment.

"I don't like this," the doctor muttered.

"*I* don't like *this*," Lamy snapped, pointing at the bandage around his eyes. "So could we please get on with it?"

"Or off with it," Petra said good-naturedly.

"Yeah," Craven agreed after a moment. "May as well." There was the sound of his medical bag being shifted and then opened.

"I'll get the shades," Petra said and began moving around the room letting down the blinds.

"That's enough, Nurse. I'll need some light to work by."

"Yes, Doctor."

El heard her soft footsteps approach and felt her presence close at his elbow.

"Don't hover, Nurse," Craven snapped.

"Sorry, Doctor."

El felt her move back. *You're a bossy little jerk,* he thought at Craven. Then he tensed as he felt the bandages being cut. The dressings had been changed, of course, but he'd been warned not to open his eyes and so he hadn't. He'd never realized what a pleasure blinking could be.

"Okay now," the doctor said when they were down to the pads resting over his eyes, "open your eyes slowly, give your eyes time to adjust—they've been off duty for a while now."

Lamy hesitated, then raised his eyelids. He might have been looking through a smear of grease.

"It's very blurry," he said tightly.

"That's to be expected," Craven murmured reassuringly. "The pressure of the bandages might do that. "Close your eyes and wait a minute, then try again."

The tone and the words were calm, but El could feel tension radiating off the doctor like heat.

El waited a moment, his muscles clenched tight. Then with a massive effort of will he forced himself to relax. Slowly, he opened his eyes. It still wasn't quite right, but his vision was clearing rapidly now and he let out a pent-up breath.

"Oh," he sighed, "thank God!"

"You're seeing better," Craven said, half question, half observation. "Excellent, good. Nurse, would you adjust those blinds, please."

When Lamy looked at her she already had her back to him; when she opened the blinds he was dazzled and forced to turn away. Then Craven was in front of him, flashing a light into his eyes and asking him to look here, look there. After about a half hour the doctor seemed satisfied and the residual blurriness was completely gone.

"Well," Craven said, slapping his thighs and then getting up from his chair. "I'll want to take you in to the lab for more complete testing, but you certainly *seem* to have made a complete recovery. Don't overdo," he cautioned El. "No reading, and I'd prefer that you not watch TV before we can determine if the flickering will bother"—a quick glance at Petra—"you," he finished weakly. "I'll want you in the lab before you try anything like that."

"I never thought of television as being dangerous to

anything but the intellect," Lamy commented.

Craven gave him a restrained smile.

"There's nothing on tonight anyway," Petra assured him.

El turned to look at her and smiled widely at what he saw. She was lovely. Strong bones framed delicate features and laughing brown eyes. Her dark, wavy hair was brushed back off her face, and her body was long and slender.

"Wow," he said and she smiled back at him.

"Don't get used to the view," the doctor said dryly. "Nurse Connoly is a specialist and costs about twice as much as Selena."

"Yeah, but I'm worth it," Lamy said smugly.

"And so am I," Petra said with a laugh. She followed Craven to the door.

"You probably will be replaced," the doctor told her.

"I expect to be," Connoly agreed. "It's just that PHN was caught flat-footed today. I'm scheduled to start another case on Friday as well, so tomorrow is the latest I could fill in."

"Good, good. Excellent," Craven muttered. Then he walked down the steps and across the yard to his car.

Petra watched him get in and start the motor, then she looked over at Lamy.

"I don't like him either," he said. "But he's brilliant at what he does."

She cocked her head at the sound of the doctor's car driving away, then gave him a glorious smile. "Alone at last," she said and waggled her brows.

El was startled for a moment; it had been over a year since a woman had flirted with him. He grinned back at her and decided to enjoy it while it lasted.

"That's my line," he growled.

Petra smiled, a bit absently, took one last look out the screen door, and walked into the kitchen. When she came back she was carrying a hypodermic and a cotton ball.

"Time for your vitamin shot," she said.

"What?" he asked, startled. "I don't get shots."

"Well you're supposed to, according to your schedule." Petra frowned down at him, then smiled slowly. "You're going to be a good boy and let me do this, aren't you?"

"Sure," he said, shrugging. "But Selena never gave me one."

"Well," Connoly said, scrubbing his upper arm with the alcohol-soaked cotton, "she was supposed to. It's right there in black and white."

The needle went in smoothly, with very little pain. Her face was close to his as she worked and she looked into his eyes, smiling gently.

"What the hell are you doing?" Craven shouted from the doorway. He rushed over to them and pushed Petra away. "What was that? What's in that hypo?"

Petra was wide-eyed, her mouth open in surprise.

"It's a-a vitamin shot," she stammered.

"I never prescribed anything like that! Who are you? Who sent you?"

She frowned, looked at El as if to confirm that this was as outrageous as she thought it was.

Craven started towards her and she back-pedaled, yammering, "I'm a nurse! PHN sent me here because somebody had an accident. Hey!" she said as her back hit the wall. Her chin went up as the doctor planted himself right in front of her. "Back up, Doctor. I am not used to being treated this way!"

"And I am not used to strangers giving mysterious hypos to my patients!" he shouted. Craven stared at her for a moment, then his eyes shifted. "Get out!" he snarled.

Petra's mouth dropped open.

"Get out," he repeated through clenched teeth.

She pulled herself along the wall until she was away from him, gave El one quick look, then picked up her purse from the couch and marched out without a backward look.

Craven went to the door and watched as she started the car and pulled away.

"I do feel a little strange, Doc," Lamy said, surprised to find he was slurring his words.

The doctor turned around, his lips tightening, and moved over to the kitchen table.

"Can you get over here?" he asked.

"Sure," El said gamely, and with some difficulty maneuvered the chair across the room.

When he pulled up to the table he was surprised to see Craven setting out instruments.

"What are you doing?" he asked. His tongue felt thick in his mouth, but his mind was sharp.

Before he could react, Craven reached around his chair and disconnected his battery.

"I'm sorry," the doctor muttered. "I don't want to do this, but I have to. I gave them my notes, diagrams, I even gave them a video of the surgery, but they want more. They want samples of the chips themselves and I couldn't get any. The damned air force has stepped up security on my lab to the extent that I haven't got access to my own work!" He gave a sharp crack of laughter. "But they said that for what they're paying me I should give them whatever they asked for, and I just couldn't argue with them. Besides''—he looked down at Lamy and licked his lips—''they scare me, you know?''

''Don't,'' El said. His head fell back against the chair; he couldn't lift his arms. He watched in horror as Craven filled a hypo. ''Why?'' he asked. ''You'll get a lot of money out of this—why sell it?''

''Yuh, sure. I'll get about one-third of what the government gets, if that, and that's *when* they decide to release my discovery. Until then I get bupkis. Hell, the battery alone is worth millions.''

Craven put aside the bottle and swabbed Lamy's arm.

''I'm really sorry,'' the doctor said, avoiding his eyes. Then he pressed the needle home.

A shot rang out and blood spattered El's face in a hot spray as Craven fell with a gargling sound. His limbs jerked spasmodically and then fell still, breath wheezing out, then stopping.

''I *knew* he was up to no good,'' Petra snarled. She glanced at Lamy. ''I've got to get you out of here,'' she said. ''Can you still move if you have to?''

El stared at her for a moment, then managed to say, ''Yuh.''

''Great.'' She rolled the instruments back into their sterile cloth and flung them into Craven's bag, which she dropped onto El's lap. Then she turned his chair. ''Go,'' she snapped.

''Can't . . . ,'' El said. ''Power cord. . . .''

''Ah. He was a diabolical little shit, wasn't he?'' she asked as she reconnected the chair.

Power restored, El aimed for the door, ignoring the sounds behind him. Then Petra squeezed around him and opened the door.

"C'mon," she urged. "We've got to get out of here!"

"Why?" he asked as he guided the chair towards her car. Lamy could feel himself fading, and he could barely move at all.

She flung open the car door and positioned the chair. Then she gripped him below the arms and with surprising strength hoisted him into the front seat and belted him in. She slammed the door and ran around to the driver's side.

"Because I said so," she muttered through gritted teeth.

She glanced over at him. El was slumped down in his seat, completely unconscious.

She smiled.

Lamy woke to the prick of a needle.

"Nnno," he groaned. He opened his eyes. Petra was leaning over him; she gave him a quick smile.

"Welcome back," she said and kissed the tip of his nose. "I've missed those baby blues."

"Wha' did you give me?"

"Muscle relaxant," she said, straightening. "Not that you *can* run away, but I've got to make sure." She started the car.

"Where we goin'?" he asked, fighting the lethargy.

"Anywhere but where we were," Petra said lightly. "Don't bother fighting it, sweetie. I gave you enough to unman a moose." She grinned. "Not enough to hurt you, mind. Just enough to keep you from distracting me."

"Why are we running?" he asked. "We could go to the police. I'd tell 'em what happened."

She laughed. "Oh, the government would love that,

wouldn't they? You going to the police. I know my employers would just hate it."

"Em-ployer's?" He felt cocooned and distant but he still struggled to stay with her.

"Yeah. I suspect they're the same people Craven had sold out to." Petra *tsk*ed. "Amateurs, I'm telling you. Stupid, useless duplication of effort." She shook her head. "Which will cost them. Nobody jerks me around like that without paying for the privilege. Still, I suspect that whatever they put in your head will be worth the price. Hell, the battery alone is worth millions."

"That's what Craven said." Lamy watched her clear profile as she drove.

She glanced at him.

"Well, he should know," she said.

"Are you even a nurse?" he asked.

"You bet," Connoly said cheerfully. "And a damn good one too. You'd be amazed what a great dodge it is." She shrugged prettily. "And if the contract killing and the industrial espionage don't work out, I'll have something to fall back on." Petra looked at him and grinned. "Go to sleep. We won't be stopping for a while. You'll only wear yourself out more trying to stay awake. Trust me. Listen to the voice of experience."

I suppose she's right, he thought blearily. *She probably tested this stuff on herself to see what it would do.* He closed his eyes and sleep came easily.

El thought he heard Petra's voice at some point, but it was too much trouble to listen to what she was saying, and then the voice faded out. When he came to himself again she was hoisting an ice chest into the backseat.

"Whazzat?" he mumbled.

"Dry ice," she said shortly and slammed the door.

El closed his eyes, his heart racing.

For my head, he thought. *That's what Craven was going to do. He was going to cut off my goddam head.* He tried moving his hands and found that though sluggish he did have some ability back. He'd always metabolized drugs quickly. *But what if she gives me another shot? Well,* he answered himself, *then I'm screwed.*

"Elwood?" she said.

He hesitated and then with more effort than he liked, rolled his head to look at her.

"Are you awake, honey?" Connoly looked him over sharply, clearly evaluating whether it was time for another shot.

"Don' wanna be." He looked at her from heavy-lidded eyes. "Wanna sleep."

"Are you uncomfortable?" she asked. "I can hoist you up or something if you want to change position."

El thought about it. Now that she mentioned it, the slumped position he was in was uncomfortable, and he would like to be sitting up.

"Nah. Wanna sleep," he mumbled.

Petra stared at him a moment longer, bit her lip. Then, "Good," she said and started the car.

Christ, she must have given me a hell of a lot of that stuff. She clearly wanted to give him another shot. It was equally clear that she didn't quite dare.

Since there wasn't anything else he could do, El allowed himself to fall into a half waking state and tried to think of something he could do to save himself. She was strong, she was smart, and she was ruthless. There was no way he was going to talk his way out of this.

Though I can see her smiling and nodding while I try to.

Without meaning to, he drifted off to sleep.

When he came to they'd stopped, it was night, and she was taking his pulse.

El opened his eyes slowly, raised his wobbling head, and just stared. Petra was naked. He blinked and she smiled at him.

"I gave you more than I should have, sooner than I should have," she said. "You gave me a little scare there for a minute."

"Naked," he observed.

She laughed. "Yeah, don't want to get messy."

He looked beyond her and saw that they were in the middle of nowhere. Grass and trees surrounded them, with not a light to be seen anywhere. Except for the headlights. They illuminated a tarp she'd spread on the grass. Craven's instruments, on their cloth, glittered dangerously where she'd laid them out.

"Yeah, it's time," she said with a rueful smile. "I've talked it over with my employers and they've agreed that they were naughty boys and that they'll meet my price."

"No way I could top their offer?" Lamy asked, with a twisted smile.

She made a moue and shook her head. "Never in your wildest dreams, baby."

He ran his eyes over her body, appreciating what he saw. She was slender but shapely, with delicately rounded hips and long legs. Her breasts were round, the nipples erect in the evening chill.

Lamy leaned forward and inhaled deeply.

"You smell wonderful," he said.

She laughed in genuine surprise and took a step backward.

"You have got to be kidding!" she said.

"Why not?" he asked. He caught her eyes. "No one will ever know."

She leaned down to his eye level.

"This won't help you, honey," she told him. "I *will* kill you. You don't mean shit to me." Shaking her head, she said, almost sadly, "Neither does sex."

Lamy took a deep breath and, raising his hands, clumsily cupped her breasts.

"Please," he whispered. "It's been a long time. Over a year." El licked his lips. "And you *are* beautiful."

She ducked her head and began to chuckle. When she looked up she was wearing the most wicked grin he'd ever seen.

"Sure," Connoly said impulsively. "Why the hell not?"

Petra wound her arms around his neck and kissed him, teasing her tongue between his lips. The kiss grew deeper and more passionate, both their breathing quickening. They broke apart, panting, and she looked at him in astonishment.

"I'm so glad you suggested this," she said.

"We need to get horizontal," he suggested.

"Mm, yes."

Petra stood in a squat and grasped him under the arms; balancing their weight, she lifted and he came off the seat. El shifted his weight suddenly and Connoly started to stumble.

"Oh!" he said and clutched her to him.

Petra yelled, "Hey!" and fell onto her back, Lamy landing squarely on top of her, with both of them saying "Oof!" when they made hard contact with the ground.

Petra gasped as she laughingly said, "Well, I appreciate your enthusiasm, but this is hardly sexy."

El looked into her eyes for a long moment, then he said, "No. It isn't."

He reached over her head and dragged himself forward, watching understanding dawn in her eyes just as he dropped his broad chest squarely onto her face. He could feel her gnawing on his flesh as she squirmed like an eel. He took hold of her wrists and had all he could do to hold onto them. She still managed to get in a couple of painful strikes. But he could feel her chest heaving beneath him and her movements began to slow and grow uncoordinated. It took longer than he'd thought it ever could and she kept chewing on him long after she'd stopped kicking, biting until he cried out with the pain. But he held on and when she stopped moving altogether he waited some more. When he rolled off her she was unconscious, her pretty face covered with his blood. But she took a breath.

Lamy looked around and spied her purse; he dragged himself over the grass to it. El emptied it out and found what he'd expected. She had a gun and a cell phone.

Then he thought, *Unfortunately I have no intention of shooting her, which she'll probably guess. And she could probably lick me one-handed in a fair fight.*

He stuck the phone in his pocket and the gun into his waistband, then rolled over to the tarpaulin, slightly downhill from where he lay. There on the cloth with the instruments, as he had hoped, was another hypodermic, already filled.

She might not be somebody you'd want to take home to Mother, he thought, *but at least she's not a complete sadist.*

He put the hypo between his teeth and began to crawl towards her, the rough grass abrading his still bleeding wounds. Petra's breaths began to deepen; there was no doubt that she was regaining consciousness. El struggled to move faster, the weight of his useless legs seeming to grow greater with every foot of ground he gained. She twitched and opened her eyes, groaning and working her hands helplessly.

"You *bastard!*" she hissed.

Lamy made a desperate lunge and sunk the needle into her hip. Connoly yelped and struck at him. El yanked the pistol out and pointed it at her.

"Don't," he said. "Neither of us has to die here."

Her eyes were already beginning to glaze.

"I hate losing," she sighed.

"You'd hate dying more," he assured her.

Her head wobbled and she dropped to the ground. The dark eyes closed and she lay still.

Lamy watched her for a moment, expecting her to burst into action as soon as his guard was down, but she was still. Slowly he eased himself backwards and called the base.

Major Klien shook Lamy's hand, while on the other side of the capsule a tech checked all the connections.

"Good luck, son," Klien said. "I wish I could be there with you."

"I'll do my best, sir," Lamy told him with a grim smile.

The tech gave them a thumbs-up and shut the door on his side of the capsule.

"See ya when ya get back, Captain," Klien said and slammed the other door.

The tech checked its seal and gave a knock to show that all was well. Klien walked over to the control hut, entered the dimly lit room, and pulled the door closed behind him.

"This better work," Ohlsen growled.

"The scientists assure me that it will, sir," Colonel Nagakura said.

Ignazio merely grunted.

"It's in his hands now," Klien said and settled in to watch the action relayed by the fighter's wing cameras.

"The satellite uplink?" Ohlsen asked.

"Secure and online, sir," one of the techs answered.

"Then what are we waiting for?" Ignazio asked. "Let's get this show on the road."

In his capsule Lamy got the go for launch. He thrust the throttle forward and rose like a bird. This was his first time flying the prototype, and Craven hadn't lied: he felt *himself* rise, felt his body move through the air. It was like swimming, only vastly more powerful. It was glorious! He put the fighter into a slow roll, then made it climb. His view was unobstructed and his sight incredibly clear. He *was* flying.

"Okay, Captain," Klien's voice said. "That's enough. We're on a tight schedule here."

"Sorry, sir," El said. "But you've *got* to try this, it's unbelievable!"

"You should be coming up on them now, Captain," a tech interrupted.

Sure enough, there before him was a speck that grew larger. Petra had told them who her employers were. With some effort they'd traced those worthies and discovered that they'd sent the information on by private jet. Now, at last they had that jet in sight, and Lamy was closing fast.

Lamy broadcast a prerecorded message to them in English, French, and Urdu. He thought he saw the wings of the plane before him twitch in surprise, but other than that there was no reaction.

"You are to turn your plane ninety degrees and descend to ten thousand feet. Go subsonic, and land when directed. If you do not respond in one minute I will fire on you."

Two minutes would take them out of international airspace. But there was no way that they could allow this information to fall into other hands. The pilot ahead of him would surrender or die.

Lamy gritted his teeth and flexed his hands. There was nothing for his hands to *do,* but the need to work them remained.

The pilot ahead of him kicked his craft into afterburner and dove, corkscrewing. Lamy followed suit, pulling up fast; it was eerie, not feeling the thrust of g-force . . . and not having to worry about greying out. *Man, this ship's hot!* The acceleration and cornering were like nothing he'd ever known.

He looked at the plane as its silhouette resolved itself and found the spot he wanted. Staring hard, he *thought* about firing, his hand jerked spasmodically on nothing, and the plane before him exploded in a magenta ball of flame.

Through his earphones Lamy heard cries of glee from home base and he grinned. Then instruments pinged and the display told him that there were two fighters on an intercept path with him. He turned to run, surprised at the narrow arc of his curve, and set off with the enemy in hot pursuit. They called on him to come under their wing. They threatened to shoot. He ignored them, fleeing with all the power his craft could provide.

Warning claxons warned him of an approaching missile and he released a decoy. The speed with which it deployed took him off guard for a moment, then he turned to face his pursuers.

"No," Nagakura's voice said in his headset. "Bad idea. Head for base."

"Let him go," Ohlsen disagreed. "We need to know if this is going to work. This seems a ready-made opportunity."

"There'll be international repercussions," Nagakura warned.

"Mebbe," Ohlsen said laconically.

Lamy aimed his craft at one of those that had been dogging him. The sky hurtled about him in a blur of blue and white, and colors without name swam before his eyes as he *looked* with the plane's radar and thermal imagers. Another *thought*—it was a little like a combination of frowning and spitting—and a missile chunked away and went into burn. There was an eerie sensation of split vision, from the plane's sensors and the missile's, and then the missile went dead, like a cold breeze at the base of his neck. The enemy plane exploded into a ball of fire that fell earthward, shedding components.

Time to go home, he thought and matched action to thought as only he could.

The enemy pilot roared after him, literally screaming as he fired missile after missile at El.

Shit! Lamy thought passionately. *No more missiles.* Lock-on alarms sounded, feeling like a maddening itch. *No more decoys . . . no more ti—*

"Shit!" Nagakura shouted. "They got him! God damn *shit!*"

"God *damn!*" Ignazio agreed.

Ohlsen and Klien shook their heads sadly.

"I hate myself," Lamy said, sitting up and pushing back the headrest.

Ohlsen laughed.

"Don't worry 'bout it, son. It's only a prototype."

Drag Race

James H. Cobb

James Cobb has lived his entire life within a thirty-mile radius of a major Army post, an Air Force base, and a Navy shipyard. He comments, "Accordingly, it's seemed natural to become a kind of cut-rate Rudyard Kipling, trying to tell the stories of America's service people." Currently he's doing the Amanda Garrett techno-thriller series with two books, Choosers of the Slain *and* Seastrike, *published and a third,* Seafighter, *on the way. He's also writing the Kevin Pulaski suspense thrillers for St. Martin's Press. He lives in the Pacific Northwest, and when he's not writing he indulges in travel, the classic American hot rod, and collecting historic firearms.*

Author's Note: "Drag Race" is based upon a true incident. While all characters are fictional, and while details of setting and time have been altered for dramatic purposes, the primary events related in this story actually occurred, no matter how incredible that may seem.

McChord Air Force Base
2141 Hours Zone Time
12 October 1953

My little black car sat out on the end of the airstrip, her top down, her front wheels straddling the centerline, and her Hollywood exhausts bubbling softly. The crash wagons and ambulances had all pulled back to the perimeter road, leaving us alone in the darkness. Beyond the windshield, the two rows of ghost blue runway lights converged somewhere out towards eternity.

It was cool, getting on towards cold. Fall nights in Washington State are like that. Yet I could still feel the sweat building up under my palms. I dropped my hands off the wheel for a second and swiped them dry again on the thighs of my jumpsuit. I also tried to come up with a mouthful of spit to swallow, not with much success.

My name is Kevin Pulaski. For the time being, gainfully employed as a Military Policeman by the United States Army. Beyond that, I own, fool around with, and race fast cars. Frequently just for the heck of it, but there have been other reasons. Back in high school I ran a circle-track roadster for two seasons, eating Midwestern dirt for trophies and heat money. I've drag raced on more back roads than you could ever name, just for the local fame and glory of it. And once, back in Indiana, there was this girl.... Well, we won't get into that now.

The thing is, even after all that, I've never raced for pink slips on a man's life before. But in just about a minute here, that's exactly what I was going to be doing.

From his station in the rear seat, Long John Truitt reached forward to tap me on the arm.

"Here they come."

I looked back over my shoulder. A constellation had busted loose from the zenith and was drifting down out of the sky towards us.

It all started in the Fort Lewis auto shop and I guess that's appropriate.

I'd spent the two previous hours contentedly hacksawing the center bar out of the Rocket's grill, just for the cool look of the thing. I was lying on my back under the front bumper, filing down a few rough edges and applying a little Mexican chrome where needed when a pair of spit-shined jump boots stepped up and addressed me.

"So, Corporal Pulaski, this is how you pissed away your overseas pay?"

"Yeah," I replied to the boots. "Sure is. What'd you blow yours on? Cheap women and expensive liquor?"

"Damn right! Sound investments for a better future!"

I slid out from under the car to find the pair of Corcorans occupied by Sergeant Long John Truitt of the 187th Airborne regiment. Resplendent in razor-creased Army greens, my old platoon mate looked a whole lot different than I remembered. But then the last time I'd seen him I'd had an ampoule of morphine under my belt and he'd been helping to carry my stretcher to the battalion aid station.

"Christ, but it is good to see you, Kev!" Long John exclaimed, extending his hand for a shake. "What're you doing with yourself these days?"

I wiped a glob of silver paint off on the front of my garage coveralls before accepting his bone-cracking grip. "Base Cadre," I replied. "Forty-four fifty-three MP, but that's temporary. I'm out in another three weeks."

"You are shittin' me! I had you picked as a lifer."

"Hell no! Four years, that's all the Army gets."

I crossed my arms and leaned back against the Rocket's black and glossy fender. "Look, I'm not saying that it hasn't been kicks. I mean, you guys taught me how to throw myself out of perfectly good airplanes and you ran a neat little war for me and everything. But still, twenty-one days from now, it is goodbye, au reservoir, or, as we hepcats put it, I am real gone, man."

"That's too bad," Long John said, going serious on me. "You were one of the good ones, Kev. The Army is going to need men like you even if the truce does hold over in Korea."

I had to sigh a little on that one. "Maybe if I could go airborne again, I'd think about it. The thing is, I can't get my jump rating back. Even with all the shrapnel dug out, the medics say my knee's torn up too bad to take jumping again. I'm cleared for regular duty, but hell, John, you know how it goes. After you've been a 'trooper, being a straight leg just isn't the same."

Long John nodded in sympathy. "I hear you. And I can't say I blame you."

There was an awkward silence that threatened to get

too long and Long John grabbed for the first convenient topic.

"So, what is this death trap and what damn fool things have you been doing to it?" He nodded sourly towards the Rocket. The little convertible grinned back at him with her newly customized grill, sleekly nosed and decked and hunkering low on her blocked springs.

I caught that train of thought. I always like talking about cars, especially my own. "This here is an Olds-mobile Rocket 88, just like in the Bebop song. She's a '49 model with the 303-cubic-inch overhead valve V-8. I've got her set up and running with dual pipes, Tornado lifters, an Edelbrock quad-jet manifold with a Stromburg four-barrel carb and a genuine mail-order-from-California Iskenderian half-race cam."

Long John managed, somehow, to curb his enthusi-asm. "I gather that incantation means it's supposed to be fast?"

"*Was* fast, oh buddy who knows not cool when he sees it. When I bought this wagon a month ago, it was indeed a fast car. Now, it is a very fast car. And down the road aways, when I'm all done growing her up, she is going to be faster than the proverbial whistlin' Jesus."

Long John could only shake his head. "The damn Reds only managed to three-quarters kill you, so now you've got to go and finish the job on your own. Hot rods! Always you and your damn hot rods! Christ on a busted crutch, Kevin, when are you going to grow up?"

"Not one second sooner than I have to."

I guess he had kind of a point though. Out on the line, I'd lug copies of *Hot Rod* and *Hop Up* around in my pack the way the other guys would carry letters from home.

"You just don't know how to have a good time, man," I continued, grinning. "That's what your problem is. Give me a second to put my tools away and we'll take this little bomb out on old 99 and I will show you what she can do. It'll be good for what ails ya."

Long John held his hands up. "None for me, thank you kindly. I'll stick to safe and sane shit like parachute jumping. And that reminds me. I'm shepherding a replacement platoon across to Japan for the regiment. We're holding here at Lewis for a few days until our transit orders come through and I'm taking the opportunity to run these newbies through a little extra training. We've got a drop scheduled out on the range tonight and I could use an assistant jumpmaster. How about you riding along? Just for old time's sake."

Why not? Likely it would be my last chance to see a stick go out the door. "You got yourself a boy, Jonathan. And afterwards, I'll stand you to a couple of foamy ones at the NCO club."

"Ha! Now you're talking! Just as long as I don't have to ride over there with you."

But it didn't turn out to be quite that simple. Nooooo way, not that simple at all.

Shortly after 2100, we lifted off the main runway of McChord Field, the big Air Force base adjacent to Fort Lewis. We were definitely going first string because the Military Air Transport Service had tied on a bran' shiny new Douglas C-124 Globemaster II as our jump ship. As all of my jumps have been made out of Gooney Birds and Dollar Nineteens, this big monster frankly impresses the hell out of me.

The Globemaster is a mammoth silver whale of an

airplane that could swallow an entire tractor-trailer rig through the clamshell doors in its bow. Standing four stories tall at the cockpit and six at the top of her vertical stabilizer and with a one-hundred-and-seventy-four-foot wingspan, the Globemaster more than lives up to her name. She's the largest production transport aircraft in the world, and when her four huge Wasp Major radials kick over, that world trembles. That's how she's earned her other unofficial title: Big Shaky.

She's capable of carrying two hundred fully equipped troops, so our lonely little forty-odd-man platoon sort of rattled around in her cavernous cargo bay, enough room being left over for a good game of basketball.

Lifting into a sky marked with stars and ragged strips of moonlit cloud, we climbed away from McChord to the south. The silver wire channels of the Nisqually River delta passed beneath our belly as we reached jump altitude and soon, the illuminated dome of the Washington State capitol building in Olympia appeared off our starboard wing. That was the aircraft commander's waypoint and he banked into a wide, sweeping turn, heading us back to the north and out over the darkly forested reaches of the Fort Lewis firing range.

It felt good to be in a jumpsuit again and to feel the hug of a T-8 chute harness, even if I wasn't going over the side tonight. As I went down the line of green troopers, snugging up straps and squaring up rifles, I found myself feeling envious. It's funny how you can become nostalgic about a time when you were frequently scared to death, shot at, and eventually shot to pieces. Pain fades, I guess. Either that or paratroopers are just naturally born crazy. Anyway, I wished these kids well.

Kids? Where the hell had that come from? I'm only

twenty-two and I still get carded when I try to buy a glass of beer. Why were these guys suddenly making me feel like the Old Man of the Mountain? I dunno. Maybe it was something in the eyes. Something that I'd lost over there on the line in Korea. Or maybe something they'd yet to gain.

Long John was back aft at the fuselage hatch with the Globemaster's crew chief.

"How'd they look?" he asked, lifting his voice over the rumble of the engines.

I flicked him an okay with my right hand.

He nodded. "Not long now."

As if in response to his words, the engines throttled back. The aircraft commander was slowing to jump speed. Next to the aft hatch, the teardrop-shaped standby light flashed red.

Ten minutes out.

"Stand up and hook up!" Long John bellowed the first command.

The platoon hoisted itself off the canvas-and-aluminum folding bench along the side of the fuselage, clipping static lines to the thin steel anchor cable running overhead down the length of the cargo bay.

"Check your static lines!" The second command. You checked your static line all right, then you checked all the rest of your gear, and then you checked the gear of the man standing next to you as he did the same with yours. On a jump, you leave nothing to chance. No . . . thing!

Five minutes out.

"Equipment check, sound off!" From the front of the aircraft and working back towards us the taut, adrenaline-charged yells came back. "Okay! . . . Okay! . . . Okay! . . ."

The crew chief popped the portside hatch, lifting the door inboard and out of its frame. The slipstream boiled in, carrying with it the head-throbbing bellow of the huge radial aircraft engines. Grabbing a safety strap, I took a second to lean out the door and have a look ahead at the drop zone.

Damn, but it was a beautiful night out there. The air blast was like a jet of ice water playing on your face, tugging at your helmet and making the chinstrap dig into your throat. The Globemaster's wing glowed pewter in the moonlight, her propellers kicking over so slowly that you could almost count the blades. The scattered lights on the horizon merged with the starblaze overhead and the forest underneath us was black velvet. Ahead was the paler patch of an open prairie, the landing area marked out by the flickering ground flares of the pathfinder team. Speed felt right. Altitude looked good. For a second, I imagined what it would feel like to drift down out of that sky under a good canopy.

I pulled back inside and stepped out of the way as Long John returned to the hatch. It was his show now.

"Stand in the door!"

With airborne, the officers always lead the way. The platoon's young second lieutenant got his hands set on the hatch frame, trying hard to do John Wayne but only managing an Andy Hardy. No criticism meant. I don't care how many jumps you ever make, that first step is always a doozy.

There was that last long pause . . . then the green light flashed on and the jump bell rang.

"Go!" With a pistoning shove of his hand, Long John launched the lieutenant out onto the night.

"Go . . . Go . . . Go!" Like bullets into the chamber of a machine gun, Long John fed the stick out the hatch. Good jumpmaster that he was, he gave each paratrooper a second to position properly, but not that extra second that might allow him to freeze in the doorway.

I stood back and watched the static lines accumulate at the end of the anchor cable. As each man fell clear beneath the aircraft, the static line, linked to the D ring on his chute harness, pulled the rip cord of his main parachute, opening it. You could tell by the way a man's static line whipped whether he'd dropped straight and if he'd had a clean pull for chute deployment.

It looked good and went good for about the first three squads . . . and then things went FUBAR: absolutely and totally Fucked Up Beyond All Recall.

It was no big deal. One kid got a little anxious, a lean and gangly private with a big nose and a haze of crew cut blond hair on the back of his neck. He crowded Long John and the guy going out the door ahead of him. There was just a little bit of a bump as the first man was going out the hatch.

But something snagged.

As the first man launched out the door, I caught the flash of a steel cable trailing after him. A rip cord. The parachute backpack of the second guy, the anxious kid, burst open in an explosion of white nylon and tangled cordage.

It was a dumb stunt, an accident, something that rated at most a bawling out by Long John and the kid's lieutenant.

Only it happened when the kid was standing with his toes out over the edge of eternity.

Parachute went everywhere! Borne by a freak eddy in the slipstream, a corner of the canopy crawled out through the hatch and caught the slipstream. Long John grabbed for the kid's harness but he couldn't get a hold, everything had happened too fast. Snared in his tangled shroud lines like a fly in a spider's web, the kid was sucked out the hatch, his scream of terror trailing behind him. Something thudded back aft along the fuselage and then there was nothing but an empty door full of night.

I was the first one to the hatch. Hanging on to a handful of used static lines, I leaned out, looking astern. Maybe the age of friggin' miracles wasn't past and his canopy had opened. Or maybe he'd managed to cut himself loose in the seconds he had. Maybe in time to pop his reserve chute before the ground came up to smash him.

Nothing. Abso-goddamn-lutely nothing.

And then something. A funny silhouette, intermittently outlined in the pulsing glow of the navigation light on the transport's belly. Something waving in the wind like a rag caught on a fence.

"Get me a battle lantern!" I yelled back into the fuselage. The light was passed out to me and I aimed it aft with my free hand.

Good God!

Long John grabbed my shoulder and hauled me back inside. "What is it?" he demanded over the engine and wind roar. "What did you see?"

"He's still out there! His chute's fouled on the airframe! We're dragging him behind us!"

We notified the aircraft commander of the situation,

asking him to keep his airspeed as low as possible. He declared an in-flight emergency and notified McChord Tower of the problem. McChord declared a base emergency and notified Civil Air Traffic Control. And ATC, in turn, declared a regional emergency and cleared the airspace around us.

We established a racetrack holding pattern around McChord Field with very wide, slow turns at either end. And then everyone involved sat back, looked at each other, and said, "What in the hell do we do now?"

The crown of the 'trooper's canopy had lapped back over the 124's portside horizontal stabilizer and had caught on something, maybe snagged on some bit of the trim tab or elevator mechanism, or maybe a shroud line had slipped into the joining between the tail plane and fuselage itself. Either way, it couldn't be held by very much.

As for the man himself, he hung from his chute risers, facedown and with his arms and legs limp in the slipstream. It was an even-money call as to whether he was unconscious or dead; we had no way to tell.

Leaving the crew chief to keep an eye on our boy, Long John and I went forward and up the ladder to the flight deck to make medicine with the pilot.

The aircraft commander was Major Walsh, a big, square-shouldered kind of man. Clad in a well-worn flight suit, he had about the coldest, grayest eyes I have ever seen. The Air Force does not hand its biggest and best over to just any greengrocer from the sticks. Coming back from the left seat, he hunched down with us next to the minute galley area. There was the smell of hot coffee in the cockpit, but no one offered to pass any around.

"I think we'd better start by fixing some initial pa-

rameters," the major said grimly. "This was supposed to
be a short training hop, so we took off with only two
hours of fuel aboard plus a one hour emergency reserve.
We have been in the air now for one hour and ten
minutes. When we are down to fifteen minutes of fuel, I
land this aircraft, whether the problem is resolved or not.
We have ninety-five minutes to develop a solution. No
more. Is that understood?"

Yeah, it was. Our guy trailed behind the Globemaster
like a raccoon tail from a radio aerial. When the plane
slowed after touchdown, he'd drop and smash into the
runway. And if that didn't kill him outright, being
dragged at a-hundred-plus miles per hour down the tarmac damn well would. By the time the aircraft stopped,
there wouldn't be anything left back there except for a
long red streak leading to an empty chute harness.

"Understood, sir," Long John replied.

"Very well then, Sergeant. How do you propose we
deal with this situation?"

"The only thing I can think of, Major, is to cobble
together some kind of line and harness rig out of the
chutes we have left aboard. You can lower me out of the
side or belly hatch and I can try and work my way back
to him. If I can swing that, I can cut us both loose, open
his reserve chute, then fall free and open mine."

Before Long John even finished outlining his plan,
Major Walsh was shaking his head. "I'm not letting anyone out of this aircraft on any kind of jury rig like that.
We could end up with two of you fouled out there. Beyond that, there's the risk of damage to the control sur-
faces. We've been lucky so far, but if we jam an elevator,
we're all in big trouble."

"But there's no way we can get at him from inside

the aircraft, Major!'' Long John protested. "I already checked that out with your crew chief. It's gotta be from the outside!''

"I concur, Sergeant," the pilot replied flatly. "But in some way that does not put this aircraft or the personnel aboard it to an excessive risk.''

Working at his station just forward of us in the cockpit, the transport's flight engineer must have been keeping his ears open. "Beg your pardon, sir," he said, turning his swivel chair to face us. "But I've heard of a deal like this once and they got the guy back alive.''

Major Walsh looked back over his shoulder. "Keep talking, Sergeant. What's the story?''

"It was right back before the war, in San Diego. A Marine or Navy jumper fouled his jump ship, and they were draggin' him behind just like we're doing with this guy. What they did in Diego was to scramble an open-cockpit training plane with a good instructor pilot aboard. The trainer came up behind the jump ship in midair and just sort of scooped the jumper into its front cockpit. They even used the propeller to cut the guy's shroud lines after he was aboard.''

The major shook his head again. "I've heard about that incident too, and I've already disregarded the idea. It occurred in broad daylight and the jumper was conscious and able to help himself. Also the drop ship was a DC-2, a hell of a lot smaller and slower than a 124. Any small plane that worked in that close to us would be bounced all over the sky by our propwash. The risk of a midair collision is too great. Especially for the sake of a man who might already be dead.''

Long John and I swapped looks for a second. That was a thought that hadn't occurred to us. Not that the kid

might not be dead—there was a pretty good chance that
he was, after bashing into the tailplane—but that it should
make any difference about what we'd do about it.

You see, a paratrooper doesn't leave another paratrooper hanging fouled. Doesn't matter if he's alive or
dead, you just don't do it. Mostly because you know that
someday it could be you up there dangling helplessly between Heaven and Earth. In places like St. Mere Eglise
and Nijmegen, a lot of 'troopers stuck their necks way
out cutting dead buddies down. A lot of good 'troopers
got killed doing it too. It doesn't make any difference. I
guess unless you pack a set of jump wings you wouldn't
understand.

"Then I guess we're down to hoping he comes to on
his own and can cut himself loose before we run out of
gas," Long John said, his voice barely audible over the
engines.

"So it would appear, gentlemen." Walsh spoke like
he was passing a sentence.

We wasted two of our precious minutes sitting there
in silence. And when somebody at last spoke up, I was
surprised to find that it was me.

"How about a car?"

That earned me a couple of blank stares.

"Look," I went on, "if another plane won't do it, how
about a car? Our guy will be torn to pieces when this
plane lands and he hits the runway, right? But what if we
have a fast, open car in position under him to catch him
before he hits the tarmac?"

The major cocked an eyebrow. "Where are we going
to find an automobile with that kind of speed?"

"Sitting in your Air Wing parking lot. I've got the
keys right here in my pocket."

"You think your heap can actually do it, Kevin?" Long John asked, leaning forward intently.

"I'm not making any guarantees, but then, I'm not hearing any better ideas either."

It took almost twenty seconds of frowning before Major Walsh started to shake his head.

"That's no good either. That would be beyond stunt pilot work. No one could fly a night approach in a C-124 and touch down with anywhere near enough precision to drop that fouled trooper into a car. Jimmy Doolittle couldn't pull it off, not even if he had Curt LeMay in the right seat and Lindbergh for a flight engineer."

"You wouldn't have to, sir. Look, this aircraft has a lot of ground clearance and our guy is streaming from the tail assembly at a pretty shallow angle. Our airspeed is blowing him back almost in line with the fuselage. Now, if you could grease her in on her nose wheel, not flaring out on touchdown, I don't think he'd ground strike. You wouldn't have to worry about dragging him until you started to decelerate because your slipstream will keep him blown up and off the tarmac. If you can maintain a high-speed taxi long enough for me to get into position under him, you could cut power and he'd drop right into our laps."

The major stopped shaking his head but he still frowned. "Let's work some numbers." We edged after him as he went to the navigator's station and dug out the West Coast approach book. Leaning over his shoulders in the dim ruddy cockpit light, we watched as he flipped the book open to the McChord Field chart.

"All right," he went on. "This is the main runway at McChord. Eight thousand one hundred feet long. That's what we have to work with. How much room will you need to get your car up to speed, Corporal?''

Good question. I'd gotten the Rocket well up into the eighties on a quarter-mile drag strip, but those last few MPH up at the high end come slower and harder. ''About half a mile.''

''Twenty-five hundred feet?''

''Pretty much, sir.''

''All right.'' He picked up a chart compass. ''The wind is from the south tonight so I'll be approaching from the north. . . .'' He used the compass's spike to mark a point on the runway chart. ''Here is where I'll have to touch down and where you will have to intercept me. Twenty-five hundred feet down from the north end of the runway.''

The compass pointer drifted to the southern end of the chart. ''Now, on the other hand, given its load conditions, I will need twenty-five hundred feet of runway to bring this aircraft to a complete stop.'' The needle tip of the compass jabbed a second mark.

''However,'' he continued, ''to abort the landing, that is, to take off again and go round, I'll need three thousand feet. That incorporates our safety margin in case we lose an engine.''

The pointer jabbed again, then swept between the third mark and the first.

''Twenty-six hundred feet, that's how much space we'll have to work with.''

The major turned in the navigator's seat and faced us. ''This brings up another point. Configured as we are, the speed of refusal for this aircraft is ninety-six knots. That is, if I reach the three-thousand-foot point of decision from the end of the runway and my ground speed is below ninety-six knots, I am required to refuse the takeoff and shut the aircraft down . . . whether you've recovered your man or not.''

Walsh turned those ice gray eyes directly on me. ''Ninety-six knots is roughly a hundred and eight miles per hour. Just how fast is this car of yours, son?''

That was another good question. I hadn't had the chance to take the Rocket through a measured mile yet to get her true top end. Sure, I'd buried the speedometer needle a couple of times road testing, but a standard Detroit speedometer starts getting wonky over sixty-five or so. The readings can't be trusted.

I did know that a butt stock Olds Rocket 88 had set a class record at Daytona Beach in 1949 with a two-way run at a solid one hundred miles per hour. I also knew that last year, Ak Miller took his full race D class 88 through the traps at Bonneville at a hundred and twenty-four plus. My car was set up somewhere in between those two extremes.

''I'll be in the ballpark, sir,'' I replied. ''That's as close as I can call it.''

Slowly, the major nodded. ''All right then, that locks it down. We will have one-half mile of usable runway, which we will cover in a little over thirty seconds. Let's hope that's both room and time enough, gentlemen. Because, as the saying goes, that's all there is, there ain't no more.''

I hadn't even seen a parachute in over a year, and a night free-fall out of a strange aircraft was a heck of a way to get reintroduced. Long John and I jumped over the base golf course, the headlights of an Air Police jeep marking our sand trap landing zone. All in all, it wasn't a bad drop, not far off target and a clean landing. I always knew that the damn medics didn't know what they were talking about.

As we tore over to the airfield, our jeep's siren merged with the wailing of a whole fleet of other emergency vehicles. The base crash and meat wagons were rolling out of their hangars and moving into position along the taxiways, their red flashers pulsing in the darkness. Worklights also blazed along the flight line as tractor crews hastily towed parked aircraft as far back from the main runway as they could. McChord was clearing the stage for the main act.

They dumped me out in the car park where I'd left the Rocket. "Looks like I have to ride in that buzz wagon of yours after all," Long John commented as I bailed out of the jeep.

"Don't sweat it, man. You're going to love it to death."

Bad choice of words.

"I'll follow you out in a second," I called after the departing jeep. "Just make sure they've got an air-to-ground radio available at the north end of the runway."

"Right."

Long John and the Air Police roared off and I sprinted to the waiting Rocket. A dewfall had started to haze her dark, polished metal and as I slid behind her wheel I had to think that it would be a hell of a note if she wouldn't start.

She didn't betray me, though. She kicked over at the first turn of the key, her eight cylinders falling into their stammering beat of power. As she warmed up, I flipped the lock lever in the center of the windshield frame and hit the retract button for the convertible top. As it folded,

I cranked down the side windows and then took another minute to snap on the tonneau cover.

Getting behind the wheel again I revved the mill, listening to the engine tone and checking my gauges. Gas . . . half a tank. Oil and water pressure . . . in the range. Ammeter . . . putting out. Manifold pressure . . . okay. Engine temp . . . just edging off the peg. I blipped the throttle, and watched the clean sweep of the tachometer needle as the revs built. Good as it was going to get.

I popped her in gear and we moved out. Going through the gate onto the flight line, I noticed another Globemaster parked nearby and I took a moment to drive around it slowly, getting a feel for the size and clearances of the massive airplane.

Plenty of room beneath the fuselage. I could drive the Rocket cleanly under it with no problem if I had to. I'd have to watch the landing gear, though. Each huge dual wheel stood almost as tall as my car's roofline. Man, what a mess it would make if I collided with one of those at a hundred and eight. And what about the propeller arcs?

I carefully studied the massive three-bladed airscrews. Yep, they were set at just the right height to take my head clean off at the shoulders.

Hey, man, but ain't we having fun now?

I parked just at the north edge of the runway tarmac. For a second I considered backing up farther into the gravel overrun area but dumped the notion. Gravel is no damn good for serious acceleration.

An Air Force radio jeep pulled up alongside me, whip antennas swaying wildly, and Long John got out of its front seat.

"The transport's in the pattern and turning base leg,"

he reported. "He's about five minutes out. You want to try it this pass?"

"Might as well."

In the back of the jeep, the RT nodded and hunched over his transceiver. Backlit in the violet glow of his dials he spoke into his hand mike, relaying the word. Apparently by default, I'd ended up in command of this show. A hell of a note for a guy who'd always felt just a little bit nervous wearing corporal's stripes.

"Pull over there ahead of me to the left," I yelled over to the jeep's driver. "Have the aircraft commander give you the word when he's about thirty seconds from touchdown. When he does, start flashing your headlights. Got it?"

"Thirty seconds. Got it," the airman yelled back. "Good luck, you guys. You're going to need it."

Long John piled in the backseat and then we had nothing to do but wait, revving the mill intermittently to keep the plugs clear. I kept my eyes on my engine gauges. If I'd let them creep over to the dashboard clock, time would lock up and we'd be stuck out there forever.

"Hey, John?"

"Yeah?"

"What's his name?"

"Whose?"

"The guy, you know? I don't know what his name is."

"Simmons. PFC Eddie Simmons. He's from New Jersey."

"Oh."

The droning of an airplane edged in over the mutter of our own exhausts. The radio jeep's headlights flashed.

"Hang on! This is it!"

My palm slapped the head of the Tornado floor shifter, socking it into low. Tires sobbed and spun and we were rolling. A reflective field marker slipped by on the right: 8000; the numerals listing the distance in feet to the other end of the runway.

Twenty-five miles per hour . . . thirty . . . thirty-five . . . The wind began to roar as it boiled over the windshield.

Clang! The transmission seemed to suck itself into second and the Rocket's tail bobbled as she tried to break traction again. I wound her out. Keeping one eye on the glowing tachometer and listening for the howl of the engine to peak, signaling the instant for the next speed shift.

Forty-five . . . fifty . . . fifty-five . . . *Clang!* We hit high gear, the blue runway lights smearing into a blur as we tore past.

Suddenly the steering wheel started to shiver in my hands. For one panicky second I figured a tire was going out on me. Then I realized the vibration was coming from somewhere else.

A mammoth shadow eclipsed the moon and a blast of landing light glare illuminated the world ahead of us. I glanced up and an undercarriage truck damn near as wide as my entire car drifted past twenty feet overhead.

Jeeeesus! That isn't an airplane up there! It's Montana with wings!

Then we saw the kid, Simmons. His face was a mask of wind-dried blood underlit by our headlights and his body had a grotesque rag doll limpness. Streaming behind the Globemaster's stabilizer on his shredded parachute, he floated and fluttered above us like an Emergio puppet from a cheap horror flick. We could also see the head of the transport's crew chief peering out and back from the bottom of the Globemaster's side hatch. Lying on his belly on the deck, he was screaming into a hand mike, trying to keep his pilot posted on what was going on under his tail.

We only had an instant to take in these impressions, though. The C-124 touched down on the runway ahead, her wheels spinning up with a puff of rubber smoke, and suddenly the roaring river of air flowing around us turned into a stone-solid avalanche.

I almost lost it, the wheel twisting in my hands as we swerved wildly across the tarmac. I'd forgotten about the goddamn propwash from the engines! It was blasting us right off the runway!

I socked the Rocket's gas pedal to the floor, backed off for a second, then smashed it down again, taking every last millimeter of play out of the throttle linkage. The 303 V-8 screamed in agony as I forced it to do things it was never designed for. Like a ship fighting heavy seas, we had to stay aimed into it! If we fell off, we'd be blown over into a death roll.

Hey God! Please don't let the friggin' windshield implode or the hood tear loose!

Finally the Rocket got her head up and her legs under her once more and we tunneled into that wall of battering wind. Out of the corner of my eye, I saw Long John stand up in the backseat. He had a death grip on one end of the passenger-side seat belt and he was using it pull himself upright in the face of the man-made tornado. In the dashlight I could see that his eyes were narrowed to slits and that the skin of his face was rippling.

We closed with Simmons again. I lined up behind the bobbling form of the helpless paratrooper and we edged into position. The kid drifted back towards us, over the hood, over the windshield, almost close enough. Long John reached up and out, stretching to the limit, fighting the air blast. His fingertips brushed the ankle of a jump boot. Long John lunged again . . . and missed clean.

The reciprocating thunder rolling back over us started to grow in intensity, a distance marker flashing past on the right: 2800. Major Walsh had hit his point of decision and had aborted the run. He was throttling back up to flight power and there was no way in hell we could keep pace with 14,000 horse's worth of Pratt and Whitney's best.

The transport pulled away and we saw its massive elevators up-angle as it rotated into the takeoff. As the tail sank, so did Simmons. Hanging facedown, and with his legs dangling behind him, he settled towards the surface of the runway. We stopped breathing.

A boot touched and an explosion of sparks trailed back from the steel toecap. Then the plane and the fouled trooper lifted clear, back into the comparative safety of the sky.

I feathered the Rocket's brakes and brought us to a stop at the far end of the runway. My hands were close to frozen from the windchill and I couldn't even feel my face. I rubbed the latter with the former, trying to get the circulation going again in both. Long John draped himself over the seat back, coughing a lung out.

"You okay, man?"

"Yeah," he wheezed back. "I just couldn't breathe back there." He took on another shuddering load of oxygen. "I almost had him, Kevin. Dammit to Hell! I almost had him!"

"I know." I put my arm around his shoulders for a second. "Next time, man. Next time we get him."

• • •

We positioned once more at the north end of the strip, setting up for the next run. Leaving the Rocket idling, I got out and jogged over to the radio jeep.

"You guys still got the transport?"

"Yeah," the RT said, passing me a headset and a microphone. "The pilot wants to talk to you. His call sign is Cheyenne November Niner."

"Right." I fitted the earphones on and keyed the mike. "Cheyenne November Niner, this is . . . this is Hot Rod, do you read? Over."

Cool even over the filtering of the radio net, Major Walsh's voice came back. "Cheyenne November Niner to Hot Rod. We read you. My crew chief says you didn't even get close. Over."

"Acknowledged, November Niner. We didn't figure on your propwash hitting us so hard. Next pass can you feather your inboard props on touchdown? That might give us some quieter air. Over."

"That could put me below refusal speed, Hot Rod."

"Roger that, November Niner. I figured that. If we're going to make this work, we're going to need for you to back your speed off a little anyway. We're going to need more running room."

"That means we lose the air abort option, Hot Rod," the major replied. "We will be committed to a landing then. We will only get one more shot at this."

I glanced over at the panting Oldsmobile. No big deal. I had a hunch my car . . . and I, only had one more shot left in us anyway. "Roger, November Niner. We're going for broke here."

"Be advised again, Hot Rod," Walsh continued relentlessly, "that my stopping distance is twenty-five hundred feet, not a foot less. Twenty-five hundred feet from the south end of the runway, I am reversing propellers and hitting the brakes. Whether you have him or not, whether you are clear or not, I am stopping this aircraft. Over.''

"Understood, November Niner."

"We are on base leg, initiating descent. Over the approach lights in five minutes. This is Cheyenne November Niner, over and out."

I returned the headset to the radioman and ran back to the Rocket. I had to get some more banzai out of her and fast. Popping the latch, I flung open the hood and studied the mill. There wasn't much I could do in the time remaining, but I tore the air cleaner off the carburetor, letting the big Stormburg four-barrel breathe easier. Then I flicked open my paratrooper's knife and slashed through the fan belt, freeing up another horsepower or two. She wouldn't have time to overheat on me tonight.

Slamming the hood shut, I crossed to the edge of the tarmac and scraped up a little mound of dirt with the heel of my boot. Scooping the dirt up, I worked it into my palms, using it like rosin, an old driver's trick from the circle track.

Then not being able to think of anything else I could do, I got back behind the wheel. "He's coming around again," I said over my shoulder.

"Uh-huh," John grunted in response. He was already twisted around, watching the sky to the north. I started to go on about how this time it was for the whole nine yards, but I shut up. It just wouldn't make that much difference. We'd do it or we wouldn't. I sat and stared down the runway until I felt the touch of Long John's hand on my shoulder.

"Here they come."

This time I could gauge it better. I was revved up and ready to drop the hammer at the first flash of the radio jeep's headlights. Rubber burned as we peeled out again. I worked up through the gears more decisively this time, knowing what to expect and where and when. Without the muffling fiber and metal of the air cleaner, the night air poured through the carburetor ventures with a piercing siren scream.

Two thousand feet down from the north end of the runway, the huge moonshadow swept over us once again. Her running lights glowing at dim-steady, the C-124 felt her way gingerly down to the tarmac, smoke streaming back from her wheels as she found it and settled onto her undercarriage.

This time there was only the briefest slap of turbulence. The major pulled pitch from his inboard propellers as I had asked, giving us a precious channel of smooth air to work in.

The 4000-foot marker blitzed past.

In our headlights we could see Simmons now, sagging closer to the runway, dangerously so, his feet almost dragging on the tarmac. We wouldn't be able to take him aboard over the windshield; we'd have to come up alongside him. I socked the spurs to the 88, trying to find that last couple of miles per hour.

I had no idea how fast we were already going. My speedometer had died of shock, the needle twisting right off the end of the cable. All I knew was that we were slowly drawing alongside the flaccid body of the fouled trooper and that we were running out of room fast.

As we crossed the 3000-foot line, I risked a glance over just as Long John Truitt rose up out of the backseat, lunging. Not saving a hold for himself, he reached out, grabbed a double handful of chute harness, and hauled Private First Class Eddie Simmons over the passenger side door and aboard the Rocket.

That still left him, and now us, tethered to fifty-odd tons of speeding airplane. Long John hit the right-hand Capwell release on Simmons' harness, cutting one set of risers loose. Just as we flashed past the 2500-foot marker, he yanked at the left-hand release.

And the son of a bitch jammed.

Amazingly, the world didn't come to an end. Not quite yet, anyway. The Globemaster's crew chief must have reported to Major Walsh that we were hung up, and that grim and gray-eyed man broke his own word, granting us a few more seconds of grace.

Leaning over the front seat, Long John doubled up the stuck risers. His 'trooper's knife flashed and he slashed through the heavy straps with a single yank of the blade, snapping it off at the hilt but still cutting us free.

And then we ran out of grace, the major's, God's, and everyone else's. There was a pulse in the airflow around us as the aircrew slammed their propeller controls into reverse pitch.

Brake smoke streamed back from the landing gear, and the portside gear truck, the one we were directly in line with, lunged back towards us. I didn't have a chance to think of my own brakes. I could only swerve out of the way to the right. Suddenly we were directly *underneath* the fuselage of the C-124 and the nose wheels were making a pass at us.

I swerved back to the left, neatly removing a couple thousand dollars' worth of spike antenna from the Globemaster's belly as I aimed for the narrow gap between the inboard prop arc and the fuselage. A wee, small voice in the back of my mind screamed *"Propeller!"* and I hugged that forward landing gear truck like it was a cheerleader who had just said yes. Something big, sharp, and invisibly fast not quite touched my left shoulder and then we shot out from under the transport's nose and into the clear.

Sort of.

We had succeeded in recovering our jumpmate.

Good.

We were now however in front of the Globemaster and, as it filled the entire runway behind us, we couldn't stop until it did. Given that, in fact, it could.

Bad. Very much bad.

I considered trying to turn off the tarmac but at the rate of knots we were cranking we'd likely lose it and roll when we hit the grass median strip. All we could do was to flee headlong, a terrified black mouse chased by a stampeding silver elephant.

It was the weirdest sensation in the world. We were tear-assing along at what must have been better than eighty miles an hour and yet the slipstream was flowing forward around us. We were riding a wall of air pushed ahead of the Globemaster by its four howling fans. With everything wide open but the toolbox, Major Walsh was making a desperate effort to slow his aircraft before he and we both ran out of runway.

Over the thundering of the engines, the C-124's brakes squealed like a sow giving birth to a coil of barbed wire. In my rearview mirror, I could see a pinkish glow low to the ground. The Globemaster's brake drums were going incandescent as they converted the kinetic energy of the transport's vast momentum into heat.

Slowly, so slowly, the big plane started to fade back. With her flaps flaring wide, she was finally losing lift, her weight settling onto her wheels and her overloaded brakes at last starting to take.

I couldn't wait any longer either. I got off the gas and went for the stop pedal, the Rocket's binders adding their piglet squeal to the howling of Big Momma behind us.

But then there wasn't any more pavement left. The gravel of the runway overrun flashed pale in the headlights. I yanked my foot off the brake but I was a shaved-second too late. Our wheels were still locked up as we hit the marbles and we just plain lost it!

We busted loose and spun out, going into a complete three-hundred-and-sixty-degree Gilhooly. I tried to catch her on the first time around, which you can hardly ever do, and I didn't. Then we were really gone, man, lost in a cloud of blurred dust, light, and darkness, and all I could do was to pump the brake pedal and pray something would grab hold somewhere.

Eventually we slithered to a halt, upright and with the world stinking of overheated metal and melting brake shoe. The dust fog dissipated and we found ourselves aimed north, back in the direction we had come from. Behind . . . ahead of us, disdainfully looking down its radome, sat the Globemaster, close enough so that you had to tilt your head back to see the cockpit.

Major Walsh cut his master switches and the transport's propellers wound down, flickered into visibility. I cut the Rocket's engine as well. Now I could hear the sirens of the crash trucks as they converged on us. I noticed that my left knee was throbbing. Now that I thought about it, it had started to hurt some time ago and I'd just been too busy to pay attention. I guess the docs were right after all.

I looked into the backseat. Long John sat cradling the still form of our fellow 'trooper in his arms with that unique form of tenderness only one warrior can show another. It took me a couple of tries before I could get my voice working.

"Hey John?"

"He's breathing."

And that's what it had all been about.

The author would like to thank the staff of the McChord Air Force Base Air Museum and the flight crew of the last Globemaster for their kind assistance in the development of this story.

Following his discharge, watch for the return of Kevin Pulaski in the 1950s suspense thriller West on 66, *coming in hardback from St. Martin's Press.*

Hearts and Minds

John Helfers is a writer and editor currently living in Green Bay, Wisconsin. A graduate of the University of Wisconsin–Green Bay, his fiction appears in more than a dozen anthologies, including Future Net, Once Upon a Crime, *and* The UFO Files, *among others. His first anthology project,* Black Cats and Broken Mirrors, *was published by DAW Books in 1998. Future projects include more anthologies as well as a novel in progress.*

As MICHAEL SLOWLY drifted out of unconsciousness, the first thing he became aware of was the heat. Suffocating, it lay upon him like a clinging blanket that covered every inch of his skin, an invisible weight on his chest, his head, his legs. He felt slick droplets on his forehead and cheeks. His chest was soaked, and his back had adhered to the bed he was lying on. As the sweat left his body, it seemed to have taken his strength with it, leaving him almost helpless.

The heat shouldn't have bothered him. He had been in hotter places. It reminded him of an episode during his military training days. For a second, he thought he might be back there, off the coast of California. He and his squad had been assigned to recon a set-up "enemy" base and gather information. One of his team had set off a booby trap. In the ensuing firefight, Michael had been captured.

The sergeant acting as the enemy commander had placed him in the "box," a three-foot-high, two-foot-deep cell of welded sheet steel. Michael remembered having to choose between sitting or kneeling. He had sat down Indian-style, with his legs crossed. It was the wrong choice.

As the sun rose, it baked the box, turning the sides into burning hot skillets. Michael couldn't rest his back against the sides, so he had to pull his knees up to his chin and arch his back so he didn't burn himself. The temperature in the box rose to over 130 degrees. Michael had been kept in the box for twelve hours, and hadn't said a word the entire time. As he remembered it, the sergeant had been impressed.

That was the hottest Michael had ever been. The way he felt now made that time seem like a cool autumn day.

He kept his eyes closed, letting his other senses gather information. He heard nothing nearby, but in the distance there were sounds of chickens and cattle. Even further out he could hear the sounds of jungle animals crying and hooting in the bush. He swallowed, his mouth, tongue, and throat feeling like they were carved out of Styrofoam. He was unbelievably thirsty.

Jungle. Southeast Asia. Laos, Cambodia, or maybe Vietnam, he thought. *The mission.*

Then he remembered where he was and why. It came back to him in flashes, the thundering booms of the mines, the splatter of blood and choked screams of the men. Michael didn't know how he had survived, but he had. The blast from the ambush had thrown him into the brush, and, half-conscious, he had seen the combat boots and fatigues of the attackers, heard them walking among the scattered bodies, stripping them of weapons and gear. They spoke a pidgin combination of Chinese, Korean, and Vietnamese. A single small-caliber gunshot echoed as one of his men was finished off. Michael tensed as he thought of the men he would never see again. Jennings . . . Altanow . . . Marco. All gone now.

But I'm still alive, and that means whoever's got me needs me for something, he thought. Michael slowly cracked one eye open and looked around.

He was the only occupant of a small hut, surrounded

by a screen of mosquito netting, then a thatched grass roof. He was lying on a metal army cot that had seen better days, but held him well enough. A crude table and one chair were the only other furniture in the room. An open doorway led to the outside and let in the only light, a square patch of sunbeam.

Without moving his head, Michael's hands scrabbled for his weapons. The pistol holster on his right hip was empty, and so was the dagger sheath on his left leg. Arching his neck, he realized that the small throwing blade usually sheathed between his shoulder blades was also gone. While his hands were exploring, he discovered that his chest was oddly numb. Lifting his head, Michael looked down and discovered his fatigue shirt was missing and his chest was covered by angry red and purple welts. There were smaller bandages on his left shoulder, and he could feel something on the left side of his forehead as well. In fact, the whole left side of Michael's body ached, from his throbbing ankle to his pounding head.

The sound of voices nearby startled him, and Michael quickly shut his eyes. He could hear short bursts of conversation as at least two people, a man and a woman, approached the hut, then passed it, their singsong voices fading as they walked away.

I've got to get out of here, Michael thought, and tried to sit up. A wave of dizziness crashed down on him, causing Michael to cling to the side of the cot and convulse, dry-heaving for several seconds. The whirling in his head subsided after a few minutes, and Michael was able to open his eyes again.

One step at a time, he thought. Swinging his legs over the side of the cot, he slowly pushed himself upright. He felt fresh blooms of sweat break out of his forehead, and if anything, it felt even hotter now. Michael put his head between his knees for a second, letting the blood gather in his brain. After a minute, he slowly stood up.

Swaying, Michael sank to his knees, bracing himself against the metal cot for a moment. His hands plucked at the mosquito netting, the fine mesh resisting his efforts to move it. Finally he found the opening, stood up, and exited the netting. He took a step towards the door, then bit back a scream as his weight came down on his left ankle. Falling to his knees again, he turned and crawled towards the back wall of the hut. Once there, he knelt in the dirt and pushed at the grass wall. It gave, and he pushed harder. With a quiet rustle a small bunch of grass came loose in his hand. Michael worked at clearing the hole he had made, wrenching dried tufts of grass out and throwing them aside, ignoring the small cuts the grass left on his hands. Soon the opening was big enough to crawl through.

Dizziness overcame him again as he was finishing, and Michael sat back on his haunches, keeping his weight off his left leg, to rest while his vision cleared. He heard faint voices again, and the sound of people coming closer.

Taking a deep breath, Michael pushed and squirmed, wriggling through the narrow space. For a moment, he thought he hadn't made it wide enough for his shoulders, but the sides of the hole gave slightly, and he scraped through. His trembling fingers dug into the dirt outside and he pulled himself forward. He had just cleared the hut when he heard the voices chatter excitedly from behind him. Although Michael was fluent in both Vietnamese and Chinese, he couldn't make out what was being said. The tone of their voices, however, left no doubt in his mind what they meant.

Dammit, they've checked on me already. Struggling to his hands and knees, Michael tried to crawl into the nearby jungle. He only managed to get about ten meters when the last of his strength dissipated, and he collapsed on his side.

He heard footsteps approaching, and saw a blurry pair of sandal-clad feet stop in front of him. As blackness rose over his vision, the last thing he heard was a woman's voice, speaking in accented English.

"You're stronger than I thought. I'm afraid you're not going anywhere just yet. Not when we've found just what we need."

Michael's eyes fluttered open at the touch of a cool cloth on his forehead. Even with his eyes open, he saw only blackness, and realized that the rag was covering the upper half of his face as well. He tried lifting his arms, only to find them pinned at his sides. His head was immobilized by what felt like a hand holding him down.

"Shhh. Don't try to move, you'll aggravate your wounds even further," the same woman's voice said with what sounded like a broad Cockney accent. "Although I admire your tenacity, it won't get you very far around here, especially in the condition you're in. Three days isn't enough time for you to be up and about, and I can't have you running around reinjuring yourself just when I've gotten you patched up."

"Who are you? Where am I?" Michael asked.

"You're safe now, in a small village just inside Vietnam."

"Please, let me see you," Michael asked, trying to move his head to dislodge the damp cloth.

"All right, but only if you promise to relax. No one's going to hurt you. Do you promise?"

"Yes," Michael said. The cloth was removed, and Michael blinked, letting them become accustomed to the gloom. He wasn't surprised to find himself in the same hut again. Michael now turned his gaze to the new addition to the room, his captor.

She was kneeling next to him, a short, slender, brown-skinned woman in her late twenties, with a broad face, almond-shaped eyes, flat nose, and startlingly white teeth. She was wary, regarding him with interest, gauging his reaction to her. Michael looked down to see his wrists locked to the pipes of the cot with flexible plastic lock-ties. *His* flexible plastic lock-ties.

"Highland Montagnards, right?"

She nodded. "You know your Asian mountains well. We're part of the Rhade tribe."

Michael smiled, although it felt more like a grimace, and nodded. "Your tribe worked with the CIA against the North Vietnamese in the first Vietnam Conflict." When he saw her eyebrows raise, he added, "This isn't my first time in country."

"For a while I was wondering if it was going to be your last," she said, mopping his brow. "Like I said, you've been here for three days. You were running a 105-degree fever, and some of your wounds had become infected. It was touch and go for a while, but you're finally coming out of it. I'll bet you feel better now."

Now that she mentioned it, Michael did feel much better. The intolerable heat was now merely oppressive, and the pain up and down the left side of his body had subsided to a general dull ache with sharp flashes whenever he shifted position. "Yes, thank you. You've had medical training somewhere, which would also explain your fluency?''

The woman nodded, although Michael saw her expression became serious as she replied. ''Yes, I trained in Australia, actually, through the Peace Corps. The village elders saw the need for someone who would use more than potions and charms to heal the sick and injured in the village. My parents volunteered me, and now I am taking care of the people who took care of me.''

''And anyone else who happens to stumble in?'' Michael said with an attempt at humor.

''Or is carried in,'' she said. ''Which brings us to you, and what you're doing here. Or were attempting to do here. Judging by the condition of your squad, I'd say things didn't go too well.''

Michael tensed at her last words, but as the pain in his body flared up again, he forced himself to relax. *Besides, she does have a point,* he thought. *Still . . .* ''I'm sorry, but I can't tell you that,'' he said.

''Can't tell me what, that you're a mercenary hired by the United States government on a search-and-destroy mission?'' The woman frowned. ''Please, don't try to hide your surprise. After all, we don't get a lot of Peace Corps volunteers out here dressed in tiger-stripe fatigues and carrying automatic rifles. What, do you think everybody who's come before you has gotten in and out clean? You're not the first, and I'm sure you won't be the last.''

Michael absorbed her frighteningly accurate summary of his mission as best as he could. Since the turn of the millennium, the war on drugs in America had turned into more of a desperate holding action than full-scale warfare. With a terminally depressed economy ever since the Republicans had taken back Washington, more and more people were turning to illegal narcotics to dull the pain of double-digit unemployment and a tumbling stock market. Of course, with the rise in drug use came all the fringe benefits: increased assault, robbery, gang warfare, and murder. With lawmakers powerless to stop the flow at American borders, they decided to take the war to the source. Again.

Only this time, instead of risking home-grown military boys who were increasingly busy quelling domestic disturbances, the Pentagon and DEA decided to exploit talent from the past. Specifically, they hired small units of ex-military men who didn't really care what they were doing or who was paying them, as long as the check was good. And while America was fading into a second-world country, it still had enough clout to get some of the best.

Which was what Michael was doing here. An ex–Army Ranger, he had served to the second Vietnam Conflict from 2004 to 2006, only to find himself seeking employment when his three tours of combat had ended. Short of joining a bangang on the East or West Coast, there weren't many opportunities in the "New America" for a man with his skills. He didn't have the background to start his own business, and he didn't want to hire on as skilled labor with another security company. After wandering from Maine to California doing everything from bodyguard work to seasonal fruit harvesting, he had answered an ad placed on the Internet which was looking for people who had "several years of military experience," and within twenty-four hours was being examined in Washington, D.C. Pronounced an excellent candidate, Michael had entered into a contract as a "special services provider" for the United States government. His job, along with hundreds of others of his kind, was to locate drug cartel operations and help destroy them. For his part, Michael had relished the chance to get back into action again, and had assembled a team of men who were loyal to him and had enough experience to get the job done right.

For a year and a half, they had done just that, in locations ranging from Bolivia to Hawaii to Singapore. Now, what was to have been a fairly routine "find-and-fuck" mission in his old stomping grounds had turned into a mission that was totally FUBAR.

And with that thought, Michael realized that there was no point in not being honest with the woman. *After all, if she had wanted to turn me in to the local drug lord, she surely wouldn't have nursed me back to health before doing so. She has her own reasons for keeping me here. She wants something,* he thought.

Michael knew he could expect no help from the U.S. government. As part of their "proactive plausible deniability" platform, no operations of this type were ever officially sanctioned or acknowledged. Members were supplied with nothing that could be traced back to the United States. If a team was lost, there would be no search, much less rescue. Any survivors would be completely on their own. *As long as I'm stuck here, I might as well try to make friends with the one person who appears to be the only ally I have.*

"You pretty much wrapped it up, so I guess there's no point in trying to hide it," he said.

His admission apparently scored, because she relaxed and almost smiled. "Thank you. Since you're going to be here for a few weeks while you recover, it would just be better if there were no secrets," she said.

"Then, as a show of good faith, would you mind?" he asked, nodding towards the restraints.

"As long as you don't get any ideas about escaping in the middle of the night. Before I do that, let's get one thing straight. You're enough of a liability as it is. The whole village is running an incredible risk in keeping you here. I had to argue for your life. If I didn't think you could help us, you'd have been left in the jungle to die. Any of the villagers here are worth more to me than your life, and I'll do whatever I have to do to protect them."

"Fair enough," Michael said with a smile. "As for me running off, well, you saw how far I got last time. As long as you're not planning to turn me in to the local warlord, I think we'll both get along just fine."

"If I had wanted to turn you in, I would have already, or, to save time, we would have just killed you and disposed of your body," the woman said as she produced a small knife and sawed at Michael's bonds. She then gave him two pills and a cup of water. "Here, take these; they'll finish off the infection. I just want you to realize the risk we're taking by keeping you here. If you're found, we're all dead."

Michael nodded after he washed the pills down. "Thank you, for all your help." As soon as his hands were free, he reached up with his right. "I'm Michael Waylan."

The woman regarded his hand for a moment, then reached for it, keeping the knife ready in her left. "My name is Xua Houng, but if I were you, I wouldn't be thanking me just yet. You see, we know what your mission was. We work for Xiang Po, the drug lord in this province. And we want you to help us destroy him."

"Excuse me?" Michael froze for a second, thinking he had misheard her. "You want what?"

"We want you to help us kill Po and take his organization down," Xua said, rising to her feet. "I have to go talk to the elders, let them know that you're going to live. We'll discuss this more later. Right now you need to rest. The second pill I gave you will help you sleep. Do you feel up to eating?"

Michael shook his head, partly answering her question, partly trying to fathom what she had just said.

"All right. Get some rest, and I'll fill you in on the details in the morning. We've got a long way to go. I'll see you tomorrow," Xua said as she walked out of the hut, knife still in hand.

Michael watched her go, then lay back down on the cot. *She can't possibly be serious. We were just supposed to recon that base and report. Now it's only me, I have no backup, no reliable intelligence, and the only native contact I have, who wants me to destroy the base, is working for the enemy. I thought this was a risky mission before, but what she wants is downright suicidal.*

Michael yawned as the drug started to take hold. *And here I thought I'd be living the rest of my days as a simple farmer tilling the back forty in Vietnam,* he thought. *But instead some villager with delusions of grandeur wants me to take down a powerful, organized drug lord? If this is a dream, I'd certainly like to wake up now.*

Michael weighed his situation against what he knew so far. *She obviously doesn't trust me, not yet. Which is good, because I sure as hell don't trust her. First thing I need to do is get a weapon of my own, maybe find out where my gear is. I hope they don't expect me to take out the base with my bare hands.*

So, he thought as his eyes slowly closed, *I might as well listen to her. After all, it's not like I'm going anywhere for a while.*

That night Michael dreamed. Although he usually didn't remember his dreams at all, especially while on assignment, this time was different.

He was with his squad; they were moving through the jungle, working their way towards Po's drug operation. Jennings, with his HK CAWS automatic shotgun, was on point. He was the best point man Michael had ever seen. Marco followed with a Steyr-AUG assault rifle. Altanow was next with the fire support, a Stoner light machine gun. Michael followed, with a new guy by the name of Caseman bringing up the rear.

The unit's normal mission would be just to parachute in and recon the suspected drug bases. Since the U.S. government's satellites were busy spying on their friends and foes alike, it was cheaper and easier to send men into a suspected drug trafficking area. Once they had visual indentification, they would mark the location and radio for an airstrike, then move to a drop zone for extraction.

The current op was going to be big, a strike at Po's rumored headquarters in Vietnam. Current intel estimated that Po had a small army on staff there, and was planning a big move in the next two weeks. Michael's squad was to go in, find them, and call in the big guns. Simple enough.

Michael's attention was drawn to Marco's suddenly upraised fist. Everybody froze in midstep, crouching down while scanning the surrounding foliage. Michael crept up to his sergeant.

"What's up, Marco?"

"Jennings, top, he just vanished." Marco pointed up the trail to where Jennings had been a few seconds ago.

Michael smelled danger. "Everybody off the trail. Spread out—" was all he had time to say before the jungle exploded around them.

This time, however, Michael was unhurt, watching as the members of his squad were torn apart by the glass shot of the Claymore antipersonnel mines they had walked right into. He saw Marco's peppered body, one arm missing, skid to a stop beside him. Altanow, his face practically torn off, collapsed in a heap just ahead on the trail. Michael didn't even have to look for the new guy. He knew what had happened to him.

Michael scanned the smoke and shredded foliage, hoping his point man had somehow survived. He saw a form walking towards him through the haze; it solidified into Jennings, with a gaping hole in his neck leaking blood. His eyes were open, their blank gaze locked on Michael.

Looking around, Michael saw that all of his men's eyes were open and staring directly at him. Even Altanow's brown eyes watched him from the remains of his face. They didn't say a word, they just kept staring at him. Michael could hear the sounds of men coming closer, a part of his mind was screaming at him to get out of there, but all he could do was look from body to body and feel those dead eyes watching him. . . .

Michael was awakened by someone shaking him roughly. "Come on, Michael, wake up!"

Shaking off the drug-induced cobwebs, Michael opened his eyes to find Xua thrusting a loose, black long-sleeved shirt and matching pants at him. "Get these on and come with me now. Po's men are doing a sweep of the village. We have to hide you."

As he dressed, Michael heard the faint baying of dogs. Ignoring the flashes of pain from his head, side, and ankle, he pulled on the shapeless garments, astonished to find that they fit him rather well. "Montagnards don't usually wear this stuff."

Seeing the look on his face, Xua helped him to his feet as she spoke. "Po's men dress us in these so they can keep track of us more easily. We figured you might have to be here for a while, so we made clothes for you. Come on." With surprising strength for a small woman, she pulled him towards the doorway.

"Where are we going?" he asked.

"To the opium fields. The smell of the poppies confuses the dogs, so they'll lose whatever trail they might find. As long as you look like you belong, you'll be fine."

"What?" Michael said. "You're going to leave me in the fields? They'll find me for sure."

Xua jammed a straw hat on his head. "Not if you keep your head down and harvest like everybody else. Po's men will look for someone in fatigues hiding in a hut, not another faceless laborer in the fields."

"What about the hut I was staying in?"

"Already being taken care of. We're burning it as a precaution against sickness. At least, that's what Po will be told," Xua said. "Walk faster."

"This is as fast as I can go," Michael said. His leg was throbbing from the sudden exercise, and he was limping noticeably on his weak ankle.

"It'll have to do for now. Once we get into the fields, no one will notice," Xua said.

The sun was just starting to break over the horizon, and the orange and gold rays illuminated the vast fields of poppies that awaited harvesting. A sickly sweet smell permeated the air. Several dozen black-clad villagers were already hard at work, moving up and down the rows of plants. Xua led Michael to a new row and handed him a short, thin-bladed knife. "Know how to use this?"

"Sure, I can kill a man five different ways with it," Michael replied.

Xua sighed and grabbed the nearest poppy while forcing Michael to his knees. "There are no six-foot-tall Asians, remember? Find the bulb and cut four vertical slits, one on each quadrant. The sap will ooze out and be collected later. Just keep moving down the row, and, whatever you do, don't look up." She turned to leave.

"Wait, where are you going?" Michael asked.

"Po's men will be suspicious if I'm not with the elders. I have to join them. Just keep cutting, I'll be back as soon as possible."

Michael watched her leave, then looked around at the other nearby villagers, all of whom were intent on their work. He noted how far the nearest tree line was in case he had to run for it, bent over, and went to work.

Although his first few attempts were clumsy, he quickly found the rhythm of hold, cut, release, and was soon moving slowly down the row. His left leg burned with pain every time he put weight on it. Michael soon found himself breathing through his mouth in an effort to avoid the overpowering smell of the poppies. Every so often, he would scan warily for armed men or dogs. He knew it was only a matter of time before Po's men would inspect the fields. *God, I hope she knows what she's doing.* He considered breaking for the jungle right then, but froze when he heard strident barking and the chatter of several voices.

Looking out from under his straw hat, Michael saw several armed men dressed in a variety of green and brown fatigues stride towards the poppy field. One of the men held the leashes of two small, wiry dogs that yapped excitedly. Three older men in similar black clothes, obviously the village elders, and Xua followed. The drug runners were yelling in angry tones, although Michael couldn't make out what they were saying. From the looks of the mostly one-sided conversation, the elders were trying to placate the other men. One time, Michael heard Xua's singsong voice, then the flat sound of a hand striking flesh. He saw three of the men point their assault rifles at the group of elders, then Xua spoke up again, and the rifles were lowered.

Michael's hands itched for his own weapon. Instead, he moved further down the row, slicing open a fresh poppy bulb. The thugs scanned the field again, and Michael's heart almost stopped when one of them took several steps into the row he was working in. His companions called him back, and the armed men walked away from the field, leaving Xua and the old men. When they were out of sight, the old men chattered at Xua all at once, then they too turned and headed back towards the village. Shaking her head, Xua walked towards him. As she approached, he could see the still-livid imprint on her face.

"What happened?"

"Po's men seem to think there may have been more Americans in that squad they ambushed," Xua said. "They've been searching the jungle for the past two days, and this morning they tore apart the village looking for evidence of you. Then, as you saw, they came down to the fields, looking to examine the villagers. I managed to put them off by saying that it would disrupt the harvesting. Your disguise seemed to work, so you're safe for now. We have a new hut for you to rest in. Come on, we'd better get you back.''

Only then did Michael feel the clammy sweat covering his body, and he realized just how exhausting the last half hour had been for him. He accepted Xua's outstretched hand and the two of them slowly followed the trail back to the village.

''Damn Americans coming in here and thinking they can do whatever they want, and everyone will just roll over and let them,'' Xua said, more to herself than Michael. ''I sure hope you're worth all this trouble.''

''So do I,'' Michael muttered.

''What?''

''Nothing.''

Once inside the new hut, Michael collapsed on the metal cot and looked up at Xua. ''Po's operation is large, well organized, and well equipped. What makes you think I can help you destroy him?''

Instead of answering right away, Xua felt his forehead. ''You're warm. Are you sure you want to talk about this now? Maybe we'd better wait until you've rested.''

Michael shook his head. ''I've rested enough. You've made it abundantly clear why you're taking this risk, now tell me what I'm supposed to do for you.''

Xua walked to the doorway and scanned the surrounding area before beginning to speak. ''In about two weeks the harvest will be done, and Po's men will convoy the raw opium down to the lowlands to process and sell. Most of the men will travel with the convoy. To ensure that nothing happens here, Po has all of the men in the village imprisoned while he is away. There is a skeleton crew left at the base, but as the days go by, they become increasingly undisciplined and sloppy. If they were sufficiently distracted, one man with the proper training''— she pointed at Michael—''could infiltrate the base and free the village men, allowing them to take the rest of the guards by surprise. When we gain control of the base, including the armory, we could equip the men and women of the village and set up an ambush for the returning convoy, eliminating them as well.''

Michael frowned. ''What would be the 'sufficient distraction'?''

Xua's face grew still, and she looked away from Michael. When she finally spoke, her voice was tight. ''There are thirty women here. The men from the base sometimes come down and take us to their quarters for 'entertainment.' Let's just say that there are several bastards around here who don't live in the drug base.''

''I'm sorry,'' Michael said.

''That's only one reason why I want them dead. Three years ago there was an outbreak of yellow fever. The base closed its doors and let a third of the villagers die. Then they still expected us to make the previous year's quotas. We had to start the children harvesting at age five to make up the losses.''

Michael nodded. ''Sounds like you've been thinking about this a lot.''

Xua's mouth sketched a sardonic grin. ''What can I say, it's in the blood.''

Michael knew she was right. The Vietnamese population had been fighting for their country for the past two millennia—everyone from Chinese invaders to the

French in the 1950s to America in 1965–75 and 2004–06. They had gained a well-deserved reputation as cunning and tenacious guerilla warriors, able to outlast and outmaneuver armies ten times their size. And of all of the native Vietnamese cultures, the Montagnards were regarded as the fiercest of all.

"Some things never change," he said.

"Not here they don't. So?" Xua said.

"You're not one for wasting time," Michael said, looking up at her.

"It's a luxury we don't have a lot of right now," she said, holding his brown eyes with her own.

"I'll tell you this afternoon. Right now I need something to eat and to rest," Michael said. For a second, he thought Xua would refuse, but then she nodded and walked to the door. Just before she left, she turned to look at him, her expression inscrutable.

"Think hard," she said, and was gone before Michael could reply.

Michael stared up at the ceiling of the hut after she was gone. A few minutes later one of the villagers brought him a bowl of rice with *nuoc nuam*, a spicy fish sauce. Michael was hungry enough to eat it all, despite how it tasted. He just hoped he could keep it down long enough to digest.

After finishing his meal, Michael examined the small knife he had hidden after his field work. The blade was maybe three inches long, but it would be enough. All he would have to do was wait for Xua to come back, take her hostage, and get out of the village. And go . . .

Yeah, go where? The only place to go within fifty miles would be Po's base. Michael pondered that for a moment. *If he could get there, and if they didn't kill him on sight,* and *if* they believed his story about a village rebellion, he could conceivably go work for them. Michael shook his head and discarded the idea. *Too many ifs.* Assuming they accepted him in the first place, he would be the low shitbird on the totem pole for a very long time, perhaps always. Besides, although he knew his working for the U.S. government had much more to do with the steady and excellent paycheck than with saving the country from sniffing its future up its collective nostrils, he had a large problem working for the other side.

If he refused, well, the villagers couldn't turn him in. *Not without admitting they'd been hiding me,* Michael thought. *But that wouldn't get either of us anywhere, neither side trusting the other. Hell, she'd probably be pissed off enough to kill me. Which leaves . . . her not-quite-insane plan.*

The more Michael thought about it, the more he became convinced that the only way he was going to get out of here would be to cooperate. *Besides, she did save your life, and not just once, but twice,* he thought. If it hadn't been for her quick thinking, Michael knew the dogs would have found him for sure.

Once the base was taken, there would no doubt be a Humvee or something he could take to the lowlands and hopefully a city where he could contact the U.S. Embassy and get the hell out of here. Maybe think about retiring once and for all. *Well, just get there first, and then I'll buy the house and yard and white picket fence,* Michael thought. *I'll tell her when she gets back.* With that thought in mind, he turned on his right side and fell asleep.

•   •   •

He found himself in the jungle again, watching his men creep towards certain death. This time, he tried to warn them as soon as he realized he was in the dream, but the men ignored his hurried whispers and gestures, moving around him as if he wasn't even there. Michael saw the whole thing again, the explosions, Po's men picking over the bodies, the pistol shot as a groaning Altanow was killed. All the while he stood in the middle of it, unseen, except by the eyes of the dead.

Michael awoke to the touch of a hand on his cheek. Reflexively he grabbed the other person's wrist and twisted it up and away from his body while his other hand grabbed for the throat, holding, not squeezing, all done in the fraction of a second. A hiss of indrawn breath was the only sound in the room.

Michael's eyes focused on Xua kneeling over him, his hand on her throat. There was no fear in her eyes, just a stoic calm. Michael released the breath he had been holding and let go of her. She tilted her head sideways and rubbed gently at her wrist and throat.

"I'd say you're getting better," Xua said. "Were you having a nightmare? You were muttering something in your sleep."

"I don't sleep very well anyway, and with all that's happened in the last few days, I'm a bit on edge," Michael replied.

Xua nodded. "Understandably so." She fell silent, waiting.

"So when do we start?" Michael asked.

"You mean you'll help us?" Xua asked.

"Yes, with certain conditions. One, I want all my gear back. Two, I'll need all of the information you've got on

that base: guard rotations, garrison strength, building layout, power supply, the works. And three, you have to trust
me and do exactly what I say if we're going to pull this
off.''

Xua nodded again. ''All right. I can take care of one
of those requests right away. We've been gathering intelligence when we've been inside, whatever we could
see, preparing for a time like this. I can sketch the layout
of the buildings and give you the strength and rotation of
the guards, which will be pretty lax when you go in.
Luckily there're no towers, so getting you there shouldn't
be a problem. From there, well, you know best, so let me
brief you and you can come up with the best plan.''

''Sounds good. Let's get to it,'' Michael said.

Xua drew her knife and began drawing in the dirt.
''Okay, here's the perimeter. . . .''

The next three days were spent in a blur of questions,
planning, and preparation. Xua and her people had done
an incredible job of learning everything there was to
know about the base. By the end of it, Michael could
walk through the base in his mind and know exactly
where he was just by the number of steps he had taken
and the direction he was facing.

His recovery was progressing nicely, but it was another four days before he was allowed to get out of bed
and move around unaided. Xua said it was important he
rest his sprained leg as much as possible. As soon as he
could, Michael tried incorporating light physical exercise
into his routine. The first time he attempted a push-up,
his left arm buckled underneath him, and he ended up
flat on his face on the packed dirt floor. He kept at it,
fighting through the stiffness and muscle fatigue to a

point where, while he wasn't at his pre-injury peak, he did notice definite improvement.

The one problem Michael did have was the dream he had every night. It was always the same, with him ending up haunted by those dead men's stares, and he grew more and more convinced that the only way to exorcise it would be to free the village by destroying the base and Xiang Po.

He and Xua talked often, refining and going over the plan, which was simple enough. She also gave him a crash course in the Montagnard language, not much, but enough to where he could pick out one word or phrase in twenty.

One afternoon he was going over the insertion phase of the operation when Xua appeared in the doorway with a large canvas-wrapped bundle. "You busy?"

"Not very. What you got there?"

She walked over and sat beside him, holding the package out to him. "Your gear. We figured you'd better have it now, in case something's damaged that we need to adjust for."

Nodding, Michael took the package and held it for a moment, feeling things shift inside, the weapons and equipment that defined him as a soldier. "Where did you hide it?"

"We wrapped it up and buried it in the jungle, figuring better safe than sorry."

Michael untied the drawstring. "Well, better see what works and what doesn't," he said, opening the canvas bag and spreading out the contents.

He checked the armor first. A lightweight ceramplast-kevlar composite, it was flexible enough, in lesser thicknesses, to be worn under clothes, but strong enough to stop a 7.62mm round. He opened the pocket on the chest-plate and extracted the flatwear computer module, designed to link all members of the squad together for communication and tracking. It was deadweight now, its battery long expired. Michael set it aside. Other than that the armor looked fine, except for the dirt and dust it had accumulated in the jungle.

"You're lucky. The armor absorbed most of the impact of whatever they used to ambush you," Xua said.

"Yeah, lucky," Michael replied. He put the armor down and picked up what looked like a pair of snap-on binoculars and flipped a small switch. He listened closely for a small whine of the goggles activating, but heard nothing. "So much for night vision."

"Couldn't you repair them?" Xua asked.

Michael looked the unit over. "I wouldn't even know where to begin," he replied, tossing the damaged optics aside. He unrolled his tactical vest and checked the pockets, laying out the tools he always carried on a mission, small bolt cutter, Leatherman, compact flashlight with red filter. Everything was there. He packed it all away and pulled the vest on.

Michael moved on to his sidearm next, an old SIG-Sauer P229 9mm pistol. He quickly field-stripped it, checking each part for misalignment or damage. Reassembling it, he slammed a magazine into the butt and chambered a round. Sighting down the barrel, he was relieved to discover that his aim was steady, with no trembling. He ejected the bullet, reloaded the magazine, and set the pistol down beside the armor.

"What's this button do?" Xua asked as she held Michael's combat knife out to him. Upon seeing the blade pointed towards him, Michael gently took it from her hands and glanced at the small stud mounted just under the knife guard. "Now, now, I can't be sharing all my secrets. Maybe someday I'll show you."

She accepted that and pointed to the last item. "I've never seen a rifle like that," she said, pointing to the boardlike weapon.

"That's because this was the first model of a design that's been revised and refined for two decades now. With the new integrated weapons systems, these older models have been hitting the secondary markets relatively cheaply. This is the Heckler & Koch G11 assault rifle."

Michael picked up the dull gray rifle and disassembled as much of it as he could, cleaning and checking the parts. Firing 4.7mm caseless ammunition from a fifty-round magazine, the G11's diminutive bullets could pierce a steel helmet at three hundred meters. When switched to three-round burst mode, the gun's cyclic rate was a staggering 2,200 rounds per minute, fast enough so that all three bullets left the barrel before the recoil could affect the shooter's aim. Constructed primarily of plastics, the G11 was lightweight, accurate, and nearly indestructible. Over the years Michael had added several refinements, including a barrel-mounted laser sight that complimented the optic sight built into the carrying handle. It was Michael's first and only choice of weapon, the one he had carried for most of his military career and during all of his government assignments. It had never jammed or misfired, and Michael trusted his life to it. Satisfied that his gear was in working order, he looked at Xua. "Not a lot of ammunition here, but it should be enough to get the job done. You said the guards mostly carry AK-74s?"

Xua nodded. "Yes, the rifles with the orange magazines. The leaders carry different weapons, but I'm not sure what kind they are.''

''That doesn't really matter, but it will be important to neutralize them without a shot being fired, especially if I'm the only one against them,'' Michael said.

''Agreed. But don't worry—by the time you get there, most of them will be so drunk it won't matter. At least, they will if I have anything to say about it,'' Xua said.

''Let's hope so,'' Michael said, strapping the armor on over his clothes. His dagger and pistol went into the custom-built sheath on his left leg and holster on his hip. ''How's the harvest coming?''

''The last of the fields will be finished tomorrow. They'll probably be ready to leave sometime in the next two days. After that, it will take two or three days for the guards to relax. Once they do, then we strike.''

''That's good, I can use the rest.'' Michael paused for a moment, staring at the floor. ''You know, I never would have believed this a week ago, but we might actually have a chance of pulling this thing off.''

Xua looked at him with a cold smile. ''It is good to hear you say that.'' Their eyes met for a second, then she turned away. ''It's almost time to eat. Someone will bring you food.''

''Why not you?'' Michael asked.

''I . . . have to meet with the elders, inform them of how things are going. We have plans to make as well. What will happen in the next few days will affect a great many things. Rest now, and eat.''

Michael watched her leave the hut, then turned back to his equipment check. He relished the feel of the armor encasing him, the weapons at his command. *It's good to be back in action.* He felt like he could march over to

Po's base and take on his army right now. With a small sigh he set his rifle down and walked over to the door, pleased to notice that his steps, even with his tightly bound ankle, were sure and steady.

He looked out at the village: the collection of thatched huts, the stone well, which Xua had told him had been there for more than two hundred years, the scattered farm animals that rooted in the dirt or roamed their crude pens.

This is what I'm fighting for, he thought. For a second he wondered if he had gone completely off the deep end. But then he shook his head, remembering his family. His own father had been a farmer, and had worked the land for decades while all around him his neighbors sold out to the farming conglomerates. His father had never given up his farm. He had died on it, in fact, right in the middle of the harvest. While overseeing the combines, he had lain down under a tree for a rest, and never got back up again. The farmland, now worth millions, had been sold and the profit divided up by greedy relatives. Michael had been traveling at the time, and hadn't heard the news until it was too late. He had actually cried when he went back one day to find the one-hundred-and-fifty-year-old house leveled, with nothing remaining except unbroken farmland. He hadn't contested the relatives' overturning the will, wanting nothing of the money they had squeezed out of his father's years of labor. He often wondered if, given the chance, he would have headed back to the farm, maybe tried to make a second life as a man who worked the land. A part of him thought it was all romantic bullshit, that killing people was all he was good at, and what he should stick to. But every so often, he wondered. . . .

I couldn't save my family home, but maybe I can save

these peoples', he thought. A noise at the door made him look up, and Michael saw that a girl had arrived with the food. His thoughts were pushed aside by his hunger, and he soon concentrated solely on the food, glancing every so often at his weapons and gear.

Two days later, Michael watched as the caravan of deuce-and-a-half trucks moved through the village. Xua had prepared him for this, and he was watching the procession from a pit dug underneath his cot and covered with a straw mat. He had a perfect view of the men and trucks as they passed by the doorway.

The convoy came to a halt, and Michael saw a Humvee Model III outside the door; a man was standing in its rear machine-gun turret. Dressed in pressed, razor-crease urban fatigues, with a black ascot, a matching beret, and sunglasses, he began speaking to a person or persons outside of Michael's line of sight. It sounded like he was giving a speech, of which Michael caught scattered words, opium . . . harvest . . . good . . . profit . . . next season. . . . He knew exactly who he was looking at: Xiang Po himself.

Michael's hands itched for his rifle, which was lying beside him. He imagined lining up the crosshairs of his scope on the back of Po's head, switching the fire selector to three-round burst, and triggering the shots that would blow off the back of his skull. His hands clenched in frustration. *Not now,* he thought. *I promise I will kill you, though, and soon.*

Po finished his short speech and signaled his convoy to proceed. Michael kept track of the trucks and whether they contained men or the raw opium sap. The total for the convoy came to seven trucks and three Humvees.

That's going to take some doing to ambush properly, he thought, *but I'll worry about that after we take the base.*

When the growl of the convoy's engines had died away, Michael got up and stretched, his muscles unaccustomed to the cramped quarters. He saw Xua approaching the hut, and sat down on the cot to wait for her. She stood in the doorway, not entering. "Did you see him?"

"That was Po?" he asked.

She nodded. "He cuts quite a figure, doesn't he?" she asked.

"Xua, he's just like any one of a half dozen drug lords I've taken down over the years, drunk on his power and overconfident. He left here the ruler of all he surveyed. He'll be coming back to a vastly different kingdom," Michael said.

"One he is no longer the master of," Xua said. Michael nodded and she continued, "It's funny how long we've waited for an opportunity like this, helpless until we got the edge we needed—you. Just be sure you can do what you've promised."

Michael frowned at her tone. "When Po comes back, it will be from the last trip he'll ever make. We move in three days. You know what to do until then. Be ready."

Xua nodded, then left the hut. Michael was left staring at the four walls and the doorway. *Now all that's left is the waiting.*

The next three days crawled by at a sloth's pace. Michael reviewed the base plans, went over the operation at least a dozen times, exercised three times a day, and thought about digging an escape tunnel just to see if he could get away with it. By the end of the third day, he felt almost as good as when he had arrived in country. He had stripped his gear of anything unnecessary, and had optimized it for the mission. He was as ready as he could be.

As the sun was setting on the third day, Xua visited him. "It's time. Po's men are having a party, and they've 'requested' that some of the village women be there. We're heading up to the base in about a half hour. You'll be there?"

"You got it," Michael replied. "Once I've freed the men, we'll come for you."

"Don't waste a minute," Xua said.

"Don't worry, we won't," Michael said.

Xua ran out of the hut, and Michael began one last weapon and equipment check. After he had finished, he peeked out of the hut to see several young women gathered in front of the chieftain's hut. They milled around there for several minutes, then Xua came out of the hut, spoke to the group of women, and, after a last glance towards Michael's hut, led them up the hill towards the drug base.

Michael let them go, noting the time on his watch. He figured it would take about a half hour for the men to really get into the swing of things, at which time he would move. The minutes ticked by. Michael made final preparations, blackening his face with charcoal and suiting up. After looking at his watch for what seemed like the thousandth time, it was time to go. He slipped out of the hut and stood there for a moment, looking at the quiet village he had lived in for the past two weeks. He glanced at the road that headed down the mountain, thinking of the freedom that lay in that direction. All he'd have to do was walk out of here, and he'd never see them again.

I'd just have to live with that choice for the rest of my life, Michael thought. He knew which direction he was going. *No matter what, I owe them at least this much.* He walked around the hut and plunged into the surrounding jungle.

Once in the bush, his old combat senses kicked in, and Michael was soon creeping silently down the path that his squad had been ambushed on less than two weeks before. The half moon out threw splashes of silver on the otherwise dark foliage, enabling Michael to cover the distance with relative ease. All the same, he checked his compass several times to make sure he would reach the correct side of the base wall.

After about a half hour of careful walking, he saw the bright glare of arc-sodium lights ahead of him. Michael slowed his pace to a crawl. Five minutes later, he was looking at the walls of Xiang Po's drug base.

While the drug lord's defenses would have been considered archaic by modern-day standards, to Michael they were formidable enough. The palisade wall was constructed of hundreds of ten-foot-high bamboo poles, lashed together with wire and sharpened at the top. Over that was strung a double strand of razor wire, its blades ready to slice into any intruder. Michael could see the corrugated tin roof of a building a few yards beyond the fence, and he knew from the plans that he was looking at the roof of the pen where the villagers were kept.

Breach the fence, take out the guards, get the men out, take the base, that was the plan in a nutshell, and Michael wasted no time. Creeping over to the fence, he tested it to see if it would hold his weight, then he took a small coil of braided line from his vest and tied a loop with a slipknot at one end. Gauging the distance, he tossed the improvised lasso up and watched the circle settle neatly around two of the bamboo poles. Michael hauled himself up hand over hand to the top, checked the other side to make sure no one was waiting for him, and wedged an arm between two spikes to support himself. He used the wire cutters from his vest to cut the razor wire, then hoisted himself over the fence to land on the other side.

This area of the base was deserted. From his vantage point, Michael saw several other concrete block buildings with tin roofs. There was noise coming from a long structure with several lit windows on the other side of the base, and Michael knew that was the men's quarters. He could hear what sounded like drunken laughter and singing coming from inside. A hot ball of anger coalesced in the pit of his stomach as he though of what Po's men might be doing to the women of the village.

First things first, he thought. Unslinging his G11, Michael crept around the corner of the prisoner compound and slowly moved towards the front of the building. He had gotten about halfway there when he heard two men talking in Vietnamese, cursing their luck for having to pull guard duty tonight. Michael heard the clink of glass and a loud belch.

Drunken guards. This might be easier than I thought. Michael had just started to move forward again when one of the men muttered something about taking a leak. An instant later, a small man in tan fatigues stepped around the corner. He had an AK-74 slung over one shoulder and was fumbling with his trousers when some instinct made him look up and see Michael standing right in front of him.

For a second neither man moved, although Michael smelled an acrid scent in the air. Looking down, he saw a dark stain at the crotch of the guard's pants. Then the Vietnamese opened his mouth to yell while clawing at the holstered pistol on his belt just as Michael stepped up and slammed the butt of his rifle across the guard's face.

The plastic stock impacted the smaller man's jaw with a loud wet thud. The guard spun halfway around and dropped to the ground like he had been hit by a truck. Michael quickly dropped his rifle and drew his knife, waiting for the other guard to investigate.

Michael had to give the second guard credit: he was at least holding his assault rifle when he rounded the corner. It didn't help. Michael grabbed the barrel of the AK-74 and pulled the guard towards him, right onto his knife. The guard didn't even have time to exhale as the blade entered his heart. His fingers scrabbled wildly on the grip and stock of the rifle as he slid to the ground. Seconds later, he was dead.

After cleaning and resheathing his knife, Michael hauled the rifles and both bodies behind the building, then searched them. Other than four extra magazines, two .45 caliber pistols, a pack of Chinese cigarettes, and two small sheafs of Vietnamese currency, the guards carried nothing else.

Shit, now what? Maybe the keys are inside. Creeping back to the front of the building, Michael looked across the compound. There was no one in sight. He stepped to the door, opened it, and slipped inside, closing the door behind him.

Inside was complete darkness. Michael slipped a small Mag-Lite from his vest and turned it on. It looked as if the large room was divided into two sections, with the back half devoted to the prison cell and the front half just kept empty. Shining his light through the wire mesh of the cage, Michael saw several dozen men packed into the holding area, with barely enough room to lie down. He shone his light on the face of one man until he blinked and opened his eyes, then threw a hand up to shield his vision from the glare of the light.

"Sanh? Sanh? I'm looking for Sanh," Michael whispered in the Montagnard language. Xua had told him that Sanh, who understood English, had been briefed on what was happening and would explain to the others when the time was right. They had decided not to tell the others until the last minute for fear that they might look too anxious or excited and tip the guards off.

The awakened man pointed towards the back of the cell. Michael shone his light there to reveal a young man sitting on the floor in the corner, wide awake. He looked at Michael and nodded, then started shaking his companions awake. He moved through the sea of villagers, motioning for them to keep quiet.

Michael waited impatiently for him to reach the cell gate. He knew that with every passing minute the chances of the missing guards being discovered increased. At last Sanh was at the cell door.

"You understand me?" Michael whispered.

Sanh nodded. "Speak little, too."

"Where is the key to the door?" Michael asked.

Sanh shook his head and shrugged.

Michael sighed, then examined the wire latticework of the cage the men were in. He took out his wire cutters again and tried them on a strand, severing it with difficulty. Michael cut a few more and passed the cutters and the flashlight through to Sanh. "Start cutting."

Sanh nodded and began cutting a hole in the mesh. Michael walked back to the door and opened it, peeking out through the crack. The sounds of revelry had gotten louder, and occasionally he could hear glass breaking.

There was no one outside. Michael slipped outside and went to the back of the building again. He picked up the rifles and pistols from the dead guards and headed back towards the front of the building.

He was just about to head for the opening when the slam of a door closing froze him in his tracks. Michael shrank back into the shadows near the wall and looked around, trying to pinpoint where the noise came from.

Movement near one of the smaller buildings caught his eye. Another guard was crossing the base, heading towards the lit building, when he glanced over at the building Michael was hiding near. Seeing no guards, he unsteadily ambled over to investigate.

Michael slowly unsheathed his blade again and twisted the handle, causing the small stud to pop up with a soft click. He watched the man from the darkness, waiting until he had approached to about ten yards away from the prison building.

"Thieu? Xan?" the man said, apparently calling for the guards, by their names. Michael groaned, softly at first, then a little louder. The man took another few steps forward. Michael knew he had only one shot at the guy, otherwise the whole mission was blown. He leaned out of the shadows, pointed the knife at the guard, and depressed the stud on the handle.

The blade shot out of the haft and flashed across the yard, burying itself in the man's chest just below his heart. The guard stared at the shaft of metal that was suddenly jutting from his abdomen. He feebly plucked at the blade, then slipped to the ground, trying to suck in one last breath. He collapsed on his back, his hands still wrapped around the knife blade.

Michael was moving as soon as the guy hit the ground.

Running over to him, he grabbed the guard's feet and dragged him to the back of the building next to the other two. Michael pulled the blade out and reset his knife, jamming the blade against the side of the building to compress the spring. He then searched the body, just in case this guy had the keys. No luck. Michael headed back inside the prison building.

Sanh had been replaced at the gate by another man, who was steadily enlarging the hole. Michael laid the rifles and pistols down by them, added his own sidearm to the pile, and motioned to Sanh, who was holding the light.

"Give these to your best marksmen, okay?" he said. Sanh nodded and began motioning to men behind him to come forward. One side of the opening was complete, and the man started working on the bottom. Michael stood guard by the door, scanning the outside for anybody else. Except for the ruckus at the other end of the base, all was quiet.

Several minutes passed, punctuated only by the click of the wire cutters. Then the light flashed on the wall next to Michael. He turned to see Sanh and four other men standing in a line, each armed with an assault rifle or pistol. Behind them, other men were scrambling out through the hole in the wire.

"All right," Michael said to the first group. "You five, come with me. No matter what, do not fire unless I fire first, got that, Sanh?"

Sanh translated his instructions to the other four men, all of whom nodded. Michael noticed they held their weapons with practiced ease, as if they had carried them all their lives. Michael grinned and opened the door for them to move out.

Outside, they trotted quietly to the long barracks at the other end of the base. The sounds were even louder now, and Michael almost had to talk normally to be heard.

"Okay. Sanh and you"—he selected another man—"will both come with me on the north end; the three of you"—he indicated the others—"will enter on the south end. Wait for us to move, then bust in. We want to take them totally by surprise so there's no chance of a hostage situation. If anybody goes for a weapon, and you have a clear line of fire, take them out. Hopefully it won't come to that."

Michael waited for Sanh to finish muttering to the other four, who nodded enthusiastically. He motioned for the second group to head down to the other end of the barracks. When they were there, Michael motioned for Sanh to follow him.

Michael moved up to the double doors and tried them. They were unlocked. He looked at Sanh, who stared back at him impassively, his grip on his pistol rock steady. The other man looked just as calm, like he was about to go for a walk through the village instead of into a room full of armed drunken soldiers.

Taking a deep breath, Michael wrenched the door open and ran into the room. "Nobody move!" he thundered in Vietnamese. He could hear pounding footsteps behind him, and knew that Sanh and the other Montagnard were right with him. At the other end of the building, there was a violent crack as the door splintered and gave way as the other three Montagnards stormed through the opening.

The scene that greeted them was total confusion. Half-dressed men and women were everywhere, some staggering around, some passed out on cots or on the floor, and all of them good and drunk. The commotion caused by Michael and the Montagnards barely caused any reaction among those guards who were still conscious. Most of them just stared stupidly at the intruders. One man reacted by passing out and sliding off his chair onto the floor.

Michael motioned to the Montagnards to search the men for weapons. He looked for Xua and found her lying on a cot next to an unconscious guard. She was awake, although she was staring off into space. He knelt by her. "Xua? It's Michael and Sanh. We're here. It's all right now."

When she spoke, Xua still stared off into space. "We didn't want to take any chances, so we drugged the wine with poppy sap. Worked well, don't you think?" She looked at him as if seeing him for the first time. "Is it really over?" Then she started to cry softly.

"Almost," Michael said.

Sanh appeared next to Michael, and he took Xua in his arms. Michael stood up and supervised herding the prisoners together and making sure they were unarmed. The ex–drug runners were docile and offered no resistance as they were led to the prison building. After locking the guards inside, Michael had three of the armed Montagnards sweep the rest of the buildings for any other personnel. They came back with several people who looked like cooks. Michael threw them in the prison building with the rest of the base population. With the base safely cleared, Michael gathered the three men who had searched the buildings together. He only had to say one word.

"Weapons."

•   •   •

Three days later, Michael crouched in the deep jungle a few meters off a curve in the road about a mile from the village. The base armory had been a dream come true, filled with assault rifles, submachine guns, pistols, and grenades, enough to outfit a group of villagers handsomely for the ambush of the convoy.

Michael hadn't seen much of Xua lately, but Sanh had filled in for her, and his mind had quickly turned to the details of wiping out the rest of Po's men. Interrogating the prisoners had given them a wealth of information, from the strength of the convoy to when they were expected back. The drug dealers didn't seem too concerned about giving up their comrades; they just wanted to survive. Michael used this intelligence to set up the ambush, then drilled a handpicked group of men to execute it. The Montagnards were quick studies, and within a day each man knew his assignment and could perform it flawlessly.

Wanting to be sure of the convoy's arrival, Michael had placed Sanh even further down the trail with a two-way radio to warn him when the trucks were sighted. His men were placed and ready. It was time.

Sanh's voice burst over the small radio. They had just spotted the convoy moving up the road. Michael told everyone to get ready. He listened for the growl of the diesel engines as the trucks came closer. After a few minutes, he heard them getting louder and louder. Before the noise of the convoy cut off any chance at communication, Michael told the Montagnards to attack on his signal.

Seconds later, the first of the Humvees came into view. Michael was sitting high in a tree overlooking the curve in the road. He had a clear view of the entire procession. Slipping off the safety on his G11, he flicked the laser light on, snugged the rifle into his shoulder, looked through the telescopic sight, and waited.

The lead vehicle rounded the bend and stopped at the fallen tree in the road. A few seconds later, several men got out of the Humvee, went to the tree, and began pulling it to one side. It was heavier than it looked, and the men were having some difficulty. There was a commotion from the lead Humvee, and a man Michael recognized stuck his head out to yell at the men moving the tree. His features were in sharp focus as Michael sighted in on his head.

"Good night, you son of a bitch," Michael said as he squeezed the trigger of his assault rifle, sending a three-round burst that split apart Xiang Po's head as if Michael had dropped an anvil on him. The shot echoed off the foothills, and while Po's men looked at their fallen leader, and some searched wildly around for the shooter, all hell broke loose.

The first and last Humvees erupted in concussive blasts, courtesy of the grenades tossed under them by the Montagnards. With the convoy effectively blocked in, the men in the trucks didn't have a chance. As they spilled out of the deuce-and-a-halfs in a disorganized rush, the Montagnards picked them off with their new AK-74s. One of the truck drivers tried to barrel over the dead Humvee and escape, but well-placed shots to the cab of the truck stopped him cold. It was over in under two minutes, the scattered remnants of Po's small army surrendering and tossing their weapons out of the trucks. Michael climbed down from the tree and watched the Montagnards round them up and lead them back to the base to put with the others. Several other villagers started putting out the small fires that had sprouted up around the ambush zone.

Michael looked up to see Xua walking towards him, wearing a belt with a small pistol holster at her side. She stood beside him and watched the cleanup for a moment.

"You should be able to clear the road with one of the deuce-and-a-halfs. I think I saw a winch on the front of one of them," Michael said.

"I'm sure we'll take care of it," she replied, still looking at the bodies and the trucks, the blood and the guns. Xua shook her head. "It's hard to believe."

"Yeah, I'm sure. All that's left is to destroy the base. But don't worry, it's finally over," Michael said.

"Yes, you've done well, except for one last thing," Xua said.

Michael started to ask her what she meant, but his question was cut off by a sledgehammer blow to the base of his neck. He heard a loud report, and realized that a gun had gone off nearby. At the same time, he was aware of a quick numbness that was spreading throughout his body, his arms leaden and useless at his sides, his trusted G11 slipping from his grasp, his legs suddenly unable to support his weight. He tried to speak to Xua, but his head and neck and jaw no longer seemed to work. Michael's knees buckled, and he slowly pitched forward to the ground. He couldn't breathe, he was choking on a coppery liquid that was filling his mouth and throat, and he couldn't swallow fast enough. His last view as darkness rose to cover his vision was of Altanow, Jennings, and Marco, all waiting to greet him as he seemed to float towards them. . . .

●　　●　　●

Sanh walked over to Xua, who was still watching the American's body. He was holding a smoking pistol. "Was it really necessary to kill him?" she asked in their native tongue.

He looked at her. "Of course. We cannot have anyone associated with this base left alive, and that included him. I want you to round up the rest of the prisoners and execute them as well. We'll burn their bodies as soon as its done."

Xua looked down at the body at her feet. "What about him?"

"Him we have to keep, as evidence that the Americans did their job and stopped the drug flow from this province. In a few days we'll take him down to the lowlands and find somewhere to drop him off, explaining that he was the last of a military squad that was found in the jungle. In a valiant battle, he and the rest of his men managed to destroy the drug base, but were themselves killed in the process. That will leave us in the clear to take over Po's trade ourselves. We now have the power in this province, and our village will be safe for years to come. You've saved our village. Be proud." Sanh turned and shouted for several other men to join him. They slung their AK-74s over their shoulders and started heading up the road to the village.

Xua knelt in the dirt by Michael's body. She flipped him over and brushed the dirt from his face. *You served your purpose well. Just like most Americans who came here, you were the perfect tool. But you have earned your rest now.* She reached out and closed his eyes, then stood up and motioned to two of the villagers.

"Take this one back to the village and wrap him up. Tell the elders we can begin moving into the base today."

Xua walked over to the other side of the road. She saw the village in a frenzy of activity, as men and women bustled about. And next to that, she saw the poppy fields, with their stalks waving gently in the breeze, and the thousands upon thousands of bulbs that represented safety and security for her tribe.

The Bodyguard and the Client Who Wouldn't Die

WILLIAM C. DIETZ

William C. Dietz has published eighteen science fiction novels, the latest of which is called By Blood Alone *(sequel to* Legion *and* The Final Battle*), three* Star Wars*–related novellas, and five short stories. He grew up in the Seattle area, spent time in the Navy, graduated from the University of Washington, lived in Africa for half a year, and has been variously employed as a surgical technician, news writer, college instructor, television director, and public relations manager. He lives in the Seattle area with his wife, two daughters, and two cats. He enjoys traveling, snorkeling, canoeing, and, not too surprisingly, reading books.*

SUB-LEVEL 38 of the Sea Tac Residential-Industrial Ur-boplex is not a very good place to entertain clients. Not unless they have a Jones for druggies, wire heads, and brain-damaged ex-marines like yours truly.

That's why it's a whole lot smarter to meet them somewhere else, like for lunch in a classy restaurant. Then, if they blow you off, you still get the meal. Pathetic? Well, hey, welcome to my life.

That particular day started the way most of them do. I awoke with the usual headache, a mouth that tasted as if something had died in it, and the memory of a strange dream. The same dream I had dreamed many times before.

I felt myself being lifted into the air and lowered onto the surface of an operating table. A distant aspect of my personality urged me to escape but that was impossible.

Time passed. There was talk of "local anesthetics," "head preps," and "neural interfaces." None of which meant anything to me. That's when it started, the general sense of inflow, of words and numbers that tumbled around me to build vast informational structures so large and complex that they could be compared with cities, except that try as I might I was unable to back away far enough to see and understand their function and purpose.

But I *did* notice that as the city grew larger and larger, I became smaller and smaller, until it towered over and around me. The air became so thick with words and numbers that I choked and couldn't breathe. That's when I decided to escape, to go where they wouldn't follow, and leave everything behind.

And no sooner had the thought crossed my mind than I was gone, drifting under the ceiling, while the bald man worked to bring me back. I watched my body jump as they passed electricity through my heart. The light grew more intense, and seemed to beckon, but I was reluctant to leave. Life had been good once. . . .

Then, like fishermen, the medics reeled me in. My head was full. So full I thought it would explode. I screamed. . . .

Weird, huh? But nothing unusual. Not if you're me . . . which I definitely am.

The shrinks call it battle fatigue, post-traumatic stress disorder, and a whole lotta other shit. All because I took a hit in the noggin. That's why the top of my head is covered with a chromed skull plate, why they kicked me out of the Mishimuto Marines, and why I take fluoxetine, buspirone, and various beta-blockers. When I remember, that is—which is sometimes.

All of which doesn't mean jack-shit, except that it explains why I'm a bodyguard instead of a rocket scientist.

The client, my only client at that particular moment, had suggested the Celestriala, a *very* high torque eatery located on Sky-Level 46, about as far from my one-room abode as heaven is from hell.

In order to get there I had to take the low-rise lift tube up to ground level, switch to the high-rise tube, and push my way in.

I stand seven feet two inches tall, weigh about two-fifty, and have lots of prematurely white hair. Add the skull plate and the .38-caliber bulge and most people make room.

Not *this* crowd, however, all of whom were service droids, and didn't give a shit what I looked like. They were on their way to work, which was more than most humans could say, since most corporations employed no more than ten or twenty people, and used freelancers for the scut work. Freelancers plus androids, of which there were far too many.

They *looked* human, well, kinda human, except for the Droidware logos on their foreheads and the spray-painted butler outfits.

I felt a sense of excitement as the platform rose. Not about the case, but about the free meal—and the chance to scope the restaurant.

That's my fantasy, you see, to open my own place, where the customers know me and the coffee is good. Good and *hot,* since most restaurants serve it lukewarm.

Silly, you say? Well, you have *your* dreams, and I have mine.

The platform paused on a service floor and the robots whined, buzzed, and in one unfortunate case clanked off to work. That left me with the entire compartment to myself. A rare occasion indeed.

The lift tube's computer scanned for targets, compared my image to a long list of criteria, and dropped a holo in front of my mug. The face jockey was pretty, *very* pretty, and wanted to make love to me. That's what her expression conveyed anyway. "Hey, baby, tired of being bald? You could have a full head of hair by tomorrow night. Just dial 888-MOR-HAIR for an appointment."

The face jockey winked beguilingly as the doors parted. I stepped through her image and out onto a transparent floor. Not *entirely* transparent, because there were what looked like clouds drifting just below my feet, but *mostly* transparent so I could see Earth the way some artist imagined it, still covered with glaciers, unpolluted oceans, and virgin forests.

The voice caused me to look up and straight down a heavenly street. It was lined with shops and paved with what looked like gold bricks. ''Welcome to Sky Mall,'' the invisible being said seductively. ''We couldn't help but notice the rather inexpensive nature of your clothing.

''If you are wealthy but eccentric, on your way to a costume ball, or here to deliver some pizza then continue on your way.

''Otherwise be aware that the police have been notified and will arrive at any moment.''

True or not, the claim was intended to send riffraff such as myself packing. And it might have worked, too, if it hadn't been for the prospect of a free lunch, and some much needed cash. I forged ahead.

The shops stood in marked contrast to what I was used to. Judging from my surroundings, the upper crust had no need of anything other than purses, shoes, and expensive jewelry.

No one noticed at first, but it wasn't long before heads started to turn and eyes began to pop.

Fortunately it was about then that I spotted the Celestriala's tasteful sign and headed in that direction. Even freaks with chromed heads can go where they please so long as they look confident and don't ask for directions.

The doors sensed my considerable presence and hurried to part company. The maitre d' was a real pro, the kind who assumes nothing and never gives offense. Too classy for the place I have in mind . . . but a study in how it's done. He saw me, raised a well-plucked eyebrow, and nodded. "Good afternoon, sir. One for lunch?"

I smiled. "Two actually—has Miss Jones arrived?"

The maitre d' gave the slightest of nods and motioned for me to follow. "I will show you to her table."

Few if any of the restaurant's patrons were as refined as the maitre d'. Heads turned, frowns creased artificially smooth skin, and whispers flew left and right.

The Jones table occupied a choice location, right by a floor-to-ceiling window where one could look out over the *real* Mother Earth, or what human beings had done to her, which wasn't pretty.

The sprawl started somewhere south of Ensenada and stretched all the way to Vancouver. There were patches of green, parks and so forth, but not very many, since the whole thing was an endless jumble of factories, hotels, refineries, slums, tank farms, landing grids, and haz dumps.

The immediate view was a study in rectangles. There were tall ones, short ones, and medium ones all jumbled together like some sort of mad puzzle.

Neon caught the eye, as did the brightly lit air cars, and the holo images that bloomed like flowers above the rooftops.

The maitre d' waited while I took my seat. "Miss Jones will be a couple of minutes late, sir. May I bring something while you wait?"

The offer was tempting but what if she failed to show? I'd be stuck with the bill. Still, I felt kind of lucky, so I nodded. "Yes, thank you. An Americano, please. *Very* hot."

The maitre d' delivered one of those infinitesimal nods

that he was so good at and disappeared. The Americano arrived three minutes later. It was boiling.

A full fifteen minutes had passed by the time Cleopatra Jones finally made her appearance. She arrived as if borne by a perfumed wind. Faces smiled, hands fluttered, and lips pouted from every corner of the room.

Jones *looked* about fifty, but, given all the miracles of modern science, may have been considerably older. She wore a pillbox hat trimmed with lab-grown leopard skin, a matching waist-length jacket, and long narrow pants. They were black to emphasize long shapely legs.

I stood the way a gentleman is supposed to. Her heels clicked like castanets and one arm was extended. No small task given the size of the diamond she wore on her hand. "Mr. Maxon! What a pleasure!"

She carried it off so well that I damned near believed it. The handshake was warm and firm.

We sat and made small talk about things I knew very little about while we waited for her Bloody Mary to arrive. She slammed the drink down, winked as if to a conspirator, and ordered another. I noticed that her face had been pretty once—and still was, in a hard sort of way. "So, Mr. Maxon . . . what do you know about my family's company?"

The truth was that I didn't know diddly about her corporation—or hadn't eight hours before. So, cognizant of how unreliable my gray cells tend to be, I had waited until the last minute to visit the company's web site.

I shrugged noncommittally. "What everyone knows, I guess. . . . Jones is a privately held firm centered around transportation. That includes three highly integrated subs known as EarthFreight, MoonFreight, and MarsFreight.

In aggregate they earned more than 20 billion credits during the last fiscal year.''

The second Bloody Mary arrived and she sipped approvingly. ''Very good. You track this stuff, did your homework, or both. I like that.

''Our conversation is going to center around the first part of what you said: Jones is a privately held corporation. My father, Jerimiah Jones, was chairman. I was president.''

''Was?''

She nodded. ''My father passed away about three weeks ago. More on that in a moment. . . . First you need to understand that the family is large and most of us work for the company.''

For some reason the image of a corpse riddled with maggots came to mind. I wondered what that had to do with me, and when we would eat. ''Yes, of course.''

Satisfied that I understood the full significance of her point, Jones continued. ''So, you can imagine how everyone felt when Daddy died.''

''Sad?''

Jones frowned. ''No, silly, of course not! The old bugger was 156 years old. We were tired of listening to endless drivel about how hard he worked to build the company.''

Our waiter arrived at that particular moment and saved me from yet another gaffe. I ordered the largest meal I thought I could get away with . . . and waited for my client to continue. A third Bloody Mary set the wheels in motion.

''No,'' Jones said. ''It was *our* turn, or more precisely *my* turn, since I was designated to replace him. That opened *my* slot to my brother, *his* slot to a cousin, and so forth all the way down the line.''

"So, where's the problem?" I inquired brightly, my eyes on the approaching food. "Is someone out to get you?"

"Of *course* people are out to get me," Jones replied matter-of-factly. "I'm the chairwoman, aren't I? That's what my security team are for."

"Then why hire me?" I asked, mouth watering as the food hit the table.

"For my father," she replied darkly. "To guard his body."

Something about the woman's tone drew my eyes to hers. "But why? He's dead."

Jones nodded. "Yes, he is. And your job is to ensure that he *stays* that way."

The platter was so hot that grease splattered the crisp white tablecloth. The steak was enormous—and so was the potato. I spoke with food in my mouth. "Make sure he stays that way? What do you mean?"

Jones ignored her teensy-weensy salad. "I mean that about two weeks after the old goat was buried he turned up at my office. His clothes were muddy and he was madder than hell. He claimed we had buried him alive! That's when he called the lawyers and went to work on the will."

I paused in midchew. "Really? How could something like that happen?"

"All too easily," came the cryptic reply. "My father didn't make it to 156 by eating plenty of carrots. He was the beneficiary of countless implants, transplants, and bionic surrogates. Artificial organs that can repair themselves. Even *after* death. That's what happened to Daddy.

He died, or we thought that he had, but the surrogates brought him back.''

I racked my so-called brain. ''I've never heard of such a thing.''

''And you *won't,*'' Jones predicted. ''The biomed firms want to suppress the information—as do families such as mine.''

I stuck my fork into the last piece of steak and used it to polish the platter. ''I'm confused. You said your father died—then turned up at your office. So, which is he? Dead or alive?''

''Dead,'' she confirmed. ''For the moment at least. When he arrived at my office he was so angry, so upset, that it triggered a heart attack. The new will, the one he and the lawyers were working on, went unsigned.''

''I see,'' I said, in spite of the fact that I didn't. ''So, where's the problem?''

''We're sending the body back to the family plot in North Dakota,'' Jones replied. ''I want you to go along. If Daddy tries to rise from the dead then shoot him—and keep shooting—till he's down for good.''

The proposition was dubious at best . . . which was why they wanted me to do it. Still, where was the harm? The guy was dead, wasn't he? So if he came to life, and I put a few bullets into him, it wouldn't matter. Or would it? My head started to hurt.

Jones, sensing my hesitation, reached for my hand. She had large brown eyes and they drew me in. ''Please, Max? I'd be ever so grateful.''

I struggled but the hook was set. I said, ''Ingo nordle doodly pop,'' realized my error, and faked a cough. The nonsensical sounds manifest a lot more frequently when I'm stressed. The doctors can't explain it and neither can

I. She had a questioning look and I hurried to respond. "Yes, well, I don't see why not. As a favor to you."

"Wonderful!" she said brightly, dropped my hand, and signaled for the check. "What's your normal fee?"

Most of the time I don't make any money at all—but even I knew better than to say that. I screwed up my courage. "Five hundred credits per day. Plus expenses."

She didn't even blink. "Done. Five hundred it is . . . with a one-thousand bonus after he's buried."

A bonus! It was as if I had died and gone to heaven. She stood and we left together. That's when I noticed the nicely dressed man with the hard eyes. He was staring at us in a predatory sort of way.

Not too surprising, I thought to myself. Cleopatra Jones is a handsome woman, not to mention a wealthy one, and I'd stare too.

Her security detail was waiting outside. There were two men and a woman. They had the sleek, well-fed appearance of family pets. They had it good and wanted to keep it that way. I was entitled to a weapons permit because of my military service. They were too damned young so there's no telling where they got theirs. I could sense their hostility.

"Here's everything you'll need," Jones said, slipping a disk into my hand. "Instructions, release forms, limited power of attorney, contact numbers, the whole nine yards. Questions?"

I had the horrible feeling that a normal person would ask questions, *lots* of questions, but shook my head. "No, ma'am."

She smiled and kissed me on the cheek. I could feel the heat of her fingers long after they left my arm.

"Thanks, Max. What would I do without you?" Then she was gone.

I returned to my apartment to check voice mail (nothing, as usual), pick up an extra set of clothes (all dirty), and print documents off the disk.

Everything I needed, including the clothes, shaving kit, candy bars, ammo for the Super, and some other odds and ends, all went into the small duffel bag.

Once that was accomplished I stepped out into the hall, checked the door, and headed for work.

I don't know how many people die in my particular urboplex every day but there must be thousands of them.

Given the fact that most of the residents are day workers, and have none of the benefits accorded to the corpies, they tend to wear out by the time they reach sixty or so.

Menials, homeless people, and professional criminals are lucky to hit thirty and most never see that.

But no matter *who* they are, or *how* much money they have, everybody leaves the same way.

It starts with a call from a relative, the police, or some shoes hung on the door. Nobody's sure where the shoe tradition came from but everyone knows what it means: We have a body inside—please come and get it.

Most droids have to be on the lookout for Jackers, but not the Takers. The Takers are easy to spot. . . . Their plastic faces are frozen into expressions of sadness, their costumes are unrelievedly black, and they move with a slow, nearly ponderous dignity.

Each machine pulls a cart capable of transporting two bodies, one stacked over the other. Nobody messes with them—nobody. Some pretty weird diseases sweep through the plex from time to time and the Jackers stay clear.

Once loaded, the carts are taken to the Level 25 morgue and held for transfer. The death train arrives once a week. After being loaded it winds through a maze of underground tunnels, breaks the surface somewhere beyond the urboplex, and heads for North Dakota.

Though controversial at first, especially to those who wanted to live there, the concept of turning the entire area into a gigantic graveyard has been enormously successful. The bodies have to go somewhere, and, like it or not, North Dakota was available.

We've all seen the footage. Mile after gently rolling mile of tombs, headstones, and cheap aluminum markers. More than twenty-five thousand square miles of them and still growing!

Maybe that's what Earth will become . . . a graveyard for the race to which it gave life.

That's where Jerimiah Jones had been sent the first time . . . and that's where he would go again.

I stepped off the escalator on Level 25, checked my back trail more from habit than anything else, and hit the jackpot. There he was, the man last seen ogling my client back at the Celestriala, now following me. I looked a second time and he was gone. Lost in the crowd.

But why? It wasn't as if I had a *live* client to protect. No, my man was dead, *twice* dead if it came to that, and supposed to stay that way. Assassins seemed not only unlikely but redundant.

That left Cleopatra Jones and her relatives. Maybe the tail belonged to *them*, an insurance policy of sorts, hired to keep an eye on *me*.

The theory made sense. So much sense that I let the matter drop.

Though somewhat ghoulish, the skull-and-crossbones icons were unmistakable and led me straight to the morgue. Like its brother and sister facilities located all around the world, the urboplex is so crowded you can't take a dump without standing in line. That being the case, there were plenty of people waiting to identify a body, say a last good-bye, or pay the inevitable death tax.

It took the better part of an hour to wait through the line and approach the open window. Rather than the droid I expected to see, there was a real live human being. She shifted an enormous wad of pink chewing gum from one cheek to the other. Her eyes were glued to my skull plate. "Yeah? Whaddya want?"

"I'm here to claim a body," I said with all the dignity I could muster. "And accompany said body to the North American Interment Center."

The clerk was just about to blow me off when I shoved a one-inch stack of perfectly executed forms under the window. I could have given her the disk, but was reluctant to part with it, and knew paper was acceptable.

For some strange reason the crats *love* paper. Maybe it's because you can't trust the electronic stuff. Files get erased, hackers alter them, and shit happens. That's why they print stuff down and squirrel it away. They like to touch it, sort it, and stamp it. This woman was no exception. She took what I submitted, scrutinized each page, and looked suitably impressed. "You're green to go. Through that door." Her nod pointed the way.

I was glad to hear it. The Jones family might have understood had old man Jones seen fit to get up and leave prior to my arrival but it didn't seem likely. I opened the door, stepped through, and heard it lock behind me.

The clerk handed me a wand, jerked a thumb over her shoulder, and deleted me from her life.

The wand tugged and I followed. First through an office filled with crats, all of whom appeared to be on break, then through a door marked "exit," but which really served as an entry to a now defunct mass transit system.

Constructed right after the turn of the century, it had been advertised as the transportation system of the future.

I knew because some badly eroded holo-posters continued to creep across the tilework walls, along with the usual collection of tiresome graffiti, 3-D advertising, and public service announcements.

My body heat triggered one of them and it sputtered into life. It was an interactive model programed to make the viewer more comfortable by keying off their appearance. The woman looked silly wearing a skull plate.

"Hello, citizen! And welcome to the future. As you move onto the escalator ahead, be sure to hold the handrail, and . . ."

I never learned the other thing I was supposed to do because sparks flew and the video snapped to black.

The escalator ran smoothly enough, but was kinda spooky due to the fact that it was wide enough to accommodate six people standing abreast, and I was the only person in sight.

Not too common in the overcrowded urboplex and a fairly good indication of how many people (those having a pulse) chose to ride the death train. Me.

The *real* subways are deeper now, down where my neighbors and I live, hauling our butts from one dead end to another.

My boots made a hollow clacking sound as I strode

the length of the once busy concourse, followed the wand to the right, and entered the one-time shopping mall.

The sign said "morgue" in letters two feet tall, but there was no mistaking the alcoves and what they had been used for.

But the brightly lit signs, busy fast-vendors, and net kiosks of yesteryear were gone, replaced by stacks of boxed bodies, the harsh odor of chemicals, and the chill of heavy-duty air-conditioning. There was a large box with two wands at the bottom. I added mine to the pile.

"Can I help you?"

The voice came from somewhere behind me and my hand darted toward the .38 Super.

I turned to discover that what I had dismissed as some sort of specialized forklift was actually an android. It had rubber-clad wheels, a lot of safety decals, and a pair of forklift arms.

"Yes, I'm here to escort a body to North Dakota."

"Well, aren't you the lucky one?" the robot asked sarcastically. "And which of the dear departed were you planning to hold hands with?"

"Citizen Jerimiah Jones."

A stalk-mounted eye whirred as it looked me over. "You got an RG-74821-4?"

"I think so," I replied, producing my somewhat thinner wad of forms.

"No frigging way," the machine replied as it backed away. "Paper isn't going to work. . . . I'm a machine, for God's sake."

"How 'bout a disk?" I asked soothingly, pulling the object in question out of my pocket.

The droid stopped. "You got a disk? Why didn't you say so in the first place. Drop it in."

A servo whined as a box was extruded from the robot's head. I dropped the disk into the slot and watched the object disappear. What if it never came back?

But my fears were groundless. The disk reappeared and I was able to snatch it back before the machine trundled away. "You can jump on the back if you want . . . or just run like hell."

I chose to ride on the back. The robot whirred down an aisle, turned into a canyon of carefully stacked cardboard coffins, and jerked to an unexpected halt. "J. J. oughtta be right about here . . . eighth from the bottom."

The forklift's arms whirred upward, stabbed forward, and pulled a box out of the rack. It looked identical to all the rest. I frowned and consulted the forms.

"Are you sure that's the correct body? The form calls for an oak casket with brass fittings and a duralast finish."

"Sure," the robot sneered, "and my specs call for chromed bumpers and a candy apple red paint job. Get real, chrome dome. The crats took the box and sold it to the scrappers. You got any idea what genuine oak is worth these days? *If* you could find some?"

"Couple thousand a running foot?"

"Bingo, big boy, so cardboard it is. Unless you'd like to file an RG-74823-5, only to have it reviewed by the same people who stole the coffin, and eventually denied. *After* a year or so."

I thought about the nature of my orders, and my urgent need for funds, and came to the logical conclusion. "Insula norgle de pop."

"Exactly what I thought you'd say," the robot replied. "Hold on, here we go."

The droid returned the same way it had come, took a

right, and followed the downward sloping ramp. It had once been used by pedestrians, but that was a long time ago, and the floor was marred by black skid marks.

The ramp emptied out onto a long narrow platform. Three freight cars were visible . . . their doors gaped open.

"She's just about loaded," the machine said cheerfully, "so you won't have to wait for long. That's important, 'cause there's some real funny folks hangin' out down here . . . and you don't want to meet 'em."

I looked back over my shoulder. "*How* funny are they?"

"Let's just say that there's a market for meat . . . and who's to say where all of it comes from?"

I remembered the steak I had enjoyed, swallowed the sudden rush of nausea, and wished I were somewhere else. "Thanks for the warning."

"Hey, think nothing of it," the droid said cheerfully, bumping over a steel bridge. "I *like* humans who know how to treat a machine and show up with the right forms.

"There, I'll put J. J. right on top, and next to the door. That way he'll be the first one off when you reach North Dakota."

I climbed down, gave the machine a pat on the cowling, and stood to one side. "Thanks, I think."

"Anytime," the droid replied. "I'll keep a sensor peeled for your body . . . and take good care of it."

On that cheery note the machine backed up, turned, and trundled away. I was left in a boxcar packed with bodies, the sweet, slightly corrupt odor of death, and some time on my hands.

Precise though they usually are, machines have no sense for the *subjective* aspects of time, like the way it drags when you're sitting on something everybody refers to as the "death train." So, when the android said I wouldn't have long to wait, there was no way to know what that would mean.

The next couple of hours passed slowly. The train jerked forward from time to time so additional bodies could be loaded, and the once elegant platform was replaced by a nondescript wall.

I didn't miss the platform so much as I missed the lights that went with it. It was dark beyond—dark and gloomy.

I heard footsteps once—two sets that passed over my head. Crew members? Heading for whatever pulled the train? Or meat jackers? Looking for prime rib? I checked the .38, resolved to keep my back to the wall, and used a coffin for a couch. The minutes dragged, my eyes grew heavy, and sleep wrapped my mind.

I awoke to complete darkness, feared I was dead, and cursed my own stupidity. Who but me would fall asleep in a boxcar packed with dead bodies? Nobody *you'd* want to hire, that's for sure.

Well, I was alive anyway, and, judging from the gentle side-to-side motion of the freight car, on my way to North Dakota. But it was dark, *real* dark, and I couldn't see. I felt a momentary sense of panic and forced the emotion away.

I fumbled for the bag, stuck my hand inside, and felt for the flashlight. It was hard and cold.

The tube threw a circle of yellow light onto the now closed door and wobbled across the cardboard coffins.

What about Jones? Was he okay? Meaning dead?

Slowly, reluctantly, I approached his box, fumbled with the release tabs, and opened the lid.

The light spilled over a handsome craggy face. The old man had white hair, a high forehead, bushy brows, a cleaver-shaped nose, and a determined mouth. True, his skin *did* seem a little waxy, but the rest looked fine.

Hell, let's face it, Jerimiah Jones looked a helluva lot better than *I* did, and he'd been dead for weeks now. Well, *mostly* dead, with time off for climbing out of graves.

I hesitated, made the decision to go for it, and placed my fingers on his jugular. Nothing. Good.

Satisfied that everything was under control I resealed the coffin, reclaimed my ''couch,'' and killed the light. Not because I wanted to, but because the power pack wouldn't last forever, and I hadn't been smart enough to pack a replacement.

The darkness closed around me, the train made the same clickety-clack sounds they've been making for more than a hundred years now, and my watch glowed green.

If I'd been sleep earlier, I sure as hell should have been sleepy then, but was wide awake.

There were some candy bars in my bag so I took one out and consumed it. That's when the noises started, or, and this is more likely, I began to notice them.

There was a clacking sound, as someone's teeth chattered to the rhythms of the train, a sigh, as someone passed a prodigious amount of gas, and the steady beep, beep, beep as a wrist term sought to remind its owner of an extremely important appointment.

The candy bar suddenly lost its appeal. I used the light to check my surroundings, was reassured to see that nobody was up strolling around, and switched it off.

I sort of ''night'' dreamed after that, remembered the way things had been, and wondered if any of it was true.

Then, after thirty minutes or so, the train seemed to slow, paused, and started up again.

I didn't think anything of it at first, until footsteps rang on the metal above, the door started to rattle, and a coffin seemed to explode.

I hit the light, pulled the .38, and fired two bullets.

I understand there were some naive types, back before androids became an everyday reality, who believed that humans would never be so stupid as to invent killer robots.

I don't think they were paying attention. Any race that would create then use nuclear, biological, and chemical weapons would love homicidal machinery, and this sucker was a beaut.

The machine had been gussied up to look like a half-rotted corpse, a ploy that would have been a lot more effective in some other context, and didn't scare me. What *did* frighten me however were the two 9mm semi-autos clutched in the droid's plasti-flesh hands.

The robot managed to get one round off before my slugs punched a couple of holes through its chest.

Unaware of the fact that it was dead, the droid took two steps in my direction.

The next pair of bullets punched holes through the robot's head, pushed the machine over backwards, and triggered an avalanche. One of the bodies flew out of her coffin and slid to the floor. Rigor mortis had set in and she was stiff as a board.

Sparks jetted down into the boxcar as a drill bit dipped through the ceiling, whined, and disappeared.

I hit the release button, caught the partially expended clip, and dropped it into a pocket. The replacement mag clicked as it locked into place.

"Maxon? We know you're in there."

Some sort of microphone-speaker thing had been dropped through the hole. It swayed from one side to the other. I put a slug into whatever it was and felt proud of my marksmanship. The object seemed none the worse for wear.

"Don't be stupid, Maxon. Why die for someone who's already dead?"

It was a damned good question. Why indeed? The only trouble was that it stimulated another: Why kill someone (me) in order to steal a dead body? Unless it possessed *more* than caloric value.

Sparks shot in through the door lock. I extinguished the light, grabbed the stiff by her armpits, and positioned her in front of my couch. I needed time—and conversation was the most obvious way to get it.

"Good point. . . . What's this all about? There are easier ways to jack some meat. Try the next car back."

"You're stupid," the voice said conversationally, "but not *that* stupid. So spare me the bullshit.

"Here's the deal—the *only* deal you're gonna get. Open the door, let our people in, and collect one thousand credits.

"Go home, tell the Jones bitch that you buried the old man, and let her pay you again. Sweet, huh? Think about it: Our offer is simple, profitable, and good for your long-term health."

This guy had a way with words, I'll give him that, but there was one little problem: I don't have much, but I do have my integrity (well, most of it), and my word is my bond. When I guard a body it *stays* guarded—even when it's stiff as a board.

"Sounds tempting," I lied, using the light generated

by the sparks to complete my preparations, "but how do I know you'll keep your word?"

"Because we're really nice guys," the voice said sweetly, "who go to church every week, give to the poor, and help old ladies onto escalators."

The lock gave, the door slid sideways, and they entered shooting. The dead body took some of the punishment, and slugs ricocheted off the walls and thumped into coffins.

I opened up with the android's handguns and watched the shooters stagger under the impact of the 9mm slugs and backpedal into the night.

My ears continued to ring from the gunfire—but there was a moment of relative silence. The train went clickety-clack, boots shuffled above, and somebody burped. They didn't bother to excuse themselves. The voice was disappointed.

"Damn, Maxon, what's with you anyway?"

"What do you want him for?" I countered. "Something for the trophy room? There must be serious money involved."

The voice was relieved—as if a mystery had been solved. "Okay, here's the deal. The geezer came back to life once—what if he does it again? What if the tech heads, our tech heads, can *help* him do it? There's all sorts of stuff locked up in that head, things that would help our company compete, and boost the bottom line. Get it?"

"Got it," I replied. "Now get the hell off my train."

The voice was angry now, as if betrayed. "You're gonna be sorry, Maxon, *real* sorry."

"Yeah," I agreed. "I think I already am."

I heard footsteps after that . . . followed by peace and quiet.

I apologized to the much perforated corpse, managed to box her up, and went back to my couch.

The train slowed about twenty minutes later, stopped, and started again, raising the distinct possibility that the opposition had gotten off, or that they wanted me to *think* they had gotten off, or that the engineer had taken a pee. Who the hell knew?

Hours passed, my eyelids grew heavy, and my head started to nod. I didn't go to sleep though, or didn't *think* I had, until the light hit my face and a hand touched my shoulder.

I blinked rapidly, peered into my own flashlight, and damned near shit my pants. The door remained open and there was daylight outside. Not much—but enough.

Jerimiah Jones looked as good as any corpse can. The five-thousand-credit suit really *was* wrinkle resistant. Even his shoes were shined. My hand sought the .38 and I was relieved to find that it was there. The dead man frowned. "Who are you? And where am I?"

"Max Maxon," I replied truthfully. "You're on the death train . . . bound for North Dakota."

"The death train?" He looked surprised, angry, and sad, all within the space of a few moments. His knees seemed to give way—and he sat on a coffin. The light took a tour of the ceiling. "I died? Again?"

I nodded. "Yeah, I'm afraid so."

I saw acceptance in his eyes followed by sudden suspicion. "You know who I am. . . . *Why?*"

I shrugged. "Your daughter hired me as an escort."

He appeared pleased, thought better of it, and frowned. His eyes went to the .38. "She hired you to kill me!"

I winced. Jones was pretty sharp for a dead guy.

"No," I answered cautiously, "not exactly. You were dead—and she wanted you to stay that way."

"So," he said, sitting up straight and pushing his chest out. "Go ahead—kill me."

And there it was—the reality of what I had been hired to do. It would be easy. Pump a couple of slugs into the old geezer, dump the body back in its box, and finish the journey.

Only trouble was that I couldn't do it. Not then . . . not ever. I returned the gun to its holster. "I should, I *said* I would, but I can't. You have nothing to fear from me."

The old man fixed me with a stare, nodded slowly, and let the air out. It didn't sound right—like there was something wrong with his lungs.

"Cleo never was a very good judge of character— which explains those husbands. She thinks the bad ones are good and the good ones are bad. My fault, I suppose."

It was a backhanded compliment of sorts, at least I *thought* it was, so I smiled.

The train took a curve, the coffins creaked, and three empty shell casings clattered across the floor. Jones tracked them with the light, brought it up, and surveyed the damage. There were plenty of bullet holes, coffins that had started to leak, and bright spots on the walls. "What happened here?"

I didn't see any reason not to, so I told Jones about the voice, the offer, and the ensuing gun battle. He laughed, started to cough, and wiped phlegm from his lips.

"Maybe Cleo's a better judge of character than I

thought! There are two or three companies that would love to take a tour of my head. Now they won't get the chance—thanks to you.''

The old man's left hand started to jerk spasmodically so he grabbed it with his right. He looked embarrassed and I felt sorry for him.

''So,'' I said, hoping to give him some cover, ''what now?''

Jones looked up from the hand. His eyes were dark and serious. ''Let me tell you something about death, Max. . . . It teaches you about what's important. It isn't money, it isn't power, and it isn't sex. . . . It's people. Helping them, supporting them, making life better for them.

''That's why I started work on my will. . . . I want to change it . . . to give my money to charity. Help me, Max, help me make it back, and I'll pay your fee.''

I gave the proposition some thought. Not a *lot* of thought, because I'd done myself out of a job and needed the money.

Besides, I *liked* Jones and here was a chance to guard a *live* body for a change. A definite step up in the world.

We shook on the deal. His hand felt firm yet fragile . . . as if his bones were cinnamon sticks. The clock was ticking. *He* knew it and *I* knew it. The train swayed—and the miles rolled away.

It was cold by the time the train arrived in North Dakota, *damned* cold, and snowflakes had started to fly. They came in at a slant, little packets of misery, propelled by the wind.

My jacket was at least two sizes too big for Jones, and

both of us shivered as we jumped to hard frozen ground and walked parallel to the train.

I've been off-planet, and fought in some pretty strange places, but none more bizarre than this. The Interment Center, as it was euphemistically named, crouched on top of a hill where it had been dug in, like a fortress against the elements.

The dead people were segregated in death just as they had been in life. Expensive monuments, memorials, and headstones marked the graves of those who had money, while further out, nearly lost in the snow, I could see the first rows of aluminum markers, the kind I would have, stretching into the distance.

Hundreds, thousands, *millions* of rectangles, each marking a life lived, and a death gone by.

"There's a visitors' center," Jones said, hunching his shoulders against the wind. "It's warm inside and there's a kiosk."

I damned near asked how he knew, remembered the answer, and kept my mouth shut.

The snow peppered our faces, crunched under our shoes, and found its way into our clothes. We were glad to go inside. It *was* warm . . . and we left tracks on the otherwise pristine floor.

The visitors' center was something to see. Plenty of taxpayer credits had been spent on interactive dioramas, a holo about the history of death, and a heat-activated narration.

"Welcome on behalf of the Center, and the Center's staff," the voice intoned. "We hope you will enjoy your time with us and stand ready to assist in any way that we can."

"Then shut the hell up," Jones growled, as he limped toward the com kiosk.

The voice heard, processed the words, and did what it was told.

I don't know what Jones did in that kiosk, or how he did it, but an unmarked transport arrived about two hours later. It circled the area, dropped through the snow, and settled on the landing pad. Snow started to melt.

"I hired a freelancer," Jones explained as we headed for the ship. "A company transport would bring all sorts of trouble down on our heads."

"Higo porla tog."

If the industrialist noticed he gave no sign of it. Jones coughed, then stumbled and managed to catch himself. I took his arm. He accepted my help.

The flight back to civilization took less than three hours. I waited till the urboplex was visible through the windscreen before I went forward, shoved the .38 into the pilot's ear, and gave my instructions. "Switch to the manual controls and pull the head jack."

She pulled the jack out of her temple, kept her hands where I could see them, and kept her cool. Ex-military? Maybe—not that it mattered. The voice was calm. "Don't tell me . . . let me guess: a different landing spot?"

I nodded. Just because Jones hired a transport that belonged to someone else didn't mean we were safe. If the pilot was on the take, *if* we'd been made, then the last-minute change could throw them off.

After all, assuming they weren't one and the same, there was "the voice" *plus* the nicely dressed man to be concerned about.

"Yeah. Put her down at Satellite Port number twelve."

"It's a *him,*" the pilot corrected me, "but no hard feelings."

I braced myself as the transport banked to starboard. Jones appeared at my elbow, eyed the handgun, and raised an eyebrow. His breath was bad—like something was wrong deep inside. "What's going on?"

"A last-minute change," I replied. "In case they were waiting for us."

The industrialist looked thoughtful, shrugged, and limped back to his seat. A client who trusted me! Life was (momentarily) good.

The landing was uneventful—which is the way I like them. The ship creaked as it settled onto the skids, Jones affixed his thumbprint to an invoice, and I wondered if dead people could charge things.

This one not only *could,* but did, and we were on our way.

The feeling that something was wrong, *very* wrong, began the moment that I started to descend the ramp. The port was not only big, it was *huge,* which meant hundreds of pads, ships coming and going, robots trundling back and forth, and lots of activity.

So why was this particular platform nearly deserted? Where was the ground crew? Maintenance droids? Baggage handlers? Hiding, that's where—which meant we should too.

I drew the .38, backed up the ramp, and hollered to Jones. "It's a trap! Get back in the ship!"

The nicely dressed man was not so nicely dressed. The blue coverall was too small and too clean. He stepped out from behind a ground tug, brought the pistol up into a two-handed stance, and triggered two shots.

My head jerked as the second creased my skull plate. I fired in return, saw one of his legs buckle, and knew I was low.

The ramp boosted me up into the cabin, sealed itself to the hull, and became one with the floor. The ship forced its way off the pod, skimmed a maintenance facility, and fought for altitude.

I staggered into the cockpit and gestured with the gun. "You could have sealed us outside. Thanks."

The pilot grinned. "No prob, Bob. They were shooting at *Homer*. Nobody shoots at *Homer* and gets away with it."

"Homer?"

The pilot patted the side of her seat. "Yeah, *this* is *Homer*, and he's mine. So, where to?"

I frowned, turned toward the cabin, and saw Jones coughing his lungs out. His body, strong though it had been, was gradually coming apart. There wasn't much time. Our plans would have to accommodate that fact.

"Check . . . see whether Jones Inc. has a building of its own . . . and whether the company put a pad on the roof."

The pilot must have used her implant because there was nothing but silence. The answer came thirty seconds later when she glanced in my direction. "That's a roger. . . . They have a building *with* a pad on top. Shall I head in that direction?"

"Not yet," I answered grimly. "There's something I need to check on. Fly in circles or something. I'll be back in a minute."

Jones had recovered by the time I reentered the cabin and used a tissue to wipe blood off his lips. "Thanks,

Max. You saved my bacon. *Again.* What now?''

"We're going to land on your office building, find the lawyers, and change that will.''

There was gratitude in his eyes. "That's all I ask, Max. You get me there, I'll handle the rest.''

I nodded. "First things first. Take off your clothes.''

Jones gave me a very strange look. I shook my head. "No, nothing like that. It wasn't the pilot . . . so how did they know?''

A sudden look of understanding appeared on his face. "My clothes . . . some sort of tracer.''

"Preciseamundo,'' I replied. "A backup in case you got away from me. Let's find the little bastard.''

It took the better part of five minutes to examine the executive's clothing, come up empty, and go to work on his no longer shiny shoes. The bug was there alright, hidden in his right heel, broadcasting our position.

I used the point of my pocketknife to pry the device out of its hole and beat on it with the butt of my gun.

Once that was accomplished we swung south, dropped into the lowest layer of traffic, and made our approach. The building was sheathed in black glass and, with the exception of a small rectangular structure, had a perfectly flat roof.

An executive-style flitter lifted off the pad, turned on its axis, and headed east.

The pilot gave the other aircraft a moment to get clear and put *Homer* on the roof. I paused for a moment, took a certain amount of comfort from the fact that nobody shot at us, and spoke to the pilot. "We'll give it a try.''

She nodded. "I'll stay till you get inside.''

I took one last look into her steady gray eyes and knew I was missing something. Something I would fantasize about later on. If there *was* a later on. "What's your name?"

"Clare."

"Thanks, Clare."

"You're welcome, Max."

I took the old man's arm and helped him down the ramp. It took what seemed like forever to make it across the roof to the small but well-appointed waiting room. A nicely dressed young woman turned, took a look at Jones, and went pale. "Grandpa? Is that you?"

I don't know where he found the strength, but Jones drew himself up, and stood unassisted. "Why yes, dear, it is. Back from the grave again. Margaret, this is Max Maxon. . . . Max, this is Margaret, one of the grandchildren for whom I still have some hope."

I nodded. "Nice to meet you."

The woman said, "Likewise," but her eyes were on Jones. He winked. "Come on, hon, you can walk me to legal."

But a tone sounded before Margaret could reply, a lift surfaced, and doors whirred open. The security types came out shooting.

Margaret raised her hands, started to say something, and spun as a bullet turned her around.

I worked from right to left, hitting each shooter with two slugs, dropping them as fast as I could.

The third might have nailed me, *would* have nailed me, except for Margaret. She pulled a two-shot purse gun, put both bullets into the last security agent, and watched her fold. Bright red blood soaked the left side of her one-thousand-credit business suit. "I'm sorry, Grandpa, what we did was wrong."

The old man shuffled over, offered his hand, and

helped Margaret to her feet. "Don't worry about it, sweetie. We all make mistakes. Let's get some pressure on that wound and get downstairs. I've got a will to sign."

It was easy after that. We got in the lift, dropped to the twenty-seventh floor, and cruised through legal. Plenty of people saw us, knew something strange was going down, and didn't lift a finger to interfere. And why should they? The family kept the *real* goodies for themselves—and fed the troops little more than scraps.

We found a couple of lawyers, scared the crap out of them, and demanded the will.

Cleopatra arrived a few minutes later, called me every name in the book, and attempted to murder her father. Her pupils were dilated, spittle flew from her lips, and the words ripped like claws. "Die, you miserable old bastard! Die!"

But Jones didn't die. Not then anyway. He just shook his head sadly, placed his thumbprint on the originals, took one of them, and left. Margaret and I followed.

The old man passed away two days later . . . with his granddaughter at his side. I know because it was on the news *and* my voice mail:

"Max . . . Jerimiah here. . . . I'll be dead by the time you receive this, *really* dead, and up to my ass in hot lava.

"There's hope for you, though . . . which is why I didn't leave you a whole lot of money. The blasted stuff *is* the root of all evil, you know . . . and you have plenty of problems already.

"What's the deal with the gibberish anyway? You should see a doctor or something.

"I did dump a couple of thousand credits into your

account, however . . . since there's damned little chance that Cleo will pay your bill.

"Take care, Max . . . and good luck. You sure as hell deserve it." (Click.)

For the further adventures of Max Maxon, read Bodyguard, *also by William C. Dietz, from Ace Science Fiction.*

Point of Decision

JAMES H. COBB

Concerning the "Splinter conflict" battlefields of the post–Cold War world, we may expect two factors to inevitably be present: speed and chaos. Enough to challenge even the enhanced C3I of the digital military. Junior line officers will find themselves mandated to confront problems once reserved for statesmen and heads of state. Per force, ensigns and lieutenants will chart the course of history.

> —Lt. Commander Amanda Lee Garrett,
> *Techno-Knight and Cyber-Ninja:*
> *The Warriors of the Third Millennium,*
> United States Naval Institute Proceedings,
> March 2003

THE NORTHWESTERN COAST OF AFRICA
0646 HOURS ZONE TIME
2 APRIL 2006

BOILING IN THROUGH the helicopter's open side hatches, the slipstream carried that particular stench of a dying city: burning wood, burning oil, burning flesh.

"Stand by! Two minutes!" the Sea Knight's crew chief bellowed over the rotor thunder. Looking back from the cockpit he held up a vee of fingers. I relayed the bellow and the gesture down the line to my guys in the cargo bay, adding my own commentary. "Load and lock!"

I scooped a handful of twelve-gauge slug loads out of a pouch on my MOLLE harness and started dunking shells into the breech of my Mossburg 590 assault shotgun. Behind me, thirty-round clips were slammed into M-4 magazine wells and carry-belts fed into Squad Automatic Weapons.

This was a security job, not a reconnaissance mission, so the whole platoon was shoehorned aboard the creaking old CH-46. Three four-man fire teams and the sawed-off command section consisting of Jake Ribitkish, my platoon Top Sergeant; my RT, Lance Corporal Joey Miller;

and me. Not all that many really, but then Marine Force Recon always works light.

"One minute!"

Flat, sand-colored rooftops flashed past beneath the helo's belly. We were coming in low and fast in an assault approach, keeping the morning sun behind us. Third World insurgents purely love to shoot at helicopters and they don't much care whose insignia is painted on the sides.

"On final!"

We looped our free arms through the safety harnesses bolted to the interior bulkheads. Back aft, the tail ramp powered down, letting in the bloody light of the new day.

"Comin' in!"

The big twin-rotor flared back steeply, bleeding off speed and sinking fast. Sand swirled in the lift wash. Over the shoulder of the door gunner, I had an impression of a dusty, walled compound, a few tattered palm trees, and an American flag defiant against a sun-bleached sky. Then the landing gear trucks whumped down on the cracked tarmac of the embassy parking lot.

"Go!"

The one best thing you can do in a helicopter sitting on the ground in a combat zone is to get the hell out of it. Fifteen pairs of boots, including my own size-twelve Danners, hit the ground running. The helo pilot didn't waste any time either. He spooled back up to flight power the instant we cleared the tail ramp, jacking the CH-46 back into the comparative safety of the sky.

I didn't yell any orders. I didn't need to. Force Recon hands don't need to be told much when it comes to warfighting. Moving by drill and instinct, my rifle teams dispersed around the landing zone perimeter. Going to ground behind what cover they could find, each man set himself an overwatch zone, peering over the sights of his leveled weapon. Hunkered down inside their body armor they silently awaited developments. Me, I stayed on my feet, taking a long, slow look around and setting my tactical awareness of environment.

The U.S. Embassy in Nouakchott was set at the vee-shaped convergence of two main city avenues, the Rue de Independence and the Rue Abdalaya, with the parking lot we were using as a landing zone set behind it at the widening of the vee. The office buildings and storefronts beyond the multilane boulevards were all pretty much new and styled in that stark European modernism that was big with the emerging African states back in the independence era.

According to our mission briefing, there hadn't been a city here at all before 1960. After Mauritania had busted loose from the French colonial empire, its new national leaders had pointed to a grassy plain near the Atlantic coast and had decreed, "Here shall be the capital."

That grassy plain was long gone now, lost to overgrazing and desertification. An arm of the Sahara had reached out and embraced the new city, the parched winds blowing in from the Sahel dropping a perpetual gritty film of yellow sand over everything.

Given half a chance, the desert would eat this whole damn place alive. And from the look of things, that chance was coming.

Street fighting had left the building fronts across from the embassy windowless and bullet-pocked. Only charred and smoldering frames remained in some places along the street, like blackened, rotten stumps in a row of diseased teeth.

Other smoke plumes rose elsewhere over the city. Off to the southwest, I could see the fire-blackened dome of a good-sized Muslim mosque rising above the low rooftops. The Mosque Saudique, according to the city maps I'd been shown, a gift from the oil sheiks to the new Muslim state. It too had been torched, and its fragile minarets dynamited.

"Yeah, boy," I heard myself murmur. "Payback is a bitch."

The streets were empty, but from the gunfire in the surrounding neighborhoods, I figured there still had to be some people around somewhere, either pulling triggers or being targets.

A brace of Whisky model Sea Cobras whup-whuped past on low sentry. Hightailed and belligerent, the helicopter gunships panned their chin turrets warily across the terrain surrounding the embassy compound. On high sentry, another pair of heavy hitters also circled, snub wings silhouetted against the sky: Marine AV-8B Harrier IIs—vertical takeoff and landing attack jets launched from our Amphibious Force mother ship, the *Kearsarge,* currently holding on station some twenty miles off the coast.

The mission planners hoped that the sight of all that flying firepower might just overawe the locals into good behavior while we evacuated our embassy personnel. And if not, our airborne Marine brethren would be ready to back our play.

Out of the corner of my eye, I caught man-movement. A figure had appeared on one of the shrapnel-chewed building roofs directly across from the LZ, starvation lean, ebony-skinned, and wearing ragged trousers and an equally ragged blanket. However, he also carried an AK-

47 easily at its balance. As he looked us over, the Sea Cobras blasted by again, low enough for their rotor wash to make his blanket flutter.

He didn't seem the least bit overawed to me.

Under my skin I became aware of other eyes watching warily from glassless windows and broken doorways. We didn't have any fight with these people that I knew of, but we were strangers in their strange land, and frequently in such places, the words for "stranger" and "enemy" are interchangeable.

I lifted a hand and gave a silent gesture-signal to my rifle teams. The security perimeter collapsed in on itself and we lined out for the compound gates, Ribitkish taking the point and Miller falling into step with me, the spring antenna of his AN/PRC119 SINCGARS transceiver bobbing over his shoulder.

After the Kenya and Tanzania bombings in '98, all of the U.S. Embassies in Africa had been rebuilt until they were as much fortress as consulate. A massive blast wall encircled the Nouakchott compound, proof against car bombs as well as angry mobs, and squat, slit-windowed blockhouses flanked the entry gate. As my boys and I snaked through the outer defense of cylindrical concrete car guards, the heavy steel grate doors cranked open.

A beat-looking Marine second lieutenant waited just inside the gate. I noticed that, like me, the young black butter-bar packed a Mossburg combat shotgun as a personal weapon. That prejudiced me in his favor from the start.

"Lieutenant Keyes, sir," he said, slapping the close button on the gate controls. "Embassy security detachment."

"Quillain, Second Force Recon. What's your situation?"

"Quiet for the moment, sir. Perimeter is secure, but man, I've got to say I'm glad you're here."

I took a fast look around the interior of the compound. A pierced aluminum security gangway circled the inside of the compound walls like the firing parapet of an old frontier fort. It served pretty much the same purpose as well. The ten men of the embassy guard were deployed around the walls, weapons up and ready, but with way too much space between them.

With the wind blocked by the palisade, the air inside the compound was stagnant and smoky. Some of the smoke crept in from the city fires, but more issued from the row of fifty-gallon burn barrels set up on the parched lawn outside the main building. Frazzled embassy staffers fed final armloads of hardcopy into the flames as I looked on.

"Top, get our boys up on the walls here! Set your overwatch sectors! Keep me advised of any changes in the tactical situation."

"Yes, sir!" Ribitkish charged off, snapping off a fast string of orders.

I held out an open hand. My radioman didn't need any further cue and he slapped the handset into my palm.

"Culverin, Culverin, this is Touch Hole. Insertion successful. We are in the compound. Situation nominal. Over."

"Acknowledged, Touch Hole," Major Clint Hacker's voice whispered back over the radio link. "Do you have a final count? Over."

I lifted my finger off the transmit key and looked over at Keyes.

"Seventy-eight, sir" he replied, "All set to go."

"Culverin, final count is seventy-eight. I say again, seven eight. Over."

"Roger," Hacker acknowledged. As the executive officer of our Marine Expeditionary Unit, he was riding herd on us from the operations room aboard the *Kearsarge*. "Seven eight. ETA first lift bird ten minutes. Proceed as per the ops plan. Culverin, out."

"Touch Hole, out."

"What's the call on the special problem, sir?" Keyes inquired as I passed the mike back to Joey.

"Special problem?" What in the hell could be more special than orchestrating an emergency embassy evac out of a capital city coming apart at the seams? "What kind of special problem are we talking about here?"

Keyes looked puzzled. "You don't have the word, sir?"

"If I did, I wouldn't be asking about it, son. What's going on?"

Keyes frowned back at me. "Sir, I think you'd better talk to the ambassador right away."

"I think I'd better."

Inside the main embassy building, the hallways and public offices were jammed with that inevitable assortment of First World refugees and hangers-on who always somehow manage to get themselves caught in the backwash when a Third World nation starts going to hell in a handcart.

There were the haggard businessmen, their briefcases loaded with the shattered remnants of their big deals. There were the blue-collar contract technicians, who until a short time ago had been keeping the machinery running. There were the wanna-be freelance journalists and war groupies who all of a sudden didn't wannabe anymore, and there were the sandaled and Gortexed tourist couples who'd found far more adventure on their adventure vacations than they'd planned on. All mixed in with a scattering of State Department personnel, who actually had a reason to be here.

The air was saturated with cigarette smoke, nervous sweat, and the low babble of half a dozen different languages. All of the foreign nationals remaining in Nouakchott had converged on the American Embassy, knowing that Uncle Sugar was their last, best chance for a ticket out. Their voices trailed off uneasily as Keyes, Miller, and I strode in from the compound.

Ambassador Evelyn Sinclair was up in the communications center on the embassy's second floor. To tell the truth, she put me more in mind of an exceptionally tough second grade teacher I'd had back in Vidalia than she did a diplomat. Gray-haired, quick-moving, and wearing Levi's and a checked blouse, she was personally supervising the knockdown and packing of the embassy's classified encryption and communications gear.

I shot her a fast salute. "Ambassador Sinclair, I'm Lieutenant Stone Quillain. Second Force Recon. We're here to get you out, ma'am."

"I'm sorry it has to be done, Lieutenant," she replied crisply. "But it seems we don't have much choice. The embassy staff is ready to evacuate and we just about have all of the critical equipment ready to load. Now, can you tell me what decision has been made concerning Colonel Ahazra and his family?"

I had to shake my head again. "I'm sorry, ma'am, but I have no idea who this Ahazra man is."

"They don't have any word for us, ma'am," Keyes

interjected. "They weren't even briefed on it."

The ambassador spat out an extremely undiplomatic word. "What in the world are they playing at in D.C.? This is a major policy call!"

The embassy Marine shook his head. "Maybe that's the problem, ma'am."

"Begging everybody's pardon!" I exploded. "But will someone kindly tell me what's going on here?"

"I can do better than that, Lieutenant," the ambassador replied grimly. "I can show you. Come with me, please."

She led us down the hallway and into the consular living quarters at the rear of the second floor. The carpeted floors and the ordered, air-conditioned cool were a pointed contrast to the disintegrating world outside of the walls. She paused at and opened the door of a small guestroom. Stepping back, she let me have a look inside.

The room's four occupants also were a contrast to the State Department–Holiday Inn issue decor as well. A man lay on the bed, a gaunt, dark-skinned Arab wearing the trousers of some kind of uniform and a formerly white undershirt. His left shoulder had been heavily bandaged and he looked shocky and feverish.

A woman sat at his side, holding two pre-school-aged children close. The kids were in grimy Western clothing, while the woman wore the traditional black chador that revealed only her bright and terrified eyes.

"This is Colonel Hassan Ben Ahazra, the assistant minister of Mauritanian State Security," Ambassador Sinclair said quietly. "Possibly the last senior government official left alive in the capital. He and his family came in through the gates last night, asking for political asylum here at the embassy."

"Yeah," Keys commented. "He didn't know that the embassy was about to get turned off on him."

Ahazra lifted his head and whispered a weak and hesitant sentence in French. Keyes shook his head and replied quietly in the same language.

"What'd he say?" I asked.

"He was asking if there had been any word from our government yet."

"About what?"

Ambassador Sinclair closed the door behind us as we stepped back into the hall. "About whether or not we're authorized to take him and his family with us when we leave."

I tilted my K-Pot helmet back a little, uneasy about the next answer I might get. "And what happens if we aren't authorized to take them?"

"Flip a nickel, sir," Keyes replied grimly. "Either they kill his wife and kids in front of him, before giving him the axe, or else he dies in front of his family and then they're killed."

"Shit! Begging your pardon, Ambassador, but what for?"

"General principles," Ambassador Sinclair replied, leaned back against the corridor wall with her arms crossed. "For the past thousand years, Mauritania has been a rigidly two-tiered society, an upper caste of Arabic Moors ruling an oppressed slave and servant caste of black Africans. That social structure has just gone into terminal meltdown. Right now, we have one of the last great slave rebellions underway outside, the black Mauritanians verses their former Moorish masters. The black Africans are winning and Colonel Ahazra is almost certain to be executed if he falls into the hands of the rebel factions. Very likely his family as well. You see, as a member of the State Security Service, he will be looked on as . . . I suppose you could call it an overseer.''

That rocked me back a little. ''The Black versus Moor angle was sort of explained to us in our briefing, ma'am, but slavery? Damn, but this is the twenty-first century!''

''Not here, Lieutenant,'' Keyes replied emphatically. ''In the back country, you could see slave traders and village slave markets operating openly, just like it was back in the bad old days in the South.''

''And just like it has been here for a thousand years,'' Sinclair added. ''Mauritania has no law against slavery, only laws denying any protest against it. We estimate that over one hundred thousand black Africans were owned outright in this country right up until the rebellion. These people have an enormous backlog of hate to work out.''

I shook my head. ''God A'mighty! No wonder the local blacks are pissed off. And no wonder that poor son of a bitch in there is scared spitless.''

I shot a glance over at my radioman. ''Tactical.''

Joey passed me the radio mike, the little RT's other hand going to the touchpad controller clipped to the front of his flack jacket, switching antenna and frequency.

''Top, this is Quillain. What do we have happenin' out there?''

''I was just about to give you a yell, Lieutenant,'' Ribitkish's filtered voice came back. ''Still no action in the streets, but we're seeing activity in the buildings to the northeast and southwest. We've got men deploying to cover the embassy compound. Multiple platoon strength, maybe a company. I'm not seeing any heavy weapons yet but plenty of small arms.''

''We taking any fire?''

"Negative. We've got some shooting a few blocks over towards the center of town but none of it's coming our way yet. It looks like they're just tightening up their perimeter and keeping us under close observation. For the moment at any rate."

"I roger that. Keep me advised." I lifted my thumb off the mike button. "Joey, get me Battalion."

As he shifted radio ranges again, I glanced over at Keyes and the ambassador. "Do the locals know we got this Ahazra guy in here?"

"They know he can't be anywhere else," the embassy Marine replied grimly.

"Battalion's up, sir."

In a fast half-dozen sentences, I sketched out the situation to the operations team.

"Stone, we don't have anything at all on the boards about this Ahazra individual," Hacker replied. "The old man is kicking this up to Second Fleet to see if they have anything on it."

"Make it fast, sir. I'm getting my first lift ship in here in a minute."

"We'll do what we can, Stone. This is Culverin, out."

"I filed a full report on this situation over eight hours ago, Lieutenant," Ambassador Sinclair said in frustration, "and requested an immediate policy decision on the matter. When I didn't get a reply I assumed that you were being briefed on the matter and would be bringing in instructions on how we were to proceed."

She straightened and started back down the hall. "We still have an active satellite link with Washington. I'll try and find out what's gone wrong."

"I would appreciate it, ma'am."

Joey had been intently guarding our commo net

through his auxiliary headset and now he looked up at me. "Lieutenant, Firelock Lead is calling. She's coming in on the landing zone and is asking for instructions."

I swore some mentally. This Ahazra deal was throwing me off. "Right. Tell her to hold and orbit. Keyes, you got everybody else set to go?"

"Yes, sir. All evacuees have been organized into twelve-person chalks. Civilians first, then embassy personnel. One piece of hand luggage per person."

"Good deal. Pull your men off the walls and escort the chalks out to the lift ships as they come in. My teams will maintain overwatch. When you get the first batch out to the LZ, pop an orange smoke grenade. I repeat, orange! Get goin'!"

"Aye, aye." Keyes dashed off.

I grabbed for the radio handset again. A pink-carpeted corridor in the embassy's bedroom wing wasn't my idea of an ideal command post but it looked as if it would have to do.

"Firelock Lead, this is Touch Hole. You are cleared to initiate approach. We are popping smoke. Sunkist, I say again the color is sunkist. LZ is cool at this time but don't count on it."

"Roger, Touch Hole," the helo jock's steady contralto came back over the static. "On final."

"Touch Hole to Musket Lead."

"Musket, 'by." The gunship boss replied from the cockpit of his Whisky Cobra.

"I want you boys to maintain a tight holding pattern around the embassy area. We got some potential hostiles lookin' us over and I want to keep their heads down. Also keep the lift ships covered on approach and departure.

You see ground fire comin' up, don't screw around. You burn 'em.''

"Rog' Wilco, Touch Hole. Yeah, we're seeing armed men on the roofs now. It's cool. We're workin' it."

"Thank you kindly, Musket. Touch Hole calling Saker Leader."

"Saker Leader here, over." The voice of the senior Harrier pilot drifted down from on high.

"Stay with us, Saker. I sure hope we don't need you, but if we do, we're gonna need you awful bad."

One by one, the evacuation flights flared in and dozen by dozen the numbers in the embassy shrank. Seventy-eight . . . sixty-six . . . fifty-four . . . The refugees scurrying to the escape offered by the yawning black tailgates of the lift ships. The embassy Marines shepherding each group out to the safety they could not yet enjoy. Walking with weapons at high port, they were aware of the watchers back deep in the shadows of the dawn, aware of the men who hadn't quite decided whether they wanted to be our enemies or not.

Forty-two . . . thirty . . . eighteen. . . .

I yanked my helmet off and swiped the sweat from my forehead with the sleeve of my chocolate chip utilities. "Joey, get me Battalion again!"

"Aye, sir. . . . Battalion up."

"Culverin, this is Touch Hole. What d'ya have for me?"

"I'm sorry, Stone," the exec replied. "Nothing new on the Ahazra situation. Neither Second Fleet nor CIN-CLANT has any word on an authorization to evacuate."

"What about the wife and kids then?"

"Stone, we have no word on anybody!"

"Then, damn it all entirely, Major, what are my orders here?"

"Until we get a decision, continue the evacuation as per the plan."

"Acknowledged. Touch Hole, out!"

I wished for a cradle to smash the handset into. The best I could manage was a hard toss back to Joey.

Lieutenant Keyes double-timed up the stairway. "Lieutenant Quillain, the last of the civilians are away and most of the embassy staff except for the crypto operator and the ambassador. The last of the classified equipment's gone out as well."

"What about the internal security sweep?"

"Completed. All hardcopy files shredded and burned. All computer files wiped and all storage disks and hard drives smashed. All we got left is the stuff in the commo room. What's the latest on Colonel Ahazra?"

"None of our people have ever even heard of the son of a bitch. Let's hope the ambassador's got something from State. Come on."

He headed back down the corridor to the communications center. Only the single, sweating systems operator and Ambassador Sinclair remained at the half-gutted main console, the ambassador with a telephone clamped to her ear.

"Anything yet, Ambassador?"

"No! Some idiot staffer didn't red flag my request for a policy call. It was incorporated into the Secretary of State's routine morning briefing and he isn't in yet!"

"Ah, come on, ma'am! We can't screw around any more waiting for Foggy Bottom to get its act together. You've got to make the call on this thing."

The ambassador shook her head. "I can't. Evacuating a member of the former Mauritania government could be construed as an active involvement in the civil war. It could critically affect our relations with the future government here. I don't have the authority to make that decision. We have to wait for the Secretary of State. He's been contacted and he's being brought up to speed on the situation now."

I looked up as the thud of rotor blades began to leak through the embassy walls again. "Too late, ma'am. That's your ride. Let's go."

She shook her head. "We only need a few minutes more!"

"We don't have 'em!" I took the phone out of her hand. "Begging the ambassador's pardon and with all due respect, but you're out of here!"

The relieved systems operator didn't need any urging but I had to practically carry the ambassador out of the communications room.

"Keyes, get the ambassador out to the evac bird. You and the rest of your team extract on this flight as well. Me and my boys will cover you out."

"Sir, request permission—"

"Whatever it is, denied! Move!"

"Aye, sir."

He only said one "aye." The proper Marine and Navy response is "aye, aye"—as in, "I" understand and "I" will obey. I should've caught that.

I turned back to the commo center. We'd got all the really good stuff out, but standard policy in an embassy evac is to leave nothing behind intact that a potential adversary could make use of. I used my elbow to bust in the glass cover on the security destruct box just inside the doorway. Removing the thermite grenade, I yanked the pin out of the squat canister and tossed it onto the opened chassis of the communications console. Ducking out, I slammed the heavy steel door behind me. A couple of seconds later I felt rather than heard the thud of the grenade detonation. Both the low-grade explosion and the ravening heat it produced would be contained inside the fireproof, reenforced walls of the communications center. Only the remaining electronic equipment inside would be slagged.

Joey was hovering outside the door, Johnny-on-the-spot with more trouble. "It's Saker Leader, sir," he piped up. "He reports the Harrier flight is fifteen minutes to bingo fuel."

There wasn't a whole damn lot I could do about that either.

"Tell him we need those fifteen minutes. The ambassador's helo is just taking departure now. Then get me Battalion again!"

The roar of the landing Sea Knight segued into the steady-state drone of a grounded helicopter. Under my breath, I counted seconds. As ten passed, the drone grew back into a roar again, lifting into the sky and drifting away. I listened past the departing aircraft for the sound of gunfire and heard none. Okay! There was one problem gone!

"Battalion sir! The exec is on the line."

I tilted my helmet to one side and clamped the handset to my ear. "Culverin, this is Touch Hole. The ambassador is clear. I say again, the ambassador is clear. Embassy evacuation complete except for the platoon and the Ahazra family. Request instructions. Over!"

"Culverin to Touch Hole." There was a hesitation in

Major Hacker's voice. "We have no situational update."

"Desperate Jesus, sir! My extraction helo is inbound and my air cover is running out of gas! I need an answer on this! Do we take 'em or not?"

"Lieutenant Quillain, the Marine Corps does not set national policy. We have no orders on this matter! This is a decision for State! We are not in the chain of authority on this!"

"I don't give a damn who's making the call, Culverin! I'm just asking that somebody quit tossing the tater and make it! For Crissakes, sir! I'm down to the wire here! Yes or no?"

"Lieutenant Quillain! Until we receive specific instructions concerning Colonel Ahazra and his family, they are not a factor! I repeat, they are not a factor! Execute the operations plan as designated. That's all we can do. Culverin, out."

I handed the mike back to Joey. For the first time since setting foot inside the embassy compound I didn't have anything to do. I looked back down the hall, noting the sand we'd tracked onto the soft rose-colored carpet, and I wondered what the place would look like after the locals had been in residence a couple of weeks.

The room that held the Ahazra family was only a few more steps down. It was funny, but I hadn't realized that I'd been drifting Joey and me back in this direction. I crossed those steps and flipped it open, letting the door swing back on its hinges.

They were still there, the high official who had been thrown down to the level of a frightened and helpless man. The woman who had committed to follow him to the gallows and beyond. The children who'd had no role to play in what had gone before and no future in what would follow.

They flinched back a little at my gaze and I didn't blame them particularly. I'm a big, raw-boned Georgia boy, a long way from good-looking at best, and when I scowl, horses tend to shy and babies burst into tears. The expression on my face wasn't meant for the Ahazras, though; more it was for the way the world can go all to shit when we don't pay attention to things.

Boots pounded in the hallway behind me. "The ambassador and the embassy guard is clear!"

I looked up and saw someone who wasn't supposed to be there. "Damn it all, Keyes! I ordered you out of here with your people!"

"I know, sir," the young officer shot back defiantly. "But, by God, this embassy was my command and I don't leave until the last chopper is out!"

I started to blow, then I realized that it just didn't signify. A couple of years back I'd likely have done the same thing.

Come to think about it, maybe I still would. "Yeah, well, I guess you don't."

Keyes gave me a grin back, his teeth showing up white against the smooth brown of his skin. "What's the bottom line, sir?" he asked, nodding in towards the bed.

"There isn't any. The boys in D.C. must figure that if they wait long enough, the problem will just go away. And I guess it will."

From beyond the walls the sound of helicopter rotors grew for what would be the last time. Ahazra knew, I could see it in his eyes. Wincing against the pain in his wrecked shoulder, he drug himself up on his elbow.

Dragging the rags of his man's dignity back around him, he gasped out a few sentences in French.

"What's he sayin'?" I asked.

"He's asking that, if we won't take him, for the love of Allah we take his wife and kids. Or that, if we won't do that, we leave him a pistol and four rounds."

Keyes hesitated, his jaw muscles working. "Lieutenant, you know, I never liked how these guys ran things around here, God knows, but that's over with now. I mean . . . what the hell, sir?"

I nodded. "Yeah, what the hell. . . . Miller!"

"Aye, sir!"

"Call Battalion, tell them we're going to need another lift ship out here."

"Another lift ship, sir?"

"Those headphones making you deaf, Corporal? Call for another helicopter and tell 'em to expedite!"

"Aye, aye, sir, but they're gonna ask why."

"Tell 'em you have no situational update on the problem at this time!"

What the hell indeed. I'd spent my first four years in the Corps as an enlisted man. I could finish out my twenty the same way. I looked over at Keyes. "Come on. Let's get 'em loaded."

"All of 'em, sir?"

"Hell yes, all of 'em. Why start making it easy on ourselves at this late date."

Keyes grinned again and slung his weapon. Maybe after I got busted back to corporal, he'd take me on as a fire team leader in his platoon. As he scooped the kids up out of the mother's arms, I heisted Ahazra off the bed. The Moorish colonel whispered *"merci"* repeatedly in my ear as I got his good arm around my shoulders.

"Forget it, old son," I muttered back. "Some of my ancestors were slave-owning sons of bitches just like you guys. And yeah, they got their butts kicked for it too."

With Joey Miller helping the wife, we started down the stairs and out of the embassy building. The Sea Knight that was supposed to be taking us home blasted past overhead, sinking down towards the parking lot landing zone.

"Think the locals would be willing to shoot it out with us to try and get this guy?" I asked as we drug through the lobby.

"I'm not sure exactly how they'll react," he replied over the sobbing of the kids. "All I know is that the local blacks really have a hard-on over the local browns just now. I don't know what they'll do when they see us lugging him out of here."

"Hopefully, they'll ask their State Department for instructions. We'll be halfway back across the goddamn Atlantic before they get an answer. . . . Top!"

Ribitkish double-timed across the compound yard to us in response to my bellow.

"Change of plans," I said. "We go out on the next bird. This one is committed to some VIP passengers. Redeploy the fire teams for maximum coverage over the LZ. If the locals are going to do it to us, it'll be on this load-out. The lieutenant and I will be walking these people out ourselves. If anyone opens up on us or the helo, hit 'em with everything you've got."

"Aye, aye, sir."

"Miller, you're with the Top. Inform all air elements that we may have trouble coming. If we start taking fire, call the gunships in to join the party."

"Will do, Lieutenant. Good luck, sir."

We paused at the embassy gates and Keyes slapped the button to retract the grillwork. "How we going to work this, sir?" he inquired.

"We don't have enough time line left for anything fancy. It's hey diddle diddle and straight up the middle. We walk 'em out, we stuff 'em in the helo, and we get 'em out of here."

"You figure the rebels won't fire on us, on Americans, that is?"

"It's a nice thought."

We got it done. I lugged Ahazra along with one arm, while packing the Mossburg half-ready on my hip with the other. Keyes hunched along, cuddling the two kids close, keeping them inside the shelter of his flack vest as much as he could. The wife trotted along between us, one hand comforting her children, the other lightly resting on her husband's shoulder.

It hadn't seemed that far out to that parking lot when we'd landed, maybe oh, seventy-five yards out from the compound gate. But now, man, it was like walking back to Atlanta. The Sea Knight sat droning on the LZ, her tailgate down and the crew chief waiting just inside the shadowy hatchway.

It's not mentioned in the Good Book, but the pearly gates are actually painted in gray-green camo, and Saint Peter wears Marine-issue utilities.

We were within fifty feet of the grounded Sea Knight when a high-velocity something tore a notch in the pavement just short of the toe of my boot.

And then the whole damn place lit off.

Gunfire hosed in on us from a dozen positions around the landing zone. We and the helo crew both would have been finished right then if counterfire hadn't blazed from the embassy walls. Ribitkish and the boys had the most likely target points already boresighted and they poured back a storm of 40mm grenades and 5.56 NATO.

Through the middle of it all, we ran for the Sea Knight. Ahazra's legs went out under him and I dragged him the last few yards like a sack of meal, all the time watching the neat little round holes magically appearing in the helicopter's aluminum skin.

Keyes literally threw the kids into the helo. Then he turned, grabbed, and launched the mother after them. I was up to the tail ramp by then and together he and I heaved the former assistant minister of Mauritanian State Security into the cargo bay, piling him up on the deck. Somehow, I don't think Ahazra much minded.

The smart thing would have been to pile in after him. Unfortunately, I don't get an officer's pay and privileges to necessarily do the smart thing, not when it meant leaving my people behind on the ground. Keyes, had the option though.

"Get in!"

"Fuck you . . . sir!"

We didn't have time to argue about it.

I swung an arm at the crew chief. "Get out of here!"

The helo guys didn't have to be told twice. At full war power, the Sea Knight broke ground and scrabbled for altitude, her .50-caliber door guns hammering. Across the boulevard, a figure sprang to its feet on a rooftop. Silhouetted against the smoky sky, he aimed an assault rifle at the fleeing lift ship. Instinct kicked in and the Mossburg swept up to my shoulder, the slide pumping back. The ghost ring sight acquired the target and the sear tripped as my finger tightened on the trigger. Scarlet blood sprayed as the big sabot slug did its job.

Then the helo was clear, sweeping away over the city towards the sea, and there was nobody left around to shoot at except for us.

We ran. I tell the world we ran! We sprinted for the embassy gates with slugs from half a dozen different rifle types screeching and whining off the pavement around us.

There was no chance of making it. No chance at all. Not without catching at least one. I took it in the back. The rear ballistic plate of my flack jacket deflected the round but the impact smashed me down onto the pavement on my face. I went glassy-eyed for a second and then Keyes was with me, swearing and dragging me up by my equipment harness, ignoring the metal saturating the air around us.

A Predator AT rocket streaked overhead from the compound walls, killing one gun nest but still leaving way too many in business. . . .

And then, the Voice of the Lord was heard across the land . . . or at least the droning snarl of a 20mm Gatling gun.

The Sea Cobras of Musket Flight popped up over the embassy compound, raking the building lines with their chin turrets.

The locals replied in kind, shifting their aim to the gunships. Lord, but they were pissed! And they didn't have any backdown to 'em at all. The Sea Cobras had to break off and evade, the ground fire striking impact sparks off their belly armor. Still, their intervention had given us our chance to reach the embassy gates.

Joey was waiting for us, couched down inside the entryway and squeezing off short bursts with his M-4 carbine. "Musket Leader wants to talk to you, sir," he said almost casually as Keyes and I piled down beside him.

I took a second to breathe and look around. The inside of the compound looked like a remake of *Beau Geste*. My guys were standing along the firing parapets, laying down rounds in reply to the gunfire that continued to rake the embassy from outside while Sergeant Ribitkish, pacing calmly along the line, was telling them to conserve ammo and pick their targets.

Damn, but I always hated how that movie turned out.

I reached over and unclipped the handset from the radio. "Musket Lead, this is Touch Hole. Go."

Hell, I could figure what he was about to say. I could hear the damn cockpit alarms going off over the radio link. "Touch Hole, be advised you got bo-koo bad guys down there! We got hosed on that pass big time!"

"Saw it happening, Musket. You got your ass blown off saving mine. 'Preciate ya. What's your status?"

"I'm losing a turbine and Musket Two's gunner is hit. We're hangin' with you though."

To hell that noise! With visions of Mogadishu dancing in my head, I keyed the mike again. "Negative, Musket, negative. Get out of here. Get yourself and that last lift ship home."

"You sure, Touch Hole?"

From across the street there came the *chush . . . boom!* of an RPG-7 firing, the focused burn-through of the antitank warhead making a heat-lightning flash on the inside of the compound wall. I took a moment to contemplate just how far up shit creek we'd be if somebody out there had a mortar.

"Oh yeah, Musket. We fine."

"Acknowledged, Touch Hole. Taking departure. . . . Final advisory, you have movement in the surrounding streets. You have additional hostiles converging. . . . Good luck.''

What son of a bitch was it that said something about no good deed ever going unpunished?

Another voice cut in over the air-to-ground net. ''Understand you've got problems, Touch Hole.'' It was Saker Lead, the boss Harrier pilot. ''I hate to add to them, but we are in low-fuel state. If you want what we got, you'd better ask for it now.''

That was the best offer I'd had all morning. We were sixteen men stuck in the middle of an increasingly hostile city, and the faster we could end this fight, the better. For our side anyway.

''Roger that, Saker Leader. We want it all, right now.''

I tore a smoke grenade from my harness. Yanking the pin, I hurled it into the center of the compound yard, purple smoke boiling up from it. ''I am popping smoke. Targets are the buildings to the southeast and southwest of the embassy compound. I repeat, to the southeast and the southwest. The ones immediately across the converging boulevards from the compound walls. We have troop concentrations under cover. Can you take 'em out?''

''I see goofy grape, Touch Hole.''

''Roger, Saker. I confirm our goofy grape.''

''Acknowledged. I have a fix on the compound. Our load-out is two-hundred-and-fifty-pound GPs and Frags. I say again two-hundred-and-fifty-pound GPs and Frags. Your called drop is close! Way close!''

I'll tell the world it was. The rule of thumb in close air support is one yard or meter separation for every pound of high explosive per weapon, and those boulevards might be twenty-five yards wide at best.

I glanced up again at the heavy blast walls that surrounded the embassy. They were supposed to be proof against car and truck bombs. You had to wonder how they'd do against the real thing.

"We've got the hard cover to take it, Saker. Just, for Crissakes, don't get lateral!"

"Your call, Touch Hole. Positioning and rolling in now. You've got twenty seconds! This is gonna be mean!"

I dropped the mike and dragged Miller and Keyes back from the gate. *"Incoming!"* I bellowed over the crackle of the gunfire. *"Get down! Everybody get down!"*

Ribitisk took up the yell and relayed it before diving for cover himself. My guys on the wall dropped flat on the firing stage, each man trying to crawl inside his Kevlar helmet and body armor like a camo-clad turtle.

Then you could hear them coming, the moaning howl of the big Pegasus turbofans growing as the Harrier IIs fell out of the sky, diving in like a pair of falcons on a prairie dog village. These were Marines doing what they do better than anyone else in the world. Precision-guided munitions? Hell, we've had 'em since 1924, munitions precision guided on target, not by computers and electronic gismos, but by the skill and nerve of the Corps' aviators.

I could visualize the stumpy little fighters dragging in, the rooftops a blur beneath their bomb-laden bellies, the flight leader's eyes narrowing, his finger tightening on the release trigger, the bombs kicking off the ejector racks, braking balloons streaming behind them. . . .

The ground came up and slugged me in the gut and the whole damn world outside of the compound exploded. My ears screamed in agony and then shut down for the duration as the first blast rolled over the wall and a gigantic shotgun blast of dust and wreckage spewed in through the embassy gate. Five more detonations followed, shock waves radiating through the ground, striking with the impact of a hard-swung baseball bat, bouncing us a solid foot in the air. An entire palm tree flipped end over end into the compound, crashing down a few yards away, and the bolts holding one section of the firing stage sheered off, dumping a couple of my guys onto the embassy lawn.

Six chunks of hell . . . then an instant's pause. Saker Leader had taken out the buildings to the southeast. Now his wingman converged and killed the ones to the southwest. Six more explosions merged into the reverberations of the first half dozen, the two strikes blurring together into one continuous chaos of sound until you were sure you'd never hear quiet again.

And then it was over, but my ears were ringing so loud I couldn't hear the jets pulling away.

I rolled over and took a look out the gates.

Damn, I could have sworn there'd been a couple of streets out there.

There was no more gunfire either. If anyone was left alive out in that debris field, they didn't want to play anymore.

"Saker Leader, sir." Joey held out the mike and I pounded on the side of my head until I got an ear working.

"How'd we do, Touch Hole?" the aviator inquired.

Tiredly, I put my back against the wall. "On the mark, Saker. When we get back to Little Creek, I'll buy you a steak dinner and introduce you to my sister."

The Harrier jock chuckled. "Done deal, Touch Hole.

See you back on the ship. This is Saker Lead. We're out of here.''

We would be too, soon. The next last-helicopter-out would be showing up presently. But just for a minute, Joey, Keyes, and I lay sprawled at the base of the wall, catching up on being alive. Glancing up at the compound flagpole, I noticed that someone had forgotten to take down the big embassy flag. A little dusty and ragged maybe, but still flipping easily in the desert wind.

I decided to let it stay. Maybe it would remind the locals that while we might be pulling out for now, we'd be back again one of these days.

Keyes armed off his K-Pot and unzipped his body armor, letting the sweat steam out. "Sir," he said, "if you don't mind me saying so, and for what it's worth, I think you made a good call here. Even with all this, it was a good call.''

I cut a look over at him as he slouched back against the concrete. "Would you have done the same?''

"I don't know, sir." His grin flashed white against the dark of his face again. "I guess that's why I think it was a good call. I didn't have to make it.''

I laughed, so I guess I was still alive, and I fumbled out the drinking tube for the water pack in my MOLLE harness.

"Hey, Lieutenant," Joey cut in. "We got a confirmation from the ship. More air cover and another lift ship are en route. Battalion's also on the line for you. They say they've finally got a policy decision on the Ahazra deal.''

I took a long pull of warm, flat water and reached for the handset. Boy Howdy, and wasn't it going to be a pleasure telling them just exactly what they could do with it, too.

Stone Quillain will be serving with Captain Amanda Lee Garrett in the new James Cobb techno-thriller, Seafighter, *coming soon in hardback from G. P. Putnam's Sons.*

In the Hunter's Shadow

JAMES FERRO

James Ferro is the author of Hogs, *a series of military thrillers set during the Gulf War and published by Berkley. The books, which include* Going Deep *and* Hog Down, *are based on the actual missions flown by A-10A pilots during the conflict with Iraq. The short story in this collection features some of the characters from those books. He believes that the A-10A Thunderbolt II—better known as the "Warthog"—is the prettiest American warplane since the B-17G. While no Hog pilot was really credited with gunning down a MiG during the conflict, he says that's only because Saddam's pilots were chicken.*

1

NO MATTER HOW he held the shotgun, it felt awkward. Jack hadn't hunted in two years, and then it had been during a trip like this, a quick visit home before a new assignment with the Air Force, when hunting was just a sidelight, something to do in the morning before the football games got going and it felt okay to drink beers and lay around the house. As familiar as the steps along the old railroad bed were—Jack had first trailed his father and older brother across these rocks when he was three— he felt awkward and unsure, slightly off balance.

But he had often felt that way here. From his first days as a toddling tagalong, familiarity and comfort had mixed with doubt and fear in the tangled paths below the railhead. The fear had grown less distinct—he knew there were no monsters here now—but it was still there, part of being the second of two sons, part of what it meant to perpetually follow someone of accomplishment and poise. It had been many years since their dad taught them to hunt, years since he passed away; no one ever openly compared younger and older brother anymore, but Jack still felt an uneasy rumble in his stomach as they walked, sharp enough to make him pray he didn't overtly screw up.

Getting the first shot or the kill . . . even in the days when he was hunting regularly, that would have been too much to ask.

Jack's brother, Mark, stopped and waited for him to catch up.

"You want some coffee?" Mark asked, unscrewing the top of the steel container.

"Drink any more coffee and I'll have to pee," he told him.

Mark nodded. He poured himself out a half cup, then sat on the edge of the embankment. Steam plumed into the air, and Jack was tempted to say he'd changed his mind. But if he took a leak when they were in the woods, his older brother would blame him if they didn't see any deer. So Jack took out some gum instead, wadding it in his mouth and chewing furiously.

His brother leaned back, eyes studying the fog as it lifted slowly from the woods. He was a doctor, as their father had been. There were a lot of other similarities— the way he stared at things, for instance; the way he drank his coffee.

And the way he pushed himself and expected others to do the same. He had high standards.

Not that that was a bad thing.

"You anxious to get over there?" Mark asked.

"Anxious?" Jack gave a little laugh. Not only was it an odd question, but it seemed like the sort of word he'd use telling one of his patients that yes, she really was going to have a baby. "I don't know if I'm going to the Gulf or not."

"You think you are or you wouldn't be here."

In fact, the squadron's director of operations had already gotten the back channel word that Jack's squadron of A-10A Warthog fighter-bombers were headed to Saudi Arabia and the war zone; the orders would be cut in a day or two, if they hadn't been already. Jack had even borrowed a beeper so he could get back to his squadron in time. He was considered a low-time flier, someone without a lot of experience who could be easily bumped from the lineup; he didn't want that to happen. It was wrong to hope for war, so he didn't—but if things happened, he wanted to be one of the guys with their hand wrapped around a Hog's stick, cranking through the lead and spoon-feeding Saddam a little American justice.

"So?" asked Mark, repeating his question. "You anxious?"

"You trying to ask me if I'm scared?" Jack said.

"I know you're not scared. You're not scared of anything."

"Well, that's not true." Jack sat down on the edge of the embankment, perching the unloaded shotgun against his leg, barrel downwards. "I'm scared of a lot of things."

"Like what? Getting shot down?"

Not at all, Jack thought. Won't happen.

Getting hit or dying was too theoretical, too far away. He couldn't explain why; if he tried, it would sound like he was just full of himself. He wasn't, so he said nothing.

What Jack worried about was screwing up, letting someone down. That was close enough to fear.

He didn't explain that either.

When Jack first qualified to fly fighters, he had tried to describe how it felt to his brother. A certain sheen came over Mark's face, as if his expression were encased in glass. The distant look wasn't disinterest, but it wasn't encouragement either.

It didn't mean that Mark didn't care about his brother. It meant that he was still disappointed, or maybe bewildered, that Jack hadn't become a doctor as he had.

He would have denied it if Jack pointed it out, so he didn't. There wasn't anything to do about it. He left it there and Mark left it there, both knowing it was something they wouldn't bother talking about.

And so when it loomed, as it did now, it was better to deflect it with a joke.

"I'm scared Saddam will back down before I get there," said Jack.

Mark gave a noncommittal snort. "I'd rather we didn't go to war," he said, still in his doctor's voice. "Killing people's not a great thing."

"War's not a great thing," agreed Jack. He waited for Mark to say something else, maybe about Kuwait or oil. What he meant was probably how ridiculous it would be if he got shot down, but that he wouldn't say.

Mark concentrated on his coffee.

Looking at them as kids, most people would never have guessed Jack would become a pilot. Mark maybe. He'd always been the more aggressive one, the first son, the boy meant to do something in the world. But then, being a pilot wouldn't have been enough for him.

A flight surgeon, maybe.

Jack was supposed to be the sensitive one. Quiet, which was definitely true. All his teachers used to say he'd make a great doctor. Mark, on the other hand— Mark they would predict big things for, great things. Had his dad lived, he surely would have been surprised— pleasantly, but still surprised—to find him still here in this small town practicing small-town medicine.

"Sure you won't have any coffee?" Mark asked.

"No, thanks."

"Let's get going, then." Mark stood up. He screwed the cup back onto the steel cylinder. Carefully, he checked his vest and his gun. "You okay?"

"I'm ready."

"You got to pee, do it now."

"I'm ready."

Mark nodded, gave him a thumbs-up, and led the way down the embankment. Their spot was about a half-hour's walk. They wouldn't speak the whole way there, probably no more than a grunt or a nod the whole morning until they found a buck, or gave up trying. Talking warned the good ones away.

The brothers plunged into the woods and the fog, Mark in the lead, Jack some paces behind. They walked as they had for years, deliberately, silently. Mark's head swayed slightly as he examined the spaces between the trees. Every so often he double-checked the wind—easy because the leaves were rustling—to make sure they weren't giving their scents away.

Jack gradually fell further and further behind, as always. And just as it had on his very first hikes, his mind began to wander. It was on walks such as these that he had first begun to imagine himself at the stick of a fighter plane. The old habits of imagination returned now. The mist dissolved into the light gray of an early morning desert sky; he began hunting tanks instead of deer.

The A-10A Warthogs—"Hogs" to their "drivers," or pilots—were ground-attack planes that flew incredibly low, five hundred feet routinely. That low in an ordinary plane, even a shotgun might bring you down. But the Hog was something special, designed from Day One as a mud-fighting, tank-busting son of a bitch, growling at antiair the way a lion might growl at a mouse. Thickly armored, it was designed not only to survive but to twist and turn better than a dirt bike while flying at treetop level. A Hog running over these woods now, cranking through the fog, could jink with the trail, plunge down over the pond, nail whatever buck was standing by the edge of the stream, then pull a one-eighty and disappear.

Something snapped in the woods to their right. Both men stopped short, waiting, straining to see through the fog and thick trees.

Nothing.

Nothing, still.

Mark motioned with his hand. They began moving forward again, slower than before, Jack paying more attention to his surroundings.

Mark never bragged when he got a buck. Jack certainly didn't. They weren't competitive in that way. But then, Mark didn't have to be—he nearly always got the first deer, just as he had always done things first and maybe slightly better when they were growing up.

Jack wouldn't feel he had beaten his brother if he got the kill. But missing or screwing up would be hell. It would mean yet one more round as the perpetual kid brother, the boy in the hunter's shadow, a six-year-old who had to be protected from bullies.

Worse: the six-year-old who had to have his shoelaces tied.

The rising sun stroked the fog, relentlessly teasing its curls, seducing it and then burning it into thin wisps. The wet scent of the air began to fall away, even as Mark and Jack approached the edge of the large pond where they always had the best success. The fall had been warmer than usual, and a few leaves still clung to some of the trees. Looking up, Jack noticed something he had never seen before, or at least had no memory of seeing—literally hundreds of tiny spiderwebs stood like nets in the highest branches, set to catch insects carried along by the breeze. The filaments glowed silver, and he realized that the woods were filled with them, each tree rigged with a dozen or more traps. Though their sizes varied, their geometry was the same; thin lines worked together to form a circle in the air, an almost invisible snare for their prey.

It was impossible for a combat pilot not to think of them as radar nets. But the webs were all empty, and as he watched them glitter Jack forgot about the metaphor, instead admiring how carefully they had been constructed, how thin and yet sturdy they were. The webs were beautiful—if not high art, hints of something transcendent.

He realized they must have been here every time he had hunted through the years, and wondered why he had never been observant enough to notice them. Maybe his eyes, honed now to detect even the slightest anomaly in the air as he flew, were sharper. Or maybe when he was younger he concentrated so much on getting deer that even a billboard would have escaped him.

The pond was only a few hundred feet away. Mark stopped at the edge of the trail, waiting for him to catch up. They were now ready to hunt, and they loaded up silently. Finished, Mark eased forward through the brush to a path that just skirted the swampy edge of the water and led to a meadow beyond. Reeds and rushes grew thick on his left, separating the trail from the edge of the water.

It had been a particularly wet year. Mud oozed around Jack's boots as he followed. One step echoed with a loud suck; he found the rocks and started up the slight incline to the clearing. But as he looked up, he nearly fell backwards from shock—a large brown shape was falling directly toward him from the sky.

Jack felt something like a 9-g pull in his chest, air sucked out by shock.

A full second passed before he realized it was a goose. The bird was oblivious to him, descending from the clear sky into the fog toward the water a few yards away. It held its wings out in a gull-like shape as it glided silently toward the water, disappearing beyond the tall punks.

Jack had seen geese here many, many times before, but something—the shock of the unexpected moment, perhaps—made this very different. It was at once beautiful and mundane, the bird so close to him he might have touched it and yet so far away it existed in another reality altogether, one he was lucky just to glimpse.

If it weren't for the splash, Jack might have thought he imagined it. He took two steps up the embankment, just enough to see into the pond. An entire squadron of geese were positioned across the surface, arrayed as a combat package ready to meet any threat.

They should have gone south weeks ago, he thought as he stared at them.

Damn ugly birds.

And yet not ugly at all. Their black masks and gray bodies seemed to glow in the fog, their bodies rounded with a symmetry of poise and power. The geese—perhaps twenty of them—floated like self-possessed angels waiting for some task to call them to action.

Suddenly, the spell broke. The birds erupted from the

lake, moving as one with a quick snap of their wings.
The loud report of his brother's gun followed. Jack turned
and saw a huge buck not twenty yards from him, rushing
away in the woods.

Any other time, he could have snapped his shotgun up
and nailed the deer; he had a pilot's reflexes, was a good
shot and standing at close range. But he didn't move. He
didn't want to; killing the big buck would have somehow
destroyed what he'd just seen.

He heard a curse, another blast. Both the deer and the
birds got clean away.

"Son of a bitch, didn't you see that buck?" Mark
asked, running up. "Son of a bitch. Twelve points, I
swear to God. Shit. Fourteen, maybe. I missed him bad.
Damn. Why didn't you shoot? You were right here. You
had him. Damn."

Brought back to reality, Jack felt something like shock
that his brother had missed. He'd always been such a
good shot, much better than him.

"Why didn't you nail him?" Mark asked again.

It seemed stupid to tell him about the geese.

"It took me by surprise," he told his brother. "I
haven't hunted in so long."

"You? By surprise? Shit. Twelve points. What crap
luck. We'll never get anything now. Shit. Right there."

They stayed out for another three hours, slowly working
their way around the edge of the meadow, back down
around the pond, and up a stream to two different spots
where they had had luck in the past. But they didn't even
come close to seeing anything worth a shot. They walked
back to the house in silence, where Mark's wife and son
were waiting for them. The rest of the day they hung

around, drank a little, and watched football. By the time
the beeper buzzed with the prearranged code telling him
the orders were coming through, Jack was more or less
ready to leave anyway.

2

JANUARY 1991
OVER SOUTHERN IRAQ

ALL HE COULD see were clouds. Thick tufts of gray filled
his canopy and worse, much worse, clogged his targeting
screen. The Maverick air-to-ground missiles were potent,
intelligent weapons, but they weren't worth crap if they
couldn't see the target. And they couldn't see it now.

Jack blew a wad of air out of his lungs and glanced
at the heads-up display's altimeter ladder. He was descending through twelve thousand feet, getting lower than
they had planned. Damn clouds went on forever.

"Devil Two, where are you?" The radio call came
from Captain Thomas "Doberman" Glenon, Jack's flight
leader. A few minutes before, Doberman had completed
his own attack against a similar emplacement just to the
east. Jack had covered him while he found a good hole
in the clouds; it looked like every one of his missiles
slammed home.

Jack ignored the radio call, holding his stick tighter
than a beer bottle at last call as the A-10A continued
toward the earth. Eleven thousand, ten thousand feet, and
the clouds were thicker than ever.

The big A-10 shook beneath him. Turbulence or something. Jack let it register in his upper chest somewhere,
focused on the four-inch television screen in the upper

right-hand quadrant of his dashboard slaved to the electro-optical seeker in the Maverick AGM-65B's nose.

Nothing, nothing, nothing.

Damn, damn, damn.

Somewhere below the muck, five or six pieces of heavy artillery were arrayed like the print of a puppy's paw. Somewhere down there, Saddam's finest were lining up their guns to take out an Army encampment just south of the border. Somewhere down there, the first military target he'd ever aimed at in anger was waving a big "hit me" sign.

Lieutenant Jack Gladstone had four Mavericks, along with a quartet of Mark 20 Rockeye cluster bombs, all signed, sealed, and ready to deliver. If he could just find a damn hole in the clouds.

Eight thousand feet. He was nearly low enough to be heard. Pretty soon he'd be within range of their antiair weapons, briefed as old but still nasty Russian ZSU-23s. The four-barrel flak dealers sat on armored vehicles and could be aimed by radar or eyesight.

Neither AWACS, the airborne radar and control ship flying far behind the lines, nor his own on-board radar warning receiver reported any threats. Either nobody knew he was aiming at them, or they were smart enough to wait until he was in range.

"Devil Two?"

The cloud cover broke just as he went to push the mike and finally tell his flight leader he couldn't find the target. Jack put all his attention on the Maverick television screen, thumbing the targeting cursor toward the middle of the screen.

But the clouds bunched back in the way before he could lock. He held tight but they seemed to get even thicker. He realized he was low—too low. He began breaking off and then his radar warning system went crazy and the Hog started shaking. In an instant, everybody in Iraq knew where he was, and wanted a piece of him.

Jack yanked his stick. His head slapped back hard against the thinly padded seat.

People began shouting at him. Missiles and bullets and bombs and doom—the world spun into a whirlpool beyond his control. Blood poured out his fingers, down his arms into his chest and stomach. He was beyond dizzy; he was gone, brain, body, and soul shriveled into a fried raisin hurtling through the air.

The Hog caught him. The big warplane wrapped him in its titanium cocoon and shuttled him through the exploding minefield. Steadying her wings, she goaded her twin GE powerplants for more giddy-up, then rocketed straight over the artillery encampment, wagging her tail at the antiair guns. She flashed nearly ninety degrees, ducking a fresh barrage, then yanked her head up to get away.

By the time Jack recovered enough of his senses to feel he might be in control, he was back in the clouds. The first thing he did was look at the arms of his flightsuit, expecting them to be stained dark with blood.

They weren't. Slowly he realized he wasn't bleeding, just sweating.

A lot. His hands, especially.

That had never happened to him before.

Check that. It had happened once. First time he ever went hunting. Sweat so bad he couldn't grip the gun right.

Missed a good buck. Eight-pointer, at least.

The deer was maybe twenty yards away, easy to hit,

a perfect trophy for a first-timer—a good trophy, really, for any hunter.

He sighted, had the shot.

His fingers slipped. The shot went wild, buckshot hitting trees well before his mark. He choked back a rush of bile to his mouth, angry and humiliated as the deer bounded off.

Mark nailed it a half-second later.

Jack moved his eyes deliberately around the cockpit, then worked them outside to survey the damage. He was sure he'd see large gaps of sheet metal gone, but everything was still there. The instruments were all pegged perfectly at spec. He hadn't been hit. Or if he had, it hadn't been serious.

What the hell had happened? His damn stomach was still doing flips, and sweat oozed from every pore.

Especially his fingers. They would have been drier under a faucet.

"Two, this is Doberman. Are you all right?"

"Uh, I'm fine," he managed.

"Climb over the clouds," his flight leader told him. "Key your mike."

The radios in the A-10As could act as primitive direction finders by homing in on one another's signal. Jack did as he was told, taking the Hog up over the cloud cover. By now he was well south of his objective. He'd completely blown the attack.

"All right, I got you," said Doberman as he broke through the clouds. "You hit?"

"Nothing serious," he managed.

"Saddle up. We're going to Al Jouf."

"I still have a full load."

If Doberman was surprised that Jack had blown it so

badly—as he had every right to be—he didn't let on. He simply told Jack to follow him to the airstrip at the forward operating area as planned.

When they landed at the Al Jouf forward operating area in northwestern Saudi Arabia about an hour later, Jack was ready to have his ass reamed. He knew he'd blown it; clouds or no clouds, flak or no flak, he should have been able to get a shot off.

But Doberman said nothing. Worse, a careful inspection of Jack's airplane revealed no damage; the plane looked like it had just rolled out of a detail shop. For all the lead the Iraqis had dished out, not one shell had exploded near enough to singe the paint.

The two pilots squatted side by side on the tarmac for more than a minute, staring at the underside of the plane. Finally, Jack muttered something about the clouds.

Lame.

Glenon nodded but said nothing. That made him feel even worse.

When word came that their second mission of the day had been put on hold because of the weather north, Glenon went to check with the local squadron commander about contingencies. Jack found his way to a tarp where two other members of the Devil squadron, Captain "Shotgun" O'Rourke and Lieutenant Sam Wells, were passing the time playing cards. It was a complicated game Shotgun had invented, a cross between War and Go Fish that only he seemed to know the rules to. Fortunately for Wells, they weren't playing for money.

Yet.

"Hey, Killer," said Shotgun. "We flying this afternoon or what?"

Jack shrugged. He didn't particularly like being called Killer; Shotgun had given him the nickname when he killed two scorpions the first night after they arrived at King Fahd, their home base in Saudi Arabia. Shotgun meant it as a benign joke; that was the way he was. But coming from anyone else, "Killer" seemed like a put-down. Most everybody still called him Jack, which was fine with him.

"Where's Doberman?" asked Wells.

"Went to see the CO. Find out about the weather." Jack plopped into one of the fabric-and-steel seats.

Shotgun slid his cards together and announced that he was going to go find himself some coffee over in the Special Ops area. "I'll be back," he said, walking away.

"He's really going to drink coffee before flying again?" Jack asked.

"Are you kidding? He flies with a thermos of it," Wells told him.

"No way."

"I swear."

"How'd your mission go?" Jack asked him.

"Shacked everything there. Even creamed an anthill or two. Shotgun says he's going to put me in for a medal."

It was meant as a joke, but Jack couldn't manage a laugh. Shotgun and Wells had hit another artillery park west of his; if anything, the clouds there should have been worse.

"How'd you guys do?" Wells asked.

Jack frowned but said nothing. Wells, another low-time lieutenant, didn't press it. Instead he changed the subject, talking about, of all things, the letters he'd written to be sent home in case he died. He wanted his relatives to party their butts off in his honor.

"There are major life insurance policies out on me," he told Jack. "My uncle bought them when I was born, see? Whole family is going to be rich."

"Doesn't war negate that?"

"Nah. No way." Wells dug his hands into his pockets. "I don't think so. I told my mom to blow ten thousand on a big party with all my high school friends," he continued. "And my teachers. Definitely them, too. In-their-face kind of thing, 'cause they never thought I'd go anywhere. Serious party instead of a funeral. No funeral. Then—each of my old girlfriends gets five thousand. Except for Kathy Haasman. I didn't get any, so she doesn't either."

Wells was looking for an appreciative laugh, but Jack only nodded. He kept seeing the damn clouds in front of him.

"I told my dad, I want him to buy a Lincoln. Piece of crap car if you ask me, but he's always wanted one. What about you?" asked Wells. "You want anything?"

"From you?"

"Damn straight. I'm worth a ton of money dead. I mean, we may be talking a million bucks, maybe two. My uncle was kind of vague." Wells spit into the sand.

"You planning on getting shot down?"

"No way. But it's good luck to talk about it. Get it? So what do you want?"

Jack thought for a moment. "How about your bike?"

Wells had somehow managed to transport a mountain bike to Saudi.

"Sorry. Promised that to my sister."

"She'll be rich," said Jack, trying to catch some of

Wells's enthusiasm. "She can buy twenty."

"Yeah, but see, the bike is good luck," Wells told him. "So she's got to get it. If you saw her, you'd know what I mean. She needs a lot of luck."

Jack laughed.

"So what did you say?" Wells asked.

"I didn't say anything."

"No, in your letter."

"Nothing," said Jack.

"Nothing?"

"I didn't write a letter."

"You shitting me? You haven't written one letter?" Wells leaned from his chair and took the barest of sips from a canteen. "Nothing?"

"Nope." Jack folded his arms across his flightsuit. "I've never written a letter in my life."

"Wow."

"What? You gonna tell me it's bad luck not to?" he asked.

Wells took him seriously. "You bet. Don't mention it to Shotgun. He's really superstitious, even more than me. Yesterday he made me throw salt over my shoulder 'cause I stepped on a cement crack."

Jack snorted. "Maybe that's what screwed up the weather."

"More likely it was you not writing a letter. You ought to at least write, you know, a good-bye letter. It's a good-luck thing. If you write it, you won't need it."

"Screwy logic."

Wells shook his head. "You shouldn't screw with luck."

Come to think of it, his luck had been kind of crappy. Like Wells, Jack had had to sit out the first few days of the air war, passed over in favor of more experienced fliers. But Wells had gotten into the mix on the fourth day, going north on a battlefield interdiction mission. Jack had also been scheduled to fly that day, but his Hog scratched when one of the gauges read serious engine problems just before takeoff.

Turned out, the gauge was screwy. Even though he'd done the right thing, Jack cursed himself; he wished he'd ignored it and just taken off. In the ten days since things got rolling, his plane was the 535th Tactical Fighter Squadron's only scratch.

But maybe things would have been worse if he had flown.

Damn, was he chicken or what?

"Colonel Knowlington said the letters were an order," said Wells. "The letters are supposed to be on file, I think. Or at least someplace where he and the death committee can get them."

Jack shrugged. Neither Knowlington, who was the squadron's commander, nor anyone else had pressed the issue with him.

"You ought to write somebody a letter," insisted Wells. "Not that it's going to be sent or anything, just to have. It's not what you say that's important. It's doing it. You can't screw with luck. I'm serious. I heard Mongoose writes a different letter to his wife every night. Tears up the old one and starts fresh. That's what kept his karma going when he got hit."

"I'm not married."

"Write your mom, then."

Jack looked out into the blank Saudi desert. It was hard to tell from here that they were at war, much less that people had been shooting at him not two hours before.

"You think we'll fly this afternoon or not?" Jack asked.

"We do, we don't, all the same," said Wells.

"I want to." He reached over and took Wells's canteen, took his own sip. He wondered how Wells had felt on his first mission—whether his stomach had turned, too. But he didn't feel like he could ask that directly. "Think it'll be hairy?" he said instead.

"Depends."

"Was it hairy the other day?"

"A little. Took me a second to realize I was getting shot at. That shook me a little. Then I was O.K."

Jack nodded. He thought about telling Wells what had happened, but quickly waved the idea away. What purpose would it serve?

"What do you think about flying wing for Glenon?" he asked instead.

"He's okay. What did you think?"

"I don't know if I can keep up," said Jack.

"What? Fuck you."

"I'm just a low-time guy and he's Glenon."

"That supposed to mean something?" Wells asked.

"He's a damn good pilot. Shit, he's the best in the wing."

"Shotgun's pretty good," said Wells. "And Mongoose."

"Doberman nearly bagged a Mirage the first day of the air war. And he brought that plane back with half a wing. I'd piss in my pants, that happened to me."

"Yeah, can't argue with that." Wells shrugged. "He's

got the touch. Except in cards. Ever play poker with him?''

"Just once. But Dixon cleaned everyone out.''

"Dixon's a lucky fuck." Wells's voice had just a hint of admiration; on the second day of the air war, Lieutenant B. J. Dixon had nailed an Iraqi helicopter in an air-to-air furball. He was a pretty good pilot but getting the helo was definitely a luck thing. "Anyway, Glenon's easy to fly with. You shouldn't get intimidated. If he didn't think you were good, you wouldn't be on his six.''

"I don't know.''

"He just wants you to hit your marks, that's all. Shit, you think Glenon's tough, you try flying with Shotgun.''

"Shotgun? He seems pretty easygoing.''

"Oh, I'm not talking about the mission itself. Not that.'' Wells laughed. "I mean, shit, he knows what he's doing, but he's unique. Damn, we're just about to mix it up this morning, he comes on the squadron frequency and I can't hear him because his stereo's too loud.''

"His stereo?''

"He's got a CD wired into his flightsuit. Plays it all the time.''

"On a bombing mission?''

"Yup.''

Shotgun had flown practically to Baghdad to rescue another pilot a few days ago. He definitely had the right stuff—but he was certainly, as Wells put it, "unique." Or just a touch crazy.

Then again, his hands probably never sweated when it was time to pull the trigger.

"Anyway, you ought to write a letter to somebody,'' said Wells. "For luck.''

"Man, let it go.''

"Your mom, at least."

"My mom died when I was five," Jack told him.

"Father, then."

"Passed away when I was in high school. The only person I could write a letter to is my brother," Jack said. "What the hell should I say to him?"

"Don't you like him?"

"He's my brother. Of course I do."

"So you ought to write."

Jack shrugged. "He knows I like him."

"You're missing the point."

"The point is, I'm not getting shot down."

"Yeah, no shit," said Doberman, appearing behind them. "Come on, grab your gear. We're flying." He was short, even for a fighter jock, and weighed barely 130, but he snapped his words with a viciousness that justified his nickname.

"What's up?" asked Jack, scrambling to his feet.

"Clouds or not, we're going back north," said Glenon. "That artillery site just started lobbing shells at one of our patrols."

Snugging himself into the cockpit, Jack felt his stomach churn. He worked through the preflight checklist, went over his navigational settings, examined his map, all the while trying to choke back the bile. He hadn't felt this nervous taking off this morning, not at all.

He told himself to relax. This time he'd have a clear view of the target. This time he'd nail it.

Everything had been carefully drawn up. All he had to do was follow Glenon, push the buttons, go home.

The Hog seemed to agree. Her engines cranked up sweetly, every indicator at precise specification.

Jack watched Glenon's Hog start down the runway ahead of him. He took a breath, checked his instruments one last time, then let her rip, edging the plane's pug nose toward the sky.

Officially, the A-10A was called the Thunderbolt II, in honor of World War II's fabulous P-47. Nobody called it that, but as ideas from the brass went, it wasn't a particularly bad one. Though designed as a long-range fighter, the original Thunderbolt had proven herself a fantastic mud-mover, helping Americans break out of the hedgerows in Normandy after D-Day. Called "Jabos" by the Germans, the tough little planes wrecked havoc with 500-pound bombs and heavy machine-guns. The generals in charge of the A-10 project probably figured congressmen would remember the P-47 when it came time to fund its namesake.

The original Thunderbolt wasn't particularly pretty, especially if compared to sleek contemporaries like the P-51 Mustang. But its modern-day replacement was a hell of a lot uglier—so ugly, in fact, that it had quickly earned the nickname "Warthog," which in turn was shortened by most pilots and crew members to "Hog." Unlike the real Thunderbolt, the plane was comparatively slow and had no hope of holding its own as an interceptor or fighter escort. With straight, stubby wings, high-mounted engines, a forked tail, and avionics largely designed before its pilots were born, the A-10A seemed not only ugly but out of place in the contemporary air wars, where speed and high-tech wizardry were prized. But nothing in the allied inventory could support troops so well. At low altitudes the Hog was incredibly maneuverable, with two-piece ailerons and a rudder so tight a pilot could parallel park. She could pack more iron below her wings than most of the heavy bombers the P-47 was designed to escort, and was the only plane in the Air Force that was really any good at firing Maverick missiles, tank-busting smart weapons that could dust everything from radar installations to main battle tanks and even Scud missiles.

But the favorite weapon of any Hog driver was the 30 mm Avenger cannon that sat in the Hog's nose. The Gatling gun spat its uranium shells so fiercely that it could literally push the Hog backwards in the air, holding the plane in place as its pilot worked the rudder pedals to tattoo his name into a target.

She might be slower and uglier than anything flying, but the Hog was, pound for pound and dollar for dollar, the most ferocious warbird in the Gulf.

Jack felt some of that ferocity as he climbed upwards after Glenon. The beast wanted to fly. Glenon checked in with their airborne controller to the south, an AWACS E-3 Sentry. Equipped with a powerful radar, the modified 707 scanned the sky for enemy interceptors, keeping tabs on the American flights and potential threats.

A good wedge of clouds lay ahead, once more thickening as they made their way north. The clouds brought some of Jack's flutters back; he edged his teeth against his bottom lip, trying to steady away the bile. There was a lot of enemy territory between them and the artillery, a lot of guys with weapons who didn't like them too much.

Lightning jagged in a furious leap across a pair of black, tufted pillows about two miles northwest as he climbed. An A-10A pilot from a different squadron had told Jack about getting caught in a lightning storm while deploying to the Gulf from Europe. The jock had lost all of his instruments—not a real fun thing under any circumstances, but especially in the middle of the night in a thunderstorm. The pilot had kept his head and managed to find another member of his flight, following him until—for no apparent reason—the Hog's instruments snapped back to life.

Jack wondered if he'd be lucky enough to have the instruments come back. Probably not.

Maybe Wells was on to something with this luck thing. Even Shotgun had a lucky charm he carried with him.

It wasn't a rabbit's foot. It was customized .45. But to each his own.

The planes trucked across the border, rising over the clouds and continuing toward twenty thousand feet. For a loaded Hog, twenty thousand feet was just about outer space. The plane took forever to get there, and wasn't particularly pleased about it, either. She was built to be a mudder, and no amount of cooing about safety calmed her.

Jack didn't mind having a good margin between him and any potential peashooters, though.

"Devil One to Devil Two, we're going to take that jog in zero-two minutes," Doberman said over the squadron frequency. "Level off at twenty thousand feet."

"Copy that," Jack acknowledged.

The maneuver was a simple turn, a dogleg due west and then a sharp jab back north to avoid the area where an SA-6 battery had been operating yesterday. Weasels—specially outfitted F-4 Phantoms tasked to strike surface-to-air missile sites—had staked out the area but Doberman wasn't positive that the radar had been neutralized. The precautionary maneuver was a simple one, giving the missiles plenty of space while still remaining more or less in a straight line toward their artillery park.

The Hog whined. The plane seemed as alive as its pilot, a medieval horse bred to take her knight to battle. She pretended to catch an impurity in her engine, fussing as they made the turn. What she was really doing was protesting: The SA-6 was a mean missile, deadly at the altitude they were flying at, but fairly clueless below fifty meters. The A-10A was simply reminding her pilot that was where she ought to be.

Doberman held the new course for precisely ninety seconds, then wagged his tail back. Jack hustled to follow, keeping the plane in a combat trail, shadowing along a half mile behind his commander's wing. He wanted to be perfect; he had to be perfect. Doberman was counting on him.

The artillery was about five minutes due north. By now the AWACS had reported that it had stopped firing. But that wasn't going to win it a reprieve.

The clouds began to scatter; they were already beyond the worst of the front.

This time it was going to be easy.

Jack worked his eyes around the cockpit, making sure everything was perfect. The Hog's office reflected not only the era it had been designed in but the budgetary constraints on the post-Vietnam military; unlike the sleek multiuse video screens in state-of-the-art sleds like the F/A-18, the A-10's vitals were displayed on old-fashioned clockfaces; you tickled her gizzards by wiggling toggles and dials. The Maverick targeting screen was smaller than a squint and the heads-up display in front of the pilot the product of an earlier generation. It wouldn't take a Vietnam Phantom pilot—or even someone who flew Sabres in Korea—too long to get comfortable with the equipment. Even an old Thunderbolt pilot would find things familiar. Hell, the biggest adjustment for the jet jocks would be getting used to how slow the Hog flew; the Thunderbolt was nearly as fast.

But this was the only combat plane Jack had ever really known. It felt comfortable, an extension of his arms and legs—flying the Hog wasn't just flying, it was a way of thinking. He saw himself somewhere in the air, and went.

This morning that connection had gotten screwed up. But that had been temporary, a flutter he was beyond now. He was back in control. And the truth was, bottom-line, he'd hung in there, come through all that flak as smoothly as anyone. Hogs didn't fly themselves. They didn't even have automated pilots for routine cruises.

It was the clouds, he told himself. They were what screwed me up this morning. Fog of war. They're gone now, or at least a hell of a lot thinner.

Easy pickin's down there.

He turned and glanced back at the sky they'd come through, pulling a routine check of their six, making sure a boogie carrying the magic BB wasn't somehow sneaking up on them. He was the perfect wingman, precise, ready, standing in the shadows and guarding his leader like a member of the Secret Service.

"Zero-one minutes to our target coordinates," said Doberman. "You ready, kid?"

"Copy," snapped Jack.

"Okay, we're going to do this exactly like we drew it up," said Doberman. "We slide into our orbit, I get the first pass, you get my back."

Jack acknowledged. The plan was a wheeling attack over the guns, one of the most basic but effective tactics for a two-ship of A-10As attacking from medium altitude.

The planes would fly a large circle around their target, opposite each other. One would attack while the other played linebacker, calling out defenses and watching for anything unexpected. They'd fire their Mavericks, then make a run with the cluster bombs. With the broken cloud cover, they shouldn't have to go below nine or ten thousand feet, well above the effective range of the ZSU-23s.

A chicken shoot. Easier than a practice drill, and Jack had done a hundred of those.

And always done well.

Doberman goaded his mount, trading some altitude for speed as he fell into the attack pattern. Jack felt bile rising in his stomach, but his arms and legs were loose. His gloves and flightsuit had dried out long ago. He could do this.

He was doing this.

"Eyeball them first," Doberman said, meaning to find the target visually before looking for it in the Maverick's targeting screen. It may have been a reminder to himself rather than Jack—he was the one in the shooting slot, after all.

Jack started to acknowledge when his transmission was run over by another broadcast. It was the AWACS controller.

They were being waved off the bomb run. Something much more important had come up.

Something another seventy miles deeper in Iraq, back to the northeast, back through the thickest clouds.

A group of British SAS commandos had been airlifted north of the border to search the low hills for suspected Scud sites two days before. Now the Special Air Service troops were in danger of being run over by a dozen Iraqi tanks.

"We're on it," Jack heard Doberman say. He had to yank the stick hard and put the throttle through the firewall to keep up as his flight leader corrected to the new course.

Jack felt the trickle of sweat starting between his fingers as Doberman tried the hail again. They ought to be right on top of the British troops, close enough to pick up their radios. Hell, he could probably just crack open the cockpit bubble and yell down to them. But there was no response.

Maybe it had all been a mistake, Jack thought. Maybe it was a dream and he was back in his cot at King Fahd.

Maybe they were too late.

"Let's take it straight down," said Doberman. "Follow me."

Jack hesitated a split second as Doberman's plane disappeared from view. Then he too tucked his wing, hunkering in the cockpit as the Hog plunged into the thick gray tundra of the clouds, falling from the calm safety of the open sky into the roiling currents of hell. The air was more violent than what he'd flown through this morning, more violent than anything he'd come up against, boiling against the plane's stubby wings as she sought the earth. Sweat surged from his fingers, and the small fire burning at the edge of his stomach exploded into his chest, flames torching his windpipe as bile bubbled into his mouth. Jack fought to hold the plane steady, focusing his attention on flying, altitude bleeding, speed building, wings trembling with the rage of the storm front.

Somewhere in the back of his mind he realized that the turbulence was not half or even a quarter of what his senses were making of it; somewhere in the back of his mind he realized fear was magnifying his perception of it. He told himself to relax, told himself this was all going to be over in just a few minutes—all he had to do was hit his marks.

The weather was immense. Jack didn't break below the clouds until roughly 3,500 feet. Still, he had done fine. Doberman was close ahead, angling to the north.

The radio snapped to life, a strange mixture of curses with an English tang to them tickling his ears.

"This is Brown Bear Thirteen to Devil Flight. We are chuffed to the fuck to have you lads aboard," cracked the British radioman.

Doberman took that as a compliment and asked the SAS soldier to key his mike so the Hogs could locate them. Jack scanned ahead, sorting the blotches of landscape into patterns his brain could understand. They were running up a crease of low-ranging hills, desert or at least open ground off their right wings. The blotches got heavier ahead, and the Euphrates River or one of its tributaries was dead on in his windshield. The Hogs had come very far north, a hell of a lot further than they had any right to fly; all sorts of antiair defenses and at least one serious airfield were within spitting distance.

The British commando tried to orient the two planes using a nearby highway; the SAS team was two clicks north of a sharp bend, hugging an irrigation ditch. One of their Land Rover 110s was on fire.

And if the Americans couldn't see that, there were a good dozen tanks arrayed in front of them, bugger-fucking the hillside with dynamite enemas.

The rest of his transmission was drowned out by gunfire.

"There, up there. Off your left wing, like, eleven

o'clock, just in front of the heavy weather," Jack said, spotting two billows of black smoke. Something percolated to their east; more tanks.

"Yeah," said Doberman. "No time to make this pretty. I'm going left. Take the stuff on your side. Watch that ditch."

Jack understood immediately, as if Doberman's short sentence had downloaded an entire battle plan into his head. This was what it meant to belong—it was like hunting with his brother, knowing where to go and what to do without being told.

His eyes shot through the cockpit glass, separating the approaching blurs into targets. He burned a trio of black shadows into his retinas, put his eyes over to the Maverick's small screen, pulled the Hog up as he found a better firing position for the missiles. The Maverick viewer was at its widest angle—six degrees; it took a half second to find his triangle of tanks, another two-thirds to swing down to the narrower view and still have it all there, pretty as a training manual, the lead tank fat and juicy for the cursor.

He recognized the long barrel from a hundred practice missions, the blur materializing into a T-72 main battle tank, a serious piece of Russian hamburger, forty-one tons of wedged steel with a 125 mm smoothbore that just now launched another hunk of explosives at the men he'd come to protect. Jack riveted the cursor on the tank turret and fired. The Maverick dropped from the wing, its rocket motor igniting with a quick flourish as the missile contemplated the best route of attack. Deciding that the shortest route was always the best, she galloped forward at just under Mach 2, the Thiokol solid-fuel rocket burning in earnest. The missile crested and fell square onto the top of the Iraqi tank's turret, where her 125-pound shaped explosive charge smashed through the relatively thin metal. The warhead incinerated the three-man crew in less than three seconds after impact.

By the time his first missile hit home, Jack had dialed up and launched a second. As he aimed a third Maverick, he realized he was pushing too close; he rushed the shot, sliding immediately into a banking turn only four hundred meters from the Iraqis. He whacked his plane level and then around into an opposite turn as he changed his mind about where he wanted to be, big-time g forces multiplying so fast the waves of pressure seemed to cancel each other out. The Hog grinned and hung on her pilot's fanny as he flogged her northeast, trying to get into position for a run that would let him fire the last Maverick and use his cluster bombs in practically the same motion. As Jack started back to the south he heard Doberman say something; his mind was racing too fast to pick out the words through the garble. There were all sorts of secondary explosions. The back end of a T-72 popped into the center of his TVM; he kissed the Maverick good-bye and corrected course a few degrees to the west, spotting a thick clump of tanks or vehicles or something to lay his bombs on. He pitched forward, working to get as steep an angle as possible, since that would increase accuracy. The preset fuses of the cluster bombs limited him; he couldn't drop too low or the bombs wouldn't explode properly. As Jack began to pickle them off his wings, he realized he hadn't compensated properly for the wind; it was too late to do anything more than push his nose slightly in the right direction as the bombs began slipping from his wings. He yanked the stick to recover; the bombs exploded almost literally right behind him, well off target.

Overwhelmed by the sudden g forces, Jack felt his head swim as the horizon replaced the ground. Only then did he realize his hands and forearms were drenched in sweat; only then did he feel the heartburn flaring in his throat. The sensations overwhelmed him, and for the second time that day he floated in the cockpit, lost.

I'm okay, he told himself. I've nailed at least two tanks and Doberman's just ahead and we've saved these guys' butts and I'm still in one piece. All I have to do is let my blood get back where it belongs and I'll be fine.

He let the jet grab hold of him, lift him back toward safety, away from the chaos on the ground. Her twin engines wound to the max, her strong wings flexing against the currents. Bombs away, she was several thousand pounds lighter than she'd been in hours; she felt frisky. The warplane galloped like a stallion let loose on the open plain, streaking through a sudden opening in the clouds.

Three miniature tornadoes appeared in front of Jack's windscreen, tiny black corkscrews. He stared at each in succession, fascinated by their perfect symmetry.

Two more appeared in front of his left wing, then four in front of his right. A fresh batch appeared and he felt the Hog slump.

Flak.

That was what Doberman had been yelling. His flight leader was trying to warn him about the guns.

Probably said something like, Don't get too close.

Too late Jack began to jink, hoping to cut the air in a zigzag and duck whatever was trying to nail him. Too late he paid attention to his countermeasures, goosing the ECM panel and hitting the tinsel and flares, trying everything but the kitchen sink to get away.

The plane groaned. Her right wing was heavy; she had a lean and Jack saw the dial monitoring the right engine spin backwards. He could taste bile in his mouth, thick and putrid, tinged with blood. Everything was going for shit and there were thousands of tornadoes now, thousands of windstorms spinning and spitting, black flecks of death trying to whirl him into oblivion. He pushed the Hog over, fell toward the ground, not conscious of what he was doing, falling and falling and falling forever, hands more water than flesh, mind a slur of jagged lightning. He needed his engine back but he was putting himself right into the black envelope of the guns, whose thick ugly shells were twice as large as the ones he'd ducked this morning. The radio blurred static and he moved in a surreal dimension, more thought than physical action.

Jack sensed that, despite the gauge, he hadn't totally lost the engine. It wasn't a logical thought, wasn't more than a hope really, and yet it turned out, as he plunged, his hunch was right. Whether it had momentarily flamed or the sensor had just freaked out, he couldn't tell. In any event, it was on line and kicking up a storm; he leveled off and took three long breaths, then saw that the tornadoes had disappeared.

Jack felt like he had just opened his eyes after a long, terrifying nightmare. He took two more breaths, and pulled back hard on his stick. He felt his butt shove hard against the thin pad of the ACES II seat, felt the dampness against every part of his skin, and realized, of all things, that he had to take a leak.

A good sign, he thought, pulling the Hog's nose back to the north as he gained altitude. He craned his head out the window, trying to see if he'd been hit. The plane felt

like she might be dragging her right wing through the air,
but he couldn't see any damage. This time he welcomed
the clouds; they made it impossible for anyone to aim at
him.

Calm now, Jack tried sorting out the high-pitched confusion on the radio. The British commando was saying
the tanks had stopped their attack. The AWACS
squawked indecipherably; a blur of other voices from
other missions intruded on their frequency. He tried calling Doberman but got overrun by a fresh frenzy of static.
Then the radio cleared, the circuit quiet. Doberman's
calm, laconic voice snapped in his ears, directing him to
rendezvous two miles south.

"Good work," said his leader when he found Jack
above the clouds. "We've smashed six or seven of the
tanks. Their helicopters are on the way. You get hit?"

"I'm not sure," Jack told him. "I don't think so."

"They had a pair of ZSU-57s covering their flank,"
Doberman explained as he closed in. "Shoot pretty high
but they're visually aimed. Big problem for the helos,
though."

Shit, Jack thought. They were out of bombs and missiles; Doberman was suggesting a low-level attack with
the cannons.

"Can you handle it?"

Hell, no, Jack thought. My body's aching in half a
million places and I'm lucky to be alive. No way I'm
going back down through that crap again.

"No problem," Jack told him.

The SAS radioman came back, asking when they were
going to "take a turn with their cannons" and wipe out
the remaining Iraqis. Glenon, after consulting with the
AWACS about the approaching helicopters, told him they

needed about five minutes to line everything up. He wanted to time the pounding so the Iraqis would be too busy with them to pay any attention to the helicopters. The choppers—two RAF Chinooks and an American Pave Low—were flying without escort, obviously on a serious improvise.

"We'll hit the guns from the rear," Doberman told Jack. "They're shooting visually and I have a hunch they won't pick us up until we're on top of them."

A hunch? Jack wanted to scream. He felt every ounce of bile return as Doberman outlined the rest of the plan— a straight-on run fifty feet off the ground right for the armored vehicles that housed the antiair guns. The low-level attack would increase their chances of nailing the targets, but it would leave them vulnerable to not just the ZSUs, but every peashooter the Iraqis were carrying.

"Copy" was all Jack said.

Turning his plane to follow Doberman's wide swing to the north, he felt the Hog stutter in midair as he pushed the throttle full bore. Maybe there was something wrong with the engine after all, despite what the gauges were now saying.

Or maybe the plane was trying to warn him. The clouds were streaming east and downward. The storm would frame them as they cranked into the attack.

Jack tried to push everything out of his mind, focusing only on Doberman's plane as they fell into the attack. He pushed his Hog through the clouds, edging right as he came clear, looking for his guns. He found them, saw he was off target, saw the first wink of the flak flying in his direction, moved his stick nearly into the instrument panel.

But Doberman had called it right. The Iraqis were

shooting way too soon, and without radar they had trouble judging exactly where the Hogs were, or rather, where they would be. The black stream of shells flared to Jack's left, high and wide, then suddenly stopped—the operator had either overheated the gun or run out of ammunition.

And now it was Jack's turn. Fingers sweating, stomach retching, he pushed the trigger on the Avenger cannon, felt the heavy, reassuring thump of 30 mm shells bursting from the nose, several hundred rounds whipping through the Gatling's barrels with a sneeze of a squeeze. The uranium and high-explosive bullets sliced through the Iraqi gun turret and its vehicle, chopping the chassis in half. The ZSU-57, its carrier, and the ground disappeared in a froth of white smoke.

Jack saw a second target, a flatbed truck of some kind, and opened up on it, pushing his rudder pedals to nudge the Hog's chin and the stream of bullets left. And now there were targets everywhere. A tank they'd missed before slid across the right quadrant of his windscreen; Jack flailed at it, missing and missing until finally he had to let up on the trigger and pull back the stick, because he was getting too low. As the Hog edged upwards the tank fell smack in the middle of his aiming cue; a split second later it disappeared under the bellowing pillar of smoke. Jack flew through the plume, then whacked the Hog sideways. The plane clawed at the air, snorting with pleasure at being down in the dirt where she belonged; she grinned as her pilot began pushing into a bank, pulling up to get more angle for another attack.

The radio yelped. Three black specs were growing on the right side of his windshield. The friendly helos. Jack grinned as he hunkered in the seat, slipping the Hog into the starting gates for a fresh strafing run.

•   •   •

Jack didn't get a buck at all the first year he went hunting. He went out with his father and brother several times after the first trip when he'd blown the shot, but was always unlucky. No one said anything about it, but in Jack's mind he always felt it was because he'd screwed up so badly the first time. The buck had been his and he'd blown it.

For nearly ten months he thought about that. Walking through the woods during the spring and summer, it was practically the only thing in his head. He planned and rehearsed and plotted fresh hunts, redemption.

The day hunting season opened, Mark and Jack went out by themselves. Their father was already ill, dying, though the boys didn't realize it yet.

Jack had seen a big buck, ten points on its rack, just two days before the season began. Incredibly, the animal had let him get within ten feet before bounding away.

It seemed like a dare.

That was the buck Jack gunned for when he and Mark went out. It was huge, a lot bigger than the one his brother had gotten on his first try, bigger than anything Mark had ever shot, in fact. He'd nail it and for once he would have beaten Mark at something, something that would stick. He'd make up for last year, for dozens of other things.

He wouldn't brag. Bragging was besides the point and, bottom-line, it wasn't his way. A buck that big was a statement on its own; Jack wouldn't have to say a thing.

It didn't happen the way he expected. Whether the buck sensed it was hunting season or had been out all night partying, it stayed away. They waited in the spot for hours. Mark said something that made it clear he didn't believe Jack had really seen such a big deer, let alone gotten close.

It wasn't meant as a mock, but it cut anyway.

Disappointed, they started to go home. The two young men had barely taken two steps from their spot when something moved in the woods. Jack dropped to his knee, sighted, knew it was a buck, got a good target, watched it stop, turn, look at him.

Look right at him.

Jack fired. The animal went down.

It wasn't the animal he had wanted. It was at most half the size. Its rack wasn't impressive, and in fact was smaller than Mark's first kill. It wasn't a statement or the one bold stroke that reversed their positions in life.

But he got it.

After that, hunting became just hunting, something to do with his brother. He still worried about screwing up, he still walked behind Mark, but he didn't obsess about it all anymore. He enjoyed hunting, and if not quite accepting his spot as second in line, at least he didn't bridle against it anymore.

The first Chinook was just clearing the landing zone when the AWACS called out a snap vector. It was the instruction for a hard-turn, a get-the-hell-out-of-there runaway call—a pair of Iraqi jets were scrambling from an air base less than thirty miles away, gunning straight for them.

Jack started to comply, then realized Doberman was pushing his Hog around in the opposite direction—toward the enemy interceptors, not away from them. Instantly he knew why. The helicopters would be sitting ducks for the Iraqi jets. The AWACS was vectoring a flight of F-15 Eagles to nail the Iraqis, but even without doing the math Jack knew there was no way they'd get there in time to keep the planes away from the helicopters. Glenon wanted to distract them, hold them off until the Brits got away.

Jack hesitated, took a lump of air into his lungs and forced it out, then urged the Hog into a fresh turn, heading north.

"Go home, kid," snapped Doberman. "I have this under control."

"Negative."

"Listen, Jack. It doesn't make sense for both of us to get shot down."

"Who says we're getting shot down?"

Doberman's response—if there was one—was drowned out by a fresh transmission from the AWACS, IDing the planes as MiG-23 Floggers and saying they were definitely coming toward the helicopters. The Eagles were eighty miles away, already painting the interceptors with their radars but still out of reach.

The MiGs kept coming; they weren't climbing anymore and Jack's gut told him they were gunning not for the helicopters but the warplanes that had cut up their tanks.

His gut was correct. The two interceptors changed course to close as the Hogs flew north.

Which was what they wanted. Kind of.

"They see us," said Doberman, putting his nose directly onto the MiGs' bearing. "They're going to try and get us to turn so they can nail us from behind with their heat-seekers. They're all speed but can't maneuver worth shit. Stay with me."

"I'm here," said Jack. The Hogs carried a pair of

heat-seeking Sidewinders on their left wings. They were
excellent air-to-air missiles, better than the Iraqi missiles
but, like them, short-range weapons; while in theory they
could be launched from any angle in an attack, to be most
effective they had to be fired at close range and from
behind.

Water poured out of Jack's hands. His stomach and
chest muscles spasmed; he felt as if he'd swallowed a
sheet of plywood. The radio jammed with all kinds of
talk; Doberman yelled for everyone to shut the hell up
but it did no good. Somewhere in the middle of the confusion the AWACS announced that it had lost the bandits
in the ground clutter.

Jack saw them emerge in the haze ahead, dead center
beneath the clouds and desert. They were two bees, fat if
deadly; any second now the F-15s would be close enough
to nail them.

Or not. The Iraqis were coming on crazy fast.

"We got them right where we want them," Doberman
said. "Break on my command. You left, me right. Take
them into the storm, then nail them from behind, just like
we practiced."

They had practiced. The whole squadron had. Several
times.

Jack remembered. But that was weeks ago, months
maybe, and he hadn't taken it all that seriously. Anything
came for them, real fighters would pound the crap out of
them.

Hog wasn't an interceptor. She was a mud-slinger. A
hell of an attack plane, but not an air-to-air fighter. That
was the Eagle's job.

Jack stared at the bee growing in the windscreen. It
seemed to wink at him.

Cannonfire.

"Break," said Doberman.

Jack pulled the Hog into the tightest turn he could manage, felt gravity smash him in the face.

His turn took him through the leading edge of the storm front. Gray clouds swirled around him, a death shroud.

Something growled. Jack didn't realize what it was at first, saw a red spark in front of him, lost it, lost himself in the clouds.

The Sidewinder. Its infrared seeker had homed in on the MiG's exhaust and cued him to fire. But like an idiot he'd blown it. The two missiles were still sitting on his wing.

Christ. A free shot. And he'd choked.

Again.

Jack pounded the throttle bar in frustration, smashing it hard enough to worry that he had broken it. His whole goddamn life came down to a stinking choke, a freeze, failure. He screamed, and as he did he realized he was in a hell of a lot of trouble. He'd lost sight of his enemy, who by now was undoubtedly angling to find his rear end. Jack pushed the Hog around, put the plane nearly straight down, came over upside down, and leveled back upright, thick in the cloud bank, jinking for his life, sensing the MiG hanging on his tail. He knew without looking at any of his instruments how truly dog meat he was, beyond yo-yo country. The pilot kicked out flares and tinsel, a desperate reflex, took a hard turn, tried to put himself in the Iraqi's face and miraculously did so. A huge wing fluttered past, then the fuselage, and the rest, maybe thirty feet from his glass; the MiG had lost serious energy and had his wings spread, flailing just to stay airborne.

He, too, had missed an easy shot. He, too, was now a fat meatball of a target.

The Hog seemed to know it, knew the Sidewinders or the cannon could chew the Iraqi to pieces, but her pilot couldn't react fast enough. Even with the missiles growling, when all he had to do was push the button, Jack once again lost the easy shot, his airspeed so low that the MiG was able to jig away.

Angry, the Hog bucked her nose down as Jack tried to find the bandit in the swirling fog. This was exactly the kind of close-in knife-fight furball she could win. Cheated, she kicked in frustration, shaking as a strong burst of turbulence unsettled her wings.

Jack cursed and yelled and slammed his controls instead of working them. The truth was, he was damn lucky to be alive. It was time to get the hell out of there, but he couldn't relax his fingers enough to actually fly the plane. The best he could do was shove it forward. The cockpit blurred around him, static pushing at the corners of his eyes as well as filling his ears. He had only the vaguest idea of where he was, only the vaguest idea that he was in a cockpit at all. The plane pitched downward and his hand couldn't pull back.

Jack tried to hold his breath and stop hyperventilating. That backfired; he gulped for more air, felt his whole body get dizzy.

If the MiG was still there—if anything was still there—he didn't care. He had to get his bearings back before he flew into the ground. He forced his eyes down to his stick, as if seeing his fingers would relax them, make them respond to his brain's command.

It worked, at least enough for him to start pulling the Hog's nose up.

A shape materialized in the grayness above him. A plane.

No, a goose. The goose he had seen hunting with his brother.

No, a MiG.

Fire.

Anger leaped up, a hot spit of lava erupting from the deep bowels of his soul. Every injury and insult he had ever felt, every disappointment surged in his body. In that instant fear left him. The cramps, the bile, the clamp that had taken hold of his body disintegrated, burned away.

But he didn't pull the trigger.

The shadow looked exactly like that goose, exactly like the unexpected flutter of beauty and grace that for just one second changed the way he looked at the world.

And then it turned into a Warthog.

Doberman.

The Sidewinder kept growling. And now that the panic was gone, Jack knew where he was, knew what was going on. And in that instant he turned the Hog almost ninety degrees and let loose, kicking the Sidewinders off after the hot exhaust of the MiG's Tumansky R-29B turbojet as it flashed overhead, its pilot lost in the thick clouds.

Sensing his doom, the MiG pilot poured on the gas, desperate to get away. As the plane picked up speed, the pilot jinked desperately, shoving the MiG so severely one of the American heat-seeking missiles missed.

The second exploded close to the ventral fin, taking away a good hunk of metal and part of the nozzle hy-

draulic system. The MiG stuttered in midair, nose buck-
ing as it started to yaw.

Two seconds later, a Sparrow medium-range missile
launched from one of the Eagles finished it off.

When they finally made it back to Hog Heaven at King
Fahd, Jack was swarmed by a mass of people. The Eagle
pilots had insisted on giving him part of the kill—damn
nice for pointy-nose go-fast jocks, everyone agreed. No
one had ever nailed a MiG with a Hog before, not in real
life at least.

Doberman met him on the ground. He smiled, gave
him a thumbs-up.

"Kick ass," he said. "I knew you could do it, low-
timer."

Jack didn't know what to say, and Doberman didn't
wait for a response. He turned and disappeared, off to
debrief with someone or see to some of the myriad details
he'd been assigned as one of the squadron's top officers.

Jack didn't have much to say to anyone else, either.
The entire encounter had lasted no more than five
minutes. All he remembered of it, all he really felt as his
legs wobbled on the tarmac, was the goose.

How to explain that?

He couldn't.

Hours later, they ended up at the Depot, an officially
off-limits bar at the edge of the desert some Hog drivers
swore sprung whole from the sand when too many guys
had too many wet dreams. Someone asked how he felt.
Jack said he had nearly puked his guts out.

Everyone laughed.

"Sure, Killer. Me, too," said Shotgun. He patted him
on the back and bought another round. Everybody was

going to be calling Jack "Killer" from now on, whether
he liked it or not. He didn't feel like one, thought it might
even whiff of being a brag, but it was beyond his control.
Blame Shotgun and his laugh.

"Sure, Killer. Me, too."

But maybe Shotgun meant it. Maybe he and everyone
else who'd made it through their first combat missions
had gone through their own initiations.

Just surviving; that was brag enough.

Later that night, Jack remembered what Wells had said
about the letter home, the letter to be sent if he didn't
make it back. He decided he ought to write one to his
brother; it was an order, after all. And besides, Wells
might be right about the luck thing.

Still buzzed from the day, he thought it would be easy.
But when he sat down on his bunk with a thick, yellow
pad and tried to tell his brother how much he meant to
him growing up, the words wouldn't come. They were
sincere but they sounded stupid.

And besides, writing the letter felt like the opposite of
what Wells had said, bad luck, not good. He'd made it
through today without one, after all.

He gave up trying.

Instead, Jack wrote another letter to his brother, one
to send right away, one about helping shoot down the
MiG. He began by describing the morning attack, honestly saying how scared he'd been. As he wrote, he felt
proud, real proud, vindicated not only for the day but for
everything, for choosing to be a fighter pilot, for getting
out on his own and following his dreams.

Jack knew even before rereading the letter that it
sounded too much like bragging. He ripped it up.

Instead, he started a new letter to Mark, one that described their last hunting trip together, the spiderwebs at the tops of the trees and the goose coming at him unexpectedly, the real reason he'd missed the deer.

He remembered as he wrote what Mark had said after missing the deer. And he realized for the first time what the words really meant. They weren't put-downs for not firing, nor reminders of his little-brother inferiority.

His brother had felt exactly the same thing he had, in reverse:

Jack's a better hunter than me. Sure, I screwed up, but him? No way.

Realizing that made him see a lot of other things slightly differently. Not much differently—he'd always known his brother loved him without reservation, and the feeling was mutual. But his perspective had shifted, ever so slightly. He remembered their hunting trips, the later ones instead of the first ones, saw them for the first time from Mark's perspective. More times than not Jack had been the one to get the first shot or had nailed the bigger buck. He was better than he thought—even if he was still, if he was always, the younger brother.

Not that he wrote about that in the letter. He just laughed at himself for missing the best buck of his life because of a flock of geese that didn't have the sense to go south at the right time of the year.

Jack thought about ripping up that letter, too. But in the end, he signed it:

Hunt with you again soon,
Jack

and sealed it into an envelope to send.